Ameke
Euersdijck
Elwartsdijck
Agger
Tbadt
Westhe
Westmae
tia

Breskin
Stuuesandt
ter Nieuse
Zaemslacht
Boschende
Steppeld
Hulst
Verbrouck
Swijndrecht
Oordam
Austerweel
Schille

Waterdijck
Biervliet
Waterduel
Philippine
Beerdijck
Beuuren
Antwerpen
Massehouen
Hoboken
Pars

Ardenbo
St. Lauris
Delborch
Lembeke
Moere
Waesmonstre
Dacknam
Rupelmunde
Schelle
Liere
Uaser Frawe
Wauer

Oost Ekelo
Waersc hot
Heuergem
Seue eyken
Durme fluui
Vlasenbrouck
Borchem
wiese
Willebrouck
Herdesem
Tolhus
Bome
Waerloos
S. Cateline Wau

Lieue flu.
Gendt
Ouermeer
Desseldonck
Grumberge
Baerl
donck
Dermonde
Londrel
Machelen
B

Meyegem
Massemen
Scelderode
S. Amand
Opwijck
Bardegem
Campenhout
Eppegem
Viluoerden
Euersbeke
R

Nazareth
Alheiligen
Gaueren
Landscotere
Westrem
Marnekerck
Morsele
AB.
Brussel
Lombeke
Waueren

ten Dale cap.
Vuersele
Dederhout
Nieneue
Afflegem
ter Alfene
A
Lumbeke
Gronendael
NT

Nokeren
Moregem
Oudenarde
Miegelbeke
Liekercke
Pamele
Sambeke
Halsenberge
Geniual

Scalasia
Watripont
Vloersbergen
Grumnge
Wendeke
Hern
Orient

Potz
Obisije
Mons Trinite
H
an-
Vianen Tolebeke
Engien
Beueren

Tornay
Conchoy
chemoir
pars
Lessene

Mouchyn
hemnion
Carchiernes
Hennon
Grunnge

Rientay
Anchyn
Viconjie
Beaupar
Valenchie
ne

Flandri... ucia celeberrim... ria flandrica 31, ... ermini sit à Septe... Meridie Hannonia et Artesia, ab Vcciaente... ab Oriete verò ab Brantia Regio est om rerú quæ hominis victui conueniunt foecuda, Vrbiú munitarú frequétia nulli cedens.

Coloniæ Agrip. exc. Joan buss.

REYNARD *the* FOX

REYNARD *the* FOX

RETOLD BY
Anne Louise Avery

Bodleian Library
UNIVERSITY OF OXFORD

First published in 2020 by the Bodleian Library
Broad Street, Oxford OX1 3BG
www.bodleianshop.co.uk

ISBN 978 1 85124 555 0

Text © Anne Louise Avery, 2020
Illustrations © Wendy Wigley, 2020

Anne Louise Avery has asserted her right
to be identified as the author of this Work.

Cover design by Dot Little at the Bodleian Library
FRONT COVER 'Renard the Fox' by Philip Reinagle (1749–1833),
from W.S. Sparrow, *British Sporting Artists from Barlow to Herring*, 1922.
© Bodleian Library, University of Oxford, 17006 d.277.
ENDPAPERS Map of Flanders by Matthias Quad and Johann Bussemacher,
Cologne, 1609. Wikimedia Commons

Designed and typeset in 11½ on 14 Dante by illuminati, Grosmont
Printed and bound in Wales by Gomer Press Limited
on 80 gsm Munken Premium Cream

British Library Catalogue in Publishing Data
A CIP record of this publication is available from the British Library

CONTENTS

For my beloved Inigo

Among foxis be foxissh of nature.
JOHN LYDATE, *The Proverbes of Lydgate*, 1510

The most successful modern princes have been
those who knew best how to play the fox.
NICCOLÒ MACHIAVELLI, *Il Principe*, 1532

The cunning of the fox is as murderous
as the violence of the wolf.
THOMAS PAINE, *The American Crisis*, 1776

A small village square and a few streets,
A statue of Christ at the crossroads,
The grey Schelde and then the tower
Which mirrors itself in the ill-tempered water.
ÉMILE VERHAEREN, *Mon Village*, 1904

A FOX FOR
ALL SEASONS

In the exceptionally wet autumn of 1792 the writer and philosopher Johann Wolfgang von Goethe found himself swept up in the brutality and chaos of war, accompanying his patron Karl August, Duke of Saxe-Weimar, on the disastrous Prussian campaign against French Revolutionary forces. Splattered with battlefield mud, deafened by cannonade, feeling like 'an outcast in a chaotic, filthy world', Goethe sought solace in reading, finding unexpected comfort and relevance, and much-needed merriment, in a retelling of the old medieval beast epic *Reineke der Fuchs* or Reynard the Fox.

For Goethe, the corrupt courtly world of Reynard and his fellow animals, ruled over by the capricious and egotistical King Noble the Lion, formed a mirror image of his own tumultuous times, of the rapacity and self-indulgence of the *Ancien Régime*. The Fox's encounters with greedy Bruin the Bear, pompous Tybert the Cat, gullible Cuwaert the Hare and malevolent Isengrim the Wolf were shaped by the same hypocrisy, the same violence and grotesque comedy of errors that he saw unfolding in real time all about him in his own society, not least in the shambolic Battle of Valmy of September 1792 and its aftermath.

Within this dissolute, disorderly world, the charismatic trickster figure of Reynard flared bright as saltpetre. Possessed of a self-reliance rooted in quick intelligence and humour and oratorial brilliance, underpinned by a sincere devotion to home and family, the Fox, despite his obvious flaws, was a character with whom Goethe could closely sympathise. A Fox of the Enlightenment, *avant la lettre*, conscience unshackled by king or church, caught in the rough amber of the old medieval texts. Inspired, describing the stories as a 'profane secular Bible', Goethe set to writing his own epic verse interpretation of Reynard's adventures, working first in the baroque calm of his home in Weimar, in the lull between battles, then back in the cannon-thunder and sludge, this time at the Siege of Mainz.

Whilst Goethe's poem largely preserves the medieval story and its satirical bite, his Reynard is equally a champion for what he called, after the retreat from Valmy, 'a new era in the history of the world'. An anti-hero for a post-Revolutionary Europe, acting only according to his own nature, without a shred of the self-deception or hypocrisy of his peers, Reynard fights for his life using neither morals, money nor position, but simply his sharp wits and vulpine cunning, defeating his enemies by employing their own stupidity or sophistry or greed against them. A foxish Becky Sharp turning all to his advantage.

From the very beginning of his literary career, Reynard the Fox has charmed his audiences, just as he captivated Goethe. He elegantly tricks us into liking him and rooting for him, just as he hoodwinks his fellow animals into traps and elaborate falsehoods. Continually in trouble with the King and his barons, a whisker away from being executed for his many crimes, Reynard nevertheless manages to squeeze out of every tight corner and triumph over his enemies. Entirely through his wiles and his ability to spin a compelling tale out of nothing, the establishment is mocked and bettered again and again, hierarchies are upended and the rich and foolish and overprivileged are exposed and thoroughly punished for their sins.

While his roots stretch back to Ancient Greek fables, no-tably Aesop's story of the sick lion tricked by a fox, Reynard's first named appearance in medieval literature was in the *Ysengrimus* (*c.* 1149), a long Latin poem about the titular wolf Isengrim, probably composed by an ambitious monk of Sint-Pieters Abbey in Gent, in one manuscript named 'Nivard'. From Flanders, Reynard then travels to France, emerging as the wicked brush-twirling lead in Pierre de Saint-Cloud's Old French *Roman de Renart* (*c.* 1175). Pierre left the enmity unresolved between Reynard and the wolf, ever his principal adversary, which laid the way open for a rich blossoming of thirty further episodes or 'branches' by later writers, the character becoming so wildly popular in France that the word for fox eventually changed permanently from the old *goupil* to *renard*.

In the 1180s Reynard lopes into Middle High German with the *Reinhart Fuchs*, written by the enigmatic Alsatian poet Heinrich, known by his soubriquet *der Glîchezaere*, 'the Trickster' or 'Hypocrite'. Based on the French branches and continuing the 'great, grim war' between wolf and fox,

Reinhart Fuchs also adds new characters and devices, ruthlessly parodying the nobility and the church and reflecting contemporary events. The unprecedented introduction of an Elephant of Bohemia, for example, stands in for the contemporaneous Soběslav II, Duke of Bohemia, who was mired in various political intrigues at the German court of the time, whilst a Leopard with a Plumed Helmet masks for Richard the Lionheart, whose emblem was of the same design.

But it was back in the Low Countries, in Eastern Flanders, in the following century that Reynard would swagger into his influential and long-lasting celebrity, across Western Europe and beyond, as the archetypal cunning and subversive Flemish trickster, whose anthropomorphised traits have barely altered over the centuries. This Reynard remains our Reynard today: the direct ancestor of Beatrix Potter's dastardly Mr Tod, the charming Fantastic Mr Fox and Disney's devastatingly charismatic Robin Hood, the drawings for which were recycled from an earlier Reynard animation, scrapped because the fox was deemed too dangerously anarchic and morally irredeemable to ever dream of passing the Hays Code, the strict set of guidelines governing American cinema.

In around 1250, *Van den vos Reinaerde (Of Reynard the Fox)* was written in Middle Dutch by an author who proudly presents himself in the poem's opening lines as Willem, *die Madocke makede*, the author 'who made *Madoc*', referring to a now lost Dutch version of the story of the legendary Welsh seafaring prince Madoc—Madoc ab Owain Gwynedd—who was thought to have reached America in his nautical explorations.

Apart from this intriguing lost work of Celtic–Flemish storytelling, we know very little about Willem, although various theories for his identity have been suggested over the years. Toponyms and linguistic idiosyncrasies point to a close familiarity with the country between Gent and Hulst, and, based on his knowledge of Latin and of Old French beast epics, the Reynardists Maurice Nonneman and Rik Van Daele, among others, have proposed that he may have been a Cistercian lay brother named Willem van Boudelo or Corthals (d. July 1261) from the important Abbey of Boudelo, close to the modern-day Dutch border at Klein-Sinaai, which is mentioned in the text.

This Willem was an influential and clever cleric of Margaret II, Countess of Flanders (called rather dramatically *la Noire* due to her highly scandalous life and cruel nature) and managed a number of her extensive properties across the Low Countries. Based on his intimate experience of the intrigues and political tides of both monastic and courtly worlds, it is feasible to attempt to match the cast of *Van den vos Reinaerde* with prominent figures from the Flemish court of the early thirteenth century. Reynard the Fox may have been based on Zeger III, Châtelain of the Count's castle in Gent, King Noble the Lion on Philip the Noble, Count of Namur and Regent of Flanders, who unjustly removed Zeger from his post in 1210, and the principal supporting animal courtiers, a thinly disguised group of malcontented barons who unsuccessfully plotted against Philip in the same period.

In England, whilst the fox was a common subject in medieval sculptures, wood carving, stained glass and manuscript marginalia—iconography which may, due to its often didactic nature, have been based on the European fox tales—Reynard enters the written literary realm explicitly only in 1250, in the form of a short poem entitled 'Of the Vox and of the Wolf', inspired by the fourth branch of the Old French *Roman de Renart*, the story of Reynard tricking Isengrim into the dank bottom of a monastery well (the manuscript of this text is held in the Bodleian Library: MS. Digby 86). Our fox then goes to ground for a century, reappearing in around 1390 with a flourish under the name of Daun Russell ('Daun' meaning Sir or Master) in Chaucer's *Nun's Priest's Tale*, again drawn from another section of the *Roman de Renart*, in which Reynard and Chaunticleer the Cockerel engage in a farmyard tussle of wits.

It was at the end of the fifteenth century, however, with William Caxton's bestselling printed edition of 1481, that Reynard the Fox would triumphantly became a principal figure within Albion's imagination, as culturally potent and entrenched as Puck or Robin Hood or King Arthur—not only fortifying the old folk perception of the fox as the cunning trickster of the countryside, but also bearing eternal trans-generational relevance through his capacity as a character to provoke and critique power, hierarchy and the status quo. As Goethe realised only too well, under his revolutionary bombardment, Reynard embodies the corrective against struc-tured, oppressive forms of society, the vent through which the steam of a bubbling pot can escape.

Caxton, a successful mercer (trader in fine textiles) before he became England's first printer, was born in the Weald of Kent between 1415 and 1424. After a youthful apprenticeship with the important London merchant and Lord Mayor Robert Large, he spent three profitable decades in the Low Countries, where the international cloth trade was based, rising to the prestigious position of governor of the English Nation in

Bruges, the organisation in charge of promoting English commercial and diplomatic interests. In the course of this mix of political and mercantile occupation, he learnt to speak and write Dutch fluently, a proficiency quite unremarkable at the time. In the busy cosmopolitan city of Bruges, and later when he moved to Gent, Caxton began to encounter the new technologies revolutionising the spread of ideas and literature across Europe, and, learning of Gutenberg's inventions, was intrigued and quickly grasped the vast economic and creative possibilities. In 1471, he travelled east to Cologne where he first learned the technique of printing with moveable type, and he was able to put this knowledge into practice back in the Low Countries, where he printed the first English book around 1474. When he returned to London in 1476, he established the first printing press in England in Westminster. He would eventually publish over a hundred editions. From Sir Thomas Malory's *Morte d'Arthur* to Chaucer's *Canterbury Tales*, all were well judged by Caxton to appeal to an audience traumatised and exhausted by the turbulence of endless civil war, eager for distraction, instruction, comfort and, perhaps most importantly of all, light relief and comic entertainment.

In the summer of 1481, having become familiar with the stories and landscapes of Reynard in Flanders, Caxton decided to publish his own translation of the Reynard story, based on the Middle Dutch prose version of Willem's earlier poem which Gerard Leeu had printed just a few years earlier. (Gerard Leeu's two editions of Reynard, one in prose and one in verse, are the main conduits for the best-known later Reynard retellings; whilst Caxton translated the prose, a Low German edition based on the verse formed the indirect source for Goethe's great epic.) Entitled *The hystorye of Reinard the foxe, done into English out of Dutch*, Caxton's translation is wonderfully readable, uneven, funny, slapdash—its hero shameless, immoral, outrageously untruthful and immensely likeable. This is no pedantic, scholarly translation, but one which races pell-mell through Reynard's increasingly shocking shenanigans; a version which begs to be read aloud, to be laughed at companionably en masse.

As he had hoped, Caxton's Reynard was an immediate best-seller, with twenty-three editions printed before 1700 alone, including his own second edition in 1489. After Caxton's death in 1491, his printing assistant Wynkyn de Worde took over his business, issuing an illustrated edition in 1495, peppered with a series of linear woodcuts based on prints from Leeu's 1487 verse version of *Reynaerts historie*. These illustrations, originally by an artist we know now only as the Haarlem Master, would influence the visuality of Reynard for centuries to come, and indelibly link the use of mass-produced graphic imagery with the fox's tales, an association which can be traced directly to modern animations, such as Władysław Starewicz's 1930s' adaption of the French branches, *Le Roman de Renard* or Wes Anderson's *Fantastic Mr Fox* from 2009.

Over the following centuries, this process of revision, modification and addition to Caxton's narrative continued. In the spirit of the fox's mercurial oratory, his story adapted to appeal to each new generation, some periods requiring a little more shapeshifting than others. From the sixteenth century, Reynard's blasphemous disguises of clerical robes and devil-may-care amorality even secured him a regular spot on the notorious list of banned books (*Index librorum prohibitorum*) deemed heretical by the Catholic Church. One way around these vulpine shortcomings was for publishers to include earnest moral expositions next to each episode in the text, producing a Reynard 'purged from all the grosenesses both in Phrase and Matter', as London printer Edward Allde put it in his heavily annotated 1620 edition. Others added new stories—Edward Brewster, for example, at the end of the seventeenth century, embroidering both a sequel to Reynard's career and a further tale of his son Reynardine's exploits, neither of which quite matches the old-established Flemish canon in their narrative power. Cheap chapbook editions were also produced, often for the rural market outside London, and heavily edited children's versions shorn of the nastier, more violent elements of the original Caxton text.

By the early Victorian period, interest in the increasingly diluted and altered Caxton editions had waned, but following the popular wave for all things Germanic, influenced by Prince Albert, Goethe's *Reineke Fuchs* came thundering into fashion, with multiple English translations being produced. One particularly influential version was printed in 1851 to accompany an exhibit of Reynardian taxidermy at the Great Exhibition, a re-creation of the vivid, anthropomorphic illustrations designed by Wilhelm von Kaulbach for an influential publication of Goethe from 1846. A series of vignettes using fox cubs and various props, the exhibit was created by a celebrated master of the taxidermic arts from Stuttgart, Hermann Ploucquet. It swiftly became one of the most visited highlights of the Crystal Palace, with even Queen Victoria remarking on its fascinating and amusing properties. In his 1852 essay in *Fraser's Magazine*, the historian and editor Professor James Anthony

Froude mused that, before the Great Exhibition, 'it was rare to find a person who had read the Fox Epic … but now the charming figures of Reineke himself, and the Lion King, and Isengrim, and Bruin … and Grimbart, had set all the world asking who and what they were, and the story began to get itself known. The old editions, which had long slept unbound in reams upon the shelves, began to descend and clothe themselves in green and crimson. Mr. Dickens sent a summary of it around the households of England. Everybody began to talk of Reineke.'

But after the Great Exhibition was dismantled, and the years passed, and fashions ebbed and flowed, Reynard went back to ground, and whilst he emerges in the twentieth century in filmic disguise from time to time, or in young children's picture books, or heavily annotated scholarly translations, relatively few today have read his tales or even know the names of the characters so close-woven within our historical collective imagination that many of them, such as Tybert or Tabby or Tibby the Cat, for example, became bywords for the animals themselves. The principal aim of this book, then, is to reclothe Reynard once more, shake the earth from his brush, and return our vulpine friend to the exuberant and provocative position he once occupied within our storytelling traditions.

My interpretation has a number of layers in its construction. Its core or skeleton is essentially my own close translation of Caxton; the story broadly following his narrative, episode by episode, as it moves from the humdrum (stealing sausages) to the wondrous (magical flying wooden horses) to the dramatic (fights and blindings and near executions). However, whilst a few passages are kept almost exactly the same, I have also extensively fleshed out and feathered and furred each section, adding new and detailed descriptions of landscapes, castles, cities, rivers and villages, and expositions of characters' backgrounds, families, motivations and occupations. Both Bruin the Bear and Tybert the Cat's pivotal journeys, for example, consist of only a couple of lines in Caxton; here we follow them step by step from Gent to Reynard's fortress home of Maleperduys and back again. Equally, whilst female figures such as Queen Gente the Lioness and Hermeline the Vixen, Reynard's wife, have long been present in the tales, their roles have been supportive or subservient to the male characters. Without diverting from the canonical plot and structure too far, I have developed their stories, giving Lady Erswynde the She-Wolf, Isengrim's wife, in particular, a more powerful and self-determined trajectory. Occasionally, I have created new characters, such as Bruin the Bear's much-admired uncle, Baron Adalbern, or given nameless animals names, christening a disgruntled courtier goat 'Chiever', for example, borrowed from Caxton's *Vitas Patrum*, printed posthumously by Wynkyn de Worde in 1495: 'The paas & way of the wylde bestes, as chieuers, beres & other.' Chanticleer the Cockerel's pet dogs Saphyrus, Mopsus, Melissa and Mopsulus are taken from the correspondence of the Brabant-born humanist Justus Lipsius (1547–1606), whose love of dogs and gardens, he claimed, was only exceeded by that of books, even lecturing with his hounds by his side at the University of Leuven.

I worked from a number of early editions of Caxton held in the Bodleian Library, including the stylish 1494 printing by Richard Pynson, one of the early Fleet Street publishers, and a wildly romantic 1629 Edward Alldee edition from the library of Robert Burton (1577–1640), the Oxonian author of *The Anatomy of Melancholy*, his elegant, ghostly initials and marginalia marking the title page and certain plum comedic passages. For the first section, particularly in terms of Flemish topographical content, I also drew elements directly from Willem's *Van den vos Reynaerde*, via the excellent 2009 critical edition produced by André Bouwman and Bart Besamusca, translated into English by Thea Summerfield.

Caxton's text offers a number of challenges to the modern interpreter, of course, not least that his language floats halfway across the North Sea, not quite Dutch, but not entirely English either. His narrative is liberally scattered with 'Dutchisms', unconscious drifts from his easy bilingualism, which a slightly bewildered William Morris, in his lavish 1892 Kelmscott edition of the work (also in the Bodleian), would place in a special appendix, a listing of what he describes as 'Some Strange Words'. Many of these words—such as 'grate' (fish bone), 'slonked' (devoured) and 'glat' (polished)—I have retained in my retelling, as this is a story of both the Low Countries and England; it straddles two worlds and the language needs to reflect that dynamic liminality. I have also kept, and indeed added, other fine old medieval words and phrases (drightfare, beaupere, drumbledore, for example), some further Flemish terms (*schuyt, waterzooi, begijnhof*), and, in the spirit of Caxton, I have tossed a few of my own onomatopoeic neologisms into the stew.

As the introductory note to the Glossary at the end of this book explains, this is not simply a fable of courtly intrigues long ago, but of a complex alternative world ruled and inhabited predominantly by beasts, by foxes and badgers and pine martens and leopards and lions and bears and otters. Humans only exist at the very edges of this zoocracy, and, apart from a few notable exceptions such as the Abbot of Baudeloo or Master Abrion, Reynard's scholarly friend from Trier, they are shadowy and vicious figures, signifying danger and persecution for the animals, who occasionally ignore that peril for a tasty side of bacon or a string of sausages. Thus, whilst Reynard's Flemish fiefdom may adeptly satirise and mock aspects of our own troubled hierarchies, it nevertheless should also be appreciated and treated as what J.R.R. Tolkien termed a 'secondary world', discrete and functional on its own terms. As such, it is logical that their language is also not quite of the human world; it intersects, but has its own patterns and lexicon. When reading this book, it is possible either to let that lyrical foxish dialect wash over you, as unfamiliar words will generally be entirely comprehensible within their contexts, or to look up precise meanings and etymologies in the Glossary.

The idea of place is as central as linguistic identity within Reynard's adventures, which play out principally in the old medieval County of Flanders (in Dutch, het graafschap Vlaanderen), ruled over with a capricious paw by King Noble the Lion from his imposing seat in Gent, the towering Gravensteen or Castle of the Counts, which can still be visited today. Whilst Caxton's account carries a strong flavour of the Flemish landscape, there are only a few specific toponyms included in his translation, such as the famous tavern halfway between Gent and Hijfte, mentioned in *Reynaerts historie* and *Van den vos Reinaerde*, where one dark night Reynard's father and a group of barons plot wickedly against King Noble.

The fox's exploits reach far beyond Noble's fiefdom, however, further than one might imagine, and in my remaking I've cast the net wider still. East of Flanders lie the County of Hainaut (graafschap Henegouwen) and the Duchy of Brabant (hertogdom Brabant), to the North the County of Zeeland (graafschap Zeeland) and the County of Holland (graafschap Holland), to the South Artois (graafschap Artesië), and to the West the North Sea (Noordzee), stern-grey and white-capped and rolling, a great heaving busyness of ships crossing to and fro to England, and up and down the coast to the whale-waters of the Arctic and the wind-blown tip of Spain and yonder, in a complicated weave of trade routes and passages, billowing the margins of our tale.

The exact location of Maleperduys, Reynard's secluded fortress, is not mentioned by Caxton or Willem, but, after travelling extensively around Flanders, I decided to site it to the north-east, around thirty miles from King Noble's castle, near the waterfront mill-town of Rupelmonde. This lies within the enigmatic Waasland or Land of Waas, a flat, marshy waterlogged domain stretching from Gent to Antwerp along the left bank of the River Schelde. The name of Waasland is somewhat etymologically mysterious, but probably derives from *waas*, meaning mud, mire or sludge, with a further sense of a haze or mist. An obscurity. For these were flooded lands, masked lands, edge lands—just the place for a renegade fox to hide. Indeed, Waaslanders have always closely identified with the plucky outsider, the wily outlaw, the anti-authoritarian rebel. The figure of Reynard thus came to typify its wild, autonomous character, and is still inextricably associated with the region today, commemorated in town and village with plaques and statues and murals and memorial trails. The master bakers of the principal town of Sint-Niklaas—bakery De Cock, bakery De Visscher, patisserie Stefan and patisserie Thierens—even developed a special Reynard cake in the early 1970s to celebrate their beloved fox, a heady mixture of almonds, pineapple, marzipan and Grand Marnier.

The most important rivers within Reynard's world are the Schelde and the Leie. The Schelde flows from its source at Gouy in northern France, through Cambrai and Valenciennes, entering Flanders near Tournai. At Gent, where it mingles with the Leie, close to Grimbart the Badger's house and Noble's castle, it turns east, then, just past Dendermonde, north towards Antwerp and the sea. It is this serpentine section of the river, bordering the Waasland, which the animals are continually following, by foot or by boat, back and forth and back and forth to Maleperduys. At Antwerp, the Schelde curves west, widening into a lonely estuary of oystercatchers and mud flats and salt marshes haunted by the old ones—the submerged altars of the goddess Nehellania at its mouth and the stooped and grey-haired god Scaldis at its turn, beading an eye over the fortunes washed up or lost with the brackish tides.

As the River Schelde ebbs and flows, so too do the temporal tides of the pastoral Flemish year, measured by the old agricultural cycles and the holy saints' days and the great church festivals. Within this perpetual calendar, Reynard the Fox's story is essentially one of early summer, of a flowering, burgeoning countryside, a tale of bright Whitsuntide, tempered by only a few icy remembrances of the deep snow drifts and black frozen dykes of winters past.

Opening with a *reverdie* or re-greening, an invocation of the arrival of spring and summer popular in medieval lyric poetry—birds and bees and blossom and the open roads—the narrative unfolds and resolves over a single month, from Whit Sunday or Pentecost itself, the seventh Sunday after Easter—here, falling on 6 June to 7 July, and the Feast day of Thomas à Becket, a very Reynardian saint, being a continual thorn in the side of regal authority.

Whilst canonically a time to commemorate the Holy Spirit ethereally descending on the disciples, Whitsun actually heralded a season of very earthy dancing and singing, processions and fairs and games and weddings, a highly sociable time of communal eating and drinking and carousing. In romances contemporaneous with Reynard, it was particularly associated with the grand feasts of kings, complete with tilts and tournaments and a full court, or *cour plénière*, drawn from across the land. In *Le Morte d'Arthur* of Sir Thomas Malory, which had its first printing with Caxton in 1485, after pulling the sword from the stone on Whit Sunday, Arthur commands 'a great feast that it should be holden at Pentecost after the incoronation of him at the city of Carlion', thus establishing the festival from the very beginning of his kingship as an occasion of great symbolic weight. As his reign progresses, it becomes the day on which his knights pledge their Round Table oaths, and when all adventures and otherworldly happenings commence, including the Grail quest itself: 'So ever the king had a custom that at the feast of Pentecost in especial, afore other feasts in the year, he would not go that day to meat until he had heard or seen of a great marvel. And for that custom all manner of strange adventures came before Arthur as at that feast before all other feasts.'

The opening scenes of Reynard humorously echo that Arthurian model, with the narcissistic King Noble the Lion holding court at Whitsun, having ordered his subjects to convene from across Flanders. All attend, except for Baron Reynard the Fox, an absence which sparks outrage amongst his fellow courtiers and plunges us straight into a fury of accusations and shocking accounts of the missing fox's wicked behaviour.

By the close of the book, whether or not we view Reynard as an amoral and irreformable Machiavellian villain, as Goethe's flaming revolutionary fighting a corrupt aristocracy from within, or, as the quintessential fox simply acting according to the laws of his own fixed vulpine nature, striving to protect himself and his family from starvation and mortal threat, is something each reader has to decide for themselves. Dutch philosopher Baruch Spinoza suggested in the seventeenth century, at the height of Reynard's early modern popularity, that all creatures naturally seek their own advantage, to preserve their own being and increase their power and that it is not only right for them do so, but that rational self-interest carries a very pure form of moral virtue. It is that benign interpretation of his character, I feel, that Reynard himself would claim, if pressed.

At the end of Caxton's translation, he addresses us directly, writing that amidst the humour, the 'japes and bourdes', 'many a good wisdom and learnings' might still be found, even leading us to new virtue and honour. For Reynard's faults, his escapades, outrageous schemes and tangled duplicities, only reflect the dense moral complexity of this fallen world of ours. No one is perfect, no one is without their faults or sins, so perhaps the best we can do is to follow his example and, eschewing all masks and hypocrisy, pursue our own inherent foxishness and hope for the best. As Froude put it in 1852, 'Lying, treacherous, cunning scoundrel as he is, there is a wholesome absence of humbug about him.'

'If anything be said or written herein', Caxton finally concludes, 'that may grieve or displease any man, blame not me, but the fox, for they be his words and not mine.' Reynard is so persuasive, so in charge of his own narrative, that even Caxton himself cannot assert authority over his own text. And neither, I'm afraid, can I. So, without further distraction or exposition, let Reynard, a fox for all seasons, beguile and entertain you with his many adventures.

CAST OF CHARACTERS

Dramatis Animales

The old tales of Sir Reynard the Fox are crowded with animals with full, busy lives and complicated relationships. For the ease of the Reader, therefore, a list of the principal characters follows, to avoid any unnecessary confusion.

King Noble the Lion
Ruler of all Flanders. His castle is situated in the middle of Gent, known today as the Gravensteen or the Castle of the Counts. Privileged, arrogant, impatient, fond of a drink and a joust. Father to the overprotected Leontius and Lenaert. Husband to Queen Gente.

Queen Gente the Lioness
Skilful in quietly retaining her not inconsiderable power. Extremely fond of fishing. Highly sympathetic to Reynard. Misses her ancestral home in Aquitaine and the company of her older brothers.

Sir Reynard the Fox
Our charming and occasionally violent anti-hero. A subversive, dashing, witty, philosophical, silver-tongued fox from Rupelmonde in the watery Waasland of Eastern Flanders. His notorious castle-fortress, Maleperduys, lies deep in woods between a wide heath and the River Schelde. Proud father to three cubs: Reynardine, Rossel and Reynkin.

Lady Hermeline the Vixen
Reynard's adored wife, a superb philologist and scribe, and a fox of great charity and goodness.

Lord Reynardius the Fox	Reynard's charismatic and dangerous father.
Sir Grimbart the Badger	Reynard's best friend and faithful supporter. Temperate, moral, kindly. An old sailor, he still keeps a boat in Brugge. A little grey around the whiskers.
Sir Isengrim the Wolf	Cruel, sociopathic, immoral. Reynard's sworn and eternal enemy, and a thoroughly nasty piece of work.
Lady Erswynde the Wolf	A sad, flint-mottled wolf with a delicate constitution and a slight limp in her front paw. Possessed of considerable skill in physic-craft and the preparation of potent medicines, but much taunted and abused by her wicked husband Isengrim.
Sir Bruin the Bear	Bumbling, vain and greedy. Lives in grace-and-favour rooms in Noble's castle. Only really interested in food.
Baron Adalbern the Bear	Bruin the Bear's uncle. Witty, erudite and much loved. Expert in both Ovid and Roman numismatics (with a leaning towards provincial coinage under Hadrian).
Sir Brichemer the Stag	Quiet and pious and dour, with many elderly relations to care for. Envies Reynard his *joie de vivre* and his freedom.
Sir Firapeel the Leopard	An aristocrat and a snob, with unpalatable beliefs.
Dame Rukenawe the Ape	One of the cleverest legal minds in Reynard's world, a powerful friend to the Fox and his family. Fond of extravagant rings and brooches and preens.
Sir Mertyn the Ape	A theologian, advisor to the Bishop of Cambrai, and great friend to Reynard and his kin.

Botsaert the Monkey	The King's Secretary. A self-made monkey from Montreuil-sur-Mer. A brilliant linguist, fluent in a dozen languages.
Sir Courtoys the Hound	Pretentious Francophile. Claims to have been a victim of Reynard's thievery through an incident with a sausage.
Bellin the Ram	A mercer of Gent, untitled, but rich and from a good family, hence his presence at Court. A busybody and a terrible bore, obsessed with his relatively minor interests in the Antwerp–Norwich wool trade.
Sir Tybert the Cat	A professor at the University of Louvain and passionate devotee of the Roman philosopher Anicius Manlius Severinus Boethius.
Sir Cuwaert the Hare	A nervous faint-voiced animal. His family farm is in Oostveld, where he pursues his passion in life, bulb gardening.
Sir Pancer the Beaver	A pragmatic and extremely tiresome lord; a know-it-all who makes a habit of explaining to others their own business.
Sir Lapreel the Rabbit	Down-to-earth, salt-of-the-earth, practical country rabbit. Accuses Reynard of attacking him.
Chaunticleer the Cockerel	Sober, sensible, head of various guilds. A well-respected cockerel from Lokeren, with a loving and large family, before tragedy strikes.
Sir Tiecelin the Raven	A pessimistic observer of courtly politics, whose great enjoyment in life lies in the misfortune, misery and reducement of others.
Sir Corbant the Crow	Noisy, tough character from the wild, flooded province of Zeeland.

Lady Sharpbeak the Crow   Corbant's deeply beloved wife. From one of the oldest and noblest families of Zeeland. Her grandmother was known for inventing a particularly delicious type of salted butterscotch or *boterbabbelaar*, which is still made today.

PART ONE

SUMMONING

In which Noble the Lion, King of all the Beasts, Count of Flanders, sends out his Mandements that Everyone should attend his Feast

Whit Sunday, 6th June

Once upon a Whitsuntide in the Low Countries, the land was white with hawthorn and the woods were blithe and greening. The trees were full hazy with new leaves and the ground with sweet-smelling herbs and flowers. All the birds were singing, singing from coiled nest, from branch, from fence, from river reed and from convent spire; songs which sang of fierce life and the kindly warmth of the sun, of journeys made and of journeys yet to come.

King Noble the Lion was lord of this watery, blossomy realm, from the leaden waves of the North Sea to the blue flax fields of Ypres. During the bright and holy days of the Whitsun Feast, he decided to open his Court, issuing forth dozens of mandements and commandments demanding that all animals should attend. And attend they did, streaming along the rough country tracks and gleaming white highways from Mons and Antwerp and Brugge, beasts great and beasts small, fearful and fearsome, rich and poor, from gilded castle and low thatched cottage they came, to celebrate Pentecost and to pay their respect and fealty to their glorious, golden-maned ruler.

All, that is, except for Reynard the Fox.

For Sir Reynard, Baron of Maleperduys Manor in the far east of the country, in the Land of Waas, the wilding waste-lands along the banks of the River Schelde, knew himself guilty of such bad behaviour at Court, of so many crimes and tricks and mischiefs against so many beasts, that he dared not show his whiskers.

And, sure enough, when all were gathered in their best finery, a chattering array of leopards and rams and cats and flitter-mouses and otters and stags and hares and beavers and unicorns and panthers and apes and squirrels and monkeys and lynxes and stone martens and pine martens and polecats and weasels and ermines and foxes and badgers and hawks squashed together on high and low tables in the Great Hall, helping themselves to the King's rich and heavily sauced dishes, there was a whispering, then a rumbling, then an uproar of indignant complaints and accusations against the Fox. At every bench of that Whitsun banquet, outrageous stories of Reynard's misconduct were told and repeated and elaborated, until the entire castle was baying for his blood and his reputation was in shreds.

CHAPTER TWO

The First Complaint made against Sir Reynard the Fox by Baron Isengrim the Wolf, his Enemy

The banquet eventually ended in a rowdy, disordered fashion with silver and maple mazers of steaming, spiced clary thumped down on each table to loud cheers. The clary, a mixture of wine and honey and herbs, was concocted each Whitsun to an old leonine family recipe by the King's butler, a snooty hare from Alsace called Witzke, who acquired all the King's wine for him, regularly making unnecessarily expensive buying trips to Paris and Bordeaux and Lisbon.

As usual, the hare had helped himself to a few cups in the cellar and, whilst serving, almost caused a diplomatic incident by sloshing some piping hot wine over a very small English weasel, the Bishop of Rochester no less, and an elderly Scottish pine marten, important guests of the Queen, scalding them grievously and ruining their hats.*

Thankfully for the hare, King Noble and his wife, the lioness Queen Gente, had already retired to their inner chamber, where their grand and highly decorated thrones had been placed. These thrones represented the pinnacle of the Flemish carver's art and had been made over a period of twenty-five

---

* The recipe for King Noble's Special Whitsun Clary is as follows. Mix very, very strong red Gascony wine together with clear honey, and generous pawfuls of cardamom, galingale, ginger, cinnamon, spikenard and green fennel. There may have been further bits and bobs accidentally added by the Alsatian hare, but this is the canonical list of ingredients, as recorded in a letter from King Noble to the King of England, who was interested in continental after-dinner drinks.

years by an enigmatic stoat, who liked to be known as the Master of Düsseldorf, despite being the son of a sausage-maker from Hulst. In any case, regardless of origins, the stoat had enormous talent in the sculptural arts, and had carved four fierce griffins for the armrests, intricate views of the towers of Gent on the backrests, and, on the wide overhanging canopy, an impressive frieze of lions performing brave and important acts in various battles of the Second Peloponnesian War.

King Noble had planned to spend an enjoyable hour or two framed by all this magnificence, being praised and flattered by his adoring subjects. All this rumpus about Lord Reynard's misdeeds had disrupted his plans, however, and the irritated lion was faced with a shuffling queue of grumbling, angry animals waiting to lodge their various complaints about the fox with their sovereign.

First up was Reynard's arch-enemy, Baron Isengrim the Wolf, who scowled into the chamber with his cowering family and a rout of slinking, snarling supporters. They didn't need to wait or push in front of the other beasts, as the queue immediately silenced then parted like ripped silk before them.

The wolf was about as nasty and brutal and frightening as they come. He had no compassion, no love, no kindness. He prayed only for himself and his own soul. He kicked his children, bullied his servants, and beat and belittled and betrayed his wife. The only lord in Flanders who had the nerve and the wit to stand up to him was Reynard the Fox. Fired by a mutual loathing which only seemed to increase as the world turned, they had a long troubled history of hostile encounters, going back decades. As often as not, these encounters would leave the surly, arrogant Isengrim in the most humiliating situations imaginable. For a narcissistic and humourless wolf like Isengrim, the worst thing in the world was being laughed at, and Reynard provided many a ripe occasion for just such mockery.

So, on this fair Whitsun Eve, the air sweet with roses from the Queen's garden, Isengrim the Wolf was determined to destroy Reynard once and for all, and he swaggered across to the thrones and stood close, too close, in front of the King, his thugs fanned out menacingly behind him. He didn't bother to bow. Even Noble the Lion was slightly scared of him, and he nervously tapped his claws on one of the carved griffins.

In appearance, Isengrim was much as you'd expect. He was tall and rangy and covered in jagged, ragged scars from his many duels and skirmishes. His fur was mottled grey with that reddish tinge which the Flanders wolves were once known for. He wore a broad scallop-edged cloak, trimmed in dark beaver fur, which swirled around him like a dirty grey rain cloud, soiled black velvet breeches and high black leather boots, laced at the side. Around his neck, a dirty scarlet kercher. Around his waist, a wide leather belt, also crow-black, hung with various sinister items—curved knives and pewter thimbles and mummified saints' fingers and amulets covered in odd runes and characters, and a tangled rosary with black Ave Maria beads and silver paternosters, which the gossips said had been given to him by one of his mistresses, a duchess from Lancaster, whose fur was as smooth and white as snow.

'High and Mighty Prince, my Lord the King,' gnarred Isengrim, his foul breath, a sour mixture of old meat and decaying teeth, trailing with each word, 'I beseech you, that through your great might, right and mercy, you will have pity on the serious crimes and trespasses and unreasonable misdeeds which Reynard the Fox has done to me and my wife.' Isengrim's wife, Lady Erswynde, a delicate, melancholy flint-mottled wolf with a slight limp in her front paw, made as though to speak at this point, but with one sharp look from her husband, stopped and hung her head.

'Last Midsummer,' declared Isengrim, 'Baron Reynard swanned into my house and befouled it. He came in against the will of my poor dear wife, and he found my sleeping cubs, and he peed on them, stinking yellow addle all over my sweet and innocent whelps! And can you guess why? Can you fathom that evil ruffin's soul? He wanted to blind them, so he did! Spoil their innocent sight with his brimstone mig!'

There were gasps of horror around the chamber. One of the rams, a devoted father to a flock of lambs, let out an audible sob.

'And where were you, Sir Isengrim? What did you do when you returned home to this terrible scene? It must have been rather shocking. Your cubs have entirely regained their sight, I see.' Queen Gente gestured at Isengrim's children, who were silently standing behind their mother. Isengrim looked at the Queen as though a worm had risen up and spoken.

Addressing the King, rather than the lioness, he continued, 'I was out finding food for my little family, as all good parents must. The fox had, er, gone by then, but I went and found him on the road, and demanded he agree on a day to come to my manor and excuse himself, and swear on my Holy Saints book that it was a mere accident, not by design.' Isengrim's tail flicked from side to side; he was pleased with the shape of his account. Queen Gente gave him a very long look.

'Well, Reynard shows up on the day, all bright and early, but when I gives him the book of saints' stories, he wouldn't touch it, let alone swear on it. And he whips around and runs away like a devil, back to his sordid hole in Rupelmonde.'* More shocked mumblings and exclamations, and Isengrim begins to exploit his audience, circling the room, all fangs and spittle and darkness. 'He didn't set much store about the matter, that fox. Blinded cubs? He didn't give a fig! And they still can't see properly—look at them.'

He roughly picked up his youngest cub by the scruff of his neck, who started to whimper and weep. 'See how he cries! Look at those tears! All is as dark as night to him! And look at all of you gathered here at the King's Court. Good animals. Honest animals. Loyal animals. Lives ruined, smashed, broken by that red-faced black-legged criminal.' Isengrim dropped his son, who landed awkwardly on the stone flags, then walked behind his wife, placing a heavy grey paw on her thin shoulder. But for her one trembling bad leg raised above the ground, she stood as unnaturally still as a stone statue in the Abbey of Saint Bavo.

'Oh, my fellow beasts, I could tell you of many other ways Baron Reynard has injured me. Stories to make your fur stand on end and your whiskers bristle. Indeed, were all the cloth of Gent gathered and unfurled as if it were parchment,

---

* Isengrim's Holy Saints book was the *Legenda aurea* or *Golden Legend* of Jacobus de Voragine (*c.* 1228–1298), a collection of hagiographies or lives of the saints. It was wildly popular in late medieval Europe, not least amongst Noble's courtiers, although its spiritual influence on the Wolf appears to have been somewhat negligible.

there would never be enough to scribe all that I now leave untold,' he rasped, stroking Erswynde's frozen back with his dirty claws, 'but the shame and villainy he has done to my wife, *that* I will howl from the highest ramparts to all of Christendom, and I will not—hear me, I will not—suffer that unavenged. Reynard the Fox will pay; by the thick blood of God, he will pay.'

CHAPTER THREE

The Second Complaint cast against
Sir Reynard the Fox by Sir Courtoys the
Hound, conveyed entirely in French

After this speech, there was a hush, pitted with a few nervous assents: 'Aye, aye, he must pay! Wicked Reynard! What a thing, eh!' Then, pushing through everybody's legs and tails, a little hound named Courtoys strode right up to the King, who was quickly having another snifter of clary to warm his blood after Isengrim's chilling performance.

Courtoys was a small dog of indeterminate breed, who was rather pretentious. He fancied himself as doyen of fashion at Noble's Court, which he privately condemned as rather provincial, spent a small fortune on his clothes and jewels, and only fenced in the Parisian style. Except occasionally to servants, he refused to speak Dutch or English, conversing in nothing but French (translated here), which he considered vastly superior in every way. Some of the animals took his appearance as a good point for a break and nipped to the closet or went to refill their cups in the Great Hall.

'I've listened to Monsieur Loup here,' gestured Courtoys, rubies glinting, best Brugge satin gleaming in the candlelight, 'and I would like to formally lodge my own complaint against the Fox. In fact, I'm very upset to impart to you all that, during the cold winter last, I endured a similar outrage.'

He extracted a frilled lace *mouchoir* from a sleeve and blew his nose. 'During that terrible hard frost, I was sore wintered and starving. My larder was almost empty apart from a single sausage—a lovely plump *boudin*, rich and fatty and salty.' Courtoys turned to the thinned crowd. 'Reynard, that scoundrel, stole that sausage. He stole it and he ate it, all by himself. My fine sausage.'

'A sausage, you say,' boomed King Noble, who could see this was going to be a long night. 'Well, well, well. A sausage.'

Suddenly, there was a flash of smooth grey fur and beautiful whiskers, and a clatter of claws on stone, and Sir Tybert the Cat, in a terrible fury, hissing like an adder, leapt half on top of the hound (who was heard by some nearby animals to bark a very earthy swear word which was definitely not French). A group of young lordly hares heading for the kitchens and three old crows, who were slipping out to go home, swiftly returned. Tybert, a professor at Louvain, was widely believed to be the cleverest animal at Court and he was a fiery and exciting rhetor when he was roused.*

'A sausage, indeed!' Tybert began, jabbing his paw at the hound, tail puffed in anger to three times its normal size. 'You are a liar, Courtoys! A liar, a gabber and a *coquin*! My Lord the King, I have been at Court all day and have heard Reynard sore complained upon, both in public and whispered in the shadows, in the stench-closet, behind sleeves. Accusation after accusation after accusation! Like flies to rotten meat! The fox is not even here to clear his name! Well, this meat in question, this sausage, minces away a wide cut of Reynard's case.'

---

* The last time being during an energetic argument with an Italian philosopher, an elderly boar visiting Gent from the University of Padua. Sparked by something to do with wine glasses and Diogenes of Sinope, it took place during King Noble's riotous Twelfth Night celebrations and, according to all, represented a high point of the dinner.

'Speak plainly, Tybert!' gruffed King Noble, 'Less of the tricksy words. Some of my courtlings are not as clever as you, Cat!'

Tybert bowed. 'What I am saying is this, Sire: the matter of which Courtoys speaks took place many years ago, not last year at all.' Courtoys shrugged in a nonchalant sort of way. 'Reynard still took my sausage.'

'But that's precisely it,' spat Tybert, 'that sausage, that lickerous pudding, that tasty *boudin*—it was mine. I had acquired it one night, I believe on the Feast of Saint Stephen, from a miller's house. I'd been taking the air, and was rather peckish, and the miller was asleep, and well, he was a fool, anyway, and it was wrapped up near the window. Anyway, I took it; it was my sausage and Courtoys stole it from me. If anyone should be sued and charged it should be that silly little hound! If he had any claim to the sausage it was through me!'

'Ha!' mocked Isengrim from the back of the Hall, where he was lounging with the other wolves.

Courtoys raced at Tybert, teeth bared. '*Bricon! Vilain! Glos pautonnier!*' he barked, as Tybert mimed eating a sausage.*

---

* Courtoys is using some rather salty old French insults he picked up in the taverns of Montagne Sainte-Geneviève, meaning 'fool' (*bricon*), low person (*vilain*) and 'gluttonous scoundrel' (*glos pautonnier*).

CHAPTER FOUR

The Third Complaint levied against
Sir Reynard the Fox, by Sir Cuwaert the Hare,
presented by Sir Pancer the Beaver

Suddenly, into the *mêlée*, cutting through the cat–dog bicker-ing, came a new voice, gruff with a strong undercurrent of insufferable smugness.

'Now, now, perhaps we should move on from the sausage incident. It seems a non sequitur, if you ask me. Sir Tybert, Sir Courtoys, calm yourselves, we are here to consider far more serious crimes.'

Up puffs Sir Pancer the Beaver, a pragmatic and somewhat tiresome lord, who made a habit of explaining to others their own business. Tybert found him particularly annoying as Pancer fancied himself a scholar and, with a certitude born from profound ignorance and the privilege of his situation as one of the richer animals at Court, would perpetually contradict Tybert on subjects which the cat had spent twenty years studying in some of the finest universities in Europe—correcting him on his Abelardian ethics, for example, or the ecclesiastical history of Flanders, and he even had the nerve to forward a contrary opinion on Tybert's beloved Boethius, on whom he was widely considered the foremost authority.[*]

---

[*] The Roman senator and philosopher Anicius Manlius Severinus Boethius (*c.* 475/7 CE–526? CE) was a highly influential philosopher whose dramatic and accessible writing spread Christian Neoplatonism to a wide medieval public, bridging classical philosophy with the early Middle Ages. For a while he was a great favourite of Theodoric, king of the Ostrogoths (454–526), largely because of his sharp and scholarly mind,

In any case, with his usual stolid confidence, Sir Pancer settled on a rush stool in front of the courtiers, who were still talking about the sausage. Once their tattle had silenced and at a nod from King Noble, he began. 'Sir Tybert, once again, I understand your concerns over this sausage, but do you really think that Reynard should not be complained on and accused? We all know him to be a murderer, a rover and a thief! There is no one, not even our Lord King here, that he wouldn't wish to lose honour, even life itself, if it meant he could have a tasty leg of roast chicken, a succulent bite of a goose!'

The Beaver paused to sip some of his fortified ale. He always used his own hedge-maple cup, which he had turned himself and which he swore had medicinal qualities, good for the liverish. Except for the wolves, the Court gathered close, sensing a scandalous story to follow.

'I shall tell you all,' said the beaver, 'what I saw Sir Reynard the Fox do to Sir Cuwaert the Hare, who stands here before us today.' Sir Cuwaert crept forwards. He was an extremely nervous creature, with a strained, worried face and a voice as faint as a summer breeze in the flax fields. Nobody could ever quite hear what he was saying, and so he lived his life in a sea of misunderstandings and missed appointments. This

---

but was executed for disloyalty, a charge inflamed by slander and betrayal by his fellow courtiers. Tybert was obsessed with Boethius and had been translating his most influential work, written in prison in the form of a dialogue with Lady Philosophy herself, *De consolatione philosophiae*, *The Consolation of Philosophy*, from Latin into a form of complicated high feline Dutch. This was taking years, begun way back when he was a student at Pavia, where Boethius was killed and his cult sprang up. It was his grand project, his legacy, for want of a wife and kittens. He talked of little else, and the other animals at Court had learned to avoid the subject in conversation.

was a great shame, for he was a gentle animal, who had much to offer the world, not least in the field of bulb cultivation, of which he was an early pioneer, importing a new type of flower called a Tulipa from Constantinople.*

'In broad daylight, it was, and one of the worst crimes almost committed in the County of Flanders from the time of Joab himself.' He paused and chewed thoughtfully on his maple bowl. Everyone waited to find out what terrible crime Reynard had almost committed. 'It was during the time our gracious King and Queen had proclaimed peace across the land, when we all laid down our swords and, more's the point, laid down old blood feuds. A time of safe conduct and a time when our weaker brothers and sisters should be able to progress around the country without dread of attack!

'It happened on the high road from Brugge. I was picking some agrimony from the fields near Knesselare to make my musket-shot water, when I saw them. Reynard seemed to be shouting at Cuwaert, so I went a bit closer to hear what was going on. Cuwaert looked all afluster and the fox was promising him that he would teach him the Apostles' Creed—"I'll show you how to sing the Credo like a good chaplain," says Reynard. And he makes Cuwaert sit between his legs—I speak the truth, Cuwaert no?' asked Pancer. Cuwaert stepped over and mumbled something indistinguishable. Pancer looked at

---

* Despite Sir Cuwaert's early cultivation, the first official mention of
a tulip by a Western European was in 1554 by the Flemish diplomat
Ogier Ghiselin de Busbecq (1522–1592), Ferdinand I's ambassador to the
Ottoman Empire, who, on the way from Adrianople to Constantinople,
described *ingens ubique florum copia offerebatur, narcissorum, hyacinthorum,
et eorum quos Turcae tulipan vocant* ('an abundance of flowers everywhere;
narcissus, hyacinths and those in Turkish called Lale').

him with a pained expression, decided he was vouchsafing his account and continued.

'Between Reynard's thighs is pinned our Cuwaert and together they begin to sing and recite the Creed. "Credo, Credo! I believe, I believe!" cries the fox, so loudly that all the birds scattered from the trees. I'll wager you could hear him in Brussels such a racket he was making. I was naturally afeared for the hare, so I stopped my hiding and went up to the pair, and just as well, as it was at that precise moment that Reynard started to play his old tune, that old sinister melody that we all know so well.

'If I hadn't stopped him, he would have killed our long-eared cousin, for he had him by the throat. Isn't that right, Sir Cuwaert? He would've bitten your head clean off?' he shouted. Cuwaert shook his head in a manner which was very hard to interpret as either 'yea' or 'nay', and whispered something akin to 'it's a long way to Reims next Tuesday.' Pancer nodded sagely. 'You can see the fresh wounds on Cuwaert's neck, look,' he pointed. Everyone looked, and Queen Gente stepped down from her throne to delicately examine the hare, but, aside from the faintest pink scratch, there was little to be seen.

Having said his piece on behalf of his imperilled willowy friend, Sir Pancer the Beaver stood up, clasping his tough little front paws lawyerly, to make his closing remarks. 'For sooth, my Lord the King, you mustn't on any account let Reynard go unpunished for this terrible crime! You mustn't let him go quietly! He who has broken your peace so flagrantly!' And he slapped his tail hard three times—a warning of great danger in beaver circles. 'If you don't act, Lord, according to our judgement as your subjects, then I fear that your cubs, and your cubs' cubs and your cubs' cubs' cubs, and even your cubs' cubs' cubs' cubs will be blamed and despised for many long years to come.'

And with this unhappy forecast, the beaver smoothed down his whiskers and took his little stool and his maple maselyn and sat down in the front row of the crowd, to hear the verdict of his king. Silence. Then a snarling yirr from the far fireplace in the shadowy recesses of the hall. Isengrim once more. 'He's right. You speak truth, Pancer. Right and justice must be done; we all know what was done to traitors and murderers in the old days. Let's not be lenient, if we want Flanders to be a land of peace and animal harmony once more.'

CHAPTER FIVE

In which Sir Grimbart the Badger speaks on behalf of Sir Reynard the Fox, his Friend

At Isengrim's words, which were greeted with a nervous scatter of applause, one of the most venerable members of the Court stood up. Sir Grimbart the Badger. Honourable, competent, sensible Grimbart. True of his words and as reliable and stalwart as English oak. Moral without being sanctimonious. Observant of law and duty, but profoundly sympathetic to the sudden upending of a life wrought by passion or the flare of temper.

He was the sort of badger you'd want as your cutting surgeon on a battlefield or guarding your gold plate when travelling abroad, or stalling a frenzied fire whipping through a city burg. And whilst he had probably performed all these services and more, he never boasted of his achievements, being uninterested in worldly glory and all its falsities. His greatest passion in life was sailing and the sea, and he'd made a considerable fortune through importing and exporting all manner of goods to England: aniseed and musk balls and garlic and frying pans and felt hats and feather beds and Cologne woad and sail thread and ivory combs and sturgeon in vats of brine. Now he was getting on a bit, he still maintained a boat in Brugge and when he took her out in a cold east wind, plunging into the vast grise-grey seas and rolling cloud-lands, he was never more content.

Indeed, Grimbart was usually unflappable, but in the midst of what he considered to be a mob trial against Reynard, his closest friend whom he loved most dearly, he was extremely angry. A roused brock, particularly a serious-minded dass like Grimbart, is a terrible sight to witness, and as he thundered to the fore the animals shaffled uncomfortably, suddenly feeling a little hasty in their eager condemnation of the fox.

Grimbart bowed in a very elaborate and old-fashioned way to the King and kissed the Queen's paw and greeted her in his excellent French, then began.

'Sir Isengrim's testimony should be discounted. It is entirely malicious and, I suspect, bears little resemblance to the truth. There is an old saying, well known by all present, that sweet words rarely fall from an enemy's mouth, and the wolf's words are, I would venture, as bitter as wormwood. Now I suggest that this equally bitter feud between Reynard and Isengrim should be settled. Whichever of the two has sinned most against the other, let him be hanged by the neck on a tree, like a thief.'

Grimbart raised his deep brockish voice to the wolf camp in the rear—'Isengrim, I fear you would be the one swinging, for you have wronged the fox more times than I can remember. If things were reversed, if Baron Reynard's standing at Court was as high as yours, if he enjoyed the same honeyed favours and condescension from on high, then, by all the saints, you would be in trouble, for, Janus Wolf, you have bitten and nipped my dear Reynard with your foul and sharp teeth many more times that I can tell. I doubt that my friend would consider it enough that you merely begged his forgiveness.'

Grimbart's face was as full fierce as a winter squall in the North Sea. Isengrim merely snorted in response.

'Let me elaborate. I will convey some points which I know well.' (Grimbart had, as a young badger in London, eaten some good dinners at Lincoln's Inn, and had retained much of that rigorous legal training.) 'Do you remember when Reynard managed to clamber onto the fisherman's cart that time, on the road through the salt marshes from Elmare? He threw down some lovely fresh plaice. And you, wicked Wolf, following from afar, ate all the most delicious fish yourself, leaving him nothing but the bones and grate.'

'Likewise,' continued Grimbart, ignoring the wolfish jeering from the back, 'I recall a similar occasion regarding a great flitch of bacon, fat and tasty, won by Reynard through his skill and hard work, and which he had graciously agreed to share fairly between you. But honour be damned! You seized it in your jaws and gobbled it all up in one gulp without a thought for the fox!

'When he demanded his share, you sneered and mocked him and said—I paraphrase—"Oh Reynard, fair youngling, I shall gladly give you your part, here's the string from which it was hung, have a good chew, it's very oily and tasty!" The string, Isengrim! The string! Shame on you, Wolf! After Reynard was almost caught and tossed in a bag for his pelt! Wagering life and limb to save his bacon, and you leave him with nothing, nothing but a lumpish curl of greasy string!' Grimbart turned to the Court, his sombre robes flapping in his agitation, 'My goodness me, by the blessed buboes of Saint Macarius, Isengrim has made Reynard suffer more than he ought to, and harm-botherings like these have happened more times than I can count on my claws!'

Grimbart folded his paws, looked down his bristly striped nose, catching the eyes of some of the more sensible animals—Queen Gente, Sir Tybert, Dame Rukenawe the Ape—and pressed his arguments.

'My ladies sage, my prudent lords, do you think this right? Do you think this fair or lawful? And yet there's more! Sir Isengrim has complained at length, to anyone who would listen, that Lord Reynard is infatuated with fair Erswynde, and has sinned against her on more than one occasion!'

'Indeed,' continued Grimbart, ignoring the growling and booing from the wolves, 'the fox had a great devotion to that lady, but that was seven years ago, long before her marriage and his, when they were scarce more than whelps. What the Florentines call a cub-*amore*, nought more. As innocent and blotless as Blandijnberg snow. I am assured that Reynard treated Erswynde with courtesy and the delicacy of young love—where's the harm in that, eh? Both were soon over their dalliance. Why are we even wasting words on't!'

The Brock glared round at various members of the Court, dwale-black eyes resting on the tattling Sir Pancer, who squirmed uncomfortably on his stool. 'If you had any wisdom at all, Isengrim,' shouted Grimbart, 'you would stop slandering your wife in this way. She has done nothing wrong and makes no accusation against the fox. You are simply stirring up trouble for your enemy!' Isengrim laughed, a nasty laugh, and pulled his wife's tail hard, forcing her back towards him and his cronies. Grimbart eyed him with savage badgerly contempt and began to pace.

'But there is more. More slander, more accusements as insubstantial as thistle tufts. Sir Cuwaert the Hare has made his very ill-advised complaint—not even in his own words, as Sir Pancer has spoken for him—and a tremulous tale it is at that. If the hare was failing and stumbling at his lessons in the Creed, then Reynard, as his schoolmaster, had every right to scold him. If scholars aren't chastised for their lazed truancy, their idleness, their prittle-prattle, how, pray tell me, Sir Pancer, Sir Cuwaert, can they ever learn?' The pair just stared at Grimbart, whose eyebrows were bristling in fury, hardly daring to respond during his rolling righteous defence of the fox's honour.

'And if this weren't bad enough, this very evening, we have Sir Courtoys the Hound, of all animals, come pushing through the flanks of his betters with one of the silliest and most duplicitous complaints I have heard in all my long years! If we were at sea, he'd be thrown in the surge for his lying tongue! First, he tells us that he had with considerable pains seized himself a nice blood pudding last Yule frost, when a good sausage was near impossible to find, by gold or by stealth. Then, he accuses Reynard of stealing this rare boudin.'

Grimbart suddenly stumbled in his pacing and sat heavily down on the steps leading up to Noble's throne. All this excitement and righteousness was making his heart jump and flicker in his chest. He was not a young badger and he was seldom this agitated. Queen Gente made to help him, but he waved her away courteously, and continued, a little ragged but just as angry.

'My friends, Sir Courtoys should have held his peace, for it transpires through the learned testimony of our whiskered brother Tybert that not only was the hound fuddling the year of the transgression, but he was the sausage thief all along! *Male quesite male perdite!*[*]

At this piece of incomprehensible Latin, which he took as extremely insulting, Sir Courtoys raised himself to his full height, which was knee-high to the badger, and stormed dramatically out of the chamber—clickety-clack-clack through everyone's legs again and past the pile of snoozing polecat guards to the main hall. As he was a tiny dog, this took a very, very, very long time to achieve, and everyone watched his curled, beribboned tail bobbing slowing away.

Badger took the opportunity to take a quick drench of hawthorn supping from his flask to ease his palpitations and bellowed after Courtoys:

'It is only good and right that what was ill-gained was also ill-lost! Who shall blame Reynard for taking a tough old sausage from a common thief! It is quite obvious that the fox was entirely in the right. No animal conversant with the law can blame someone as well-born as Reynard for confiscating stolen goods! Why, not a single noble beast of Gent would think it unreasonable if Baron Fox had slow-hanged Courtoys when he found him with the pudding. Menour are menour and thieves are thieves after all, and it was only for the sake of the honour of the Crown that he didn't gallow him there and then, on Christmas Day in the snow.'

He paused to glare at Sir Pancer the Beaver once more.

'But Sir Reynard, whom you malign so unreservedly, is a far finer fox than you imagine. He did not wish to do justice

---

[*] This is Grimbart's slightly garbled version of *male quaesita male perdita*, an appropriate reference for the sausage incident, meaning literally 'badly acquired, badly lost goods' or 'stolen goods never do well'.

24

without proper leave, and out of his respect for King Noble he forbade hanging that trindle-tailed little cur. And what reward has he received for this gentle act of mercy and fidelity? Little thanks from his fellows, and only garbled lies from the hound himself! And what wounds my dear friend the most, what scathes him to the bone, is the fact that he, Reynard, is the one being complained upon!'

Grimbart started to step and pace again, and spoke earnestly now, front paws folded, looking more like a Beaupere than ever in his simple dark robes and girdle.

'My dear friend Reynard is a gentle and true fox. He suffers no falsehoods and detests liars. He does nothing without his priest's council. Since my Lord the King hath proclaimed his peace, he has never thought to hurt anyone, feathered, furred or, indeed, human-shaped.'

Grimbart glowered at Sir Bruin the Bear, who was leaning against a pillar noisily gorging a ham hock and a bowl of preserved cherries, his fashionably tight gipon and breeches—both in an expensive puce silk velvet—straining at the laces whenever he moved.

'Unlike many other animals I could mention, Reynard eats no more than once a day, from a very small trencher, and lives as a recluse. It's been over a year since he ate flesh of wild or tame beasties. He chastises his body regularly and even wears a shirt of hair. Fleas march through his ruffled fur, his whiskers are greasy and unwashed, mud chokes his white brush, all for the love of God. And, what's more, I just heard from some sheep from Antwerp, who passed by Rupelmonde only yesterday, that Reynard had left and given over his castle Maleperduys and built a simple hermitage near the river, with a few beehives, where he now resides, quite, quite alone. He has stopped hunting and, aside from the honey and a few hindberries from the forest, lives only by alms and takes nothing but what he is given in charity.

'In sum, Baron Reynard has waxed most pale and thin from all his fasting and praying and harsh disciplines and long vigils to be one with Christ. Indeed, peace with God is his only purpose now in life.'

Aside from the sounds of a dice game in the wolf's quarters, Bruin's scoffle-munching and a few gentle snores from the guards and some of the other bears, the entire hall was gripped by Grimbart's words. Gripped and entirely bewildered, as this portrait of Reynard as a penitent fox ran contrary to everything the Court had seen and heard of his behaviour for many years. They might, however, given the upstanding moral character of his defender, have accepted this new pious figure, had the blanched, bony claws and dark feathers of Death herself not entered the castle grounds.

CHAPTER SIX

The Final Complaint by Chaunticleer the Cockerel and his Family, who tell of their Great Sorrow

It was late. Servants had brought in dozens of yellow candles to light the chamber and clouds of moths were drifting in from the dark summer night, whirling and flickering around the flames and the Whitsun wreaths of whitethorn and quince blossom and apple blede.

Outside, grasshoppers were singing themselves to sleep, and the castle moat, filled that morning from the river sluice to drown an encampment of summering rats, lapped against the high stone walls.

As Grimbart came to the end of his speech, there was a sense of anticlimax, of exhaustion, of the embarrassment and awkwardness that linger after a fever of collective outrage has cooled. Perhaps they had been too hasty to condemn Baron Reynard; perhaps they could simply put his absence down to his new complicated religious devotions—after all, a rich feast was not something a fasting, godfrighty fox would be keen on attending. Some whispers were even beginning to circulate of possible sainthood, of similar sudden conversions from dissolution to sanctity; an elderly mole mentioned Saint Francis.

And so, the fox redeemed, and his accusers routed, the Court was slowly starting to gather itself to bed, when, just as the solemn compline bells were beginning to toll, Queen Gente's godson, Sir Íñigo-the-Black-Ears, a popular young fox from Navarre, known for his skill with a longbow, shouted out—'Look, look, coming down the hill, look!'

Everyone rushed to the arched windows which looked across to the corn fields and the Great White Road to Antwerp. Under a brilliant gibbous moon, a grim procession was slowly moving towards the castle gates, casting in and out of view as it passed through the deep, angular shadows of the poplar trees.

It was led by an anguished Chaunticleer the Cockerel, arrayed entirely in black. Behind him was a bier, a funeral cart, draped with swathes of orange velvet, on which were laid the mortal remains of a little hen, head quite removed from her body: brutally murdered by Reynard the Fox. Following the bier came a drightfare of chickens, chanting and wailing and groaning and sobbing.

King Noble ordered some of the animals to assist Chaunticleer, and the little hen's catafalque, as light as a May mist, was carried into the Great Hall, then through to the Throne Room, where it was placed, in all its horror, in front of the lions' thrones.

Chaunticleer was a sober, well-respected cockerel from Lokeren, head of both the Master Weavers Guild and the Poultry Guild and a dozen other companies and fellowships and fraternities. He wore a little pair of spectacles on the end of his beak, kept careful records in a round, careful script, and was an important lynchpin in the complex networks of mercers fanning out like lace bobbins across Noble's kingdom and abroad.

This Whitsun night, however, he was a wreck. A hollow shell of a bird. For the remains were those of his best beloved daughter, Coppen, a sweet young hen on the cusp of life in all its joys and sorrows. He staggered in front of the King, piteously wringing his feathers and twisting his feet this way and that.

By either side of the bier stood two equally sorrowful hens, Coppen's sisters, draped in exquisitely embroidered veils, black as their tail feathers. The elder hen was named Cantart and the younger Good Crayant. Widely believed to be the two fairest hens between Holland and the Ardennes, their beauty paled, however, beside that of their recently departed sister, whose spotted hazel and cream feathers had been spread angelically either side of her limp, cold body.

Each sister held a burning taper, long and straight, the flames sooting their plumes as they wept. So wretchedly they cried for Coppen, so heavy were their tears, that sympathetic sniffles could soon be heard around the chamber, Sir Bruin blowing his nose noisily on his sleeve.

On receiving the news of her little daughter's murder, their mother, Pertelote, had collapsed in coiling pain at home in Lokeren, plucking her own feathers out in her agonies, and it was said that her screams of loss could be heard that night all those miles away in Noble's castle in Gent—carrying like shards of brittle light over the fields and dykes and waterlands.

Shaking, Chaunticleer addressed Noble the Lion, who had called for some brandewine to try and settle him a little. 'Merciful Lord, my Lord the King,' he stuttered, 'please hear our bitter complaint and abhor the great scathe, the great wound of all wounds which Baron Reynard the Fox of Maleperduys has done to me and my children, who stand here weeping before you and the Queen!

'It was in the beginning of April of this year, when the trees were budding new and the weather was so fair. I was feeling very proud and very bold and hardy. I'd been thinking, you see, about my noble lineage, going all the way back to Baron Chaunticleer the Numerate, whose skills with an abacus are still praised in Lokeren today.' He smiled sadly.

'All these distinguished fowl rowed behind me, and before me,' his voice cracked, 'eight fair sons and seven beautiful daughters which my wife had hatched. All strong and healthy and plump. And they spend their days in our farmyard, which is protected not only by a strong high wall, but also our six great dogs living in a shed by the main door—

'Saphyrus, a jewel of a hound, with white fur and purple-brown ears, and the leader, Mopsus, chestnut coat, speckled with golden hair, and Melissa, their mother, the colour of quicksilver, and Mopsulus, a real old rascal with one yellow eye and a snub nose, and Arnoldo, a handsome canis given to us by a dear lawyer friend from Antwerp, and last but not least dearest Pimpernel, who has a fondness for wine, which has caused him a little bit of gout, which we've been trying to address with poultices...'

Queen Gente coughed pointedly. Those shocked by grief, she knew from experience, were apt to ramble for hours, and it was important to hear the cockerel's testimony. Chaunticleer looked at her blear-eyed, then continued.

'Our dogs, you see, are our dear friends, but they are also fearsome guard dogs, and have torn and plucked many a beastie's skin, and so my children have never been afraid, and have always peacefully played and pecked in our yard.' He swallowed hard, his wattle swifting from side to side. Each time, it seemed harder to utter the name of his Coppen's killer.

'Reynard the Fox, knowing they felt certain he couldn't reach them, was even keener to get his long teeth into them. Oh, he cast a greedy eye on my children and wife, so he did.

'Night after night, we heard him creeping around the walls, scratching and sniffing and knocking over the old milking pails. Sometimes he was silent as the grave, lying in wait for us to come out. We set the dogs on him many a time to hunt him away. Once they caught up with him by the dyke, and in the dark they leapt on him, and it cost him hard. I saw his very skin smoked off, yet he managed somehow to escape, howling all the way home. May God grind him low for his crimes!'

The cockerel paused as a small liveried mole, one of Noble's servants of the bedchamber, helped him take a snifter of brandewine. Sir Grimbart, the fox's protector, face as stern as a stone bishop, came up to assist, conveying some words of comfort and succour and patting Chaunticleer on the back, returning afterwards to the alcove where he was making dense notes on a scrip of parchment as the chicken continued his tale.

'After this incident, we were quiet of Reynard for a long while. But then, one bright May morning, there was a knock at the gate, and there he was, dressed in the likeness of a hermit, in dusty brown robes and a rope girdle and broad blue hat. He gave me a letter to read sealed with the King's seal—a lion risen up, just like that'—he pointed with his wing at one of Noble's banners, embroidered with the red lion rampant of Gent. 'The letter said that all manner of beasties and fowls should do no harm or scathe to one another anymore. That you, my Lord, King Noble, had proclaimed peace throughout the land and from now on there would be no more fighting or feuds or killing.'

'Quite so,' said King Noble, 'I did indeed proclaim as much.'

'Then Reynard sank down on his knees and told me he was a cloisterer now, a closed recluse in the Abbey of Baudeloo, the main house at Klein-Sinaai, and he told me he would perform great penances for his sins—very, very serious pilgrimages to Rome and Canterbury and Jerusalem and the like. And he showed me his mantle and his fur pilche and his hair shirt thereunder—all the things you need for a pilgrim's walk. And then he says,' the poor, grieving father's voice broke once again, and he took his spectacles off and dabbed at his eyes with a plume, 'he says, "Sir Chaunticleer, you and your kin don't need to be frightened of me no more, don't even need to take heed of me anymore, as I've decided to eat no more flesh." And he looks at me with those lamber eyes of his, looks at me straight and says "I'm weary of the world now, Sir Chaunticleer, I am tired of sensation, of the endless chase. I am old. I am old, and I want to concentrate on saving my eternal soul. That is my only concern. Now, I must part with you and say farewell, for I've yet to say my sexte, my none and my evensong." And he grasps my wing, so sincere he was. I don't know. I'm such a fool.'

He started to shake, his beak hidden in his trembling wings, not even crying now, just a complete capitulation to his tragedy that was desperately upsetting to watch.

'And off Reynard the Fox went, singing his Crede all holy and loud. But he didn't go. He didn't really go. Foolish bird, I am, stupid bird. He didn't go, did he.' Chaunticleer looked around the room, as though begging the animals to tell him different. 'No, he didn't leave. No, he went round the back of the farmhouse, didn't he, slunk under a spike-tangle of white albespyne by the trough. He didn't go away, did he.'

The Misses Cantart and Crayant gave their tapers to two kindly hares, delicately eager to help, and went to comfort their father as he staggered on with his terrible testimony. Their sweet cinnabar faces, still framed in pinfeathery fluff, were so pained and so serious, with a look of much, much older hens, that Chaunticleer clutched at them. 'Courage, Papa!' they urged, 'Courage! You've almost told! Our Lady Mary will help you; she lost her child.'

Chaunticleer looked at his daughters with dazed adoration. 'I thought he'd gone for good, that fox. I thought that was the last we'd have to worry about him. I was so glad and so happy and took no more heed of him. And I went to my darling children, and I, and I clucked them altogether, I did, and, then—stupid bird, Chaunticleer, foolish bird—I took them out of the yard for an evening stroll, I was so happy, I wanted them to know that they were safe outside and were free, finally free. I said that, I said, you're free, my chicks. Stupid bird, foolish bird.

'Then, the harm came at us so fast. Reynard was lying under his thorn bush and he came creeping out between us and the gate, and he caught one of my children, he did, he caught one, one of my littlest chicklings, dear little Colijn, my youngest son, and he killed him, he killed him in front of us, and put him in his pouch, like he was nothing, worth nothing, nothing at all. Oh Colijn! Oh! Your snepe and witless father, what a foolish, stupid bird I am! And then, with the taste of my little son in his mouth, the fox went mad, he went quite mad, mad as a woodman he was, no hunter nor hound in the world could keep him from our little family after that! He lay in wait night and day, slouching around the wall; crazed and cunning he stole baby after baby after baby, he slaughtered my family—O Father King, O Mother Queen—he killed them chick after chick after chick, my darlings, he killed fifteen of my darlings, as though they were nothing, worth nothing at all. Of fifteen, I have only four left, only four left. And yesterday, the worst, my best beloved, my little Coppen, so good and kind, the pippin of her mother's eye, her little body that lies there on the bier was rescued by the hounds. Gracious King have pity on me, on my great damage from that wicked vos, I have lost almost everything, almost everything. What means money or flax fields or wool sacks or lineage, when your precious chickling lies dead before you.'

The candles were guttering low now and the moon was sinking in the sky and there wasn't a dry eye in the castle. Everyone was moved to tears by the cockerel's account, from the most insignificant little ewery mouse eavesdropping en route to the kitchens, to Noble in his satin finery on his great kinestool, rough-wiping his face with his sleeve and then gruffly snapping his paw for another stiff drink for Chaunticleer, who was barely standing now, propped up by his daughters and Sir Grimbart, who was talking to him with his usual tact in the gentlest of voices. 'There, there, all will be well now, you've made your telling, Coppen would be proud of her father, so she would; there, there, old chap.'

Things did not look good for Reynard the Fox.

CHAPTER SEVEN

The King summons his Counsellors

After Sir Chaunticleer had been settled, King Noble the Lion, smoothing his mane with an enormous paw, began to speak, his booming blunderbuss-tones stilling the chamber.

'Sir Grimbart the Badger, you have heard these charges laid against your friend Reynard the Recluse. You have seen the body of Fair Coppen. By Saint Arnold of Soissons, if I live until next Whitsun, he'll pay for his crimes, however much he fasts and prays and says his Creed.' Grimbart nodded. He was still making copious notes of the proceedings on his cross-hatched and increasingly ink-blotted parchment.

King Noble then turned to the chickens, his voice gentling as much as a lion's can. 'Now hark Sir Chaunticleer of Lokeren. Your complaint against the fox is enough to act on; you have shaded the gloom landscape of the fox's crimes well. But even a king cannot resurrect your daughter and we can bind her no more to life. Think now of betaking her to God. We shall tonight give her the death rites, we shall sing her vigil mass and bury her worshipfully on earth.'

He paused. If left to its own devices, Noble's mind rested naturally on jousting and drinking and frike tales and gossip, and, just like his father and grandfather before him, he always felt exhausted by difficult decisions, sinking into a mental torpor when prevailed upon to rule rather than simply luxuriate in the pomp and riches of his rank. Nevertheless, he had been deeply moved by the chickling's death and concerned by Reynard's wild behaviour, so he rallied somewhat. 'Sir

Cockerel, we shall speak with these lords gathered here and take counsel on how we may do right and justice on this massed murder, and bring this false thief, this wicked fox, to the law.'

So, as night began to thin into dawn, and the day star rose over the rooftops of Gent, King Noble the Lion ordered the Court, young and old, exalted and humble, to begin the *officium defunctorum*, the office for the dead, for the soul of the little hen Coppen, whose eyes had now been covered by a pair of the smallest silver coins from the King's mint. The first antiphon, *placebo Domino in regione vivorum* ('I will please the Lord in the Land of the Living') was intoned very loudly by the high meadow voices of the hares, who felt deep kinship with the chickens, being equally afeared of the fox. It would take too long to recount all the other verses and hymns and psalms and readings, and who sung them and when, but suffice to say Coppen's wake was as thorough and as mournful and as dignified as that of a royal duchess.

After the vigil and the commendation, Coppen was laid in a grave dug with great care under a lime tree, in a little patch of grass starred with celandines. Upon it was laid a marble stone, engraved with the following gloomy inscription:

Coppen
Chaunticleer's Daughter
Whom Reynard the Fox Hath Bitten
Here Under Lies Buried
Lament Her Well, for She is Shamefully Come to her Death

After the melancholy interment, the King sent for his lords, those whom he thought were the canniest of his Council—Sir Grimbart, Sir Firapeel the Leopard, Sir Brichemer the Stag, Sir Mertyn the Ape—to take advice on how Reynard the Fox should be punished for this depraved and cankered murder. Their deliberations and conclusions were swift. Any considerations of his new-found godliness were dismissed. It was quite obvious that Reynard must be sent for immediately and brought to appear in the King's Court to hear the judgement against him.

He would, they thought, inevitably try his usual foxerie to evade arrest, and so they decided to send the strongest, heftiest figure in the castle—Baron Bruin the Bear. He wasn't the brightest of animals, but he was certainly the largest and, judged the Council, more than able to trump Reynard in brawn and muscle, if not in wits.

This all seemed good and proper to King Noble, who was very fond of wrestling and wraxling and jousting and all sports which loosened teeth and broke noses and smashed collarbones, and so favoured strength over intelligence any day of the week. 'Sir Bruin,' he declared, 'I would like you to assume the position of Royal Erindbere and take our message to Reynard in his hermitage at Maleperduys near Rupelmonde. It is a long way and it might be a bit difficult to entice him out, but we all trust you and place this very important task in your, er, capable paws.' He stopped for a moment, looking over at the sleeping bundle of grieving chickens tucked up under blankets next to a tapestry of the Walls of Jericho.

'You must take care, Sir Bruin, we don't want you to end up on your own funeral cart. Look after yourself as best you can, for Reynard is an evil rascal and a tricksy old shrew. He's dangerous, Sir Bruin, you understand, Bear, dangerous! He's full of so many wiles and he will lie and he will flatter you, oh my goodness, he will flatter you, and he will think of all the ways to beguile and deceive and bring you to mockery. D'you hear, Bruin, mockery!'

Sir Bruin was trying to pay attention to Noble's advice, but was drifting off a little, thinking about which tasty morsels to pack and wondering whether the cooks in the kitchen were up or whether they had gone to bed and which hat to wear on his journey and how grand it was that he'd been picked for this extremely important mission. 'It's a bit late for Reynard to deceive a Bear such as myself,' he replied, 'I know my law, I do, I've learnt my cases. He's come too late to mock me!'

CHAPTER EIGHT

The First Summons: In which Sir Bruin the Bear, Royal Messenger, is dispatched on a calamitous Mission to bring Sir Reynard the Fox to Court

Whit Monday and Whit Tuesday, 7th and 8th June

At sunrise, Sir Bruin the Bear, Royal Messenger, Erindbere to the King, entrusted with the task of capturing the errant fox, marched down the long straight road leading from the castle. It was a glorious June morning. The birds were pippering in the trees, the hedgerows were white with May blossom and frory banks of cow parsley, and the bells of Gent were singing out across the fields for Whit Monday.

In one fat paw, Bruin grasped a tightly rolled sheet of parchment still dripping with black wax from the King's great seal—a warrant for Reynard's arrest—and in the other he carried a stout walking staff. Over his shoulder was slung a worn leather bag, stuffed full of leftovers from the feasting the night before. He had a very big appetite, even for a bear, and this was what he had packed for a light morning repast:

Five roast capons, crispy and succulent.

A small basket of sweet red cherries.

Several pawfuls of sour green gooseberries.

Four loaves of soft, floury payndemayn bread.

One big round cheese like a ball, with a waxy pimpernel-red rind.

Two pats of sweet yellow Eindhoven butter shaped like fen flowers.

Two fatty veal pies with the lightest of pastry.

Two oily lamprey pies that stank high of river weeds.

Three marzipan lions, moulded *en couchant*.

A few rich morsels of roast swan (as the *pièce de résistance* of the banquet, Bruin could only rustle up a few leftover scraps, stuck to the base of a fancy ornamental silver *nef* in the shape of a three-masted sailing ship).

A clay pot of squirming, wriggling earthworms (with a few gleiming slugs thrown in for good measure).

'Such a handsome figure I do make,' thought Bruin as he rumbled along, biting the head off one of the lions and nodding imperiously at a group of peasant hares passing by on a cart, singing their country songs, dressed in their unbleached smocks, worsted stockings and heavy wooden *klompen*. Sighing with satisfaction, he admired, in contrast, the rich silver embroidery on his tunic, glittering in the morning sun, and the sleek curves of his fine Spanish boots. Perched at a rakish angle on his head, a scarlet velvet cap sported a peacock feather, which wagged and trembled as he walked.

'Such lordly and fashionable apparel!' he exclaimed to himself, 'Why I dare say I look just like a most heroical knight from one of those long-ago Romances! By Our Lady, that ungoderly fox has met his match! I'll be able to see straight through his sneaky, meechering ways!'

And along he went, humming to himself and steadily scranching his way through his many elevenses.

The wide, busy road passed under avenues of whispering poplar trees, through red-roofed villages, *en fête* for Whitsuntide, round old apple orchards festooned with pale blossoms as delicate as Alençon lace, and over shallow fords, until it reached the edge of a great forest.

The bear stopped and contemplated the dark sea of trees before him. The smooth stones of the King's Way stopped abruptly here, yielding to a rough, twisting path, riddled with gnarly roots and puddles and fallen tree trunks. The sun, which had been shining so merrily, swept behind a huge storm cloud, the sour yellow of a traitor's gown. Bruin shivered.

'I'll have a little sit down for a moment,' he mumbled, and, perching his wide bottom on a mossy oak stump, made himself an enormous roast-swan-skin-and-slyppery-earthworm-and-cream-cheese-and-gooseberry sandwich, and washed it down with a swig of mead from his flask.

Somewhere deep within that ancient wold was Reynard's fortress of Maleperduys. Maleperduys, the most notorious castle in the kingdom, the fox's favourite burg—the most secure and impenetrable of all his properties. And running through the forest like tangled wool were Reynard's secret tracks. Some were bypaths to escape from his many enemies and victims, others were hunting sties to spring upon mice and birds and rabbits undetected, others were pretty little ways that he hacked out for his own amusement—to promenade on a slumbery summer's day, chewing on a plume of meadow-sweet, or to contemplate the heavenly spheres on a winter's night, when the planets and constellations progressed sharp and cold across the black sky above the trees.

As he stood up and walked gingerly towards the trees, thoughts swirled around Bruin's mind like mayflies. He thought of the tales he'd been told about Reynard's viciousness, how he would torture and maim and kill without a second thought. How there were whole chambers in Maleperduys piled high with bodies, the floors crunchy with bones. 'But no one could really be that wicked,' he muttered, 'not really. No, I shall be stout and brave. No sinny foxes will beguile Sir Bruin.' And, after a quick mouthful of roast-capon-with-squashed-slug-sauce and another nip of mead and one more marzipan lion and a pawful of cherries and the end of the swan and some bread spread very thick with butter and the last lamprey pie, he stepped onto the crooked forest path determined once more to capture Reynard and bring him to justice.

Even on a June morning the forest was cool and dark, like the eely depths of a deep green river. The oak trees were in flower, the silvery birches were in their summer leaf, and forget-me-nots as blue as Mary Maiden's cloak were pooled under the spreading branches. But the bear saw nothing of this beauty. The deep leaf-shadow of the woods felt dour and sinister to Bruin and he held fast to his staff in one paw and his dagger in the other, jumping at every sound in the undergrowth, imagining the murderous Reynard ambushing him in the gloom. On he stumbled, tripping over logs, swatting away flies buzzing around his food, splashing though puddles and once, frightened by a cross-looking partridge bursting from a thicket, falling sideways into a clump of particularly nasty stinging nettles.

After a couple of hours, the path grew steeper, edging up and over a low hill. Huffing and puffing and mopping his brow, Bruin staggered along, too hot and tired to be scared any more. As dusk descended, he found himself wading through thick, sticky mud. 'An easy stroll, they said!' he humphed, examining his ruined leather boots, 'There and back again in no time, they said! By pious Saint Corbinian, I shall be very stern with that Fox when I find him.'

The poor old bear comforted himself with his remaining morsels. By the time he had slipped and sliked down the other side of the mound, he had finished the lot, even licking the inside of his bag for the drosens of earthworm juice and the last few pie crumbs. Exhausted and tummy rumbling, when the path finally descended back into the woods, Bruin bedded down for the night at the edge of the track, covering himself with pine needles for warmth, cap (now missing the peacock feather) pulled over his eyes.

Long before daybreak, Bruin woke with a howl, giddy from the most horrible nightmare. A ferocious dream-Reynard had been stealing, from right under his nose, a very, very fine Parma pastry pie (with seven thick buttery layers of pork and mutton and veal and chicken and eels and pike and carp, all mixed up with plump raisins and figs and dates, and painted in gold and tin leaf and drenched in the best Sicilian sugar). Bruin wheeled around looking for the fox, hurling punches into the night air, until he came to his senses.

Sighing heavily, he decided to labour on; big salty tears dripping from the end of his furry nose when he remembered, with a sickening lurch, that he had no food and no mead left. Trudge, trudge, trudge he went, through the endless forest, the sky gradually lightening to a rosy dawn. Trudge, trudge, trudge, through ever narrowing hollow ways overgrown with hemlock and stitchwort. Trudge, trudge, trudge, images of tasty French dishes and slavering foxes dancing wild rounds in his tired mind. Trudge, trudge, trudge, SPLASH!

Not looking where he was going, Bruin had tumbled into what he had thought at first was a forest pool, then swiftly realised, as he scrambled out, was actually a moat. A stagnant, foul-smelling, pus-coloured moat at the base of a high stone wall, covered in monstrous tangles of ivy.

The bear stood on the bank looking up at the wall, fur dripping, his beautifully embroidered tunic slimy with green scum and frogspawn. Up and up it towered, punctuated by black arrow slits, until it reached high crumbling battlements. A large gargoyle in the grim shape of a fox ripping the throat of a wolf cub poked out from the greenery, a thick rusty liquid trickling from the side of the fox's mouth onto the leaves and the stone. Protruding into the trees was an *échauguette*, a turret in the modern style, decorated with a frieze of foxes marching into battle, enarmed with helmets and shields.

Bruin gulped: here, at last, in this dismal, stinking grove, was the dreadful fort of Maleperduys.

The path had come to an abrupt end, the moat and wall disappearing into the forest on either side, blocking any further progress. Bruin tried to brush off some of the frogspawn and blew his nose noisily on his sleeve. He thought of his own cosy chamber at home, of a clean, soft linen shirt and a full belly. He imagined himself tucked up in his best feather bed eating a slice of pear tart with fresh cream and sipping a cup of sweet Putou wine. But then, with a shudder, he remembered how much the Court would mock him if he returned without Reynard, what a fool they would think him, how disdainful the ladies would be, and he reluctantly turned to wrestle through the thicket, muttering a prayer to kind Saint Romedius, friend to sinful bears, as he went.

He blundered into the left-hand wood-shaw, thick-woven with hazel, which seemed to have some sort of faint track through the nettles and the bramble bushes. Using his staff, he slowly battered his way through the undergrowth, getting more and more stung, fur bristling with burrs, tunic torn by thorns, following the snaking boundary of Maleperduys until he finally reached a clearing, where a little stone bridge led over the moat to a gatehouse, portcullis half-down in a threatening row of metal teeth and its doors closed tight shut behind.

The gatehouse had two high towers, each with a swallow-tailed standard, gently waving in the spring breeze. (Lord Reynard's coat of arms—two foxes counter-salient gules on a field of argent—was a source of inordinate pride to him, its origins lost in the fogs of vulpine antiquity. It adorned every chamber in Maleperduys; painted upon plaster, hammered onto shields, woven into vast tapestries by the very best atelier in Geraardsbergen, and embroidered across dozens of pennons, banners and standards, which he kept lovingly in a deep chest, ready for battle.)

Between the towers, in a niche usually reserved for the Blessed Virgin, perched a painted statue of a fox dressed as a bishop, crozier in paw, standing on the body of a very dead-looking wolf, who looked suspiciously like Isengrim, tongue lolling unsavourily out of his mouth. But there was worse. A collection of long iron spikes thrust up from the battlements, topped with the bloodied, chopped-off heads of dead animals, in varying states of decay. Bruin stared up in horror as he found himself counting the heads of six coneys, three cats, four wolf cubs, two polecats, six boars, six moldiwarps, one unicorn and a worried-looking brown bear, who bore a strong resemblance to his Uncle Adalbern.

Feeling a little sick, Bruin lumbered across the bridge, and began to knock resolutely on the big oak doors. There was no answer, although Bruin could have sworn he heard a faint chuckle. He sank down and, sitting on his tail, called aloud to Reynard:

'Sir Reynard! Are you at home! It's Bruin, your kinsbear, whom King Noble has sent to summon you to Court to answer a number of accusations exhibited against you. I have the royal warrant here'—he retrieved the now torn, food-and-mud-splattered roll of parchment from his belt—'You must come to plead your case, Baron, for the King has taken a deep vow that if you fail to appear at this summons, then your life shall answer your contempt, and he'll confiscate all your goods and all your honours. You'll, you'll... lose this, er, splendid castle, Reynard!'

Silence, just the sound of the flags flapping in the breeze. Unnerved, Bruin nevertheless carried on.

'Therefore, Sir Reynard, do please be advised by your, um, friend, and go back with me to the Court to shun the danger that will otherwise fall upon you.'

Silence. Bruin tried again.

'I must be blunt, Reynard. King Noble will hang you, or he'll set you on the rack or the wheel, for sure. You must listen to my counsel and return to the Court with me straightaway.'

On the other side of the wall, Reynard had been lying in his favourite warm spot by the gatehouse, sunning himself as he stretched out on a pile of green velvet cushions and idly turned the pages of a new book, delivered just that very morning from an English bookseller in Gent (a thrilling collection of the tales of the Trojan War, all glinting swords and thunderbolts and hideous revenge—most enjoyable, thought Reynard, as he compared his walls favourably to those of Troy).

At Bruin's knocking, however, he leapt up, and looked through the spy hole in the door, chuckling at the bedraggled figure of the bear. He then tiptoed softly across to a little round door in the walls, scarcely three feet high, which he opened with a rusty key from his belt. It concealed a narrow earth tunnel, one of dozens winding in and out of Maleperduys— here one and there another—which Reynard opened or closed according to need.

Some were escape routes traversing deep under the forest, from which Reynard could then flee across the heath beyond the trees, sometimes running for miles and miles, even deep into the desolate salt marshes towards the sea. Others led to warm, snug holes, impenetrable to anyone other than Reynard, where he could go to ground with his books and some cold chicken and ham, until whatever the latest trouble he had got himself into had calmed down.

This particular route (an ancient tunnel dug out by Reynard's great-great-grandfather, who had a flair for engineering) swooped under the moat and led to a stone-lined hole with a chaise longue stuffed with the softest goose feathers, a lovely copy of the *Decamerone* from Ferrara,* and a dry, cool pantry filled with fat hens and red apples and walnuts and his precious store of dried figs. However, as he was trotting along, listening to Bruin's muffled cries, Reynard, that arch-deceiver, suddenly thought of a delightful way to fend the Bear off. He flicked around and, clapping for a servant (one of his many

---

* After his death, Reynard's precious book was passed reverently down, fox to fox, eventually crossing the North Sea to Norfolk, entering the Earl of Leicester's collections at Holkham Hall and thence to the Bodleian Library, where it resides today as MS. Holkham misc. 49.

impoverished nephews), had the gates opened wide and the portcullis lifted to reveal an astonished-looking Bruin, scrambling to his feet.

'Welcome, welcome, Uncle!' exclaimed Reynard, 'I heard you well before, but,' he put one black and russet paw to his heart in a pious fashion, 'I was saying evensong, and so tarried a little, dear old friend. But, by the horn of Saint Hubert, you have been led a merry dance to get to my humble little hole in the forest! You've been given a great deal of trouble by whoever sent you over our long hill—I can see how weary you are from the sweat running down by your cheeks. Or perhaps you went for a little swim to cool down from your tramps, most sensible!'

Bruin started spluttering, but Reynard smiled serenely. 'Well, I'm afraid there was absolutely no need—you've rather wasted your time, Uncle, as I was in any case coming to Gent tomorrow morning, bright and early.

'But there we are... I shall not shed any tears over your kind visitation, as I do believe someone as wise as you, dear Baron Bear, will no doubt help me immeasurably in Court. But it is a great wonder to me that our gracious Noble couldn't find a less important messenger to run this fool's errand? Apart from our dear King, you are the noblest, and the wealthiest, of all the courtiers.' Reynard smiled pleasantly, as he watched Bruin adjust into a more chivalric pose, head up, tummy in and sword gripped in the fashionable French manner.

'I wish we were already at Court, dear Uncle, but I'm afraid I can't accompany you right now, as I've eaten so much today that I'm afraid that my belly will break or cleave asunder.' Reynard patted the glistening white fur around his trim middle and winked at Bruin, whose own tummy started rumbling noisily at the mere mention of food.

'But what did you lunch upon to make you so full, Lord Reynard?' slavered Bruin, eyes wide.

'Oh, simple fare suitable for an impoverished old fox such as me... You wouldn't know with your riches, Baron Bear, but we poor folk must eat things sometimes that we wouldn't touch if we had any better—a few dry bacon rinds and a dish of peas—and for afters,' Reynard examined his well-manicured claws, 'a great heaven-high pile of sweet forest honeycombs... as plump and golden as if Helios the sun god himself had gilded them at the behest of the bees... quite pleasant at first.'

He sighed deeply and looked mournfully up at the bear, 'But on account of my terrible hunger, dear Bear, I ate far too many. Indeed, I choked down so much of that fresh sticky honey that I thought my belly might burst.'

'*Nomini Dame, Cristum file*,' gasped Bruin in wildly inaccurate Bearish Latin, the grumbling in his stomach echoing around the gatehouse, 'By the dulcet tongue of Saint Ambrose, Sir Reynard, how can you think so little of honey? Why it's the very best thing! It is a food for the greatest emperor in all the world! I love it more than meat, more than syllabubs, or pears in syrup, or apple fritters, or Christmas goose! Dear Reynard, will you not tell me where you got it from? Dearest, gentlest Sir Fox, help me to get some of this honey, and as long as I live I shall be to you the truest and most loyal of friends. More than that, I shall... I shall be your servant everlastingly.'

Reynard twirled his whiskers, and contemplated Bruin.

'Very amusing, Baron Bear, very droll,' said Reynard, sternly, 'I presume you're pulling my leg, which is very unkind to a poor simple fox like me! Really, Uncle, nobody could possibly like honey that much!'

'No, no, no,' gasped Bruin, his voice getting higher and higher, 'I am in serious earnest, Reynard! For just one lick, I shall become the most faithful of your kindred! I shall protect you at Court! Fight your corner with King Noble and your accusers! Put your neck before mine! I entreat you, Sir Fox, take pity on me and let me have a mere smatch, a mere scraping of that nice fresh honey!' He sank to his knees in front of the fox, who beckoned magnanimously for him to stand once more.

'Hmm... let me think on it...' said Reynard smoothly, turning to admire his courtyard, which was pleasingly scattered with petals from the quince trees close by the curtain wall. 'If... if it's true that you do indeed love honey so well... I could give you enough honey that ten bears, even bigger and tubbier than you, couldn't eat in one sitting...' 'Please don't say ten bears, Baron,' interrupted Bruin, 'I could eat all the honey between here and Portugal on my own, without any help, honestly I could.'

Reynard suppressed a wicked smile, 'Well, Bear, if you swear your eternal friendship and help me against all my enemies in the King's Court'—Bruin nodded feverishly—'then I'll lead you to the honey... Not far from here is the cottage of an old forester called Lantfert. He has so much honey that even you couldn't eat it in seven years. Indeed, you can have seven stout barrels of that honey, as much as you can carry, and more if you clear my name.' Bruin clasped both paws to his muzzle, then laughed so loudly that he startled a black cloud of rooks from their nests in the castle tower, who cawed down rude insults as they circled overhead.

'We'll need to travel a fair few miles to get there, so follow me, and do try to keep up,' said the fox, clapping to his snoozing nephew to secure the gatehouse, and leading Sir Bruin briskly across the inner ward, damp blossoms sticking to their boots.

Faster and faster Reynard sped, a blur of red fur and leather and keys, Bruin lumbering in his wake. Up and around the battlements they went, then down a rickety ladder stained with tar from some old siege or other, past his wife Hermeline's study (they could hear her scratching away with a quill on some important translation or other as they tiptoed past), and under a crumbling, mortared archway, leading to a carved elm door, which took three elaborate keys to unlock.

Then, through the Chapel (where Reynard made Bruin kiss one of the family relics—which the fox said was a toe once belonging to Saint Hubert), and down a flight of stone steps, worn smooth with centuries of padding fox paws, into the Crypt, where, behind the tomb of one of Reynard's great-great aunts, they entered a long dank tunnel, lit with little coiled *candélou,** the earth roof so low that a panicking Bruin came close several times to being stuck. After almost an hour of squeezing and hurkling in the dark, Reynard finally stopped and opened a trapdoor, from which they emerged, blinking in the sunshine, into woodland, some distance from the walls of Maleperduys.

---

* Small curled French candles, historically associated with mourning and death, not a particularly good omen for Bruin.

CHAPTER NINE

In which Sir Bruin the Bear ate the Honey

As Bruin panted and wheezed, Reynard nonchalently kicked some leaves over the trapdoor, and leant against a tree, observing the Bear with amusement. Casually pulling a little yellow slug from his tail, and popping it into his mouth with a flourish, he thought how well his plan was progressing.

'Buck up, Uncle,' he cried heartily, 'we still have a few miles to cover. Think of the honey, of your seven golden barrels...' And off they went, through the bramble-brier and the hound's thorn, until they reached Lantfert's timber yard, still within the woods, but on the outskirts of a lively little village—the sort of village where everybody paid their rent on time, mended their thatch before it got too mossy and knew everybody else's business—the sort of village where bears and foxes were most decidedly unwelcome.

Lantfert was a beetle-browed, stocky man; face and temper both pitted by smallpox. He was considered well-born, for his father was Macob the bucket-maker (a similarly taciturn man, brave and stout, as long as he had smaller fry to fight) and his mother was Dame Pogge of Chafporte (a beauty in her youth, the toast of Rupelmonde).

Aside from his passion for strong cheese, Lantfert was known for his great skill as a carpenter of huge thundering pieces of timber—timber for ship's masts and cathedral roofs and trebuchets. Just the other day he had hauled a great oak into his yard, which he had begun to split in half by hammering in two wedges (which Reynard, an interested amateur carpenter, had observed the day before on his morning constitutional).

Picking a sliver of the slug from between his gleaming white teeth, Reynard whispered to Bruin, 'See that gaping oak over there by the trough... the long one, like a spar for an admiral's warship...'

Bruin licked his muzzle, eyes as wide as saucers, legs trembling.

'In the centre of that tree is so much honey, Baron Bear, that it is immeasurable... combs upon rich amber combs of the stuff... see if you can climb into it... but, my dear Bruin,' and Reynard smiled as innocently as a young cub, 'you must take care not to eat too much. It's all very sweet and delicious, but do eat temperately, otherwise you will get the most terrible collywobbles, and, alas, I shall be blamed as usual.'

'Sir Reynard!' exclaimed Bruin, voice faintly tindery, 'Do you take me for a foolish bear! I shall be most sensible and only eat as much as can fit in my belly! Moderation in all things is my motto!'

'True, true,' said Reynard, winking at Bruin, who lumpered over to the oak faster than he had ever lumpered in his life, and gingerly thrust his brown furry snout and two brown furry front paws deep into the cleft of the tree; Reynard shouting encouragement from the sidelines, 'Open your mouth a bit wider! That's the ticket! Put your paws in too! Your muzzle's almost touching the honey now! Oh bravo... *bravo!*'

Whilst he was calling out cheerfully to the bear, Reynard sprang lightly across the yard and, once Bruin was in as far as he could possibly go, knocked out the two fat oak wedges keeping the log split open. In a flash, Sir Bruin—Knight errant,

Erindbere Royal—was stuck fast with his broad bottom in the air: head, ears and paws caught in Lantfert's oak as securely as a coarse-furred, bumble-brained peasant bear trapped by hunters for baiting. And, however much he flattered or promised or chided Reynard, nothing would move the fox to help poor foolish, greedy Bruin, imprisoned smack in the middle of the busy timber yard.

And all that dreamy, gilden honey? As the fox knew full well, no combs or hives had ever treasured that particular tree; and even if they had, Lantfert would have whisked them into his pantry and onto a nice crust of bread before you could say Saint Ambrose.

It didn't take Bruin very long to grasp that he had been thoroughly tricked by the wily Reynard. Not so much as a lick of honey, and now he was horribly, painfully stuck. He tried to heave himself out, but all his considerable ursine strength, ever constant in the past, failed him.

Furious and terrified in equal measure, he began to howl and bray, scratching and kicking his hind legs so that clouds of dust rose from the dry earth. He was making such a terrible racket that, before long, Lantfert himself came hurrying out of one of his workshops carrying a sharp hook in his hand, to see what on earth was happening in his normally peaceful domain. Bruin remained stuck in the cleft of the log in terrible fear and dread, bellowing, wrestling and crying, and all for nought, as he simply could not budge an inch.

Lounging on a bed of mulchy leaves in the undergrowth, Reynard watched the emergence of Lantfert and Bruin's worsening predicament with immense satisfaction, taunting the bear with tricksy remarks, 'How's the honey, Bear? Good, is it? Be careful not to eat too much! And, now that I have delivered you to your heart's desire,' he performed a most elegant and ornamental bow, 'I must, regretfully, leave you to the good care of Monsieur Lantfert.'

And off Reynard the Fox scampered, back to his castle, planning to rouse Hermeline from her scholarly pursuits, gather up his little sons, Reynardine, Rossel and Reynkin, from their play, and celebrate his triumph over Bruin with some roast rabbit and a bottle or two of their finest red wine (brought back from a fair in Saint-Pourçain by Grimbart the Badger as a gift for Hermeline, who had assisted him on a tricky point of maritime law).

Meanwhile, back in the timber yard, discovering the miserable, wailing Bruin stuck fast in the oak tree, the horrified Lantfert had raced, stumbling over his own feet, to his neighbours in the village, shouting all the way 'BEAR! BEAR! THERE'S A BEAR IN MY YARD! EVERYONE COME QUICKLY! BEAR! BEAR! HELP!'

It was just past dinner time (curling woodsmoke and frying fish and family chatter) and word whipped around the bustling little thorpe in moments. And from cottage and barn and church they poured. Without a pause, every man, woman and dog came running as swiftly as they could to rout out the evil bear from Lantfert's place. Each villager carried a makeshift weapon—cudgels, axes, flails, hawthorn sticks and anything they could quickly grab from kitchen, hedge or field—forming a raging, raggle-taggle bear-hunting procession.

Lantfert was in the lead, still carrying his hook, followed by the priest of the little village church of Saints Protus and

Hyacinth, who'd picked up the second best cross on his way out from midday prayers.

Next came the clerk, clutching the weather vane he'd been fixing onto the church tower (in the dangerous shape of a sea unicorn), and the oldest lady of the village and her best friend, both completely toothless, both waving rakes.

Close behind were Julocke the priest's wife, brandishing her distaff (she'd been in the middle of spinning some yarn for her granddaughter), old Hugelin with the crooked leg shaking a heavy hammer, and Ludolf with the broad, long nose wielding a leaden ball.

In the middle ranks came handsome Sir Bertholt with the long fingers (son of the even handsomer Lord Giles) and tall Ottram (who, people said, had strangled two wives), carrying tough ash staves, well-leaded at the ends.

Bringing up the rear were Tigiers, the village baker, waving a muddy fork—he had been out muck-spreading in the fields all morning and smelt like a pigsty; Hughelijn, the best lantern-mender in the Waasland, carrying an old bull's horn; Baetkyn, the comb-maker, flashing a good sharp saw; Dame Bave with a skimming spoon and a meat hook; and, finally, Ende and Abelquak drumming their rods together at the tail end.

Hearing the horrible great noise and cries of the villagers as they approached through the woods, Bruin became desperate—'how can I stand alone against that mob... they'll break my spine!' he panicked, 'they'll kill me... *mon Dieu*, what an ignoble end for such a delicate and honourable Messenger of the King!'

The terrified bear realised that it would be far better to lose his muzzle than fall into their clutches. He wrestled and strained and pulled so hard that he managed to pluck his head out of the log, but unfortunately left most of his fur and both of his ears behind. (There was not even enough fur left around his face to make a pilgrim's purse.) Poor old Bruin! Blood running over his eyes so he could barely see, he looked like a monster or a red devil from a chapel painting—no one had ever seen a fouler or more loathsome beast.

Hearing footsteps on the cobbles at the entrance to the yard, Bruin made one final gigantean effort to free his trapped paws and ripped them out, losing all the claws and most of the rough pads. Oh, the agony! Thick black blood everywhere! Hardly able to stand, Bruin stumbled backwards from the oak, just as Lantfert and his neighbours reached him.

Big and small, young and old, the entire parish of that sweet little forest village started to smite and strike Baron Bruin on the head and face with their peculiar but effective weaponry. Groaning and howling in pain, Bruin tottered around the yard like a grotesque dancing bear, battered from every angle. One particularly vicious blow from the priest knocked him right over onto the ground; another, from Lantfert's brother, whacked him so hard on the head that for a while he could neither see nor hear.

Eventually, Bruin managed to stagger out of the yard, crashing through hogweed and wild garlic down to a deep, swift tributary of the Schelde fast-running to the north, the villagers haring behind him, pelting him with stones. Seeing stars, head spinning, Bruin tripped over an eel trap and then a large rock, and with an enormous splash fell into the water, pulling some of the women with him, including the priest's wife, Dame Julocke, whose dress became entangled with another eel trap, drenkling her in the weedy depths.

With a terrible cry, the priest tumbled after her, screeching to the other villagers, 'That wicked bear is drowning my dear wife in the river! Full absolution for any who can save her! Any sin assoiled... yes, yes, even for you Baetkyn... no, no, no, by good Saint Warinus, stop throwing stones... save my poor Julocke instead!'

At that, the villagers (thinking of the many bad and risqué things they'd done recently, rather than from any particular love for the priest's wife, who was a disagreeable, cross sort of woman at the best of times) stopped attacking the poor old bear, and started dragging the sodden Dame Julocke, the eel trap (complete with one very surprised eel) and the other bedraggled ladies out of the river.

Meanwhile, Bruin had managed to paddle into the fastest current and was being swept downstream on his back at a considerable speed, the icy water washing the blood away and stinging like Saint Sebastian's arrows.

Lantfert and his neighbours started yelling again as the bear rushed away: 'Come back you false thief, you vicious bear!' But faster and faster he went, past woods and fields and hamlets, half-delirious from pain, cursing Reynard and the honey-tree, sobbing for his lost ears and ruined paws, until the river narrowed and slowed by an old jetty, not far from Maleperduys and, indeed, from the fox himself, who had taken the quiet but scenic riverine route home to pick Hermeline a bunch of wild flowers and keep out of any trouble.

As Reynard was kneeling by a bed of yellow flower-de-luces, whistling a merry tune to celebrate the demise of his would-be captor, he suddenly realised that what he'd thought was an overturned coracle bobbing around in the river was in fact the Bear—bloodied, bruised but annoyingly alive.

Furious at Bruin's escape, furious at his brilliant plan being foiled, furious at Lantfert's incompetence, Reynard was now as darkly depressed as he'd previously been happy. He scrambled onto the dilapidated jetty, and started shouting down the river, shaking a paw in the air, whiskers bristling—'You fool, Lantfert, you ignorant, unlettered fool! May God give you a shameful death! You've lost good bear meat, rich and fat and oily, and let the brute escape, when he was right there! Stuck in your log! Wounded! Oh, you foolish wood-hagger!'

Then, hearing the moans and groans from Bruin's great furry, watery, bebled mass, Reynard turned his rage bear-ward and let loose a tirade of spiky and sarcastic taunts. 'Cher Priest,' he sneered, 'Dieu vous garde! Which order are you joining, Uncle, with that new hood of yours... and you've shaved your crown too... and nipped off those ears... and are those new gloves! Tell me, are you going to be a monk or an abbot?' (For the ripped raw skin and clotted blood mottling Bruin's head and neck resembled, if you were very short-sighted or very cruel, a monastic tonsure and hood.)

Bruin didn't answer, but said to himself 'I hate that red rascal, I hate him, hate him.' And Reynard continued nastily, skimming a few stones as he snarled, 'I hope you paid Lantfert for all the honeycombs you stole from him, Baron... what a great shame, if not, and so dishonest... Happy to be the messenger and pay him for you if you're otherwise engaged... I'm inclined to suppose you must be floating off to sing at compline...' And Reynard sent one last stone hurtling across the river, which splashed close to Bruin's nose, before it disappeared into the cold, clear water.

With that, Reynard took his leave, flicking his magnificent white-tipped brush as he turned. Bruin raised his head painfully and saw him disappearing up into the undergrowth, a huge bunch of sweet irises in paw.

Once he was safely gone, the bear slowly paddled to the bank, and crawled ashore, wheezing and spitting blood mixed with foul water. In the distance, between an avenue of elms, he could see the straight white path leading back to King Noble's castle—he had been carried a fair number of miles along the river. It was evening now, but the sun was still warm on his fur.

He staggered to the road, wincing in agony with every step. It was no use, he thought, he couldn't walk back to the Court, his feet were still raw and bleeding; he would have to shuffle there on his tail. And shuffle he did, mile upon baleful mile, painfully rolling and tumbling, thick treacly blood oozing from his wounds.

All his finery was lost, even his leather pouch had been ripped from him by the villagers, and a more bedraggled and drabbled bear it would be difficult to imagine. He forced himself to keep going by imagining King Noble's gleaming kitchens and his jolly cooks preparing some rabbit stew with prunes or fresh fried eel or a creamy blancmange when he returned. He didn't even care anymore if he was mocked by the Court for his failure to bring Reynard to justice; he simply wanted sanctuary and to never, ever, see that mocking red mask again.

He slept for a few hours in a ditch by the roadside, as the moon rose full in the sky above him, and woke in even more pain than before, but persevered in his tormentous journey, until finally, at noon the following day, the gleaming turrets and wind-flickered pendants of the lion's palace appeared.

It was just after dinner, and King Noble, Sir Firapeel the Leopard and Sir Tybert the Cat were taking a turn on the ramparts as a digestive, when a sudden burst of frightened shouting rose from the sentries below (two tough-faced foins and a polecat). 'Monster! Hell-devil! Approaching from the east on the highway! Sound the alarm!' And the liveried polecat scurried up the watchtower and started to ring the alarm bell.

Its solemn clang–clang–clang sounded across the fields in warning, and the loathly bloodied figure drew closer to the gates, crawling unnaturally and groaning like a soul in welling-woe, the fires and torments of hell. As it neared the moat, and rubbed one eye pathetically, it slowly dawned upon King Noble that there was something very familiar about the figure.

Leaning over the battlements, he exclaimed 'Mon Dieu, it's Sir Bruin the Bear, my old friend! My loyal Erindbere! Lord God, who has wounded him? His head's gushing blood, he looks on the brink of death... Look! He's lost those fine Spanish boots... and that ridiculous hat of his... but where,' he roared, recalling Bruin's mission, 'where is that fazartly fox? Where is Reynard? Where is Reynard the Fox?'

CHAPTER TEN

In which Sir Bruin the Bear makes his Complaint against Sir Reynard the Fox

The Feast Day of Poor Tortured Saint Maurinus of Cologne, Thursday 10th June

The castle was in uproar. King Noble's furious roars echoed round the ramparts like thunder, loud enough to turn the milk sour in the dairy.

His guards, two sharp-whiskered pine martens, rushed down to the cellar storerooms to find the one working stretcher. It was shoved in a cobwebby corner, underneath piles of the sort of things that nobody in the castle wanted to throw away exactly, but nobody could be bothered to mend either: blunt, rusty sword blades; broken longbows; the stone heads of statues of Charlemagne and Louis the Debonaire (both decapitated during a trebuchet practice which went horribly wrong—one of Noble's great-great-aunts lost an eye during the incident and had to wear a patch for the rest of her exceedingly long life); old jousting equipment (dozens of vamplates and splintery red and yellow lances) and a tangle of Queen Gente's fishing rods and nets.

The stretcher had last been used in a skirmish with the French and the woven willow was mouldy and patched with unpleasant brown stains, but there were no tears and the poles were intact, so they dragged it to where poor Bruin had collapsed by the East Gate. The pine martens were proud of their physiques, but the task of heaving the bloodied bear onto the wicker bed was one with which even the famously strong knight Marshall Boucicaut would have struggled.*

Eventually, after a considerable amount of effort and many rude words, a moaning, bleeding Bruin was carried up through the gate to King Noble's sumptuous Throne Room. Word about the bear's terrible injuries had spread quickly around the castle, from Armory to Oratory, and a huge crowd had gathered, which immediately fell silent apart from a few shocked gasps, as the two groaning stretcher-bearers entered with their groaning stretchered bear.

They staggered across the flagstones and collapsed in front of the high dais on which King Noble and Queen Gente were seated on their grand thrones. The hard wood of the chairs had been softened with a length of crimson velvet embroidered with golden bees, which contrasted horribly with Bruin's raw face and paws, his gaping wounds still oozing blood.

'Well, Baron Bruin,' said Noble, nodding at kindly Sir Grimbart the Badger, who was supporting the bear's head and giving him something to drink and eat to keep up his strength, 'Tell us what has befallen you! You have so many hurts and blechures and sores, I wonder if you've fought a thousand great giants in battle!'

Bruin looked feebly up at the King, and, after dolefully gulping down a stiff measure of cowslip wine and a sweet

---

* All of Noble's guards were huge admirers of the Marshall, otherwise known as Jean Le Meingre, who was renowned for his military skill and powerful physique, and liked to copy his gruelling training regime by running around the castle walls every morning at dawn wearing full armour, waving hammers. At parties, they would always make a particular point of dancing in their chain mail, even though it slowed down their salterellos considerably.

rice tart, pastry crumbling into his fur, he began his long tale of woe at the paws of Reynard, his voice thin and trembling.

'I appeal to you, Sire Leo, *mon Roi*, to avenge me upon Reynard, that foul beast of a fox, for this all happened in your service. He made me lose my handsome cheeks, my feet, my ears, *and* my Spanish boots, by his false deceit and treason. Look at my wounds, they will never heal. By Saint Drogo, this is the end of Bruin."* Huge tears of self-pity trickled down his face, making him wince in pain, as they stung his poor broken skin.

Frowning in sympathy, diligent Grimbart began to dress Bruin's wounds with a little warmed honey, as the bear recounted the horrors of his journey to an increasingly outraged Court (skimming over some of the more embarrassing vignettes and moments).

When Bruin had finished describing his last encounter at the river with the fox, of Reynard mocking him and stoning him like a common criminal, and how he had to crawl all the way back to the castle on his haunches, wentling and tumbling over the rough stony road, Noble let out another cry of terrible fury, making some of the smaller animals jump.

'How dare that scoundrel Reynard assault my messenger!' he bellowed, tearing at his coiffured mane in rage. 'I say to you Sir Bruin, and I swear by God and by my crown' (he removed his sleek gold coronet, and kissed it with a flourish) 'I shall avenge you on him to such effect that you will prostrate yourself before me not in anguish, but in thanks.'

---

* Poor Saint Drogo, born in Epinoy in Flanders in 1105, was stricken by a terrible skin complaint, and became patron saint of the unspeakably repulsive, but also of coffee.

The lion sat back heavily on his throne. 'Now all leave—go, go, except for my wisest advisors,' he muttered, and with a flick of a great paw dismissed the courtiers and the servants and the quietly sobbing Bruin, who was heaved out by the pine martens, the willow stretcher beginning to split dangerously under his weight. The whispering, gossiping crowd shuffled out slowly behind them, leaving just the members of Noble's Council and Queen Gente, who regarded them all with studied disdain, dabbing her nose with a large silk handkerchief.

(The lioness knew well the superficiality and prejudice of power and was careful to always wear a haughty sneer on her face, important for establishing her rank as arched above all others in Court, and, more importantly, equality with her husband. This had worked well over the years, and she had managed to hasten through many of her favoured laws and droits with her terrifyingly contemptuous stares. This, in turn, left her time to enjoy her sole true passion in life, fishing at dusk—'biting time'—for toothy pike in the wide grey River Leie as it flowed north-east of the castle.)

The Council pressed close to the King in a tight cabal, led by a grave Sir Grimbart the Badger; a furious Sir Brichemer the Stag, who had always harboured a deep envy for Reynard's freedom from the strictures of the Court; a somewhat sympathetic Sir Firapeel the Leopard, who disliked Bruin's bumbling disregard for hierarchy and form; and Bellin the Ram, whose curly cream wool was tingling in sympathy with the skinned Bear.

As they argued and vacillated over the best course to take in the thorny matter of Reynard, a sleepy dusk fell over the castle and the stars brightened in the clear sky. Swallows and martinets darted in and out of rough nests woven into the eaves and arches and castellations, and little bats flickered over the moat in the half-light.

On and on they talked, as the constellation of Ursa Major, the Great Bear, wheeled slowly over the countryside, over the long rows of pollarded willows and the windmills and the reedy marshland edging the German Sea, and, miles to the east, over a tranquil Maleperduys, where Reynard and Hermeline were lying on top of a tower, drinking Portuguese wine and sucking on brightly coloured marchpane.

Eventually, the wise lords decided their course of action. Reynard must be summoned a second time and brought to Court to answer charges. 'But who should be tasked with retrieving him from his dark hole?' asked the King. 'Sir Tybert the Cat should fetch him,' pronounced Sir Grimbart, and the others nodded in agreement. 'He is clever and well-versed in rhetoric; he, of all animals, may be able to entice the fox to face his accusers.'

CHAPTER ELEVEN

The Second Summons: In which Sir Tybert, Eminent Scholar and Proud Prince of Cats, is dispatched on a Second Embassy to Sir Reynard the Fox, with Equally Disastrous Results

The Feast Day of Saint Barnabas the Haymaker, Friday 11th June

Without further ado, soldiers were dispatched to bring Sir Tybert from his manor house next to the Abbey of Saint Veerle in Gent. The cat was furious at being disturbed, having been deeply entrenched in his books and manuscripts, diligently at work on his translation of Boethius, surrounded by guttering candles, a half-drunk pitcher of thick cream, and a trencher piled high with garlicky sun-roasted mice, which he gobbled down whenever he was stuck for a word or had a difficult philosophical thought.

Tybert, I'm sorry to say, was ravenously addicted to mice. Apart from his overweening sense of intellectual superiority, they were his one great weakness. The sweet-natured, peaceable field mouse; the melancholy wood mouse; the greedy, wary city mouse; the tough-talking salt-marsh mouse; the rustic harvest mouse, skilled in weather lore; the lean and fearless alpine mouse; the good-omened white mouse, who feasts sumptuously on winter snow and sleeps in nests of goose down; the plump, languid dormouse; the humble, hard-working house mouse; the formidable, scabbed and flea-flecked brown rat; the sensitive, faint-hearted water vole; the fine-whiskered, artistic Egyptian mouse; the briny, seafaring whale-mouse—each had their own distinctive and delicious flavour, their own clutch of recipes stowed away by Tybert in a well-used oak box in his study. He even relished those strange, difficult-to-catch mice from the land of Chalybes, who spend their days eating iron from the local mines, the rough nuggets filling their tiny mouse bellies, adding to their exquisite yet subtle blooded taste. And, as we shall see, despite his keen erudition, that problematic predilection for rodents would be his downfall.

By the time Tybert was finally escorted into the Throne Room, the sun was rising in the east, and blackbirds were singing in the hornbeam trees in the castle yard. The exhausted members of the King's Council were yawning and stretching and beginning to think about breakfast, followed by soft beds, and Noble was grumpily ordering yet more pitchers of spiced Rhenish and bone-dry La Rochelle from a drooping, bleary-eyed pine marten.

As Tybert was marched along the cobbled roads leading to the Castle his anger at being dragged from his work had been gradually replaced with a sense of terrible foreboding. Like all kings, Noble was prone to fits of irrationality and spite, and on occasion loyal animals were imprisoned or banished or executed with very little provocation. Only last month, a dear friend of Tybert's named Rygaert, a yellow-and-black cat from Hasselt, an expert on Seneca, had been exiled simply for making a complicated joke about herrings. Noble prized intelligence in his courtiers, but it also made him feel slow-witted and paranoid, and one tenacious rumour, one false note, one misconstrued witticism could destroy a beast's career, if not his very existence.

Bowing low, holding his black clerk's cap in one paw, Tybert gingerly asked the reason for his summoning. Told of his mission by Sir Grimbart, he looked utterly horrified at the prospect. News of Bruin's disastrous encounter with the fox had reached him through the gossipy Abbot of Saint Veerle, with whom he'd dined *à deux* that very evening.*

King Noble waved a paw. 'Whilst he's foul to all the other beasts, he trusts you, Tybert, he trusts you well, and will bide by your counsel, I have no doubt. You can tell him if he doesn't come, then he will receive a third summons. And if he doesn't come then, well, we shall proceed against him and his family without mercy!'

Tybert regarded the King in disbelief, as though he had completely lost his mind. 'My Lord, my King, those who counselled this are not my friends!' He glared at the gathered company of lords, who shuffled uncomfortably. 'What on earth shall I do there, in those monstrous halls of Maleperduys? That fox will neither return to the palace for me, nor abide by anything I say. I beseech you, dear King, send some other animal to command him.'

Tybert sunk to his knees pathetically before Noble's throne, his whiskers drooping, ears flattened. 'I am little and feeble. If Bruin the Bear, who is so great and strong, could not bring Reynard here, how should I then take him in paw?'

King Noble slurped noisily from his favourite goblet, brought back from Syria by Gente's father, and held it up to the morning light, admiring the etched lions on the thick blue

---

* Sautéed river eels in a sorrel sauce and an extremely rich almond cheesecake.

glass. 'No, but you're wise, Tybert, and well learned. Though you are certainly not great in size, with your craft and cunning you can do far more, I am sure, than many with might and strength. You're a scholar, a clerk, after all. You know your Aristotle and that Bothus fellow and whatnot. You've been educated at all those damned universities.'

Tybert sighed. He had boasted to the King many, many times about his long and impressive scholastic career, his many published works, his innovations in the synthesis of classical and feline idiom, but Noble never seemed to remember a single word he said.

Standing up to his full height, tail lashing with irritation, he addressed the King in clipped syllables.

'I was indeed fortunate enough to have received, as a mere kitten, my *Magister Artium* at the University of Pavia. And, as you know, I wrote my first treatise, on the *Batrachomyomachia*, at Cologne, and my second, which has been much admired,' he glared at the King, who was pouring himself some more wine from a pitcher, 'the *Tractatus felino-philosophicus*, at Montpellier, where I also compiled my seven-volume history of the city of Bubastis in Lower Egypt. And I have taught at Louvain for many, many years. However, none of this will be of the slightest use in bringing that red-faced, black-nosed, spike-whiskered rascal to Court.

'At Whitsun, I listened at length to Grimbart's defence of his friend, and I was initially sympathetic, but think of the mindless slaughter of little Coppen and her family, think of poor Bruin! Reynard listens not to reason nor logic nor moral insight; he twists everything back to front and upside down. I am honoured to be considered for the task, but Reynard is as wily as the Teumessian fox and only brute force will work, mark my words.'

Noble looked at Tybert rather blankly; he had been thinking about an exciting jousting tournament at a friend's castle just outside Reims the previous summer and, as usual, hadn't been listening to anything the cat had uttered. 'Very good, Sir Tybert, very good points, but *precepta regis sunt nobis vinculo legis*,* and all that, so off you go. Do pop into the kitchen on your way, I'm sure Cook will provide you with some fish for your journey.' And with the gesture of a huge paw, curved claws gleaming in the coarse golden fur, Tybert, for all his indignation, was dismissed.

The cat made a sad figure as he walked slowly down to the kitchens. 'Might as well get something for the journey, I suppose,' he thought. The cook, a portly old badger named Godefroot, flea-bitten fur tinged with grey, fifteenth-cousin-thrice-removed of Grimbart, gave him some smoked pike and a couple of hard-boiled eggs, neatly wrapped in a cheery red napkin.

'Off to find that tricksy old Reynard, eh!' he boomed at Tybert, conversationally, 'rather you than me, eh! You want to be careful with that fox, Professor! He is a cunning one and no mistake. He'll trick you, Tybert, even with all your fancy book learning.' And he laughed until he wheezed, and slapped Tybert jovially on the back. 'Yes, well, thanks very much for the food and the advice. I am well aware of the

* 'All that the king ordains, binds us with legal chains.' A variant of a maxim of Roman law shouted out to the King as a public acclamation in William Langland's *Piers Plowman* (1370–90). Used ironically and somewhat threateningly here by King Noble.

dangers in my task,' replied Tybert through gritted teeth at the beaming cook.

Leaving the kitchen and passing through the dark tunnel under the gatehouse, he nodded at the guards, who smiled at him with grim sympathy as they heaved open the heavy doors. Word of his expedition had spread fast. Pausing by the moat, Tybert gloomily tied his meagre food parcel to a willow stick and, resting it on his shoulder, made his reluctant way to the beginning of the long white road to Maleperduys.

CHAPTER TWELVE

The Wheel of Fortune

Tybert walked through the flat green landscape, past the castle fish ponds, past a group of tired peasant rabbits scything hay, past the stinking pigsties, the dappled swine rooting for acorns in the mud—all the while, his mind turning and tumbling like a creaky old butter churn.

How had his quiet, scholarly, ordered life been upturned so abruptly! How had things come to this precipice, this soul-shaking point of no return? He might as well have been exiled or sentenced to a horrible death, so suicidal and fruitless was his mission. Why was he, a loyal and diligent subject, being toyed with so cruelly? He had often performed odd tasks for the King—smoothing out tricky diplomatic ruffles, helping to organise the distribution of food when famine lashed across the land one wet summer, composing fancy writs and charters and contracts—but had never before been dispatched in such a rough and thoughtless manner.

With these disagreeable thoughts chafing and churning, cursing Noble's advisors—particularly Sir Grimbart, his duplicity mirrored in his black and white mask—Tybert roughly finished washing his face and then curled up in an elegant ball to take his nap.

But he slept fitfully, the half-sleep of a condemned cat. And, as he dozed and twitched, the perfect June sky began to darken, great plowngy rain clouds sweeping in from the sea with a cold northerly breeze, the dark-wetting-brown-grey of water ouzel feathers.

Tybert woke with a start. Bleary-eyed, he picked his way reluctantly back onto the stony path, his fur all rumpled and his whiskers drooping. He looked up aghast at the clouds. Like all cats, he loathed rain. More evidence of my ill fortune, he thought, as he began his miserable journey once more.

After an hour or so, the rain holding off, but a dull thundery ache weighting the air, he reached the little wayside village of Lochristi.

The crow-stepped houses and church and *béguinage* were festooned with garlands of sweet white woodruff and fat pink and cream roses, all for Saint Barnabas's day, and there was a merry atmosphere with excited animals spilling out onto the road with pitchers of frothed ale, and trays of cheese poffertjes and *pain d'épices* and crisp fried wafers, piping hot out of the coals, piled with swirled pats of butter and dark honey and cream so thick you could stand a silver spoon in it.

Tybert slunk moodily through the crowd, hissing at a carousing weasel in a straw hat who trod on his tail. He bought a bowl of cream, and licked it dainteously, whilst frowning at the appalling noise of the rabble outside the church, who were singing loud, very rude songs and performing a wild dance called the 'Reynard Round'. (For the fox's many and various exploits were known throughout the population, not simply amongst the courtiers.)

Poor Tybert's blood ran cold at even this lighthearted reminder of Reynard, and he had to stop to compose himself for a moment on the outskirts of the village, where the fields opened out once more under the vast lour sky; flatlands of ripening wheat, edged with poppies and yarrow.

He perched on a stone waymarker by a dike, ate a hard-boiled egg from his picnic and stared at the long, level view, at the strange thundery light slanting sharply across the crops. The laughter and hurdy-gurdies and singing were now faint in the distance.

A couple of sturdy brown hares were working in the corn, trying to weed out some of the thistles before it began to rain in earnest. One of them raised a gloved paw, and Tybert nodded in response. Oh, he sighed, Nature and her seasons are so simple, so regular, so predictable compared with the vagaries and mishaps of animals' lives.

He finished the crumbling orange yolk, which had a faintly unpleasant tang of sulphur, washed his face and paws, and was just about to start off along the path again, when he saw a great bird coming from far in the distance, swooping and twisting above the road.

It was one of St Martin's birds—*un oiseau de Saint-Martin*—a *Sint Martijns vogel*—a Harrow-hen—a fierce Jean-le-Blanc with a hooked eagle's beak and vast tawny pinions patterned like old Roman armour. A strange, ominous, cursing, cursed bird. A bird who eats snakes and frogs. A bird whose eggs are the colour of cinders. A bird whose talons are the colour of plucked cinquefoil.

Tybert shuddered and crossed himself. He knew the bird was an augur, a diviner of the close future, and could turn his journey to the good or the bad in one plumy twist of white and black.

If it flew to the right, all would be well, Reynard would be surprisingly pleasant and Tybert would escort him back to the Court to the everlasting gratitude of King Noble and the grudging admiration of his advisors. (He briefly imagined Sir Grimbart's marvelling countenance at their entry into the Throne Room, his tufted eyebrows raised high at the submissive figure of the tamed fox led by an insouciant Tybert.)

If, however, the bird flew to the left, Reynard would play tricks and hurts upon him even crueller and nastier than those with which he had tortured the bear. Tybert's mind juddered and crept swiftly away when he started to imagine *those*.

As the bird continued to circle the road, Tybert called out as loudly as he could, his voice cracking and ragged in panic, but managing a few erudite flourishes, gleaned from his extensive and thorough education:

'All hail, Gentlebird! Honoured fowl of Saint Martin! Of the pale eastern skies! *Aetos Dios* of the Reedy Lowlands! Carrier of lowly poets from the deep earth to the tangled transfiguring stars! Great Eagle-Seer of the Marshes and the River Velts! Feathery King of the Grass Snakes and the Wart-Toads and the Mersk-Rats! Turn your wings hether-wards, I beseech you, and fly on my right side! I beg you, to the right, Sir, to the right!'

With a disdainful flash of a golden eye and the heavy beat of a manicured wing, the St Martin's bird completely ignored the cat's cries and alighted on an old ash tree to Tybert's left and then just sat there, looking at him, the branch swaying with its weight.

Tybert, who was unusually superstitious even for those superstitious times, was frozen in horror. Left was bad, very, very bad. And not only that, but that bird was looking at him in the same way Tybert might look at a harvest mouse.

There was an eerie silence for a few moments. The hares stood up from their toil, thistle pincers in their paws, looking up at the blackening sky. Then the air seemed to crackle, and suddenly everything happened at once. A great clap of thunder rumbled across the corn-lands, followed by a fork of lighting spearing the oak copse at the far end of the wheat fields. The St Martin's bird swooped, claws outreached, Tybert dashed away from the road, south towards the river, only just escaping the bird's talons; half-running, half-tumbling through long grass, his heart thundering, his whiskers quivering, his packed lunch and hat strewn behind him. And then the heavens opened, the torrential rain swiftly hardening to hail like cold lead snaphance fire.

Barely able to see, bombarded with a thousand icy arrows, he tore through the downpour, sinking into mud and slipping on fat slugs and wet hay and slopped cowpats for the long miles until he reached the river path. He felt the curse of that bird like a physical blow, its violence seeping into blood and bone and sinew.

Then, all of a sudden, as Tybert could run no further, the hail stopped and the River Schelde spread out mistily before him, silvered and wettering still. Tybert collapsed next to a clump of green irises and tried to catch his breath. As he lay there, shivering, on the wet ground, listening to the dripping trees, he wondered at the violence of hail, at how quickly the sheet metal of the sky had parted in response to the bird's flight.

Finally, he roused himself, and sat by the water for some time, warming his fur in the hazy sun. The colour of the Schelde reminded him of the looking glass he'd bought in Brugge last winter (a beautiful thing of cased bronze, made in Florence and used by Tybert to arrange his whiskers in the morning). How carefree life was then. He'd met a good and old friend—an English mercer and sometime publisher—and they'd sat in a tavern in the town square and talked about the idea of printing his translation of Boethius and drunk much sack and laughed and laughed at the foibles of the publishing trade and the merchants of Brugge and the generally dire state of academia and the cloth trade.

'Oh,' cried Tybert wildly to some passing ducks and swans, 'it is the worst, the most miserable misfortune to have been happy once!' And with this melancholy conclusion, he spontaneously composed a poem—rather a good one, he felt—which he intoned to a doleful-looking stork snoozing by its nest. I will spare you the brunt of it (it was *very* long), apart from the last few lines to give you a sense of his worsening mood:

The mists which rise from the steaming water
Recall those troubling the dreadful Styx
How Fortune deserts the most innocent of cats
Turning in the flight of a bird,
In favour of false villains and janglers and callous kings!
In a sudden storm, a stour cast by hidden, angry stars,
My exile is plotted!
Ah! This life is fleeting!
We are but storm-kindling
floating on an unknown course.

Eventually, having committed his lamentation to memory (to jot down the moment he happened upon a quill and a spare scrap of parchment), and mustering a grim sense of duty, if not bravery, Tybert left his secluded spot, and began to pick his way along the riverbank towards the fox's manor, following the fenny, overgrown path eastwards. It was now late afternoon, and the bad weather had vanished with the hail. The sky had brightened to the colour of flax flowers, pale and clear and cloudless. Across the water, the windmills dotting the floodplains were turning slowly in the breeze.

Fleeing from the St Martin's bird, he had run much further than he had imagined, and before long he reached the outskirts of the bustling fish town of Rupelmonde, where the River Rupel, carrying a dozen other streams and tributaries—the Zenne, the Dender, the Thyle, the Dijle, the Nete, the Leie, the Demer—flows into the Schelde.

This was a trading town, a smuggling town, a feisty, salty, watery town, a town of news and gossip and hard work and laughter, of heaving nets of brown trout and flounder and baskets of slippery pimpernol eels, and, whilst it was only a mile or so from Maleperduys, there was comfort in its rough, riverine busyness.*

It put a spring in Tybert's step and a high lift to his tail. He stopped at a low tavern by one of the quays and ordered some salt-crusted *stockfisch* and some Jerusalem figs and a dish of warm yellow milk, spotted with cream, and took them outside, where he settled amidst the barrels and oars and ropes. For a short while, listening to the tall tales and rude

---

* Goods made their way to Rupelmonde from every corner of the kingdom and beyond, from Picardy and Antwerp and Mons and Brussels, carried by flat-bottomed river boats through the drowsy water meadows. Here, not two miles from Maleperdys, landed every kind of treasure to tempt a hungry and house-proud fox—fat currants and white herrings and Nuremburg mirrors, writing tables and jet beads and oranges. And, indeed, Reynard and Hermeline often nipped down to shop at the weekly markets when the river was packed with *marktschepen*, market-day barges, enjoying a nice plate of fried perch before heading home.

jokes of the river folk, he forgot the curse and Reynard and was lulled into a happy state of forgetfulness, then a deep, dreamless sleep.

He woke with a start a couple of hours later, and everything had changed. The night had drawn in and a full moon had risen over the creaking barges. The tavern was rowdier and felt dangerous. There were cooking fires down by the water, and the air was thick with a choking, oily smoke. Somewhere, a dog was howling.

Tybert tiptoed away, pacing swiftly along moonlit alleys and boardwalks, hiding from a drunken, ale-blown cogboatman stumbling to find his way home, until, turning a corner, he suddenly found himself in front of the vast fortress-castle of Rupelmonde, with its seventeen tall towers, dark with ivy, and its bloodstained executioner's block.

He'd forgotten all about this place. Used by King Noble, and generations of royal lions before him, as a prison for traitors and murderers and witches, it was almost as notorious as Maleperduys—a forbidding place, a place of torture and hopelessness and stasis. Hard by, across the moat, was an old tidal mill, its wheel stilled for the night, silken river weeds trailing from its cogs, creaking and groaning in the lapping water.

'By Saint Gertrude, it's Fortune's Wheel!' muttered Tybert to himself, leaning on an old stone pier, feverish with tiredness and nerves. 'And next to a prison, a house of justice, no less!'

He imagined the goddess Fortuna turning the waterwheel slowly round with her hand-crank, St Martin's bird perched on her shoulder, Sir Reynard standing triumphantly on the top, whilst he, Sir Tybert, slipped and stumbled to an undeserved, capricious fate, crushed at the bottom, drowning in the sullen green depths of the River Schelde.

Tybert shuddered; then, as he listened to the Rupelmonde night—the stray dogs, the drunken bargees, the call and response of owls from the lofty towers—a surge of scholastic logic replaced the panic.

'Ah!' he shouted at the old mill, at the bats skittering overhead, 'Ah! But the definition of Dame Fortune's wheel is its constant motion. What is cast down must be raised high, as she makes her cycle. We are all subject to its vicissitudes. As the tide ebbs, so it flows! As the moon wanes, so it waxes! Out of happiness, She brings sorrow, but also from sorrow She heralds joy!' Behind, in the undergrowth, he thought he heard a muffled laugh. 'So even if something terrible happens to me tonight, then the fox is still bound to fall. Punishment comes to all wicked wrongdoers in the end, even to Reynard, and,' he looked around, and lowered his voice, 'to cruel, ill-advised kings.'

And with these somewhat reassuring thoughts, he turned away from the river and the castle and the mill, and ramped into the tangled forest where Reynard's wicked hole lay.

Thrutching through sharp bramble and hogweed, brushing off spiders and moths, deftly leaping over fallen branches and roots, Tybert quickly—far too quickly—found himself looking up at the sinister towers of Maleperduys, lither and fraked in the moonlit wold.

Just like Bruin before him, he gasped at the grisly tableau of severed heads which flickered in and out of view between the leaves. He couldn't see any cats, but he blanched at the black furry head of a large male bear who closely resembled

Bruin. He rubbed his eyes, and saw that it was actually a much older bear—elderly even—and suddenly realised it was Bruin's uncle, Baron Adalbern, whom Tybert had always liked immensely. Adalbern was charming, witty, erudite. He collected Roman coins, played the psaltery like an angel and was fond of quoting Ovid. In short, he was very like Tybert. The difference being, however, that Adalbern had been built like a furry mountain and was known across the kingdom for his expert skill with a sword, honed on two crusades, and Tybert was a small grey cat, skilled only at rhetoric.

Once again gripped by the horror of his situation, forgetting all previous thoughts of divine justice, Tybert decided then and there to flee from Reynard's accursed hollow and go into exile. That was it for him. Abandoning his fine library, his glittering career, his standing at Court, none of these worldly trifles was worth being speared on one of those cankered spikes.

'Going somewhere, Monsieur Chat?'

Tybert leapt in the air with horror, landing awkwardly on his back, his paws flailing. It was Reynard the Fox. Reynard, who'd been following the cat with amusement for some time, having been enjoying a nightcap at the same rowdy Rupelmonde tavern. Reynard, who had watched him sleeping on a pile of old turnip sacks after his supper. Reynard, who had listened to him muttering and shouting about waterwheels outside the castle. Reynard, who knew exactly why Tybert was here and, moreover, exactly what to do about it.

'Well, Tybert, Prince of Cats?' said the Fox, bowing in a sneering, exaggerated sort of way, 'Why are you creeping around my manor in the middle of the night? Have you come here to exchange pleasantries? Or, perhaps, to duel with me? You want to show me some of those fancy fencing moves you learnt in Italy? Which is it?' As he spoke, Reynard gripped the hilt of the dagger which hung at his waist.

'The rich God give you a good evening, Reynard,' replied a trembling Tybert, picking himself up off the ground and brushing dead leaves from his fur, 'but... but surely you know why I am here? I am sent by King Noble, who has menaced you, for to take your life from you! If you don't come with me right now to the Court, to Gent, he will surely send you to the gallows!'

Reynard grinned, his sharp white teeth gleaming in the moonlight, 'Tybert, Tybert, my dear cousin, you are most welcome at Maleperduys. Of course you are, my dear Baron Mew. And may I wish you much good luck!' He lightly put his arm around Tybert's back, though it made him cringe to do so.

Poor Reynard, while his plan was to employ his considerable charm to beguile the erudite but witless Tybert, it caused him actual physical pain to use kind words to the cat, and his heart felt the opposite of all he uttered—a duplicity which will become only too plain, I'm sorry to say, as this part of our story unfolds.

'Look, Professor, dear Sir Greyfur,' smarmed Reynard, patting Tybert, 'why don't we spend the rest of this fine evening together? I'll put you up and entertain you—we'll drink good wine, have good cheer, you can tell me all about that impressive book of yours—I worship Boethius, as you know—and then tomorrow, early in the dawning, we will go together to Noble's Court.'

Tybert looked at Reynard. For some reason, he felt a little calmer than he had before. Perhaps Reynard wasn't quite as bad as everyone made out. After all, Bruin was neither virtuous, intelligent nor of good will. How reliable was the bear's account of his injuries? Maybe it wasn't the fox's fault that those marauding villagers had attacked him. Perhaps it was just his own stupidity.

'Good nephew,' the fox continued, as he led Tybert towards one of the overgrown forest gates to Maleperduys, 'let us do as I say, I beg you.' He sniffed theatrically, extracting a silk handkerchief embroidered with the curled red initials $R.F.$ from his breeches. 'I have none of my kin whom I trust as much as I trust you. Here, HERE, in my dear home, was Bruin the Bear, the traitor, who treated me so shrewdly, so wickedly, and was so strong and so brutish, that I would not for a thousand marks have gone with him'—he coughed delicately and dabbed his shiny black nose, looking sadly at Tybert—'but dear cousin, I will tomorrow, *bien sûr*, go early with you.'

As Reynard was talking, he placed a paw again on Tybert's back, and began to guide him over the little wooden bridge skimming the oily-black moat.

'Wait, wait, Sir Fox,' cried Tybert, his old fears flaring again as the moon cast grotesque shadows of the severed heads onto the pale timbers. 'I... I... I think it's best that we go now, for the moon...'—he gestured wildly at the sky—'the moon is shining as brightly as if it were day and I... I... never saw, um, um, better weather!' Tybert stuttered to a halt, his famed eloquence failing him in that wraithful shaded place.

Reynard smiled, but his brush began to flick faintly from side to side. 'No, no, dear cousin, you're not used to these parts.

There are some folks who if we met by day would make us very good cheer, but by night,' he paused for effect, 'even such a night as this, peradventure they should do us great harm! It is very suspicious to walk at night, dear courageous Tybert, very suspicious indeed. So, there will be no argument, you must bide this night here at Maleperduys with me.'

With that, as though it was the end of the matter, the Fox extracted a great ring of keys from his belt, selected one (blackened, elaborate) and started to unlock the gate. Tybert blustered on, 'but... but... what should we eat, cousin, if we abide here?'

The half-rotted gate to Maleperduys creaked open to reveal an unlit tunnel, a damp, musty smell of old stone and old urine seeping into the night air, mixing with the brackish water of the moat. Tybert shuddered. Reynard leaned elegantly against the door, and, brushing some imaginary dirt from his sleeve, said, in a purring sort of voice, 'Oh dear Baron Pouncer, here is but little to eat, unless you fancy a honeycomb, good and sweet? What say you, Tybert? Will you sample one?'

It is quite obvious to us, of course, that sly old Reynard was teasing Tybert, knowing full well that the Cat would have heard all about the disastrous consequences of Bruin's lust for honey. But Tybert was prone to adding two and two to reach five, and instead of interpreting Reynard's invitation as a simple warning, dripping with sarcasm, he reasoned that that reading was far too obvious and if the fox was offering honeycombs, perhaps he really did have some? Perhaps that whole business with the tree trunk was entirely down to Sir Bruin's foolishness? Moreover, the intimidating weight of Tybert's learning undoubtedly meant that Reynard was compelled to be honest and straightforward in a way he would never be with that scant-witted, cloud-brained bear.

So Tybert warmed to Reynard and lost some of his fear of his wickedness. 'I don't care a fig for honeycombs, Baron, but perhaps you have something else in your larder? If you could give me a good fat mouse, I should be better pleased!' he ventured, remembering how long he had suffered without sampling his most favoured dish.

'A fat mouse, you say?' replied Reynard slowly and nonchalantly, vizying his claws, 'Well, my dear cousin, close by, only a little way from here, on the edge of my manor, dwells a priest and he has a barn by his house which is full of so many mice that a man could not lead them away on the mightiest of harvest wagons. In fact, I have heard the priest complain many times of the terrible harm and damage they do.'

Poor Tybert! Already lulled by Reynard's charm, the mention of this cornucopia of mice—and probably the plumpest of harvest mice at that—sent him quite giddy. 'Dearest Reynard,' he cried, 'lead me there! I will do anything—anything!—for you in return!'

Smiling sweetly, Reynard carefully closed the gate to Maleperduys again, which screaked like a lost soul. 'Tell me the truth, Tybert,' he whispered, as though seeking a profound and unmentionable intimacy, 'how well do you love mice?'

'Oh, oh, my dear Fox,' exclaimed the cat, his mouth watering, his mind filled with spinning platters piled with flaky mice pies with the sweetest raisins of Corinth, and mice in spiced gingery caudle, and crispy mice fritters and rich mouse broth, 'I love mices better than anything the world could give me! Don't you know that mices taste better even than venison!

That a fine mouse flan or pastry is the tastiest thing you will ever eat!' He grasped Reynard's paws, eyes wild, stomach audibly rumbling, 'So lead me thither where the mice be, and you will win my everlasting love! Even if you kill my parents and all my kin!'

'Is that so? All your family, eh? Nah, you're mocking me, you're japing me, cruel Cat! How can I, a poor humble country fox, skirm with your claw-sharp mind! Tut, tut, tut. Shame on you!' replied Reynard sternly, extracting his paws from Tybert's grip, and locking up the gate with his huge key.

'No, I'm not, so help me God, I'm not!' urged Tybert, somewhat desperately, his mind feverously imagining the limp, plump bodies of those rosy-cheeked barn mice.

'Oh, Tybert, had I known that, I would have made sure that you would already have had your fill.'

'My fill of mice! Oh, I could eat hundreds!' drooled the cat, scarcely realising that he was being gently guided by the fox, away from the moat and the castle walls, and along a dark path winding further into the forest, a heavy full moon flittering in and out of view through the thickly woven trees.

'Oh Tybert, how you tease me! How you pull my leg!' exclaimed Reynard sadly, as they pushed through low branches and brambles and overgrown ferns.

'No, no, no, I do not, good Reynard!' gasped Tybert, 'If I had a fat mouse, I would not give it up even for a golden noble!*

---

* Tybert is making a little pun here, parried adroitly by Reynard in his reply. As well as being the name of the flaxen-maned king, a noble was also an English gold coin, first minted by Edward III, usually valued at 6s 8d (half a mark).

'How very noble *you* are, dear Kinscat, how very dedicated to the rumblings of your belly,' beamed Reynard, increasing their pace to a trot. 'Come on then, let's go, and I'll take you straight to that mouse-stuffed barn!'

'Oh, dearest Reyner,' said Tybert, visions of pink-eared mice wallowing in galantine sauce having treacled the last vestiges of unease which had so troubled him since Gent, and as for the St Martin's bird, he had entirely forgotten the incident, 'with your safe conduct, I would go with you as far as Montpellier! A university I believe your honoured father, being learned in the medical arts, knew well.*

'Ah, my dear old dad! Such leechcraft! Such Physic! And what a neat surgeon! He once operated on the Queen of Spain, you know, sewed her up with the most delicate stitches in Christendom!' sighed Reynard. 'And,' he adopted his silkiest, most serpentine voice, 'is that not the place where you composed your magnum opus on old Ægypt?'

Tybert blushed pink under his grey fur, 'Quite so, dear Fox, quite so!'

Reynard smiled engagingly, 'Let us fly then, old Gibbe, to the priest's barn; come, come, we tarry all too long.'

And off they went, arm in arm, without lingering, along the shadowy path through the forest to the very same village where Bruin had met his bloody fate. The village of beetle-browed Lantfert the carpenter and old Hugelin with the crooked leg and hawk-nosed Ludolf and dreamy Sir Bertholt

---

* Montpellier was one of the main centres for the teaching of medicine in Europe: Jewish, Arabic and Greek scholarship flourishing in the tolerant trading city. In 1180 the lord of the city, Guilhem VIII, proclaimed that 'anyone, no matter their religion or roots, could teach medicine in Montpellier'. This, of course, included foxes.

with the very long fingers and murderous Ottram with the two dead wives.

And if you've been paying attention, which I am sure you have, then you would already have realised that the barn was owned by the very same priest from the little church of Saints Protus and Hyacinth who had felled old Bruin with his second best cross, the very same priest whose disagreeable wife, Dame Julocke, had been dragged into the Schelde by the bear, her best frock all tangled up with river-wreke and the village eel pots. Poor Tybert was skipping happily and greedily into a terrible trap of his own.

After a while, the dark path widened, then left the forest and began to meander through salt marshes until it reached a sombre line of black poplars, leaves whispering in the night air. As they walked, Reynard took a greenish chaperon from his pocket bag and pulled it over his head. 'Just feeling a little chilly,' he whistered to Tybert, who nodded, deep in thought. The avenue of trees had reminded him of the Heliades, the seven beautiful daughters of the sun god Helios. Zeus had slain their brother with one of his jaggedy fire bolts, the poor golden boy tumbling into the depths of River Eridanos, as limp and charred as a dead crow. In the thunderlight, the girls had gathered to weep by his watery grave, turning one by one into amber-teared poplar trees. The cat shivered and, prick by prick, tree by tree, his old fears began to return.

Soon, all too soon, they reached the main track to the hamlet, deep-rutted by carts. The steeple of the church was gilded by the full moon, and moonlight poured into the priest's farmyard close by—the high gabled farm house, the granges, the stables, swine-cote, dove-cote, hen-cote as brightly lit as if Tybert's merciless Helios had already risen in the eastern sky.

Reynard, shrouded and mysterious in his soft velvet cowl, pointed to a smallish barn with a rough thatched roof. Apart from one notable gap, the base of the barn had been freshly walled about with a thick layer of mud. This was on account of an unfortunate incident the night before, when the fox had sauntered down to the farm, broken in and stolen two good fat hens for his supper. The priest, discovering that his best layers had been killed, was furious, and spent the morning huffing and puffing and forging a trap, setting a gryn directly in front of the hole through which Reynard had squeezed, ready to snare him on his next night-time raid.

Dear cunning, thieving, clever old Reynard knew all about the priest's trap, of course. Chuckling to himself, he turned to the hesitant Tybert, who was trembling and fitful again, crouching behind a tall clump of yellow ragwort.

'Sir Tybert, cousin!' signalled Reynard, gently nudging the cat out from the weeds. 'See over there... creep into that hole, and you won't tarry long before you can catch great heaps of mice! Hark how they pipe and squeak already! Can't you hear them, Baron Puss?' Tybert strained to hear the salutations from his longed-for dinner, but heard nothing but the wind in the trees and the call of a distant nightjar.

'Come, come,' chivvied Reynard, 'stop this, er, quavery-mavery and go and eat your fill. I'll wait here for you, right here next to the hole. I promise I won't move until you return. And tomorrow, as planned, we'll go to Court together. Look, see, I have a book to read, so take your time. But don't tarry *too* long, so we can return to Maleperduys and my Hermeline, who will, no doubt, be waiting up for us, and will make us most welcome before our journey.' And he pulled out a little volume of Cicero's *De Amicitia*, beautifully bound and embossed with his coat of arms, and started to turn the pages thoughtfully, as though that should put an end to all of Tybert's vacillations.*

'Reynard, cousin, is that your counsel, then, that I go into this... this muddy hole?' asked Tybert. 'I don't know, I really don't. These priests are so wily and cunning and shrewish. I dread something terrible happening to me!' He started washing himself in a violent sort of way.

'Goodness me, Tybert! My fierce courageous captain! I never saw you so afraid! What on earth is ailing you?' Reynard's innocent eyes looked so appalled at his cowardice that the cat felt deeply ashamed, and, muttering a swift prayer to Saint Gertrude of Nivelles, sprang into the hole. All in a trice, he was caught in the priest's snare by his neck, bound tight by its horse-hair rope. Poor, poor Tybert, flattered and shamed and tricked by Reynard, his supposed cousin and host.

As soon as Tybert became aware of the gryn, he started to panic. He tried to spring back out again, but the cord held fast. Terrified, he began to wail and wraw and struggle, for he was close to being strangled. He tuggled and struggled, but the harder he pulled, the tighter the noose became. In deep despair, he cried and caterwauled, his desperate miaowings echoing around the hushed barnyard. It was only a matter of time before the whole village was woken up.

---

* Cicero's *De Amicitia* is a treatise on friendship. Reynard's volume was a thoughtful present from Grimbart the Badger on the occasion of the birth of the Fox's third cub, Reynkin.

Reynard strode over to the hole and looked down at the pitiful Tybert, listening with enormous satisfaction to his plaintive appeals for help. He was delighted with the way his plan had gone. How arrogant King Noble was to think he could outwit Reynard with that milksop wiseacre! Living with the brilliant and self-effacing Lady Hermeline, with her razor-sharp mind, remarkable wisdom and universal knowledge, he had very short shrift with characters like Tybert, full of intellectual vanity and pomposity, but little original thought. Fired up with disdain and triumph in equal measures, Reynard began to sneer at the cat, his voice darkening as he spoke.

'Tybert, you love mice so much, as long as they're fat and good! If the priest or Martinet, his son, are generous, maybe they'll bring you a nice sauce. What kind do you like on your mices? Sharp, poignant? Sweet, creamy? Say, Tybert! How about the speciality of the house, a bindweed *jurvert* or a honeycomb almond *velouté*? Goodness, Tybert, you're even singing as you eat? Is that the done thing at Court? Well, well, well, I am out of touch with the current modes. Lord God, you feeble, gluttonous fool.'

Poor, poor Tybert wasn't listening. Roped in his prison, fast-fettered, past all comfort, he writhed and strained, crying and calling on all the saints and the goddess of fortune to save him. The terrible fate which had plagued his thoughts on the long journey to Maleperduys had come to pass. Disorientated, he thought he felt the creaking wings of the St Martin's bird circling him, and prayed for release from this terrible nightmare.

Unsurprisingly, with all the miaowing and galping, young Martinet, the priest's son, a light sleeper at the best of times, woke up and, springing out of bed, cried loudly to his snoring father: 'God be thanked, Papa! Our snare's taken the thief who's been stealing our hens! Come on, come on, get up! Hurry up! Come on, Papa! Come on! We can give him a big reward for his efforts!'

With all this shouting, the priest hauled himself up, blearily registering his son's cries. Six foot four, hair standing on end, bloodshot eyes, and stark naked, he was in the foulest of moods and immediately woke up everyone else in the house, booming out with the loudest of voices: 'The fox is taken! The fox is taken! Old Reynard's in the trap!'

Everyone staggered from their various beds and ran to the barn. Some pulled on robes or breeches, but the priest didn't bother, and, with one hand over his private parts, was entirely *tout fin mere nud*, as naked as a nail.

Wheezing and bellowing, he grabbed a heavy church candle and hurled it at Julocke, shouting at her to light it by the kitchen fire. Then, fumbling for some sort of weapon in the dark, he seized his wife's distaff, still wrapped up with wool, and strode out into the cold yard, brandishing it like a spear. And, despite his wife glaring at him and rolling her eyes, he still managed to strike Tybert across his back with a very heavy blow.

One after another, the priest and his family bludgeoned the cat this way and that. Just as his beloved Boethius had been unfairly arrested, then tortured to death in a hot, dusty courtyard in Pavia, clubbed then strangled with a twisted rope, so Tybert was battered and tormented in Reynard's place.

Martinet in his zeal had been the first to reach the hole and was the worst tormenter. Fired up by his sentimental fondness for the two recently departed hens (whom he had sung to sleep and had lovingly named Lynken and Lysbet), he struck the cat so violently that he knocked out his left eye.

It hung grotesquely on Tybert's cheek for a few seconds, before another blow severed it, and it rolled into the mud. Without a pause, the priest raised his arm ready to cudgel him into the ground, once and for all.

Half-blinded, blood pouring, the cat saw death coming for him; a common, lowly, sordid death, a comedic death administered by a woolly distaff brandished by a naked fool, which made a mockery of his discrete life of scholarship and philosophy. With one last burst of strength, Tybert sprang between the priest's legs with his sharp white claws spread and his sharp white teeth bared, and he ripped the priest's right cullion straight from him. There was a sudden shocked pause in the proceedings, as everybody watched the holy stone fall down and join the eyeball, two grim spheres in the slike.

When Julocke realised what had happened to her husband's delicates, she began to yell and scream and shake her fist at the sky, and she swore by her father's soul that she would rather it had cost her all the offerings of a whole church year than her dear priest be subjected to such harm and shame. 'That there trap was set in the Devil's name!' she sobbed, 'look Martinet, love, your poor father's stone lying there on the floor.' She threw herself down by the priest, who was now prostrated on the ground, covered in blood, howling in pain. 'Oh, this is a wicked shame and a great hurt, and even if he's healed he will never be my dear husband again!'

Reynard, lounging quite unnoticed at the edge of the hole, listened to all this hurly-burly with enormous amusement, snorting and laughing until his belly hurt and he could barely stand. 'O Dame Julocke,' he whispered to himself, 'be still, be still, let your great sorrow pass. Losing a clapper should not hinder your priest. You can still be man and wife together. After all, there's many a chapel in this wide world which is rung with only one bell!' And so, with this vulgar witticism, Reynard mocked and scorned the torments of unpleasant old Julocke, doubling up again with ill-covered guffaws at the scene of confusion, lost balls and bloodshed laid out before him.

By now, the sky was slowly brightening to the same clear watery blue as the borage flowers which edged the yard, and the farm cockerel had hesitantly begun to crow. It was the end of the Battle of the Hole. Trying to get up, the priest had swooned again, and his family had heaved him into the house, up the stairs and back to bed.

The drama over, and Tybert successfully routed, Reynard silently padded away from the village, and back to Maleperduys, where he was greeted most affectionately by his loving family, who had prepared him a light breakfast of his favourite stuffed eggs and barley tisane to soothe his nerves after a most trying night.[*]

As for Tybert, the fox had left him in a state of terrible jeopardy and dread, body limp with brattle-blows, blinded in one eye, his beautiful grey fur caked in blood and dung and mud. As far as Reynard knew, Tybert was dead or dying. But

* Reynard the Fox's favourite recipe for stuffed eggs was as follows. Cut each egg in half when it has been well cooked and is hard. Then remove the yolk and mix with marjoram, saffron and cloves. Mash thoroughly, adding a little cheese and one raw egg for every eight. Fill the cooked egg whites with this mixture, fry in pork fat, and eat with a tart green sauce.

when Tybert had seen everyone busying themselves around the priest, he furiously began to bite and gnaw through the snare, tearing at the stringy black horsehair until it suddenly gave away, and he was free.

He scrambled out of that cursed hole and staggered from the farm towards the Schelde, rolling and wentling the last few yards down to the trailing willows, where he washed as best he could, sobbing for all that he had lost. He sat there for some time, shocked and hurting, then, gathering his wits, fearful of priests and foxes, began to limp back towards the Court. Past Rupelmonde, at the little fishing village of Temse, he rested again for a while, and watched a group of yawning eel-men pushing out their flat-bottomed schuyts onto the river. It was high tide and the water was lapping over the banks. You could smell the sea in the cold morning air—salt and fish and spices from the Antwerp docks. The sun had risen over the meadows, and was refracted in the water, like shattered gold, cloaked and bleared and rippling.

It was the most beautiful dawn Tybert had ever seen, its loveliness brightened by the black tempest of the night. He had failed his mission and had lost an eye. Reynard had gone to ground and King Noble would be furious. He had been as stupid as the bear—worse, really, as Bruin was so stupid to start with.

He hung his head and wept again, when suddenly he felt a presence behind him on the path. He turned wearily and there, glimmering in the gilden dawning, was the figure of a vixen, tall and unearthly in that hushed light. Tybert cried out and began to cower, trying to shield his remaining eye. But she shushed him, and bent down to gently stroke his head. Awestruck, the cat peered up at her. All at once she seemed diminutive and twenty-foot tall, as though the heavenly constellations were her diadem. Her tawny face was wise and noble and as ancient as the earth, and her dress was a deep blue, embroidered lavishly with gold and silver thread. Later, he found out that she had woven and decorated it herself, with her own two forepaws.

He thought he was dreaming, perhaps dying, and clutched at her hem, which was oddly embellished with the Greek letter π (*pi*), and, higher up her skirts, was deft-woven another letter, θ (*theta*), and between the two was a pattern of steps, spiralling like a staircase from the lower to the upper.

She was carrying some books, which she placed carefully on the ground, as she knelt next to Tybert. 'Tybert,' she said, 'fellow scholar and servant of Philosophy, I have come to comfort you, and clear the fog that clouds your vision.' As she spoke, she lifted the rich, soft folds of her lovely dress, and delicately dried the cat's tears. And the cat was astonished to recognise the kind, intelligent features of Hermeline, Reynard's wife.

They walked together, the cat and the fox, for many hours along the Schelde, and then north through the King's orchards, where they plucked ripe red cherries, to the Great White Road to Gent. All the time they talked and talked, and Tybert basked in the glory of Hermeline's wisdom and learning. She was the only animal alive who had read all his books and treatises, and she spoke so generously about his work that his eye misted once again with tears. They spoke of happiness and of free will, of cruelty and of consequence, of the ebb and flow of power and kings. Somehow, such was Hermeline's skill, Tybert began to understand, if not forgive, Reynard's motives and the reasons for his cruelty, and, just as she had intended him to, he began to look at his own shortcomings and his own sins, and he resolved to change and to improve.

At the busy crossroads at Sint-Niklaas, they parted. Tybert prostrated himself before the fox and kissed her feet and the dusty hem of her philosophical gown. Weeping yet again, his soiled eye stinging, he thanked her for her charity and her comfort. She had soothed him and fortified him, and he felt as though he had been swift-apparelled in a delicate golden armour, enough to shield him from the worst of blows and barbs to come. He felt brave enough to return, to weather the ridicule from those two-faced courtnolls, and the worst of the lion's inevitable rage.

The afternoon was as fair as the dawn and he almost enjoyed the last miles of his journey. The sky was a deep midsummer blue, relieved by huge wool-sack clouds making their slow and stately progression across the heavens towards the city. They reminded him of the painted clouds carried on poles in a procession he had once watched in Umbria on the Eve of the Feast of Saint John the Baptist, and he sighed, regretting happier days, then recalled Hermeline's admonition as they had said their goodbyes, that only God was eternal, and the relentless trajectory of time and experience, measured in bells and holy days by animals, was mere illusion, fleeting and insubstantial.

And so, with these temporal thoughts skittering through his battered temples, Tybert finally reached the Court. He limped into the Great Hall, a pitiful wight, eye socket gaping, body beaten, fur bloodied and ragged.

Quite contrary to his expectations, he was received with a horrified silence, followed by tutting and sympathy and care, and a wawish swell of anger against Sir Reynard the Fox.

Without his looking glass, Tybert had simply no idea how loathly he looked, how shocking his injuries. Baron Bruin's battering was one thing, observed the horrified courtiers, but for the cleverest amongst them, a renowned scholar, a wise professor of Louvain (appointed by the noble-nosed, leather-booted Duke of Brabant, no less), to have been tricked and mutilated in this way by that wicked Reynard the Fox was an abomination.

Far from scolding Tybert, or banishing him as he had feared, King Noble, once he heard the full story of how the cat had been misused by the fox, was sore angry, as furious as only a royal lion can be. He raged and menaced Reynard, calling him a thief and ruffin and a host of other ungodly names. Tybert's tentative excuses for Reynard's spite, gleaned from his counsel with Hermeline, were dismissed as the humble-wise ramblings of the ill and he was packed off to the infirmary under the care of one of Noble's nieces.

Noble immediately summoned his Council, who had last met on the dark night of Tybert's departure. They sat down on the long benches at the High-Board, looking at the cheese and bread and clary wine left over from dinner, and not one word was spoken. Sir Brichemer the Stag, Sir Firapeel the Leopard, Sir Grimbart the Badger and even Queen Gente were silent and sober, united in their guilt at Tybert's grisly fate. 'Well,' boomed King Noble at last, 'how will you advise me! How on earth can I bring this wretched fellow to the law? And by the blessed goose of Saint Pharaildis, how on earth do we fetch him?'*

Eventually, Sir Grimbart spoke up. Truth be told, he felt as culpable as Reynard in Tybert's misery, having urged his mission. Oh, how he had misjudged the cat's skills and the fox's wiles! But, nevertheless, he still loved the fox dearly and worshipped dear Hermeline and the cubs (he was godfather to Reynardine, the eldest).

'You lords,' said the badger, 'even if my old friend Reynard were twice as bad and shrewish, there is still a remedy. We can still repair the timbers, as they say, we can bote the beams without building the gallows quite yet.' The table of councillors and Noble looked at Grimbart. 'Go on,' said the King.

'You must treat Reynard,' and the badger tapped his claws rhythmically on the table to emphasise his point, 'as a free animal! Don't drag him here or threaten him, but let him be done to as a free fox. As Baron Reynard of Maleperduys, of the Hermitage of the Blessed Relics of Saint Amalberga, *not* as a common criminal. And when he is tried and judged, let him be tried and judged as would be any of the worthly lords of this hall.'

He raised a tufty black paw, as everyone started to speak at once. 'He must, of course, be warned and summoned a third time. And if he doesn't come then, well, he will be deemed guilty by default of all the offences and trespasses laid against

---

* Saint Pharaildis was one of King Noble's favourite saints, and in the centuries to come became a patron saint of Gent. He particularly loved her miracle of the goose, in which she resurrected a cooked bird working only from its skin and bones.

him, every single one of the many complaints with which we are all so uncomfortably familiar.'

The members of the Council nodded at Grimbart's speech. With his clarity and good sense, the badger was always very reassuring. King Noble, knocking back the last of the wine, started to laugh, 'But my dear Lord Grimbart, 'who will go and dare Reynard to come? Who will risk losing his ears, or his eye, or indeed his life? Who has that kind of courage? I don't think there is anyone here who would be such a complete fool!'

Grimbart stood up and made a half-bow. He looked tired in the evening light. 'So help me God, I am so much a fool that I will fetch Reynard myself, if you will command me, good King.'

CHAPTER THIRTEEN

The Third Summons: In which Sir Grimbart the Badger calmly and sensibly, without any Fuss, brings Sir Reynard the Fox to Law

The Feast Day of Saint Basil of Caesarea, Monday 14th June

After the decision had been made, Grimbart spent a little while carefully talking to each lord in turn, and to the King and the Queen, until he was happy that any reassurances he might offer to Reynard would be honoured. 'Now go forth, Grimbart,' warned Noble, before he left, 'and be careful. Reynard is so false and so subtle and so good at trapping a fellow, you need to look about yourself at all times, and be aware of him. Remember what happened to our first emissaries.'

Grimbart bowed to Noble and kissed Gente's paw, and then went down to visit Tybert in the infirmary. He found him propped up on a fat bolster covered with a cool linen sheet—one of the best sheets in the castle linen store, woven by a family of rabbits in Rennes.

His empty socket was now shaded by a satin eyepatch, which had been swiftly embroidered with periwinkles and a very tiny Virgin Mary by Noble's niece, and covering his bloodied fur was a thick fragrant ointment of myrrh and rose and poppy. Sir Adalbern the Bear had brought back the recipe from Damascus many years ago. It had worked admirably on one of Noble's jousting wounds, and everybody in the castle swore by it, although Grimbart often preferred a simple dressing of warmed honey on more superficial wounds. He looked cheerful and rested and was even attempting to eat a little mouse blancmange.

'I brought you a book, Sir Tybert,' said Grimbart, offering him an extremely well-worn copy of the *Voyage of Saint Brandan*. 'It's my favourite tale. Very exciting. Lots of action. Lots of rowing about. There's a very good bit with Judas Iscariot on a rock.' Tybert nodded—he had already read it a hundred times and had presented a much-praised series of lectures on ideas of quiddity in the original Latin text at Cologne, but he bit his tongue, and smiled and thanked the badger profusely.*

'Good, good,' beamed Grimbart, patting Tybert gently. 'Now, I must take my leave, and bring my poor troubled friend to justice. You concentrate on getting better, Tybert, and all will be well, soon enough.'

After making sure that Tybert was being properly cared for, Grimbart looked in on Bruin, who was under a pile of blankets snoring like a dragon. He smiled and went back home for the night. No point in rushing, he thought.

Grimbart's house, Dassenburcht, lay in the heart of Gent, next to the walled gardens of the Abbey of Saint Bavo. It was a rather mercantile mansion, but he loved it. It was very tall, six storeys high, built of grey Tournai limestone and warm red bricks, shipped downriver by the industrious monks of Baudeloo.

---

* On his voyage, Saint Brandan comes across Judas being lashed by frozen waves in the middle of the ocean. Judas explains that he is granted a day of respite on Sunday, also from Christmas to Epiphany, from Easter to Pentecost, and on the feast days of the Purification and the Assumption of the Virgin Mary.

It had been built by his great-grandfather, Old Sir Dass, set firm by the deep and foam-clashed confluence of the rivers Leie and Schelde. The water lapped gently at its sturdy foundations and, in a flood year, rose up to wet the lowest shutters. Grimbart kept a small boat tethered to a jetty running alongside, from where he spent many a happy hour fishing for his favourite whiskery burbot fish. Once he caught so many that he invented a delicious stew, which he named *Waterzooi*, thick with heavy cream and egg yolks, and flavoured with parsley and thyme and carrots and celery and leeks. The first time the badger made it, on a particularly cold March afternoon, when the wind was whip-cold from the sea, he ladled a dozen steaming-hot wooden bowls, and took them to all the members of the fishmongers' guild, shivering in the fish market. They declared it a triumph, and before long it had become one of the great dishes of Noble's watery kingdom.

On the fifth storey of Grimbart's house, just where the crow-stepped gables began to rise, there was a little sheltered balcony, on which he tended pots of yellow and orange nasturtiums. Here, high above the city, the badger could sit on a comfortable stool, water his plants, espy the comings and goings of the river folk far below, and on dark, clear nights observe the heavens. How he loved watching the constellations wheel in all their silvered glory across the Flemish skies! How satisfying they were in their constancy and order, so unlike the moon with her waxing and waning and wanderings! And he would sigh, and mutter half-remembered lines from old John Gower—'We that dwell under the moon, Stand in this world upon shifting ground,' and worry about his dear friends and kin, particularly Baron Reynard, whose wanings, he hoped, would not lead him to a swing from the gallows.

Like many badgers in that floody, streamy, brackish salt-licked land, Grimbart's greatest passion in life was the sea, and his regular stargazing was, in part, to fine-tune his celestial navigation. In addition to his river boat, he had a fine hoy, strong and well trimmed, which he harboured in Brugge. He often sailed down the coast to Calais, or up to Hindeloopen or Ribe, a favourite port where he would treat himself to a hearty sailor's breakfast of blueberry pancakes and cream.*

On this bright June morning, however, his journey was, he assumed, to be a short and straightforward one, even if the ending was uncertain, and, as his boat was out being caulked and pitched by an old chum of his, a straight-talking fox from Maastricht called Lodewyk, he decided to walk to Maleperduys instead.

After breakfast, Grimbart carefully packed his overnight bag with some sensible supplies—three turbot pies, each the size of the crown of a parson's hat, a couple of pawfuls of hazelnuts, a pottle of fresh milk, a sharp penknife, some parchment, a quill and his ink horn, a pewter amulet against the plague, it being the summer months, and a scarf, in case the weather turned, or he needed to sleep outside. He also squeezed in a small purse of silver florins, two small toy boats

---

* One mild December he had even taken sail to the far north, to Bergen in the ice-lands. En route, he saw a great black whale singing in the Karmsund straits. Its back was so huge and flat that Grimbart could have sworn it had earth and grass and corn growing on it. Returning home through a frozen sea of bergs and ice floes, he stood in wonder at the helm, as strange lights danced and swooped and flickered across the vast night sky. Whether they were angels or demons or the souls of lost sailors, Grimbart scarcely knew.

he'd whittled for the fox cubs, and Hermeline's favourite black ink, ground by the monks next door from a rare charcoal made from young grapevines. For Reynard, he packed a nice strong bottle of Putou and some of his favourite marzipan.

Thus well prepared, Grimbart put on his brown monkish travelling robes, tied with an old rope, and took up his wide-brimmed hat and the stout staff he used for pilgrimages (nailed proudly with lead badges from Bromholm and Canterbury, Chartres and Wilsnack). He then bade farewell to his housekeeper, who was just starting for the day, and set off through the busy streets of Gent to bring Reynard the Fox to justice.*

It was a delightful journey. Uneventful and calm. Grimbart strode happily along the Oude Veldstraat, then crossed down to the King's Great Highway, greeting all with courtesy and good humour. At about four o'clock he sat on a bench outside the church in Lokeren, having first said prayers for Reynard at the dark-lit shrine of Saint Laurentius inside, and ate a couple of pies, and shared some of his provisions with a chatty, itinerant mole. Then he set off again, singing a Norwegian sea shanty, and planning in his mind how best to help the Fox and his family.

At around half past eight in the evening, having followed a pretty forest path, lined by a tangle of sweet wild roses, Sir Grimbart the Badger arrived at the main gatehouse of Maleperduys. He looked up and waved at one of Reynard's nephews, who was mending some of the sculptures of animal heads he had deftly carved up on the battlements. 'Good

* Grimbart's housekeeper was a busybody, busy-idle hedgehog named Mechtild, all bluster and prickles, who had been with the family since Grimbart was knee high to a grasshopper.

evening, son! Be careful up there!' shouted Grimbart, wondering as always how much like real heads they looked. They could give a nervous animal a real fright on a dark night, he chuckled to himself.

Before Grimbart had even managed to admire the swans siling in the moat or knock on the great oak doors, they were flung dramatically open, and there, paws outstretched stood Sir Reynard, fox cubs wriggling shyly at his side, pulling on his clothes. 'Reynard!' cried Grimbart, happily, embracing his old friend, and kissing him repeatedly. 'Rossel! Reynkin! Reynardine! Come and give your old godfather a big hug!'

It was a touching scene, as Reynard ushered Grimbart into Maleperduys—the grown-ups laughing and japing and slapping each other on the back, the foxlings stumbling and running and jumping in excited circles and telling the badger all about their sleek new toys from Antwerp (pairs of high stilts and bags of brightly painted clay marbles and flag fans and a little miniature windmill which turned gently in the breeze) and how a family of warty moat toads had set up home in the dungeons. They squeaked with delight at their presents, and climbed the old badger like a tree, tickling him and pulling his fur and riding on his shoulders, until he begged them for mercy.

They walked across the courtyard, which was cluttered with chisels and hammers and saws and blocks of veiny marble. 'My nephew Nivard has a great talent for sculpture,' observed Reynard proudly, gesturing up at the hammering on the battlements. 'We just let him get on with it for the most part. He has a nice job in Ypres next year rebuilding old Saint Martin's—he's very good with heights, you know. And he's a dab hand with drapery—you should see the robes he did for Saint Hubert in our little chapel, just like real linen, folds and everything. Now, you'll be wanting a good dinner, dear Grim, after your arduous journey.' The fox clapped and shouted for yet another nephew, a scrawny young fox with a pox-splotty mask, who scurried off to the kitchens.

Leaving the cubs playing hide-and-seek in the fading light, Reynard took the badger through a low door and up the steep winding stair towards the Grand Hall of Maleperduys. He called to Hermeline as they passed the passage to her closet, and she emerged, ink-blackened, tired and worried-looking, dark moths fluttering around her lantern. On her head she wore her favourite velvet writing cap: hawthorn-red, with embroidered apertures for her fine black-tawn ears.

She embraced Sir Grimbart, and he was struck hard, as he always was, by the wisdom and goodness of her rather long, beautiful face. Hermeline in turn was chilled to her bones to see the concern thin-lying underneath Grimbart's jovial greeting and smiles.

Up to dinner they went. Everyone knew, of course, why Grimbart was here, even the pustular cook-nephew in his fat-splattered smock serving the venison, but nobody wanted to broach the subject, and talk roamed and rambled on other matters: the badger's boats, Hermeline's ongoing translation of Abū Bakr Muhammad ibn Zakariyyā al-Rāzī's alchemical texts, Reynard's growing wine cellar and the highly peculiar weather.

At twenty past nine, at the tail end of the cheese course, there was a sudden lull in the chatter—Hermeline was reclining in a dark corner of the Hall with her three sleepy cubs and some of the badger's marzipan; Reynard was deep in thought, sipping on a stiff cup of willow wine and piling *fromage de Herve* on a thickly buttered hunk of bread—and so Grimbart finally grasped the nettle and spoke.

'Now Reynard,' Grimbart began, clearing his throat and taking a long swig of tea, 'To put it bluntly, you must be aware that your absence from Court is very damaging, with all these terrible accusations being laid against you. Now if you both think it's a sound idea, then I think it's high time that you come with me to Gent. Going to ground here in Maleperduys is not doing you any good with complaints flying in from every direction, and this is, after all, your third warning.'

The badger regarded Reynard very, very sternly, his feathery eyebrows bristling. 'Now I'm telling you the truth, old friend. If you stay here all day tomorrow, no mercy can help you. In three days, your house will be besieged, and a gallows tree and a rack will be built in front of it. Please listen to me, dear Fox, you will not escape with Hermeline, nor with the children. This is deadly serious, Reynard. The King will take all your lives. It will be the end of your happy home, Hermeline's scholarship, your gilded nest; even your little foxlings will be in danger.' Hermeline clutched the cubs who were now fast asleep, ears and paws and brushes twitching with their gambols in sweven-land.

Grimbart suddenly got up and walked round the long table and sat next to Reynard on his bench. He took hold of his paw and patted it and fixed him with the same look he'd give a panicking young sailor in a sudden wave-thundering, timber-rattling tempest in the Bay of Biscay.

'Reynard, my best advice is that you come with me straight-away to the Court. No doubt—*no doubt*—your cunning... your subtle and wise counsel will prevail and you'll escape in the end, as you always have done in the past. You have had far greater adventures, far worse scrapes than this and have always survived, always triumphed. I'm sure it will all have a happy ending, and you will be acquitted of every one of these awful *acoupements*, and all your enemies will be put to shame, but you must come, d'you see? You must come.'

Reynard looked for a long moment at the old brock's familiar stripy face. He was getting on a bit now, his friend: fur flecked with yellow-grey, as though fine-sprinkled with chamber soot, and glim-black ash-bud eyes a little rheumy and full of care. At these wear-worns of age, a faint tremble of sadness suddenly came upon the fox, who was tipsy from the willow-shrab. Grimbart the Badger was the only animal outside his family that, despising the hypocrisy of most creatures on earth's shadowy plains, he truly trusted and respected and loved.

So, Reynard the Fox answered, and answered, for once, with complete sincerity. 'As always, you speak the truth and nothing less, Grimbart,' he exclaimed with a deep sigh, rising up and brushing crumbs from his handsome whiskers. 'Everything you say is true and you're quite right, it's best that I go with you to Gent. I've no more japes, no more swikes, no more tricks up my sleeve, and I'm getting damned tired of hiding. Perhaps the King will be merciful to me if I come and talk to him animal to animal, and I'm right there under his eye, so to speak? And Noble understands, *oh he understands only too well*, that his Court simply couldn't keep going without my wits, not even if I caused worse harm than I have already.'

Grimbart nodded encouragingly. 'That's the spirit, Reyner! Well done!'

'And even if some of those courtiers are full foul to me, you know what, I don't care, it doesn't trouble my heart one bit.' By now Reynard was in full flow, flashing around the Hall in a blur of russet, wine a-splashing. 'All might judge me, but where great courts are gathered of crown-heavy kings or sabled lords, where subtle counsel and fine-woven plans are needed, it is always Reynard the Fox whom they seek! Noble's barons might swan around with their own fancy schemes and *ruses de guerre*, but in this stormy world of deceit and blasphemy and sin, a fox's cunning and ingenuity are always best! And by God's Armies, my wise sayings and politic strategies will always be looked to above all others, in war and in peace!'

Hermeline exchanged looks with Grimbart, and the badger quietly lifted the sleeping Reynkin and Rossel from her lap and, a long strip of cub draped over each shoulder, took them to their chamber; the older Reynardine stumbling behind, crying with tiredness, brush drooping. Reynard followed them down the winding passage, moonlight quartering through the window bars, whispering loudly. 'And in that lion's Court, there are some, nay many, who have sworn to do me the worst they can.' Reynard paused to tuck the little foxes into bed and to bid all the saints in heaven protect them in the night, and when he continued he had tears in his eyes. 'And, dear Grimbart, it does make my heart heavy, for many enemies can hurt me so much more than one. Nevertheless, it is better that I go with you to the Court now, and answer for myself, than put my family in any more danger and peril them in a venture which we are bound to lose.'

He tenderly kissed his little foxlings and stroked their ears, then tucked Grimbart's toy ships—carved by the badger with so much affection—into the folds of their blankets, to keep them safe from harm. 'Let's go now, dear Brock. King Noble is too mighty for me, I must do as he will, and if I cannot better my situation, then I shall take it patiently and, by the blessed torments of Saint Aldegonde, I shall suffer it with as much courage as I can muster.'

And Reynard went to Hermeline, and sweetly kissed her and hugged her as tight as he could. And he told her to take great care of the children, 'my dearest Reynardine, such a big boy and so clever with his books already, just like his mother, and precious Reynkin, my youngest son. He is so very, very like me and I do hope he follows in my footsteps. And there is Rossel, already such a passing fair thief, snatched two fat poulets from the Abbot of Baudeloo last week, in broad daylight no less!' He looked around proudly, but was met by an unfavourable glower from Grimbart and a faint head-shaking from Hermeline. 'In any case, I love them as well as any animal could love his little ones, and if God gives me grace and protects me from harm, when I return I shall thank you, my dear wife, with a multitude of fair words—for I know how much you love the skein-frill of a fine fox-turned phrase.'

Thus, with these brave words, Reynard the Fox, Lord of Maleperduys, took leave of his adored Dame Hermeline. How they all wept. Sentimental Grimbart blowing his nose like a wheezy sackbut, Reynard roughly wiping tears which flowed without still, and Hermeline quietly lamenting with the clear-eyed knowledge of what lay before her husband, and the equally pragmatic realisation that the larder-house was completely empty and so were the various little pantries kept in hidey-holes around the manor.

CHAPTER FOURTEEN

The Confessions of Reynard the Fox

The Sober Feast Day of Saint Landelin the Confessor, *
Tuesday 15th June

It was past midnight when the fox and the badger finally left Maleperduys. Grimbart quietly pressing the pouch of silver florins into Hermeline's paw at the gate, and Reynard rushing up to kiss his cubs once more, and to change his hat for the third time.

Reynard had no intention of skulking into Gent like a common wandelard, and so had ordered his nephew to fetch his finest piece of clothing, a highly dramatic and wildly fashionable houppelande in a deep, woadish demon-blue.

The houppelande had been made the previous year by a renowned atelier of lynxes, their workshop a dark, cool, tiled house by the river in Seville.

Their cloth was widely acclaimed as the finest silk velvet in Europe, which retained the faintest signature scent of orange blossom and Guadalquivir fish heads, always noted with pleasure by their many discerning clients. This particular piece had been skilfully woven with a stately silver-gilt design of

---

* Saint Landelin (*c.* 625–686) was a ruffian and a brigand, who became most devout after his conversion to Christianity, and set about trying to right some of the terrible wrongs he had inflicted on others during his wild youth. In Hainaut, for example, where he had committed many a foul crime, he founded an abbey in around 650, to benefit his former victims. He was a particularly popular saint in Cambrai, a town which Reynard liked immensely, and visited often to study its complicated system of defences and meet with his cousin, the famous architect Goupil de Honnecourt.

snarling fox heads and curling grapevines. Huge sleeves trailed almost to the ground, their edges elaborately petal-scalloped, and the great voluminous folds of the main garment, lined in the softest of miniver fur, were tucked rakishly into a jewelled belt of the softest leather, into which Reynard also jammed his best scabbard and dagger.*

This was no ordinary cloak, but a cloak for kings or popes or emperors, and as such it demanded appropriate headwear. Rushing up and down the stairs to his chamber, Reynard tried various approaches before settling for a silk cocket in the same startling hue, which he arranged carefully around his ears, securing the folds of material with a gnarly old chicken foot, into which a fancy peacock's sword feather had been roughly glued.

Privately, Grimbart thought that a subdued, pious outfit in drab browns and greys, even a hair shirt, would be more suitable for the occasion, but he bit his tongue and waited patiently whilst Reynard and his nephew draped his velvets and fastened his hood.

After all the bustle and emotion of leaving, the forest was still and calm, the moon lighting their path through the roses. 'We'll go the road way I think,' said Sir Grimbart, pausing for Reynard to tie his sleeves to stop them being ripped by brambles. 'Through Belsele and Lokeren, and then enter Gent through Destelbergen. Should be quiet at this time. I should think we'll make it by morning, if we keep the pace up.'

---

* The head of the atelier, an enigmatic lynx named Ysabel Arantzazu de Mendoça, had grown up on a rambling vineyard in Valdepeñas and was particularly skilled in the realistic representation of the grape.

Through the dark trees they went, following Reynard's crooked paths which skeined through the forest in a bewildering and intricate network of tunnels and tracks and sties so narrow that Grimbart could barely squeeze through. One burrowed down through the mushroomy roots of an ancient oak; another ran along a tenfold plank bridge through a stinking bog, thick with mosquitos; and one was so completely enfolded by thorn apple that they had to crawl like adders on their bellies. Grimbart took all this in his stride; as a sailor, he enjoyed mapmaking and chorography, and took a keen interest in the complex architecture of Reynard's woodland labyrinth, even though he disapproved of its nefarious purpose.

When they finally emerged from the woods into a wide, open field of nodding barley, golden and whispering in the dark, the fox suddenly stopped.

'Grimbart, dearest,' he said, grasping the badger by his shoulders, 'I have to tell you, I am shuddering and shaking like this barley-corn. I am in agonies, AGONIES! In the very greatest of fear, TERRIFIED from ears to brush, right down to my poor fox bones. Here we are, striding happily away through the woods and fields, as though we're on an idle midsummer jaunt, and yet with every step I descend into even greater dread. My very life is in jeopardy, Old Brock, MY VERY LIFE!' And stepping back he elaborately crossed himself, and then sank dramatically and foxily to his knees.*

'Being so close to the end—so close I fear I can smell a whiff of hell-smoke—I am wracked, WRACKED, with repentance for

---

* Being in mortal fear of one's life, *in periculum mortis*, was an accepted reason for making a confession, and this type of lay confession would have been allowed in exceptional circumstances within Reynard's world.

my sins. Sins which I must confess to you, dear Grim, as there's
no other priest near here to confess to,' snuffled Reynard. 'If
I were shrived of all my sins, I would feel a great burden lift
and my soul would be clear.'

Grimbart looked down at Reynard, kneeling in all his
sumptuousness in the dusty barley-rig, poppies ringing him
like drops of grail blood, and sighed. 'Will you confess,
Reynard? You must be serious about this, my friend. And
you must begin by promising to leave all that stealing and
roving and plundering behind.'

Reynard nodded gravely. 'I will, God wot, I will. Now hear
me, cousin Brock, hear what I say!' And, still kneeling, he
produced a miniature gold and purple psalter from the folds
around his belt, which he proceeded to clutch to his heart.*
Clearing his throat slightly, he began:

'*Confiteor pater, mater* of all the misdeeds that I have done.
And gladly will I receive penance for them.'†

'Now, just stop right there, Reynard,' interrupted Grimbart
gruffly, 'None of that French fance now. Unless you want to
confess to yourself, then say it in Flemish, or English even,
so I may understand you. And come on, let's keep walking,
you can tell me as we go.' He pulled Reynard up, dusted him
down, picked some barley awns from his fur, and they carried
on, heading for the village of Belsele.

---

* This psalm book had been made and transcribed by Dame Hermeline,
who had taken great care with the illuminations and dyed the parchment
a rich and unusual purple with a powder made from crushed sea snails
she'd bought from a dour Italian count in Leuven one Christmas Eve.
† Here Reynard is corrupting the usual opening to a confession, *Confiteor,
pater, peccavi* (I confess, Father, for I have sinned). Grimbart, a seaward
badger of practicalities and pragmatic action rather than scholarship,
mistakes his jumbled fox-Latin for French.

'Well,' said Reynard, 'I have trespassed against all the beasts that live. Every single one of them, may God pardon me. I tricked Uncle Bruin the Bear into having his crown and paws rough-bloodied, so he had to crawl back to Court on his bare fundaments. And I taught Professor Tybert to catch mice, and fleeched him into a snare at the priest's house. I have also greatly wronged Chanticleer and his children, of whom, I'm sorry to say, I've supped on a good many. I haven't even spared King Noble. I've slandered him on many an occasion and,' he paused, re-pinning a sleeve, 'shamed Queen Gente too.'

'Is that so, Reynard? The Queen?' asked Grimbart, a little shocked, as they clambered through a crab-apple tree, trying to avoid a papery wasps' nest which hung like an old lantern in the leaves.

They were leaving the fields now for the wild heaths which circled Belsele. A single pathway crept across this strange desolate wasteland, where only the heathflower bloomed, even in midsummer. This was the realm of spiteful adders and wandering ghosts and wolves, a grey, still, sandy place, which muddled the eyes and scared the wits. The moon was still bright, but a heavy mist had risen, and as they walked it was difficult to tell where they were going or where they had been. Grimbart thought it looked a little like his nurse had described purgatory when he was a cub, and he shivered despite himself. He took the last turbot pies from his bag and passed one to the fox. 'Carry on,' he said.

'Well, I have beguiled and tricked Isengrim the Wolf more often than I can tell. I always call him Uncle, but really he is nothing of my kin, he's no family nor friend of mine.' Reynard, looking cross, took a big flaky bite of fish and pastry. 'Once, a couple of Michaelmasses ago, I made him a monk at Elmare, when I was tonsured for a while.'

'Reyner, what d'you mean, you made him a monk?' worried Grimbart. Reynard sniffed. 'I was enjoying a brief respite from my worldly toil with the brothers there, and I asked Isengrim to join me. He was most flattered, as he delighted in the sound of the great bells in the priory steeple ringing out over the salt marshes, and I grant that they did have a certain dark cadence, which might appeal to a wolf. That first evening, before I'd even introduced him to the abbot—a nice man, but completely obsessed with writing his damn annals, always complaining about the sloppy records they kept at Sint-Pieters,—anyway, Isengrim said he wanted to learn to ring the bells as they were so sweet to his ears in that windswept old place, so I bound his feet to the bell rope to start him off. Before long, he was ringing those bells like nobody's business. Ding, dong, ding, dang, dong. You could hear them right out to the deep-lashed sea! You could hear them halfway to the Suffolk coast! Isengrim rang them until he was sore and dizzy, and his ears were bleeding; he rang them so hard that the folks in the street and for miles about were afraid and thought there was a demon swinging on the clangers.' They both laughed, Grimbart trying to look disapproving as he chuckled.

'This was all before he'd asked to join the order, so the monks rushed in and found him bobbing up and down, the bells a-clanging and the very tower a-shaking and a-shuddering. They say that bells are jealous of the presence of evil; well, they almost slaughtered Isengrim that September night. He was beaten black and blue, almost to the death.'

The mist was close around them now, swirling and trammelling and moiling their fur and clothes. At the edge of the heath they passed by a stagnant pool which smelt of old fish and dead things. Reynard nodded towards it and continued his confession.

'There's more, for I taught the wolf to fish as well. It was Midwinter Eve, just before Rossel was born. Ham-salting time. Bitter, bitter cold and the snow lay deep across the land. Rime-frost on the willow trees like sugared subtleties, and a great copper moon hanging low in the sky. D'you recall, Brock, all the rivers had frozen hard—you could dance down the Schelde all the way to the sea. Anyhow, past three, at the holl of the night, Sir Isengrim and I crossed paths in the turnip fields up by the Baudeloo fish ponds, the ones all the villagers use. The biggest pond was thick-cast with ice, except for a single hole, axed out each day by one of the farmers for the cattle to drink. Every night, he and his friends would drive their cows down, and have a drink and play some dice. Earlier on, I'd seen that they'd left one of their buckets down there.'

The badger sighed and rubbed the tufts between his eyebrows.

'I told Isengrim that if he came along with me to the ponds there was an easy way to catch a mess of good fish—the very choicest ones, I said—lampreys and barbels and tasty troutlings, I told him. And I showed him the bucket and the hole, and then I, er, I tied his tail to the handle. As tight as I could. With his own belt.'

'Oh Reynard,' muttered Grimbart, who could see what was coming next.

'Go on to the ice, Brother Wolf, I bade him, and dip your tail and your fishing-pail into the hole. Off Isengrim went, slippering and sliddering across the pond. When he reached the middle, he lowered his haunches, settling down to fish his catch. Down into the freezing icy water goes the bucket and that stormy grey tail of his. His face, Grimbart, when he felt the cold, by Blessed Arnold of Soissons, I thought he might die right there on the spot!'

'I suppose he got stuck, Reyner, yes?' said the Badger, stumbling a little in the thickening mist.

'Dangling down the hole, the bucket fills right up to the brim with gobbets of ice—not fish, of course, not even a miserable prickleback'—Reynard took a beautiful larkspur silk handkerchief from inside his brocade folds and delicately blew his nose—'and then the water all around begins to freeze up solid, holds the bucket fast, and along with it, our dear wolf's tail, knotted up with the handle and sealed into the pond ice like a feather in amber.'

Reynard tried quite unsuccessfully to turn a wide, white-fanged smirk into pious contrition. 'Completely stuck he was. He started to wriggle, then tried to stand up, then tried to pull the bucket out, but to no avail. He was smashing his claws down onto the ice and barking at me to help him, proper 'ghasted he was, proper 'ghasted!' Reynard carefully tucked his hankie back. 'He hadn't realised he was bedded in; he thought he'd fished his catch and more!'

'And did you help him, Reyner?' asked Grimbart.

Reynard made an odd spluttering sort of noise, 'I admit, Cousin, I was cruel, but Isengrim is so loath and greedy and spiteful, I simply couldn't stop myself. I called out to him that those who covet everything lose everything, and laughed at him struggling away with his frory tail. Then it was dawn, and the sun rose up over the snow and everything was a-glittering in the light and Isengrim was wailing and howling. Men would be abroad soon, I thought, even in the deep snow, and sure enough, at first bells, that rich young lord who lives in the manor at Meulevijverstraat, Constant des Granges, came galloping up with a mottled pack of hounds, blowing on a horn. And he wasn't alone. He'd risen his whole household for a midwinter hunt, behind him followed a merry ramshackle of people, shouting and hallooing. Well, the moment I saw them, Grim, I smolted, up behind the poplar trees on the rise to watch the show: Sir Isengrim still trapped like a cork in a bottle—heaving and tugging with all his might, and almost ripping off his tail in the process.'

Grimbart and Reynard had now reached the outskirts of Belsele. A lamp was burning in the window of a farm cottage, eerie in the fog. The world feels without substance, *sine materia*, thought the badger, remembering his cubhood Latin, hoping that the fox's confession was more substantial than the heath mists.

Reynard carried on in a loud whisper as they passed the farm. 'Then, one of des Granges's servant boys, wrangling a couple of dogs—Norfolk tumblers—on a leash, spots something strange and unnatural in the pond, comes closer, and starts to shout "Wolf! wolf! there's a wolf stuck in the fish pond!" Down gallops Constant, muffled by the drifts, crying to his huntsmen to follow suit. Well, I can't say exactly what happened next, old friend, as my view was rather obscured by a holly bush, but I can tell you that there was the greatest of hullaballooing, barking and howling and screaming, and a few moments later I saw Isengrim shoot off in the direction of his dismal berg, tail gone, scarlet blood dripping behind him in the white snow.'

They rested for a while in Belsele marketplace, leaning on the horse troughs and munching hazelnuts and a couple of disorientated earthworms Reynard had picked up on the heath. Apart from the baker, a portly ram in a crisp linen apron, who nodded at them as he trundled past, the village was still very much abed. 'That it, Reynard? D'you have any more misdoings against Brother Wolf to tell me?' asked Grimbart as they set off along the lower, quieter road to Lokeren.

Reynard took Grimbart's arm companionably. 'Couple, pr'aps. Any more little nuncheons, Badger? It makes me hungry, all this confessing.' Grimbart passed him some cold roast venison he had packed as they were leaving Maleperduys.

'One rainy September morning,' said Reynard, 'I persuaded Isengrim to come to the house of the priest of Bloys with me. Do you know Bloys? Charming little village—cows, pirates, very good herring pâté—couple of leagues past Brugge?' The badger nodded without speaking. Many, many years ago, he'd walked there from his boat, to collect a posy of sea lavender from the tidal marshes for the funeral of his sweetheart, Lady Slopecade, who had died of lung-fever one terrible spring.

'In all of the fat, green lands owned by the Abbey of Saint-Quentin of Vermendois,' continued the fox, 'and those monks own property all the way from Poitiers to Bremen, there was not a richer priest.

'And this priest, his name was Lambrecht, I believe, he had a big larder where many a good flitch of bacon was hung. That summer, I was attending to some very important business in Brugge—staying in Hermeline's grandmother's pied-à-terre by Saint Donaas—and stocking up on books and wine and maps and whatnot, and getting those hangings made for the best bed—those ones with Orpheus on. Anyway, after my affairs were dealt with each morning, I would trot over to Bloys for a bit of exercise and to fill my belly from the priest's cupboard. By the swine of Saint Anthony, that bacon was so damn good, I forged a hidden hole into the larder from the street, so I could slip in and out without anyone being the wiser.'

'And Isengrim?' asked Grimbart.

'I bumped into Isengrim, quite by chance, in a tavern on the Hoedenmakersstraat, and after a few hands of cards and a few flagons of ale I enticed him out to Bloys with juicy talk of hook after hook of bacon. I showed him the opening to the hole and suggested that he crawl in. I *might* have given him a bit of a push.' Reynard paused to pick some venison out of his teeth. 'In he crept, and there he found salt beef in barrels and so many good sides of pork, which he ate and ate and ate like a starveling, bolting down the most extraordinary amount of meat. He ate so much, without thought or measure, that his belly, flat as a flawn coming in, had swelled out like a windball, and when he tried to squeeze back out again through the hole he found that he couldn't fit. He was stuck. Well, I'd had a few beers myself, so I tumbled away to the village square and made a right old racket—shouting and yelling, until all the townsfolk were wondering what on earth was up at the priest's house… Any more venison, Grimbart? And perhaps a drop to drink?'

Snaffling down the last of the meat and gulping some fortified yarrow wine, good for the liver, which Hermeline had passed to the badger before they left, Reynard continued.

'I was a bit wild, I admit. You won't believe what I did next! Lambrecht the priest was sitting at the table in his front parlour, eating as fat a capon as any man might find in the whole of Flanders. I dashed in, stole the capon, and raced away as fast as I could. "Thief! Thief!" he cried, running out into the street, "Grab that fox and slay him!" My goodness, he was angry. "I've never seen the like!" he wailed, bright red and flailing around like a windmill. "A fox coming right into my very own house and taking my very own hen from my very own table! Whoever saw such a saucy, hardened thief!" And he took his table knife and he cast it right at me—it was as blunt as a sack of squirrels, mind—it flew straight past my nose, and landed in the gutter.

'I ran even further away, and he shoved the table over with a thunderhorn-clatter-bang, and then came after me, limping and shouting, "Kill him! Slay him! Kill that fox!" And after him came half the good men and women and children of Bloys, up in arms against poor Reynard, waving their sticks and staves. I ran and I ran, roast chicken in chops; I loped right around the ramparts and out onto the salt marsh, leading them all on a merry dance, until I ended up back at the larder hole, Sir Isengrim still very much trapped inside. It was at this juncture that I had to drop the hen. That lovely, crispy, golden-skinned capon,' hanky out again, Reynard daintily mopped some drool from his whiskers, 'it was far too heavy for me and much—MUCH—against my will, I left it there. Right there in the dust next to the once secret hole into the fulsome pantry. Secret no more. For rushing up behind me came Lambrecht the priest and the citizens of Bloys, wheezing and panting and gasping with the chase. I slipped silently away when they were catching their breath.

'The priest slowly picked up his capon, then spied my little tunnel, and, bending to look in, came face to face with the bloodshot yellow eyes and grey muzzle of Isengrim the Stuck, and he bellowed and hallowed and took many a saint's name in vain. "Hit down here, friends," he shouted, "Smite the hole! It was a wolf, not a fox, and he's squatting inside my meat pantry! The nerve of it! See that he doesn't escape!"

'And they went at him in a fury, hitting and poking and prodding and lashing, making such a noise that the rest of the neighbours came out to see what was what, and they joined in too, giving him many a shrewd stroke and throwing stones and rocks and turnips. Eventually, they heaved and squeezed him out of my foxhole and threw him onto a patch of grass by the church and blindfolded him and beat him and tortured him until "noble" Sir Isengrim rolled over with his legs in the air as though he were quite, quite dead. Everyone cheered, and the children clapped and made merry, and they pulled him onto the second-best bier with the wobbly wheel and jolted him over stone and scrub to a wasteland of crows, high-ponging of gong, outside the village bounds.'

'And what happened to Brother Wolf, Reyner? How did he escape?' inquired Grimbart, who was beginning to feel thoroughly exhausted by his assumed role of confessor.

'Why, they rolled him into a foul ditch, and left him there.

Stark dead they thought he was. And there he lay all night long, grave-flies buzzing around his battered body. I don't know how he eventually got away, as I was long gone by then, back to Brugge, where I had a very nice poultry supper at the Ter Buerse inn to make up for the lost capon; good pudding as well, I recall, prunes and English custard.' Reynard tapered off at a frown from Grimbart.

They were just coming up to the gallows pole on the outskirts of Lokeren. It stood at the crossroads leading to the little hamlet of Rozen and the Great White Road between Gent and Antwerp, along which so many summoners from King Noble had trudged. The grisly remains of an elderly squirrel—a notorious nut thief from Limoges—hung in the gibbet cage, thin bones rattling in the breeze. Reynard shivered as they passed by, and the badger patted him kindly on the back. 'Courage, Reynard, *mon ami*, courage.'

Reynard nodded curtly, sniffing loudly, and loped a bit faster, his head hanging down and his brush feathering dust on the road. Grimbart breathed hard to catch up with him, stopping a couple of times to hold his chest, a familiar pain around his heart.

After a while, the fox, then the badger, wiping his brow, came to the steep sides of a grassy ridgeway. This high path, prettily scattered with white cottonsedge flowers, marched past Lokeren above the watery fenlands, which now spread for several miles to the south.

It was the first point of vantage they'd had for some time. The sun was rising now, and slowly drawing the last of the mist from the meadows and the marshes. Reaching almost to the horizon, the shifting water was glittering in the golden light. The hushed confessorial intimacy of the heath, the fog screening the fox's shriving as thoroughly as a Lenten veil, was fading too, and would soon be torn completely asunder for King and courtiers to inspect and judge the depths of Reynard's soul under a much less forgiving beam.

For a while, though, they rested there quite peaceably and looked out across the reed banks and the pollarded willows and the rows of yellow alders edging the fens. The bells of Lokeren were ringing lauds, which drifted like thistledown across the farmland to busy its congregation to prayer.

'You know, some animals say it's bad luck to pass even one alder tree on a journey,' Reynard suddenly announced in a bleak voice, 'and there's a whole parade of 'em down there. And do you know their bark bleeds when you cut it, gushes red as mulberries, like the blessed death-wounds of Christ.' He sighed heavily and crossed himself.

'What utter nonsense, Reynard!' cried Grimbart, giving him a stern look. 'The alder is a good tree, Cousin Fox, a good, sensible tree. He gives us our walking clogs and our water pipes and our herring barrels. You can't walk a mile in Flanders without passing one! Now come on, you buck up and try to finish your confessions by the time we get to Destelbergen.'

Reynard sighed again, but began his shriving once more, as they set off along the ridgeway. 'Where were we? Well, I think Isengrim must have had his rem'brances knocked out of him that fateful day in Bloys, for at Martinmas, when the wind was nipping from the north, he comes knocking on the doors at Maleperduys as though nothing ill has happened between us and he'd never heard of any priests or sides of bacon.

'He was in a bad way, Grim, thin and rakey; looked like

he hadn't had a good meal for quite some time. Hermeline, charitable as ever, even to the likes of Isengrim, welcomed him inside and gave him one of her knitted shawls and a glass of eau de vie and he sat in the hall by the fire for ages. Had a funny look on his face, as though the world itself had come to an end. Eventually, he turned to me and says, "Reynard, I will be your good and faithful friend for an entire year, till Martintide next, if you could fill up my belly with chickens." What could I do, Cousin Brock? He looked quite mad and his stomach was rumbling like a thunder blast. So, I snuffed the candles, and we sneaked out of the castle. Hermeline had gone to bed by then.' Grimbart shook his head and tutted. 'I took him down the road to a cloth merchant's house in Terlinden. A grand house it was, with seven fat feathery hens and a scarlet-plumed cockerel, who sat on a high beam all day right next to a trapdoor by the chimney.

'It didn't take much to persuade Isengrim to climb up there with me, but he was so weak from his empty belly that he could barely crawl, let alone scale a wall, so I pushed him from behind and he dug his claws into the mortar, and clung onto the thick ivy, until somehow or other we were both sitting on the highest roof in Terlinden. It was a bird's eye view, alright. You could see for miles and miles from there, all the way to the lighthouse at Westkapelle in the north, fisher-boats sailing by, piled high with herring, and far, far south across the river, to the bolsty walls of Brussels. I swear I could even see some soldiers doing their rounds, helmets and pikes and everything.' Reynard grinned, pleased with his scene-setting.

Grimbart was combing his eyebrows with a slightly shaky paw, stopping to pierce a flea and flick it into the dyke. 'I very much doubt that, Reyner, dear, both Westkapelle and Brussels are miles away. Even in the case of a tall building like that lighthouse, I can't imagine you'd be able to spy it from a cloth merchant's house in Terlinden.'

'Well, you could see at least as far as my cousin's brewery in Buggenhout, then, which is a considerably long way away,' snapped Reynard. 'The point is, we were sitting there, next to that fall-door, *very high up indeed*, and I told him to believe me and to trust me, that if he were to creep through that door, he would find as many hens as he could gobble up, just sitting there snoozing inside. And he laughed and laughed—a mad-hungry laugh, with about as much mirth as a moon-howl—and opens up the door with his great black paw, and creepy-crawls inside and, very carefully, begins to cast around here and there for chickens.

'After groping around for quite some time without a single fowl for his troubles, out he pops, glaring at me, a growl in his voice, and spits "Reynard, are you just toying with me? Are playing one of your tricks? I cannot find any birds in there, fat or no!"

'Hold on, hold on now, I don't quite understand, Reynard,' said Grimbart—they were passing Lokeren proper now, the little town full of its morning business. A group of hares passed them nervously, heading off to the flax fields. 'Why didn't he just fall straight through the trapdoor? Where is he rustling for chickens? I can't picture it.' Reynard groaned, 'It doesn't matter to the story, Brock, but there's a half-beam right under the fall-door, couple of meat hooks on it.' 'A weight-bearing platform?' asked Grimbart.

'By Saint-Loup-de-Sens, yes, a weight-bearing platform!' barked Reynard, exasperated. 'Anyhow, I said to Isengrim, "Uncle Wolf, you need to creep further in to find your prize! I've already scoffed the hens at the front! The really plump and feathery ones are nesting at the back. And he that wants to win," I told him, "needs to take a little trouble, a smatch of effort, a *petit pois* of courage, put his paw in the fire, so to speak, and see how many crispy poulets he can pull out!"

'So, between me and the pangs of his grumbling thin-shanks stomach, old Isengrim was persuaded to try again. The moment he pushes his muzzle through the trapdoor once more, I gave him a shove so hard that he fell right off the beam (and, if you're wondering, Grim, it was a very, very narrow perch and was all wood-wormy and splintery at the end). Down he tumbled, smack onto the stone floor far, far below, at least twenty feet, with a such a thump and a wallop and a howling that he woke up the entire household.

'Everyone that was fast asleep sprang up. The spit boy who'd been lying next to the fire was shouting that the trapdoor was open and something heavy had fallen in, but he couldn't see what it was. Then the goose girl found a candle and lit it from the fire, and the screams when they saw it was a long, grey, fang-toothed wolf—well, all the chickens started squawking and the merchant and his daughters came rushing in with pokers and candlesticks, and someone else grabbed the clothes pole, and together they beat him and kicked him and threw him into the millpond by the house. Almost flogged to death again, he was, and hungrier than ever before. And that was that. Yes, dear Grimbart, I have brought Isengrim much, much trouble and jeopardy, more than I can say or even remember.'

It was past tierce now, mid-morning, and the fox and the badger were threading carefully through the undergrowth of some dismal woods, a shortcut past Lammeke. Wych elms twisted their heavy branches over a mottle of poxy stagnant pools, and the laurel flowered here as dark as blood, its sweetness mingled with a rasp of decay. It made for unpleasant going. Angry wasps buzzed around their ears and ticks burrowed in their fur and their paws were muddy and torn from all the brambles.

It was an old, old place, this place of mulch and shadows, and even the badger tried to be silent as they struggled on, fearful of waking its inhabitants. Whilst named the Nonnenbos, the Nun's Forest, after the nearby convent of black nuns who owned the land, it was no frith for Christian souls. For across Flanders, these woodlands were well known and well avoided as elf-land, haunted by *la mesnie Hellequin*, the wild attendants of the King of Faerie, who liked to thunder through the trees on their moon-white mares, dressed in their black velvet finery, blowing their curled silver horns and trailing the newly dead in their wake, shrouds flapping in the frenzy.

As Grimbart was using his pilgrim's staff to flatten down some particularly vicious nettles, Reynard suddenly stopped dead and started to sob, covering his eyes. Grimbart paused his bashing, and patted him gently on the back. 'There, there, don't despair, Reyner, we'll be out of here soon, and I have a protection here, look, good for plague and for the ghosties.' He pulled out his amulet and pressed it upon Reynard, who pushed it away and collapsed on the bracken.

'It's not the ghosties, Grim. It's worse, I've done far worse. I haven't told you everything. I have betrayed my Hermeline with Dame Erswynde, Isengrim's wife.' He sobbed even louder, blowing his nose on the silk ties of his cocket, which had unravelled in his agitation.

'I am sorrier for this sinning than for all the other wrong-doings put together. I have shamed her, a good kind wolf—so unlike her husband—*and* my dearest wife.' He began to hyperventilate with his upset, and Grimbart looked nervously around, expecting a troupe of fairies to emerge at any moment.

'Dear Eme!' he whispered, 'Dear Uncle Reynard! I'm not sure I completely understand. What d'you mean exactly by betrayed? For a confession, you do seem to be holding back a bit. I confess, I don't know this language, as an old bachelor, please explain.'

'Oh Badger, isn't it obvious! I have trespassed with the wolf's wife. I kissed her last Baptist Day, in her still room, when she was making her famous rose sugar. Hermeline had sent me to fetch some for the cubs. Poor Erswynde had a black eye and broken ribs from that husband of hers, who'd been at the yarrow mead all day,' Reynard looked up at Grimbart slantily, 'and I felt so sad for her that I kissed her.'

'Well,' said Grimbart, 'Well, I never.' And he sat down next to Reynard on a knarry old root, scuttling with earwigs. 'Well, I never,' he repeated again.

Grimbart had, of course, defended Reynard against the adulterous accusations levelled by Isengrim, dismissing them as nothing more than the false ravings of an envious and immoral wolf, desperate to see a rival baron killed, his jewels and plate and vineyards and flax fields confiscated, his wife compromised, his family and bloodline in ruin.

Any doubts, however, regarding Reynard's conduct had never even occurred to Grimbart, having observed the fox's singular devotion to his Hermeline over the long years of their friendship. He knew that Reynard had been sweet fond of Erswynde many years before either he or Isengrim had been married, but had assumed, and, indeed, had argued vigorously at Court, that this was a mere sparrow fever of youth and was innocent and chaste, Reynard the model of gentle knighthood.

Tears pricked the badger's eyes and he muttered a quick prayer for guidance to his dear Saint Piran (whose first disciple he knew to have been a badger, and a courtly badger at that, just like him, not a wood-dweller or anything).

And then, all of a sudden, he recalled a book Tybert had shown him in his study in Gent, on an airy May evening many years ago, when the breeze blew sweet from the fields and the lilacs were in bloom along the river path. It was a beautifully decorated volume on long loan to the cat from the abbot of Sint-Pieters and had been written by an extremely clever and pious fox named Peter the Chanter of Notre Dame of Paris, whose great-granddaughter was coincidentally good friends with Tybert's second cousin twice removed, from Poitiers.

A great thick doorstep of a book it was, and much used in all the abbeys in Gent and all their houses scattered throughout the countryside. Its subject was *Moral Dilemmas and How to Solve Them*. It dealt with confessions and broken oaths and corruption and all those kind of things, and was a highly enjoyable and thrilling read, claimed Tybert, as well as being of important practical application in the uneven, troublesome lives of monastic Flanders.

On one silky vellum page, there was a faint drawing of an old-fashioned ship, and the following passage, which Tybert had roughly translated from Latin for Grimbart, due to its nautical bent. Grimbart had liked it very much indeed and had tried hard to learn it by heart. These were the lines, then, by Peter the Chanter of Notre Dame of Paris, translated by Sir Tybert the Cat, and half-remembered by Sir Grimbart the Badger, which flickered like moths through the latter's mind as he sat on his knotty stump next to the sobbing Reynard:

'Those brave animals who go to the sea in their boats, they witness all the Lord's wonders in the deep waves... Down they go into the world's torrent, to all the doubts and sadnesses which it brings. A channel as wide as the North Sea lies between a philosopher in a university thinking hard about the vast questions of life, and those humble folk—the village shrift-fathers and penancers—who are obliged to help those struggling along in this weary weeping-dale.'

What Peter the Chanter of Notre Dame of Paris was saying, thought Badger, was that all of God's work was mysterious, and that only a few of us can sometimes see its true workings, such as us sailors, and that the practical business of hearing confessions and dealing with animals' souls is very different from the work of learned scholars. Elsewhere in the book, Tybert had told him, Peter the Chanter of Notre Dame of Paris had asked some very prickly moral questions. Can one burn consecrated church furniture to keep the poor warm? Should a bishop send troops to a king's war which he knows is cruel and unjust? Grimbart couldn't remember the answers to those questions, but the point was that life is hard and complicated and never clear-cut, and sometimes one needs to just try to help those who are still thin-streaked with good, like a well-hung bacon.

And the badger, taking his role as Reynard's confessor very seriously, shook himself out of his reverie, ate a handful of earwigs, and spoke kindly to the fox, who was lying prostrated at his feet.

Reynard swiftly gathered himself up, swatting away a hornet. 'I should have told you back then, Grim, I should have said it openly, FLUNG it out into the clear air after it happened. But you know how upset and angry you get if anyone speaks ill of the ladies.' Reynard brushed the twigs from his tail and unravelled his hat, which was torn and muddied, and threw it into a frothy clump of wild parsnip.

'I have told you everything now, Grimbart. All I can think on. All the wrongnesses and sins that I have done.' Reynard clasped his jewelled psalter once more and looked sadly to the ground. 'You must set me my penance and absolve me, dear friend, for I am truly repentant.'

Strengthened by his prayers and brief meditation on the complexity of crime and redemption, Grimbart was subtle and wise in his judgement. Very solemnly, he stood up and snapped a branch from the wych elm, and swift-stripped the leaves.

'Reynard,' he said in a grave voice, 'You must smite yourself three times with this rod on your body. Then,' Grimbart paused, desperately trying to think what a priest might suggest, 'then, er, lay the branch down on the ground—best away from the nettles and the stink-balm—and spring three times over it without bowing your legs and without stumbling, and, um, then, um, take up the rod, and kiss it friendly-like in a token of meekness and obedience to the, er, penance that I give you.' Reynard looked at him in wonder and started hopping around with the stick. 'That it, Cousin Grimbart?' he asked a couple of moments later.

'Yes, that's it, Reynard. Herewith, you are forgiven for all the sins you have committed up to today. I forgive them all.' Grimbart, rather embarrassed by his role, did his best to bless the fox, and hugged him awkwardly, and they both laughed and Reynard was as glad and giddy as he'd ever been.*

Grimbart looked at him closely. 'Now, Reynard, this doesn't mean that you can go back to your old ways again. You must be a good fox from now on. This is what you need to do.' And Grimbart rustled in his overnight bag for the long strip of coarse parchment and his writing things, which he pulled out triumphantly. He perched on the wych elm again and, hushing Reynard's questions, laboriously scrawled across the vellum in his dense, black, antiquated script. And this is what he wrote:

'Having in the name of God, been considering and contemplating my soul and my future life, so that I might deserve to receive favours before the great pious Lord, I, Sir Reynard the Fox of Maleperduys Castle near Rupelmonde in the Waasland in Eastern Flanders, henceforth do solemnly swear to:

* It should perhaps be mentioned that Grimbart's role as priest was without any proper authority and his penance was comically mild. But, whilst this was partly because of inexperience, it was also given both from a very real wish by the badger to rehabilitate Reynard through kindness, rather than cruelty, and from his great dislike of Isengrim, who he felt was a truly evil animal.

Do good works
Read my psalms
Go to church
Fast and keep my holidays
Give all my alms
Be gentle to Sir Bruin the Bear
Stop murdering my chicken cousins, especially
    the kin of poor Sir Chaunticleer the Cockerel,
    to whom I will make amends
Stop tormenting Sir Isengrim the Wolf
Leave my sinful and ill life behind and all my thefts
    and treasons and naughtinesses
And so I may come to mercy.
Enacted in the middle of the Nonnen Woods,
by Lammeke, by the big wych elm and the hornet nest.
Signed by the paw of:
Sir Reynard the Fox of Maleperduys Castle,
    near Rupelmonde in the Waasland in Eastern Flanders.
Witnessed and scribed in the name of God and
    His Majesty, King Noble the Lion by:
Sir Grimbart the Badger, of Dassenburcht, Gent.'

They both signed, Reynard with an elaborate and flamboyant paw; Grimbart in his careful, elderly Gothic.

'I do promise I will do all these things,' said Reynard, handing Grimbart back his quill and bowing in a worryingly jaunty manner, thought the badger. But he kept his counsel and with his fox clean-shriven, off they went on their journey to Court once more, pushing through the spite-dank faerie wood, through the stingers and the fallen branches, occasionally stopping to look round at an odd sound or the gleam of a watchful yellow eye in the tangled thyvel.

At midday, twigs and blossoms and green snails in their fur, the two lords stumbled out from the trees onto a wide, friendly road. Busy with animals going to and fro, it led towards the priory of black nuns who owned the woods. Almost immediately, they met an elderly ape of Grimbart's acquaintance: Anselmus, a retired apothecarist from Mechelen, travelling to Mons for a wedding. Whilst the badger was discussing possible cures for his sciatica, Reynard sauntered on ahead until he reached the nuns' whitewashed cloisters. It was a homely place, pink flat beans and culverfoot in brightly painted pots, damp linen hanging on a line and the faint strains of sweet singing from the little chapel.

Reynard hid behind a bush, unable to believe his eyes. Everywhere there was poultry. Just idly swanning around, ambling in and out of the nunnery walls without a care in the world. Ducks and geese and capons and hens and pullins and cockerels and some plumy little brown birds he'd never even seen before. Poor Reynard! Faced with this exquisite temptation, this clucking cornucopia of fowl, all his oaths, his confessions, his promises, his signed and witnessed charter, his pledges to his wife, to his dearest friend and to God vanished in a sudden frenzied cloud of blood and feathers. By the time Sir Grimbart had bade farewell to his friend and reached the convent gates, he found Baron Reynard the Fox sitting in a puddle, tail feathers from a plump capon sticking out of his drooling chops, with an irate crowd of birds, including the outraged but intact capon, hurling abuse at him from the safety of the convent barn roof.

Grimbart was furious. 'Reynard! You accursed Fox! What have you done! Will you fall into your old evil, sinning ways, into those dark sins we have just shriven away, all for the sake of one little capon!' ('Oy!' cried the capon in question from the chapel tower.) 'Reynard!' continued the badger, clutching his chest, heart pounding in his outrage, 'Reynard! You have broken your oaths not only to me, but to the Lord Almighty! I am ashamed of you, ashamed. You made a confession and you should be sorely repentant, not chasing chickens who are just getting on with their day!' And Grimbart nodded curtly to the gathered poultry, who were all agog at his fierce defence of their honour, and rumbled off towards Destelbergen, thumping his staff angrily on the ground with each step.

Reynard hung his head and slunk miserably after the badger, brush between his legs, ears low-drooped. 'Cousin, I'm sorry. I don't know what came over me. I had forgotten. Please, pray God he will forgive me for I will never do it again. I promise. Wait, Grimbart, wait.'

Grimbart carried on without stopping. Reynard weaved around him wringing his paws, casting forth a scattershot of protestations and excusements. Grimbart brought to such anger was a shocking and grievous sight to behold, and it deep-rattled the fox, more than he cared to admit.

Before long, they reached a little arched wooden bridge over the River Durme, and the badger, who'd been thinking again on the tenets of Peter the Chanter of Notre Dame of Paris, paused over the rushing water, to talk with Reynard and to try to forgive him once more, when he suddenly realised that the fox was twisting and turning to look first at a family of eider ducks who were gently snoozing on the sandy river bank, then at some soft-plumed baardkriel hens, pulling up worms by an outhouse of the nunnery.

Grimbart leaned on the bridge and watched Reynard struggling with his urges, and, very much despite himself, suddenly began to chuckle and swiftly fell into a case of the morbid giggles, rather like those which strike without warning at the most solemn part of a royal funeral. 'He simply cannot restrain himself,' he thought, mopping his eyes, 'He simply cannot stop chasing those chickens and making his mischief, however hard he tries. Well, that which cleaves to the bone cannot be cut out of the flesh. Even if my poor friend is hanged, he'll still be eying hens from the gallows and planning a nice waterzooi for his last meal!'

By the time Reynard had sheepishly joined him on the bridge, Grimbart had pulled himself together, swallowed his mirth and had dwelt once more on the moral seriousness of the situation. Mindful again of his responsibility for the fox's poultry-raggled soul, he issued a stern series of admonishments to Sir Reynard, who shifted around from foot to foot like a cub being ticked off for firing chestnuts from a sling in the schoolroom.

'Foul, false, flighty deceiver!' bellowed the badger, 'not once, but twice after your pardoning do I find you stalking chickens, your eyes moving featherward on all and any of the good fowl of Flanders! Why should you place yourself so far above them, Reynard, that they should submit to your insatiable hunger! They are equal souls under God's watchful eye, Reyner, equal. You must think hard on that.'

Grimbart waved his staff like Moses at the bewildered eider ducks, who launched themselves onto the Durme, which was—thanks be to Saint-Amelia, they mutter-quacked— flowing swiftly away from the monkish, raging badger and peculiarly dressed, darty-eyed fox towards the wide waters of its great grey mother Schelde.

'Cousin Brock,' puffed Reynard, as Grimbart marched sternly away, his brown serge flapping like a sail behind him. 'Cousin Brock, you've got me all wrong and you greatly misdo to say to me all your cruel words. Wait for me, WAIT FOR ME.'

Grimbart eventually paused for him half a mile past the bridge, at a quarefoure on the Destelbergen road, where a charming wayside shrine to the Virgin Mary stood under elder trees in full flowering.* Someone had just placed a tray of fresh custard tarts as an offering. Reynard moved them with exaggerated care, and then knelt piously on the brick platform in front of the worn statue.

'Badger,' he said sadly, 'you may mean well in your tellings-off, but you *have* been distracting me from all my devotion and prayers. Let me say a paternoster for all the souls of the poultry and geese that I've betrayed and, er, well, eaten, and for the poor little bald capon whose tail feathers I stole at the house of the holy nuns.' And Reynard the Fox prayed and muttered and rosaried for an impressive amount of time, then managed to persuade Grimbart to share the custard tarts. 'They'd only be eaten by corn mice otherwise, Grim, and they're far too rich for delicate mouse bellies.'

Munching his tart, Grimbart was not well pleased with any of this, but he reasoned that Reynard had indeed confessed

---

* It had been built many years ago by King Noble's grandmother and was crowned with a stepped roof decorated with tiles of the Gent arms of a lion rampant.

and performed his penance with good grace, and if he had slipped a little again, well, he had apologised and he had said his prayers. He is a fox, after all, and it is difficult for all of us animals to transcend our God-given natures. And he thought about the hundreds of worms he had eaten in *his* life, and wondered if worms had souls, and then said a prayer for them anyway, whether they had them or not.

The sun was waning when they finally reached the cobblestones and woodsmoke of Gent. At Destelbergen they had stopped by the great lake to share some fried crabs with a group of earnest young rams who were just starting out on a long pilgrimage to Rome. Once their eager chatter was left behind, however, the two animals fell into a silent reverie on the last few miles to the castle. Grimbart thinking about legal precedents and Reynard quaking with fear, knowing that, whilst the badger loved him dearly, he would soon have to face a Court full of lords who wished him ill, if not dead and buried, and whether he liked it or not he would have to answer to them for his many crimes and misprisions and foul deeds.

PART TWO

GALLOWING

CHAPTER FIFTEEN

In which Sir Reynard the Fox comes to Court
and excuses Himself in front of the King

The Feast Day of Saint Lutgardis of Aywières,
the Miracle-Worker, Wednesday 16th June

Reynard and Grimbart crossed the River Leie by the
Boudinsbrug. It was the day of the dairy market and the
streets were packed. Everyone stopped and stared at the fox,
whose ashened reputation had spread far and wide.

Some of his old audacity and hardiesse had returned by this
point, however, with the visceral thrill of entering the heaving,
stinking, noisy, glorious city; his cape swirling around him
like Robyn Hood the Outlaw or Fair Lancelot, he swaggered
and sauntered through the streets, dagger flashing, brush
waving high, winking at the ladies and exchanging sparkling
conceits with the sober burghers of Gent.

By the time the pair had reached the moat, Reynard's
charm had thoroughly bewitched the crowds, who had begun
to whisper that those snobby grandlings up at the castle had
got it all wrong—how could such a witty and unpretentious
fox be a murderer or a thief! By contrast, when it was first
known in the Court that Reynard had finally been brought to
justice by his old friend Grimbart, there was none so poor nor
so lacking in kin or friends that they didn't ready themselves to
make an accusation against the fox. The queues were growing
even longer than those at Whitsun, snaking out of the main
Hall and into the courtyards.

Brave Reynard pretended he didn't have a care in the world, despite the gnawing fear inside, and walked along the great and famous streets with his head held high, only faltering when he caught a sudden vignette of the infamous Onthoofdingsbrug, the low stone Execution Bridge, where King Noble and his fore-lions had beheaded criminals for centuries. Two of Reynard's ancestors, his great-great-grandfather and his great-grandfather, had almost been killed there. They both wriggled out of it at the very last moment, he wasn't quite sure how.*

When they finally passed under the gatehouse into the castle, Reynard carried himself as proud and mighty as though he were the King's own son returning in triumph from some foreign skirmish, as though he'd never sinned against another soul, and was a fox of the purest and most unwemmed character.

In he marched, as bold as latten-brass, straight into the heart of the Court, through the yelling, lance-wielding guards, through his furious massed accusers, until he was standing square in front of King Noble the Lion. Reynard bowed, a

---

* Reynard is referring to the very famous incident of a young fox (his great-grandfather) and his father (Reynard's great-great-grandfather) arrested unfairly during some riots and tortured by the then king, who wanted to ascertain whether parental or filial love is stronger. He determined in his verdict that one of the two had to behead the other. The poor executioner would be subsequently pardoned. The father managed to convince his little cub to perform the beheading. They were dragged to the bridge and the son was forced to heave the sword to strike the deadly blow to his father, but the blade flew out of the hilt and landed with its point in the wooden bridge. Since an execution could only take place once, father and son were immediately released, but the terrible strain weakened their hearts and they both died young, Reynard's grandfather never really knowing his father.

magnificent bow, a bow of old romances and high fluttering flags and half-forgotten courtesies. Then he began to address the astonished Crown in his most silken voice.

'May God grant you great honour and worship, my Lord Noble,' declaimed Reynard in a formal manner, followed by another complicated foxish bow. 'There was never a king that had a truer servant than Reynard has been to your good grace. Nevertheless, dear Lord, I know well that there are many in this Court who would destroy me if you would believe them.' Cries of 'Thief!', 'Murderer!', 'False fox!' echoed around the Hall.

The main part of dinner had just been cleared away, and the Lion and his Queen were seated at their high benches, the rest of the Court rabbled around in their various cliques and alliances. Puddings were being served and some of the animals were split between their greed and their grievances. There were *appelflappen*, apple fritters, with thin English cream, and delicate tartlets of apricots, and a very large and impressive cake in the shape of the Ruins of Antioch, carried by a team of mice wobbling dangerously as they set it down in front of Gente, who waved them away.

Reynard nonchalantly grabbed a fritter, dipped it in Sir Tybert's cream bowl without asking, and continued his speech. 'But, God thank you, it's not fitting to your exalted position, to your crown, to believe these false deceivers, these purr-tongued liars, so lightly! I should complain to God himself that these deceitful flatterers,' he motioned a paw at the angry crowd, faces smeared with pink crumbs and clotted cream from the Ruins of Antioch, 'are believed above an honest fox! Let loose to do their worst to God-fearing animals, to harm and scath a poor country-lord! A simple hermit attacked by velvet-clad vultures!'

King Noble was angry. He had been planning to have a nice long nap in a sunny spot on the roof after his nice long dinner and he felt no inclination to spend the rest of the day listening to Reynard's twisty words.

'Peace, Lord Reynard! False thief and traitor!' he boomed, 'How well you bring forth your fair tales! But I don't care a straw for what you say, Fox, I know what you are! Since we were cubs, you have used all the flattering words to be my friend, you, who have served me so ill over the years, have oiled and unctured your way out of every misdemeanour and into my fellowship. O Reynard, you know full well what you have done! My Great Peace—my Great Peace commanded across all Flanders beasties, my heralds sent across the land, even to Maleperduys, d'you keep it, eh? Did you observe the Great Peace! Did you, miserable, unfaithful Tod!' By now Noble was red-roaring, and Reynard's ears were blown quite back in the gusts.

Witnessing his King's righteous fury, Sir Chaunticleer could no longer be still. The death of his Coppen was as jangle-bone-raw as the east wind, and his mind, once so unemotional and mercantile, was quite upturned by grief. He had spent each night since her burial encamped in a little military tent next to her grave, 'to keep her safe from the bad ones,' he would say to his daughters when they tried to urge him home.

Faced with the murderer of his gentle chickling, he had to speak, and he crowed wildly and desperately, hopping on a table to be seen: 'Think what I have lost in this Peace! Think of it! Think of my dead chicks in their graves!'

Noble turned to him, not unkindly, hushing him down, 'Be still, Sir Chaunticleer, be still, hold your beak, let your King answer this foul thief on your behalf. You do your Coppen no favours by interrupting here.'

Reynard had been mouthing something at Grimbart during Chanticleer's cries, and at Noble's response merely looked haughtily down his muzzle at the trembling fowl, as though he were a mere servant bird or a hind from the field squawking out of turn in a theatre of his betters.

Noble bellow-flared at Reynard once more—'Snatcher! Coward! Villain! You told me you loved me well, you sent word of how well you treated my messengers, my Erindbere Bruin, my counsellor Tybert the Cat, and yet look at the pair of them,' he signalled for them to rise, 'look at their bloody wounds, Tybert half-blind with his patch, Bruin skinned and tonsured!'

Reynard looked to the King with outrage; orange eyes as striped and eerie as one of Sir Cuwaert the Hare's rarer tulipa flowers. '*In nomine pater christe fili*—In the Name of Our Father and Christ the Son! Lord and Mighty King,' he spoke in refined and elegant tones, delicately removing a loose thread from his houppelande, 'to be quite frank, what's it to me if Bruin's crown be bloodied? Not my fault he was caught scoffling honey in Lantfert's yard. He brought that beating entirely upon on himself. He could have fought those peasants back, avenged himself with those thick, strong bearish limbs of his, but no, no, no! He went stumble-splashing into the river, pulling old Julocke with him. Really! What did he expect! And then comes Professor Tybert the Cat, whom I received with the greatest accord and friendliness. I can't help it if he goes wandering off without my counsel to steal mices from a priest's house. My goodness, you don't need the quadrivium to know that's a foolish course of action! And can Reynard truly be blamed for the priest's blows?'

The fox had been walking up and down between the long tables, in a very legal sort of fashion. He suddenly whipped around to face the Crown again.

'I am not happy about such an unfair accusation, my Lord. This matter is clear and good, as far as I am concerned. I have done no wrong to the Cat or the Bear. But you, and your Court, with your power mired in prejudice, can do what you will with me, I suppose. Siede me! Burn me! Hang me or make me blind! I know I can't escape now. We all stand under your correction—you so mighty and so strong. I am but a feeble fox, and if you put me to death I have no one to help me, no friends here, no family.' He almost imperceptibly shook his head, as Grimbart made to speak and the badger sank back down. 'I have but a small neck, and vengeance would bare take anything at all, bare anything at all.'

As Reynard was speaking, the low grumble of the disgruntled courtlings was getting louder like storm waves across the shingle, and even before he'd finished his accusers were beginning to rage. Up sprang Bellin the Ram and his wife, Dame Oleway, who started bleating their complaints in their surprisingly loud sheepish voices, then Lord Bruin the Bear, creaking up from his invalid's chair, with all his fellows and bear kin around him, like a copse of swaying oaks. Then one by one, from every bench and stool and quarter of the Hall, they stood to damn the fox.

'*C'est tout le monde!*' smirked Courtoys the Hound to Grimbart. Tybert the Cat, Isengrim the Wolf, Pancer the Beaver, Cuwaert the Hare, Musart the Camel, Boudewijn the Ass, Bore the Bull, Hamel the Ox, Muushot the Weasel, Eghel the Hedgehog, Chiever the Goat and all his kids, sprang to their feet, yelling and calling out their dishonours and complaints. In the front were Chaunticleer and his wife Pertelote, close feathered by their remaining young.

Everyone was pushing and shoving and shouting—King Noble's fortress had not witnessed such an uproar since the Herring Riots of his great-great-great grandfather's reign. Led by the shaking rooster, they came in front of the lion and demanded, in one unified voice, the immediate apprehension and arrest of Sir Reynard the Fox.

CHAPTER SIXTEEN

In which Sir Reynard the Fox is arrested
and condemned to Death

The Afternoon of the Feast Day of Blessed Saint Hervé of Finistère, the Eloquent, Trickster of Wolves and of the Feast of Corpus Christi, Solemnity of the Most Holy Body and Blood of Christ, Thursday 17th June

Enflamed by his courtiers, King Noble the Lion immediately called a parliament to consider the Matter of Reynard.

It was a thrilling trial, retold for many years in the taverns and manors and abbeys of Flanders. Mercury was well aspected that lovely June day, for the Court had never heard charges put so well, narrated with such clarity and crafted with such wisdom. Each wounded beast stood and proclaimed his or her complaints of woe and violence with such subtle invention that the fox seemed doomed, his future sealed.

And yet, and yet—the fox, still in his Sevillian finery, answered each point against him like the sharpest swordsman from King Ferdinand's Palace of Alcázar in that fiery city. Reynard's responses to each accusation were formidable. He defended himself with such brilliance, parrying and thrusting and appelling with sudden emotive exclamations (intoning one phrase—'O FALSITY THY NAME IS BEAR!'—or clapping his paws or dramatically stamping a foot) that all were held, albeit briefly, before him, wondering at his resplendence, if not his innocence.

The King and the Council heard all the witnesses for the prosecution; they listened to the long and sorrowful accounts of Reynard's misdeeds from the fanged and the woolly, the elderly and the full-toothed, the fashionable and the farmers. Despite Reynard's glittering defence, the die was long cast, however, and, as is typical in such cases, whether just or not, the Court's mind had been decided before the trial had even begun.

There was a low rumble of thunder and the sky was thestering with dark rain clouds when Reynard received his sentence. In a hushed silence, the parliament barely hesitated before they decreed that the fox should be put to death. 'GUILTY! GUILTY AS CHARGED!'

King Noble the Lion covered his mane with a black felt cap and pronounced that the fox should be taken from the castle to a place of execution, and there hanged by the neck until all present considered him to be dead.

At this savage ruling, Reynard's brave and flamboyant defiance, the thin-skim-rendered confidence trick which had been carrying him for the past couple of days, abruptly vanished, and he went limp and low-tailed, suddenly seeming a much smaller creature. There was no swagger left in him. His flattering words and deceits could not help him now. He longed for his Hermeline and couldn't bear to look for Sir Grimbart's face in the crowd.

The judgement had been given and was now set in judicial stone. Grimbart felt violently sick, as bilious as if he'd gorged on a full pail of bad worms. Leaning on his staff, he looked around at his fellow lords—a dense, baying mob relishing Reynard's destruction. It was profoundly shocking to watch their glee, and the badger decided to have no more of it. He could not help and he could not bear to watch the hanging.

He beckoned to Reynard's other supporters and extended family—for there were many more present than the fox had realised. Among them, Sir Íñigo and his band of young Spanish mountain foxes; Reynard's old drinking partner, Sir Firapeel the Leopard; and the lawyer, the eminent Dame Rukenawe the Ape, an old béguinage friend of Hermeline. Together they left the Hall, and then the Court. The badger hurrying to his townhouse to think hard on what, if anything, could be done.

Watching them leave, King Noble was surprised to see so much quiet distress; the small coterie of younglings, in particular, were weeping so hard that their frilled lace sleeves were dripping with tears. He looked at Queen Gente, and she shook her head sadly. She was fond of Reynard, too. He glanced at the fox, who was staring bleakly at the flagstones, head lowered. Noble thought about it all, as deeply as he could, and then he said to himself that, whilst Reynard is certainly a shrew and a cad, he has inspired loyalty in many; there are good lads there, good lads, Íñigo is a fine archer and Sir Firapeel is a most enjoyable companion of an evening, the most jovial leopard this side of the Schelde.

Just as the lion was beginning to consider whether a hang-ment was really necessary, there was a sudden lull in the hum of conversation and Sir Tybert the Cat (his eyepatch—blue Brugge satin embroidered with yellow lilies—a horrifying reminder of Reynard's crimes) could be heard clearly above the rest, lecturing the wolf and the bear, his fellow victims: 'Sir Bruin and Sir Isengrim, how can you be so slow! It's almost evening! There are so many hiding places around here, bushes and hedges and cellars... if he escaped from us, if he was delivered from this peril, if he gained even three *voete*, three feet of freedom,' Tybert sniffed and adjusted his patch, 'he is so subtle and so wily, so full of deceitful tricks, he would never be taken again and his wickedness would go unpunished. Why don't we just hang him! Why are you all just standing around! The gallows can be made ready before night falls!' O how swiftly Tybert had forgotten his Boethius, his sympathy for the imprisoned vanishing with the pop and roll of an eye!

Sir Isengrim's voice, sour and disquieting as usual: 'Not far from here, between Lochristi and Lokeren, there's a gibbet, an old gallows at the quarefoure with Doorgangstraat. By the hamlet of Katte, Cat, in your manor lands, no? We could use that.' Then he sighed, a broad, rattling sigh which in Flemish wolf-tongue spelt deep contentment. Tybert, however, misunderstood entirely. Having cast Reynard as the only villain in the county, he had no scruples in screwing noble intentions to every rough-souled beast in Gent.

'Lord Isengrim,' gasped Tybert, 'are you frightened of punishing Reynard! Is it against your will to hang him? Is your heart troubled, noble Wolf! How can you hesitate! Remember it was Reynard who devised that plan to hang your dear beloved brothers, Rumen and Wijdelancken! If you're wise, you won't tarry with this hanging, you won't tarry one cockcrow!'*

---

* This was true, and two nastier, more bloodthirsty wolves it would be difficult to find under our great starred firmament. One Martinmas they had killed three small children and an overworked washerwoman in Tielt, then gobbled up five newborn fox cubs from Aalst, offspring of a well-liked brewer named Dirk, known for his fiery nettle ale. With a number of other lords, Reynard had written to Noble over the murders, as indeed had Tybert, who is gilding the truth quite considerably here to further his revenge.

CHAPTER SEVENTEEN

In which Sir Reynard the Fox is led to the Gallows

*The Night of the Feast Day of Blessed Saint Hervé of Finistère,
the Eloquent, Trickster of Wolves, and of the Feast of Corpus
Christi, Solemnity of the Most Holy Body and Blood of Christ,
Thursday 17th June*

Isengrim balked and growled at Tybert. 'You misunderstand
me, Cat,' he spat-snarled. 'Had we a good halter to fit his
scrawny neck, and the rope were strong enough, I'd be the
first to swing that pestilent Tod.'

At this unpleasant jab, Reynard, who had been standing in
a dazed silence, with the words 'hanged by the neck, hanged
by the neck, hanged by the neck till dead' marching through
his mind like night guards on the ramparts, finally spoke up,
his voice flat and grey and miserable.

'Isengrim, shorten my pain, just shorten my pain, for the
sake of God's bones. Tybert still has that strong cord which
caught him in the priest's house—he was showing it off this
morning, as he does every day, no doubt. Well, even scholarly
cats are good climbers, and swift, so let him bear the line, and
attach it to my hanging-tree.' He wiped his eyes and paused.
Some of the more compassionate animals exchanged looks.
Not a rustle nor a cough nor a word was heard. 'Isengrim,
Tybert, it becomes you well to treat your nephew in this
way—I am sorry that I have lived this long.'

And he bowed his russet head, and half-whispered, 'I am
resigned to my fate, please tarry no longer. Bruin, go forth

and lead me. Isengrim, follow fast behind, and you can make sure that I won't escape.'

The uncomfortable silence was loudly interrupted by Bruin's jolly, insensitive boom. 'Well, that's the best counsel that I've ever heard, what Reynard there says. Good fellow, good fellow, eh!'

Baron Isengrim was already slinking towards Reynard, followed by his mangy cohort of nephews and cousins and hangers-on. 'Grab hold of him, for he's wily and false,' he growled, and in a trice Reynard was surrounded by a weaving sea of grise-black fur and drool and teeth. Two wolves held him by the feet, another by the beard. Isengrim seized him, painfully, by the brush, and pulled, trying to get Reynard to whimper. He made his wife stand by him and watch on. This they continued until they were certain the fox could not escape.

Reynard lay passively as the wolves were doing their roughing, and he listened to Isengrim's snarls with polite interest. 'Och, dear Uncle Wolf,' he said, 'I think you'll do yourself a damage, all this relentless scathing of a poor fox. If I could, I would pay you a pile of silver for you to be more merciful, though it seems that you're rather enjoying my hurt and suffering—it's rather pleasant to you, ain't it, Sigrim? You know your wife wouldn't want me to suffer, we were sweethearts once, if she's allowed to remember the old times. She's as gentle as you are murk, she is, foul Lupus!' There was a faint broken cry, and from the awkward angle in which Reynard was pinned he could see Isengrim quietly nipping Erswynde's back leg, hard, before plitching his own brush again.

He shouted at the wolf to distract him, 'Hey now! Do with me what you will! I am at your mercy! Isengrim! Bruin! Tybert! May God himself strike you down, if you don't do your worst to me! I know where my path leads. I know Death he is coming for me, I can see the glint of his sickle, the hempen twist of his cord! I may die but once, but I wish I were dead already! I saw my father die, it was over so quickly, a spirit gone in a breath.'

Isengrim, feeling the familiar squirm of being mocked in a way he couldn't quite grasp, kicked Reynard in his soft white belly, and snapped, 'Let us go then if you're cursing us for taking our time. We'll not abide here a moment longer.'

The strange and morbid group made to leave the castle. It was a bleak tableau. A furious Isengrim guarding one side; on the other, Bruin, lumbering along and chewing on some crispy mackerel skin. And so, in this way, they led Reynard the Fox to the gallows ward.

In front, Tybert, running ahead, bearing the hanging rope, mighty pleased at the way things were playing out. His throat was still sore from the trap, and his gullet from all the priest's blows, but the *Rota Fortunae*, the whirling Wheel of Fortune, had turned once more and now he, Sir Tybert, was on the rise, and Reynard on the plunge. Oh, thought the cat, how the goddess Fortuna has abandoned you now, Fox, how she will discard you, how she will cast you in agony beyond endurance.

There was no jubilation as they left. No cheering, no yells of triumph, just a broad sense of unease and anticlimax. King Noble and Queen Gente and the rest of the Court slowly followed after Bruin and Isengrim and Tybert, and the procession snaked along the Great White Road to Katte and the Doorgangstraat, the sinister place where felons were put to death.

The storm, which had been rumbling around the fields all day, finally broke as they began the journey, rain hammering down on the roofs and towers and spires and flèches of the city, swift-flooding the dykes and swelling the streams, water sheeting across their path, drenching their clothes and fur, the light strange and purple and unchancy. And so they trudged, bearing the fox along to his terrible fate.

And what of Reynard's mood? During this torturous march to Katte, being jolted and pulled and pushed by three of his most despised enemies—the cruel wolf, the arrogant cat, the greedy bear—he nevertheless was able to think deeply on his precarious situation and how he might still manage to save himself from the gallows. He pondered on how to deceive those three, how to turn things around, bring them to shame, how to manipulate and trick the King into coming onto his side. How, in essence, to put away his sorrows with his wiles.

Plans and schemes trambled through his mind as he was yanked slowly through puddles and pools of water, through brambles and spidery copses, walking the same tiresome miles he'd only just covered with Grimbart. And, as the sky blackened with night, and the rain stilled to drizzle, these thoughts became more and more inflamed, like a sudden fever, with his old insolence, his brazen, foxish hardiesse.

It's no wonder the King and everyone are so angry with me, he thought, I have well-deserved their hatred. And yet some of them certainly merited their punishments. That stupid Bear fr'instance. No, I can't trust any of them, and I swear I shall never help them nor do them good, no matter

how strong the King be, no matter how wise his counsel be...
but, but, nevertheless, if I can become Noble's best friend...
what marvels could I achieve... I am the master fox of so many
deceptions and juggles, I shall rise, rise as high in the lion's
Court as they want me to swing on the gallows!

It was near midnight by the time they reached the lonely
crossroads where the Great White Road intersected with the
Doorgangstraat. And there stood the pair of gallows. Elm-
made. Animals had been hanged here and suicides buried
here for many a long year.

When he saw the hang-fork, the fox involuntarily stepped
backwards, and made an odd coughing noise as though he
were trying to swallow something lodged in his throat. Sir
Bruin, without thinking, turned to assist, but Isengrim immediately growled at him.

'Bear, you dumb hulking creature, you greasy fat Urse,
think about your bloody crown, your ripped paws, all man-
flayed by Reynard's means. Now's come the time we can
reward him for his toils against us. Tybert, up you go, you're
the lightest, climb up hastily and bind the cord fast to the
cross-beam. Make a riding knot or a strop. A noose, Cat, a
noose, have you never tied a noose before? Come on, One-eye,
think on't, tonight, you'll get your revenge of that evil lowrie
who made you suffer so.' Poor Reynard started to struggle.
'Bruin,' gnarled Isengrim, 'don't let him escape! Hold fast!
Hold fast, Woolsack, hold him, by God's bones! I'll prop the
ladder for him to go up.'

'I'm holding him, I'm holding him well fast,' shouted Bruin.
Queen Gente called, 'Be gentle, Bruin, for goodness sake, he
is still a lord.'

It was at this point, when Isengrim was nipping his back flanks and Bruin was trying to force his feet onto the bottom rung of the ladder—a Jacob's flight by which he would swiftgain either heaven or hell—that the fox launched desperately into the most important speech of his life.

'My heart is heavy with the greatest dread and I can see Death standing there before my eyes. He is coming for me, in his tattered cloak, and I can't escape him now.' He gestured across the dark fields with a paw wrestled from Bruin. Thoroughly spooked, the courtiers nervously looked for the figure of Death in the flat shadowy wasteland beyond the road. Sir Cuwaert even took out his rosary he was so frightened. After just the right amount of dramatic tension, Reynard continued, his beautiful voice effortlessly engaging all before him.

'My Lord King, my dear Queen, and all you who bear witness. Before I depart this stormy world, I pray for one thing, and one thing only, that I be allowed to make my confession openly and tell my sins as clearly as I can, so my poor weak soul isn't encumbered with their burdenous weight and, of more importance, so no other animal is blamed for my theft, nor for my treason.

'If you grant me my wish, then my death will be so much easier, and you may all attest that I meet my fate as a Proud Fox of Maleperduys, as a Loyal Fox of Gent, as a Free Fox of Flanders.' He looked to the distance again, a haunted look in his eyes as though he were halfway to the vaulted heavens already, then he glanced up to Tybert and the hanging rope and sighed heavily. 'Lastly, I implore all you good beasties to pray to God to have mercy upon my soul.'

CHAPTER EIGHTEEN

In which Sir Reynard the Fox makes
his Confession openly in front of the King
and before Anyone Who Would Hear It

The Feast Day of Saint Elisabeth of Schönau,
Narrator of Irregular Insights, Friday 18th June

Silence. Everybody stared at Reynard, as he dusted down his ripped clothes, having been released by the bear and the wolves. All of a sudden, a barn owl swooped like a white ghostie from the poplar trees down to a low stable roof, so close they could hear the creak of its wings.

Aside from Sir Isengrim, the entire Court had been moved to tears, pitying the fox greatly after his eloquent pronouncement, impressed by his iron fortitude, his courage at the hinges of life. His request seemed so little, such a small concession for a condemned fox, that a sudden cacophony of voices broke the hush, begging the King to grant it. Noble the Lion readily agreed, his doubts about the sentence returning once more.

Reynard, of course, was delighted, thinking that perhaps, just perhaps, things were swinging his way again. He coughed delicately and then began. 'Help me, *Spiritus domini!* For I see no animal, neither friend nor foe, whom I have not harmed in some way or another. Many years ago I was one of the gentlest cubs that anywhere in the kingdom could be found, from the moment I was weaned from my mother. Indeed, I used to delight in playing with the lambs who dwelt in the fields and cherry orchards around our manor of Maleperduys.

I loved to gambol and frolic and sport with them, and how gladly I heard them bleat with their delight!

'But then, one Eastertide, one Long Friday, I was chasing a young rambunctious friend and he tripped head over tail on a root, and I bit him. Oh, how I remember the strange red flowers blooming in those white curls. I learnt on that fatal day how to lap blood, and it tasted so damn good, so damn savoury. And so, in this way, after a mere innocent game of chase, I acquired a terrible lickerousness for flesh, a terrible hunger.

'When my mother was at vespers one night, I sneaked out of Maleperduys, and followed some goats into the wold; deep in the forest they went to where they kept their kids safe, and I heard them bleat; and then I, then I, I murdered them, right there, in the ferny bracken, right there in front of their mothers.' Reynard stopped and raked his paws up and down his face and ears as though to screech and scrape the deed from memory.

'I came home and went straight up the stairs to my bed-chamber. My teeth were dripping blood. When I woke in the morning, the bolster was scarlet. And then I started to get all cocky and crouse. I was so fierce and angry, I just didn't care anymore, didn't give a Sienese fig what my parents said. I killed and I killed and I killed. I killed geese and pullaile and hens. I killed whatever I came across, whomever I could catch, whenever I felt like it. Even childhood friends. I slew 'em all.'

The fox, who'd been pawing his psalter during the telling, looked up at this point, and if you knew him inside out, if you knew him as well as Hermeline, say, or Grimbart, you would have immediately recognised that Reynard was trying not

165

to laugh, that he was adroitly hiding the broadest, toothiest of grins, the spirit of which flickered over his mask. But he swiftly reassumed a face of weary penitence and continued apace.

'Some time after, in the deep winter, walking out by the frozen ponds in Belsele, I happened upon Baron Isengrim, hiding under an old yew tree.' The wolf, pacing, irritated at the crowd's captivation, snorted loudly. 'Isengrim told me, he reckoned to me quite conspiratorially, that he was my eme, my old friend. That we were family. That he was just like me. We became close fellows, good fellows, outlaws even. I repent of it now, but back then we were as thick as thieves. We promised each other to be true.'

'Rubbish!' cried Isengrim, 'A fable, he's gabbing his foxish fables again.'

'We promised each other to be true,' Reynard repeated, ignoring him, 'and we began to wander around the Waasland together from Antwerp to Gent to Hulst and back again. Best friends. Allies. He stole all the big things and I the small ones. But whilst all was supposed common between us, he always seemed to arrange it so that he had the best deal, and I barely had even half of my share. Whenever he seized a calf or a ram or a wether, he would grim me with the meanest looks, growling, swearing like a herring-man, keeping both my part and his. That's the sort of animal he is, if you'd care to know. Wouldn't even split the meat fairly with his closest pal.'

'You lying lop-bitten churl!' shouted Isengrim, but he was hushed down, as it was clear to everyone that the fox was nearing a thrilling episode within his confession, the most secret and sensitive part. 'When an animal is close to death, he keeps nothing back! And he has no need of falsities!' whispered Bellin the Ram to his wife, Dame Oleway, who shushed him in turn, in case she missed anything.

Staring once more into the middle distance, a touch of the hermit, of the mystic, about his expression, the fox carried on. 'Yet this was the least of it all. Whenever we were lucky enough to take an ox or a cow, Isengrim would bring his wife with him, and their seven children, and, while gentle Erswynde would try to pass me some scraps, he would force and urge his family to eat up all the flesh, so not even the smallest rib would come my way. But what could I do, overpowered by a bully? I tried to be content with my lot, considering that I had no great need for food nor drink nor any little treats, no great need at all, for... you see... I...' Reynard stuttered to a halt.

'Keep going, old chap!' urged King Noble, 'Why had you no need for food, eh? What's this all about, Reynard?'

'Well, you see,' said Reynard, 'I have so much treasure, so much precious scat, glittering towers of gold like the sun and glimmering heaps of silver like the moon—piles and piles of it—so much that seven broad wagons couldn't carry it all away.'

The courtiers gaped. The Queen gasped. The wolves growled. But the King, oh the King was entranced, enthralled, enraptured by Reynard's description, and deep inside he began to burn, just as Reynard knew he would, with the most powerful greed and covetousness for the fox's vast treasure.

'Sir Reynard,' he croaked, 'where are these riches now? Might you tell us, dear Fox?'

Reynard carefully rearranged his tattered sleeves, their delicate pong of Seville fish and orange blossom scenting the cool night air, then beckoned to the King and the Queen to move closer. Everyone else shuffled forward too.

'I shall tell the whole sorry and complicated tale, my Lord,' stage-whispered Reynard, 'All my treasure, all the gold, all the silver, it was all stolen—first by my father, then, I'm sorry to say, by me. But! If it hadn't been stolen, it would have cost you your life and you would have been murdered, which, God forbid, would have been the greatest hurt of the world.'

When Queen Gente heard these words, she was grievously afraid for her husband, of whom she was very fond, despite his faults, his laziness and boorishness, and his grindingly tiresome obsession with tilting and tournaments. She roared in her clipped, elegant way, and clasped the fox's smooth paws. 'Alas! Wellaway! Baron Reynard, what are you saying? I conjure and beg you by the long, high way your soul is going, to tell us the truth of everything you know about this great murder which, you say, was planned against my Lord Noble!' She beckoned the other lords and ladies even closer, so all were whiskers to tail around the fox. 'And Reynard, speak openly, speak loudly, that we may all hear the matter!'

And now, you must hearken, clever Reader, you must listen even more attentively than Sir Tybert the Cat, or King Noble, or even poor Lady Erswynde. *Nu hoert!* Now hear! (As they say in the Low Countries.)

Listen below the words. Listen through them. Listen around them. Listen behind them. Listen to Sir Reynard the Fox on that moonlit night on the Doorgangstraat, on the road to Antwerp, in the yarrow and the sheep sorrel, underneath the gallows, all those centuries ago, as he performs one of the greatest acts of deception and swikedom fair Flanders has ever seen. Listen to the skill with which he flatters the King and the Queen. Listen as he wins both their goodwill and their love. Listen to how he hinders those who labour for his death. Listen as the fox slowly and deftly unbinds his whole pack of tricks—his flattery and fine words, his warm and sugary russet charm, his bold-faced blandishments. He has brought forth a spool of raw lies and spun them into a glittering web of truth to trap them all. Every last one of them.

With a sorrowful countenance, Reynard spoke to the Queen.

'My dear Lady, I am in such a case, so many bad things have befallen me that I cannot now escape death, and even if you hadn't begged me in such distress, I would not have set my soul into jeopardy by keeping quiet. I can burden it no longer. Otherwise, the torments and pains of hell await my poor foxish ghost. I will say nothing that I cannot prove for sure, but this I will say, that there was a plan afoot to murder the King, a secret plan hatched by members of his own Court! His very own folk!

'And most unpleasant of all, and the reason why I have been as mute as a hermit for so long, is that the principals in the plot, the main players, have been friends, members of my own kin. Believe me, I would never have betrayed their names, had I not been departing on my long journey, and wished to avoid the anguish of the fiery pit!'

The animals gaped wide-mouthed at Reynard and then started whispering and eyeing each other suspiciously. They all, of course, assumed that one of the suspects was Isengrim, but who were his secretive accomplices? Reynard was connected in some way or other to most of the Court; the murderers could be any one of them.

King Noble, who had always happily assumed that he was one of the most beloved and popular rulers of his age, if not of every age, looked very deflated, his sandy mane, tangled by the rain, rather greasy and thin. 'Reynard,' he asked, heavy of heart, 'are you telling me the truth?'

'Yes, I am,' replied Reynard, in equally wretched tones, 'Can you not see how it stands with me, my Lord? If I tell the truth, then I damn my fellows. But if I were to say anything other than the truth, then I would damn my soul and forfeit my place in the sweet pastures of that better land to which I beg entry! Death is nigh, dear Noble, he waits patiently in the fields for me, there amidst the worms and the poppies and the flittermouses—I have no need for friends nor gold nor prayers now.'

Reynard started to violently tremble, from his ears to the white chape of his tail, possessed with an aspen-fear which was not altogether manufactured. It was profoundly disturbing to watch. More than any words the fox had uttered, it brought home to the courtiers the great horror of the situation, the quiet violence of their night-time gathering under Reynard's gallows-tree.

It upset Queen Gente in particular, and she felt enormous pity for the fox. When she was a young lioness in Toulouse, she had witnessed similar involuntary trauma in a number of her kin-lions, who had only just escaped with their lives after a ferocious battle with the Aragonese. She had sat for hours with one of her brothers, who had been unable to stop shaking and grimacing after seeing his best friend slain beside him. So she went to the fox. And she calmed him. And she told the animals to leave him be, and not to cause him any more harm whilst he told his tale of the lost gold and the plan to murder her husband.

King Noble sat down heavily on the hanging platform, adjusting his crown, which was slipping on his wet mane, and commanded each of them to be still, and let Sir Reynard the Fox tell his story without interruption or fear. Still trembling slightly, Reynard felt his fur stand on end, in a frisson of excitement, the thrill that came not during his many last-minute escapes—his frenzied spinning of stories or squeezing through of tunnels and trapdoors, but in the fragmentary moments just before, in the edge-time of his escapades, when a sudden internal vision of the right path to follow was perfectly revealed to him, the mass untangling then fast-weaving of his various deceitful possibilities until they formed a perfectly woven tapestry, a bright cartographic landscape of falsehood and trickery laid before him.

'Then,' said Reynard, stepping from the edge to the centre of his story once more, feeling his luck changing, the old *Rota Fortuna* cranking around once more, 'be you now all still, since it is the King's will, and I shall openly tell you the treason. And I will spare no one whom I know to be guilty, though my heart be ripped out in the telling.'

CHAPTER NINETEEN

The Fox's Treasure

Now listen carefully to how Reynard begins his testimony, for it was the first of the cords of his tale to be tightened. Listen as he accuses his dearest friend and cousin Sir Grimbart of Gent, the badger who has always bravely supported and defended him in times of direst need, extracting Reynard from many a tight corner, often at great risk to his own position at Court, his own reputation.

The fox knew, of course, that the badger was widely respected as one of the most trustworthy lords in Flanders. The last animal whom anyone would ever expect Reynard to betray. Citing him as a scheming villain was thus a risky but brilliant device. Casting Grimbart into his account endowed it with a gleaming veracity, which would colour all the other fabrications and accusations with a similar sheen of soothfastness.

Reynard also knew that Grimbart loved him more than any other creature in this darkling world, aside from the badger's poor dead sweetheart in her mossy grave. He loved him so dearly, without bound nor end, that the fox was quite certain Grimbart would relinquish his liberty, even life itself, for his Reynard should the opportunity arise. Well, here and now, under the gibbet, in the moth-fettered moonlight, was precisely that opportunity, and Reynard roughly kicked aside any notions of guilt or betrayal, banished thoughts of the shades of Gethsemene clustering around his own piles of silver, and convinced himself that not only would Grimbart approve the ruse to save his friend's skin, but he would also be able to easily fish the badger out of the hole he'd dropped him into, once he himself was free himself from the shadow of the noose. Finally, and crucially, Grimbart was not there. He was miles away in his Dassenburcht. By the time they sent a messenger to call him, by the time he reached them, the whole matter would probably have been ended one way or another, anyway, thought Reynard, as he prepared himself to fight for his life.

'Many years ago,' began the fox in his bardic voice, 'my own father, Reynardius, discovered the fabled treasure of King Emereric, that wolfish old warrior, buried deep down in an old pit.* However, once he took possession of it—once he laboriously dug it all out—pile after tottering pile of gold and silver and jewels—and heaved it home to Maleperduys, something changed. Something fractured deep inside him. I won't say the treasure was cursed, but day by day, hour by hour, his character altered out of all recognition. He became so proud and haughty that he began to despise and look down on all the other beasties, beasties who had once been his fellows, his friends, his equals.

'One cold September morning, he called for Sir Tybert the Cat, who owed him a favour (something or other to do with my father acquiring a manuscript of homilies for him from

* Reynard is referring to the famous King Ermanaric (d. 376). A Gothic Alexander figure, belligerent and land-hungry. Ermanaric became a popular character within Germanic heroic legend, and was widely believed both to have built the fortress of Gent, King Noble's castle, and to have possessed an enormous treasure, lost after his death at the advanced age of 103, which is frequently referred to within epic poems, such as the *Nibelungenlied*.

the Bishop of Rochester), and sent him off into the wild forests of the Ardennes to search out Bruin the Bear, who was living in a secluded manor there, high on a peak overlooking a deep curve of the River Meuse.*

'So off Tybert went, a journey which must have been very perilous at times in that fierce region, and he found the bear and paid homage to him, and, following my father's instructions, told him that if he wanted to become king, then he should come with Tybert post-haste back to Flanders. Well, Bruin was delighted and flattered to hear this plan, for he had long desired—*long desired*—to usurp Noble and rule in his stead. He packed a trunk, and they set off. When they finally arrived at our castle of Maleperduys, my father received him right friendly—as friendly as a fox can be to a bear who'd spent a year on his own without a well in the middle of the Ardennes, with just a few morose charcoal burners for company.

'Oh, how my father pulled out all the stops! Bruin's favourite dishes for dinner! Fifteen courses of the best food in Flanders! Our broadest table heaving with roasted river swans and birds of Juno! Sweet jellies in the colours of Bruin's family crest— part yellow saffron, part black elderberry! One hundred-and-twenty-nine hard boiled eggs studded with cloves! Soft figs and damascene plums stewed in rose water!

---

* Reynard's tale strongly and very suspiciously resembles the late-twelfth-century *Four Sons of Aymon* (*Quatre fils Aymon* or *De Vier Heemskinderen*), which recounts the adventures of the knight Renaud de Montauban (in Dutch, Reinout van Montalbaen), his younger brothers Guichard, Allard and Richardet, and their magical horse Bayard as they revolt against the emperor Charlemagne, on whom King Noble likes, in his better moments, to model himself.

'Whilst Bruin was feasting, my Lord Reynardius sent a servant to fetch wise, reliable Grimbart and grey-masked Isengrim the Wolf and Tybert the Cat, still tired from his travels. These five lords met in a tavern halfway between Gent and Hijfte, a rough, sullen place, where no one would know their names nor their faces. There they held their counsel through the long, dark night. There under low beams, in the dim light of a sickly, embering fire, they plotted and schemed: the fox, the bear, the badger, the cat and the wolf. With the Devil's help and craft, and with my father's riches, they conspired to kill our blessed King Noble and swore to that purpose.

'Now hearken and hear this wonder,' Reynard paused histrionically, one elegant copper paw raised to an ear in a gesture which he held for several moments.

'The four lords stood in that lowly, sordid place, walls dark with smoke and cooking fat, and they placed their paws upon the top of Isengrim's head and swore that they would make Bruin the Bear lord and king, and bring him to the stone at Aachen, and set the crown of Flanders upon his rough, undeserving fur. If there were any of King Noble's friends or lineage who kicked up a fuss, mounted resistance, then my father would, with the endless gold and silver of King Emereric's treasure, destroy them, take from them all their wealth and all their worldly power.

'Weeks passed, and the leaves fell from the trees, and mushrooms bloomed in the forests, and the Michaelmas moon, moon of reckonings and accounts to be settled, rose high and white in a sky the black of hornblende. One morning, Grimbart and my dear wife, Dame Hermeline, were walking, well muffled, across a bleak and addery heath, returning from their pilgrimage to the Shrine of the Magi in Cologne. Grimbart had been drinking spiced wine to keep warm, as there was a sharp chill in the air, and (*in vino veritas*) was moved to tell the whole sorry story to her, point by point, detail by despicable detail—the plotting, the oathing, the players, everything. Hermeline, who is a rare and truefast lady, gave the badger her solemn promise, swearing on the fragrant bones of the Three Kings, that she would never, not for love nor for hate, tell another soul, but would keep it secret.'

Reynard sighed. He would not tarnish Hermeline. He thought fast and twisty.

'Hermeline returned to our manor and went to the chapel to place her relics from Cologne, and to pray for guidance. And after her vigil, she came to me in the woods, where I was gathering truffles and beginning to put those palings around our bounds, and she told me all that she had heard, with so many tokens, so many particulars, that I believed it at once. Not that I could ever doubt her! *Mon dieu!*

'My judgement, then, was that this account was the hard and brutal truth, and for dread and fear my fur stood right up and my heart became as heavy as lead.' Reynard examined his audience. Despite the thrill of his revelations, some of the larger animals, particularly the bears, were nodding off. A quick change of tack was needed.

'Frogs! Frogs! Frogs!' he barked, to wake up the snoozers and the shut-eyes. 'Not too long ago, I recall the same thing happened to a group of frogs, from, um,' Reynard searched around for an impressive-sounding kingdom, 'Thebes. Yes, some Theban frogs. Well, these frogs were free, up to their eyeballs with liberty they were, and yet they complained that they had no lord, no one to govern over them, no one with authority over them. A country without a ruler was no good, they cried. So, they joined together, young and old, and in a great chorus croaked to God in heaven with the loudest of voices to ordain a new king. This was all they desired—a new king to look to.

'God heard their request, and thought it was very reasonable, and so he sent them a blanch-winged, black-legged serpent-necked stork, a venerable king of storks, no less. Well, that king proceeded to eat those frogs, young and old, without distinction. He swallowed them whole, as many as he could find, wherever he could find them, in the lakes, in the fields and in the cool wells. He was unmerciful to them. And the poor frogs complained that they were hurt and their children were hurt and their grandmothers were hurt, but it was too late. It was all too late. The frogs, who were once free and afraid of nobody, were now cruelly obliged to simply strengthen and feed the pitiless King Stork in his reign of terror, subjected to him for evermore, existing in an anguished state of eternal fear in their once carefree land. Only the cleverest and quickest survive in the Court of the Crane.*

'Recalling this chronicle of froggy woe, I was gripped by a terrible unease that a similar fate would also befall you, gentle animals of Gent, whether rich or poor, weak, powerful or simply rusticating. Thus, my Lord, King Noble, I was desperately worried, a concern for which, I may say, I have been rewarded with little thanks.' Reynard managed to look

* The tale of the frogs who desire a new king is one of Aesop's fables, buoyantly popular stories in Reynard's world.

simultaneously stern and wistful for a moment, and waited for everyone to say 'Go on, Sir Reynard, please,' which of course they did. All apart from Bruin and Tybert, who were looking completely bewildered, and Isengrim, who was lying down glaring at Reynard with his usual malevolence.

'I know Bruin the Bear,' resumed Reynard, 'I know him well. He's a wicked rascal, a fool of the highest order, a base, uneducated thief who thinks only of himself, plump with vanity, only interested in plundering whatever he can. I thought, nay I knew, if he should be king, we should all be destroyed and lost, utterly lost within a year, if not a month.' Bruin raised himself up, looking at the fox in amazement, bandages still wrapped tight on his crusted wounds.

Reynard ignored him and bowed so low to the King that the black tip of his nose touched the toothy dandelions blooming in profusion around the royal couple. 'I knew my sovereign Lord Noble to be of such high birth, so mighty, so benign and merciful, so gentle towards all his subjects, that I thought, truly I thought, that to replace such a ruler for a foul, stinking thief of a bear would be an exchange of great evil.

'The very idea of forgoing a mighty, stately lion for a bear with more mad folly in his unthrifty head than a froth-mad dog, and a trail of lumpen ancestors just as barmy as him, well, it is not to be borne, thought I! Dear Noble, I felt wretched. My heart was fluttering with sorrow like a flax-wren at summer's end. I knew I had to act and fast. I thought hard on how I might break my father's false counsel, how to put a stop to his wicked plans which would fashion a lord and king out of a peasant and a traitor.'

Without warning, Reynard sank to his knees, and gestured solemnly to the starry sky. 'Always I prayed to God. I prayed without still, without pause. I prayed that He would keep our Lion King in high repute, keep his name in shining honour, and preserve his good health and grant him a long life.' Some of the animals at this point, roused by Reynard's fierce loyalty, shouted out 'Amen! Amen! God bless the King!' The fox smiled innocently and continued.

'Despite my prayers, I realised that with his vast ill-gotten treasure, my father and his false accomplices would always find a way—a way paved in silken pearls and silver coins—to depose and set aside our beloved King. The treasure was the key. I thought very hard about where my father might have hidden it. I secretly went through his documents, his plans, his letters, through his books in the library. I listened outside doors and through open casements. I searched in the tombs in the crypt and in the spidery attics and up the cindery chimneys. I bribed the servants to tell me his movements and kept a close guard on him at all times. I followed him into the woods, into the fields. I hid under hedgerows, under bushes. Day or night, cold or wet, dry or marshy, I was always by that crafty father of mine, always spying on him to find out where that treasure was laid.

'Then, one night—at All Hallowtide—I laid down flat on the ground and covered myself with coppery ferns to hide my bright fur, and I saw my father, Lord Reynardius, come running out of a hole! Now hark very carefully to what I saw him do.' The courtiers nodded sagely; everyone was on tenterhooks.

'When he first emerged from the hole, he looked around quickly to see if anyone was near, if anyone had seen him. I held my breath under the ferns and tried not to move a whisker. When he was sure he was alone, he began to stop the hole up with sand, making it even with the surrounding ground. He had no idea his son was watching him do all this. Next, he took his tail and he stroked and dragged it over where his paw prints had been, covering them with earth, and then he licked and smoothed over them again with his mouth. He obviously wanted to make certain no one should come across this hole, either accidentally or by following his tracks. By Saint Wilgefortis's beard, in that there beech wood I learnt such cunning, such tricks and subtleties from my father, of which I knew nothing before.

'Satisfied that all was as it should be, he then left for Rupelmonde to run his usual errands and visit his favourite watering hole for a strong pint of spikenard ale. As soon as I saw the last of his red brush disappearing into the thicket, I sprang up and leapt over to the hole, which was easy to find, despite all his efforts to disguise it. I scratched and scraped the sand out with my front feet, and crept in.

'And there I found the most extraordinary treasure—towering, glittering, tumbling heaps of silver and of gold. Ewers and goblets and chalices! Crowns and chaplets and circlets! And the gems! Oh, the gems were magnificent! Esmaragdes the colour of grass snakes and fire beryls as red as blood and rubies as black as nightshade and margarite pearls and white sapphires and Ethiopian schrysoprases as big as apples, flaming yellow in the darkness of that secret burrow! There is no one here present so old that they have ever seen such riches in one place!

'Quickly, I rushed home and told Lady Hermeline everything. She was shocked and worried, but returned to the wood
with me, and we worked night and day, without stop, without
sleep. With the greatest of labour and pain, we dragged and
carried the treasure away, as quietly as we could—no cart or
wagon, just our bare paws and some sacks. We found a new
hiding place, better than my father's—a deep hole thirled
down under a thick hawthorn hedge—and slowly filled it with
every last florin and seed pearl of King Emereric's vast hoard.

'Whilst we were labouring away, Lord Reynardius was
meeting with his co-conspirators, in a tavern down by the
Schelde. They had thrashed out an ambitious plan of action
over their beers and fried eel. Bruin and Isengrim the Wolf sent
word out across the Waasland and beyond, to all the manors
and villages and abbeys about Maleperduys—down the river
to Antwerp, up to Hulst, past Dendermonde to Brussels and
south-west to Tournai, Lille, Lens, Arras, Amiens. Bruin told
everyone that he would pay piles of gold and silver, good
soldier's wages, if they would join him and fight for him. My
father ran all over the countryside bearing letters set with
Bruin's seal in thick brown wax, little knowing that he'd been
robbed of his treasure and wouldn't find a penny of it even if
he wandered across the whole world. He could have bought
the entire City of London, and now his mighty hidey-hole was
rich only with mud and dry leaves and wood-louses.

'After Reynardius had ranged across all the lowlands between the Elbe and the Somme, mustering many a young
soldier to come to help Bruin the following summer, he
returned to the bear and his fellows. He was always a marvellous raconteur, my father,' Reynard sighed a little, wiping

away a sudden tear, 'he could hold a room in his paw with just one word from his gilden tongue. By Mercury's wings, he held those traitors captive, telling them the ins and outs of all his adventures, all his news. How in the boroughs of Saxony he'd been daily pursued by hunters and packs of hounds, the cold earth quaking with their thundering iron hooves and the still air ringing with the baying of the dogs. He had to pull out all his tricks to flee, barely escaping with his life each time.

'After recounting these daring tales of cunning in the nip-teeth of death, my father passed round some letters to the four false beasts. They pledged much to Baron Bruin. On one were written the names of twelve hundred wolves of Isengrim's family, with sharp claws and fierce maws, not to mention all the other noble and not-so-noble badgers from Dresden and foxes from Hamburg and cats from Leipzig and bears from all over Thuringia, who had sworn that the moment they were called for they would put on their armour and take up their swords and come to help the bear. That is, the letters continued, in their various inks and paw-writing, if they were paid one month in advance. No exceptions.'

A gentle laugh rippled through the courtiers at this, but Reynard didn't even smile, and there was a look in his eyes, a look which transcended the tale. A look of pain which had nothing to do with his fabrications, but led back many, many years to a sudden bark and a scream one winter night, when the berries were scarlet against the snow, and he lost all that was once safe and dear to him.

'I saw these letters, thank God. I can swear to their contents. I know who wrote them. Well, after these words with his goodfellows, my father went up to the woods, to his secret hole, to get the gold for Bruin. As soon as he got there he knew. We'd forgotten to cover it back up with the sand, and the entrance had fallen away, the hole collapsed. He knew the moment he saw it that his treasure was gone. He knew that the plot had failed. He knew that his bold swagger, his tales of muster, would be mocked. He knew it was the end. But he searched and searched just in case, digging in different places between the trees, a flicker of hope that he was mistaken, that he'd come to the wrong place, the tavern wine had addled his memory. After an hour or so, he sat down and he began to sorrow and to howl. And then, and then...' Reynard started rocking and shaking again. 'And then he took the rope that we'd left behind, the rope we used to pull along some of the treasure sacks. He took that rope, my rope, it was my rope he took, and he lashed it to a rowan tree, and he hanged himself. I found him there the next day, a furred weight of copper-rust in that hard blanche-frost. I took him down and I carried him back to Maleperduys.'

Reynard stopped and bowed his head. Queen Gente went to him and comforted him. After a long moment, he thanked her quietly and made to carry on.

'Thus was the end of Bruin's treason, undone by my subtleties and sealed by poor father's death. Now see, can you see, my misfortune? After everything I've told you, that these traitors—Bruin the Bear and Isengrim the Wolf—should be so close to you, King Lion! That they should be your privy counsellors! Sit with you at high table, at high bench! Whereas I, Reynard, am the scapegoat! I have no thanks, no reward.' His voice shook. 'I have buried my own father so that the King should live, yet I am cast out and sentenced to death myself. My Lord, where amongst these animals gathered here before us, who would do as much as I have done, who would destroy themselves to keep you safe!'

And Reynard sprang to his feet again and stood proudly in front of the Crown, head held high: a courageous, discrete and self-sacrificing fox, betrayed by a world quite undeserving of him. It was a brilliant performance. And it worked.

Without taking counsel, the King and the Queen beckoned Reynard to one side, and together they picked their way through the long grass to behind some tumbledown stables, which stood out of earshot at least ten long paces away from the gallows. They both, for very different reasons, hoped to win Emereric's treasure. The King wallowing in his un-trammelled avarice, the Queen determined not simply to acquire the newest English fishing tackle from her friend and fellow enthusiast Dame Juliana the Otter, an abbess from St Albans, but also to perform generous acts of contrition, of grace and charity, across Flanders, ameliorating the harm of that evidently cursed and cursing hoard. One after the other, the lions purred to him, and circled him, and asked him if he would very kindly tell them where the treasure was now buried.*

'With the greatest of courtesy,' cried Sir Reynard, 'why should I tell! You, my Lord, Lady, for the love of traitors and murderers, would have me hung! I would be out of my poor

---

* Dame Juliana the Otter was also a talented writer, and her practical treatise, dedicated to Gente, on the arts of *Hawking, Hunting and Heraldry, or the Blasing of Arms*, sometimes known as the *Boke of Seynt Albans*, is still consulted today. Later, an essay on angling was also added, including many insights and observations from the Queen.

foxish wits to reveal where I hid the treasure!' And he folded his paws and looked at them both.

The Queen spoke in her soothing, imperious voice. 'Nay, nay, nay, Reynard. Worry not. The King will let you have your life, he will pardon you of everything, forget all ill feelings, as long as you shall henceforth promise to be virtuous and loyal, a wise counsellor to my husband, and sensible, Reynard, sensible, as sensible as your wife.'

'Dear Lady,' answered Reynard, a great joy welling up inside, the familiar felicity of a perilous, last-minute escape, 'dear Lady, if the King will believe me, and will pardon and forgive all my old trespasses—even those not cited in my trial,' he added, cleverly, 'then there will never be a king so rich as I shall make him, for that ancient treasure is unimaginably and incalculably vast.'

King Noble looked at Reynard's hopeful face and abruptly remembered the terrible lament of Sir Chaunticleer, his little olive mourning tent pitched at the side of his daughter's grave. 'Ach, Dame, are you sure?' he roared, the old distrust of Reynard tempering his greed. 'Do you believe the fox? Do you believe his whole account? Why he is born to rob and steal and lie! Deceit cleaves to his very bones; it can't be cut out so easily!'

Irritated at his questioning and brimming with pity for the bereaved and traumatised fox, Queen Gente glared at her husband and gravelled back, 'Nay. Nay, nay, nay. You are completely wrong, Noble. You may certainly believe Reynard. Whilst he behaved wickedly before, and fell far, very far, it is obvious to the meanest intelligence that he is a changed and reformed animal now. Remember, he has been concerned with nothing less than unburdening his immortal soul! He accused his father and his most loyal supporter, Grimbart, of the plot to murder you, which he might very well have laid on one or two of the other beasties if he was continuing on his usual pad-way of treachery and lies.'

Noble knew better than to contradict the Queen and, in any case, he wanted to believe the fox. Treasure-lust was writhing inside his chest like a green-eyed asp. So he capitulated. 'Lady Gente, if you think this be the best course, then I'll follow your tail, so to speak. Despite the fact that he may very well end up hurting us, I will pardon all these damned trespasses of Reynard and believe his words. But I swear by my crown, if he breaks the law again, if he ill-uses his fox-craft one more time, kills one more chick or steals one more bloody sausage, then he and his lineage will pay for it, to the ninth degree!'

Reynard briefly closed his eyes. He fancied he could feel the gentle strokes of Dame Fortuna's fingers on his battered body, the light breeze on his fur and the rough jolts of movement as he began a slow and steady ascent on her milling-wheel. He knew he had won—he could see straight through the King. He could see the tasses of gold plate in his eyes, see his lion-heart pounding for the love of rubies and topazes and ancient carbuncle gems shining like devilish lanterns in the earth. To the King, he simply said, 'My Lord, I would be a most unwise fox, a stupid fox indeed, to say things that were not true!'

King Noble grumphed and humphed and nodded and said a few things under his breath, then he picked up a straw from the ground and ceremonially pardoned and forgave the fox for all his misdeeds and all those of his father, Reynardius, too.

No wonder Reynard was so overjoyed! Word by gleaming word, he had fine-crafted his own miraculous escape out of nothing but the night air and a string of syllables. He was free from the threat of the gallows, and free from the grubby claws of his enemies. 'My Lord, the King,' he exclaimed, words rattling out of him like a jackdaw, 'my noble Lady, the Queen! May God repay you for the great honour you have done to this undeserving fox, and the memory of his poor, unhappy father!' A pause. 'I know how to best thank you though,' Reynard trod lightly, 'I will thank you in a such way that you shall be the richest King and Queen in the world. For there are no animals living under the sun to whom my treasure is better entrusted than you both!'

And Reynard the Fox picked up another straw, and wiped the mud from it, and proffered it with a flourish to the King, pronouncing in a loud and stately voice 'My most dear Lord, please receive here, with this, er, symbolic flax straw, the rich treasure trove of King Emereric, for I, er, give it to you with my free will and acknowledge it openly.'

The King took the straw from Reynard and threw it to the ground in a merry way, and he started laughing with his great lion-laugh, and the Queen started laughing with her side-of-the-mouth self-conscious yawps, and then Reynard started laughing too, but in the strained way of someone who knows full well that the joviality might turn in a whisker.

But for the moment, at least, the fox had the two lions entirely under his spell. And they waited patiently, washing their faces, for him to tell them exactly where he had buried the loot. And a little further off, the rest of the courtiers, who had crept as close as they dared, leaned in to hear as well.

'In the east of Flanders,' whispered Reynard in a conspiratorial, fireside voice, 'there stands a wood named Hulsterloe, near a long, low ridge of sour-black poplars. In the middle of that damp, gloomy wood, there lies a lake called Kriekeputte. A lonely and melancholy place and so great a wilderness, so eerie and deserted that often a whole year can go past without a single passer-by, save those who know about it. A fisherman or an old woodcutter now and then, perhaps, but *I've* never met another living creature there, save for a few night owls and blue jays who have their nests in the tangle.

'This is where I hid the treasure. Remember the name. KRIE-KE-PUT-TE.* He spelt it out to them, enunciating each syllable precisely. Noble and Gente repeated it after him like a spell. 'Now, I would strongly advise you and your lady to go there together, and not to send any other animal in your stead. After my story, you must realise that you can't trust anyone, especially around such a vast and precious hoard.' Reynard stepped up to the King and Queen and dropped his voice even lower.

'Now, when you come to the pool, you will see a grove of delicate young birches, as white as snow and as green as glass. There are two trees in particular: you can't miss them, their branches touch and part over the water, the treasure is buried under the one on the left. You'll need to scrap and dig some moss away, then underneath you'll find beautiful and priceless jewels set into gold and silver, and pawfuls upon pawfuls of

---

* I have myself been to look for Reynard's treasure and I can confirm that the land lies exactly as the fox tells it. There *is* a tangled wood and a dark lake and gorse bushes and thin silver birches, and it *is* a very strange and lonely and melancholy place. It now lies exactly on the border between Belgium and the Netherlands, just east of Clinge.

loose gems and the finest goldsmiths' work—work which once cost many a thousand mark. And, as I should have mentioned before,' Reynard looked around to make certain the other courtiers couldn't hear, 'the fabled crown of King Emereric! The one he wore on his very own head in his very own throne room in his very own palace. The very one which Bruin Bear would've worn if he'd had his wicked way.' Reynard sniffed and observed the covetous face of his King.

'My dear Lord Lion, when you have all this exquisite gold and silver, all these rare riches in your possession, piled high in your safe house in Gent, how often shall you say in your heart, how often shall you declare to yourself, "O Reynard, how true art thou Reynard the Fox! How honest and full of honour! How unusually clever! That with your subtle wits and wiles you should find this secret place to bury away the greatest treasure the world has ever known or will know! May God look after you and feather you with happiness wherever you may be!"' Noble muttered and started to shake his mane at this point. The fox had gone too far.

'Well, Sir Reynard,' he said, 'you'd better come and help us to dig up this treasure, then, for I don't know that wraith-addled part of East Flanders, I should never find my way. Poplar trees and ghosty birch woods and dismal ponds are ten-a-penny round Hulst, Fox. I know Paris and I know London and Aachen and Cologne, but I am beginning to doubt you a little, Reynard. That name, what is it, Kriklepit, Kreckelputle? Eh? It sounds made up. I think you're tricking us again, what?'

Reynard was horrified. Caught up in his hushed theatrics, he thought he'd been painting a highly convincing picture, and Hulsterloe and Kriekeputte were, after all, real places! He hadn't made them up. The very idea! He began to get very angry with the stupid, greedy, ignorant lion, who didn't even know his own kingdom, and he spat back indignantly, trying to ignore the faint tugging feeling of gallows rope around his neck once more, 'You are about as close to the truth as Rome is to the merry month of May!' he swore, 'For heaven's sake, my Lord, I'm hardly leading you to the Leie pretending it's the River Jordan! Or beguiling Gent into Jerusalem! Or, or, or ringing Antwerp with the bludgeoned walls of Troy!' The fox turned to the other animals, who were, of course, trying desperately to listen to every word of his private audience with the Crown.

'I will prove I'm right and trample on your suspicions, King Noble. One cannot trust anyone but eyewitnesses—in olden times, no one was allowed to chronicle events unless they'd seen them with their own clear eyes! As we all know, the word history—*hystoria*—is derived from *hysteron*, which means "to see" in Greek.* And I have my own eyewitness right here—over there, lurking at the back! Sir Cuwaert the Hare! Come forward! Come in front of the King!' Everyone turned to look, wondering what the King was going to do. The snatches of conversation between the fox and the lions were very confusing and nobody was quite sure what was going on.

The little brown hare, silky ears flattened in fear, trembling like a lute string, emerged from the back row. 'Cuwaert, are you cold?' shouted Reynard, 'how you shake and quiver! Be not afraid, little wood-cat. By the allegiance you owe to the

---

* Reynard is quoting from a book much loved by the entire Court: *De Lekenspiegel* or *The Layman's Mirror* by Jan van Boendale, a clerk and poet from Antwerp.

King and the Queen, come now and tell them the truth and nothing but the truth, as I demand of you!'

Sir Cuwaert the Hare hurckled down, whiskers twitching, and managed to whister in his thin wavery voice, 'I shall tell the truth Reynard, even if I lose my neck, and if I'm damned then I'm damned, and I do worry that might happen, but I shall not lie a single word, if I know the truth I shall be truthful, even about a bad crime if it comes to that. You've charged me so forcefully, I will do as you ask, but what if the criminals come after me, I am only a flower gardener, I don't have any fancy swords or armour to fight any bad animals, I have my gardening tools, I suppose, I have a big rake I could use, oh dear, Saint Monacella, please look after me, this is not what I was expecting this night, not at all what I was expecting...' He trailed off. Reynard smiled; calling the hare was a stroke of genius. It was so rare that anyone could understand his endlessly dull whitterings.

Sir Reynard started to stride up and down, in his most lawyerly fashion. 'Sir Cuwaert the Hare, pray tell us, do you know where Kriekeputte is? Can you see it in your mind's eye? Can you describe where it stands?'

Cuwaert nodded nervously and began, the Court straining to follow his whispering stream of consciousness. 'Yes, I do know Kriekeputte, I do know it, Lord Fox, that is true. Twelve years ago, I knew it very well indeed. Why d'you ask me? I don't know why you're asking me that. It makes me sad to think of it. It stands in a wood named Hulsterloe, a very boggy place. Muddy. Green gnats everywhere. Had so many itching bites on my ears, my fur rubbed off. Lots of brambles and crab apples and those birches that my grandmother Haazie used to say have the ghosties in their trunks. Built on old warren lands in the wilderness. Used to be owned by some count or other. He was ill, something to do with his liver. He was very yellow in the face. Like a buttercup. Lots of us hares and rabbits, and squirrels, and otters, yes, otters too, they used to live there a long time ago, but no more. Funny place, it is. A bad place. I don't like even thinking about it. I have suffered the most terrible sorrows there. When I lived there, I was so hungry all the time. I used to dream about carrot fritters and creamy parsnip soup and cheese soufflé. I remember that. So hungry. And I was so cold that winter and thin as a cricket, I thought I would freeze to death. Freeze solid in my bed. That pond was all frozen too, thick ice, the fish all died and the gnats. The otters moved away then. And the squirrel families. Lot of their kits perished. They *were* dead in their beds, ten in a row, stiff as stones. Terrible grief and rues they had, them squirrels.' The hare stopped for a moment, gasping for breath. He was very asthmatic, and this sort of stressful occasion brought it on.

'That was before Pater Symonet the Frisian moved in with his 'complices. Clergyman, right, but he'd fought in all them wars up north by the sea, lost everything he had. He set up this business of counterfeiting money. There in the woods. Heaps and bushels of it. He supported himself and all his fellows with it. They paid for wine and lace-boots and schools for their children and everything. There was three of them. Symonet and this fox called Reynout, sounds like Reynard, but nothing to do with the Maleperduys lot or our Baron Fox here. And the last fellow was Rijn the Hound, he was my special friend in those days. He was a poet, you know, he used to write me these verses about the spring and plantings and herbs and vegetables that I liked. He was a good poet, Rijn, he knew a lot of words and where to put them, but he also helped me escape many a danger, which he could tell you about if he was here. Which he's not. No, he's not here, no. But we didn't do nothing against the King though. Nothing. Nothing wrong and we only did our escapes within the law. Within the arms of the law.' During the poor hare's next bout of rasping and wheezing, Reynard took the opportunity to nip his testimony in the bud, which would have carried meandering along its winding peculiars for hours if unchecked. (He also wanted to stop any more talk of faking gold; that was *not* the subject he wanted Noble to dwell on at this juncture.)

'Thank you very much, Sir Cuwaert,' said Reynard, 'you can return back to your grassy seat, the King doesn't need to hear any more from you.' 'Oh,' said the hare, who had been beginning to enjoy himself. 'Oh, I see, that's all you wished for. I understand. I'll go back now. I beg to be excused, my Lord King.' And he ran unsteadily back to his anonymity behind the other mostly taller lords, where he could be heard trying to manage his unruly lungs for some considerable time.*

Reynard stalked over to the stables again. 'Lord Noble, was it true, then, what I said?'

'Quite true, Reynard, forgive me. It was wrong of me to mistrust you, eh,' replied Noble, who was fairly certain he'd understood the wispy narrative of the hare. He'd certainly heard the bit about the pond and the wood being real. He

---

* Eventually, the poor hare found some coltsfoot in the hedge, which he started to chew, eventually calming his ragged breath down to its usual trembling regularity.

wasn't as sure about the whole counterfeiting poetry business. It all seem very unusual and he couldn't make head nor tail of it. He must remember to ask Tybert about that part later. To the fox, he bellowed happily, 'Well, Reynard, my old friend, lead us to your wood and your dreary pond, and show us where to dig up the treasure! It'll be dawn in a few hours, we'd better get on our way to Hulst before it gets too busy on the roads. Don't want anyone to follow us, what.'

Reynard the Fox looked at the lion lounging in the yarrow. Steeped in privilege like a sop in Limburg honey. Never had to fight or scrap or beg for anything. Never known hunger. Never known grief. Never known despair. Reynard thought of his Hermeline and he thought of his little cubs, alone in their shabby castle, and his old friend Grimbart, tucked up in his sturdy box bed in Gent. They must be in anguish, all of them, thinking he was dead and hung up for the flies and the sharp-owls and the prurient passers-by to gawp at. And so he gathered and shuffled his wits together like a pack of spilt cards for the last big push of the night.

'Oh dear, oh dear, oh dear. By the walking staff of Saint Drogo,' said the fox, shaking his head with an air of mournful resignation, 'it would be a thing of wonder if I were able to accompany you to the woods, but alas I am not in that happy position. I should savour nothing better than breaking the good brown earth to reveal its many treasures, to crown the glorious Lion of Gent, to nobly ornament our King of Beasts, our Leo Belgicus with the fabled jewels of Emereric! But, alas!' Reynard clutched his heart in sorrow, 'I'm not available for the task anymore.' Noble began to mutter, but the fox put up a paw. 'No, wait, please my Lord, and listen to the reasons for our shared disappointment. It is a tale, I'm afraid, of villainy and shame. But it must be told, and its consequences accepted. I should have told it before, I know, but with the death-beams raised above me, the rough coils of the rope gathering in.' He shuddered.

'One Whitsun, around the time my middling cub Rossel was born'—at the thought of his son, Reynard's voice wavered, and the Queen urged him to rest whilst he did his telling, but he continued to pace up and down, dizzying the lions with his wild to-ing and fro-ing.

'Isengrim the Wolf, in the Devil's name, found religion and entered the priory up in Elmare, in the peat bogs. A god-forsaken place, wild and grey, just sea-mews and fog and black sucking-mud. He became a monk and his crown was shaved, but he found very quickly that the provend of even six monks wasn't enough for him. His lust for flesh was simply not satisfied by their thin rations of salt herrings and potage, and he came to me and complained so much of his hunger, wailed so sore, that I took pity on him. He was thin and sick; his fur was falling out and you could count his ribs. As a kin-beast of mine, I counselled him to leave Elmare, run away, forget his vocation, come back to civilisation and good, hearty food. You can pray just as well after a roast chicken supper, I told him.

'Unfortunately, that advice, which he followed in a trice— he loped straight down to Hulst for a pot of beef stew—cost me dearly. The abbot wrote to Rome, and the Pope excommunicated me four months later, by return messenger.* I am cursed and outcast, dear King, cursed and outcast!' Reynard

---

* The papal bull excommunicating Reynard is preserved in the Vatican Apostolic Archive (Vulp. Lat. 1512), a little stained and folded, but intact.

pulled out his beautiful psalter, in a carefully absent-minded way, as though the book scarcely left his pious paws.

'Tomorrow, when the sun rises, I shall follow its slant-light through the poppy fields, through the greening corn, to the long and dusty road to Rome to be pardoned. After I have gained my indulgence, I will not rest, but will take sail for the Holy Land. I will cross the Mediterrany Sea to Jerusalem and will never return again until I have done so much good, that I may accompany you with honour and propriety. What should the world say, King Noble, if you associate yourself with an excommunicated fox! A fox mired in disgrace, under sentence, cast out by the Bishop of Rome and all his cardinals!'

'You have a point, Reynard, a worthy one,' answered Noble, who had never much liked the sound of the Pope, who was the son of a cobbler, of all things, from Troyes.

The lion suddenly remembered a visiting minstrel singing a story about the Pope refusing to pardon a poor poet who had been dallying with fairies, but was very penitent about his frolics. Or perhaps the Pope *had* pardoned him but it was too late? That was it! thought the king. The Pope had declared that forgiveness was as likely as his papal staff blossoming, and then it did—the minstrel said it sprouted almond blossom as sweet as sugar—but the poet had already fled dejected back to the sinful elf-lands, despairing of his future, his soul damned for all eternity. With this terrible tale in mind, Noble thought Reynard a courageous fellow for risking disappointment himself at the end of such an arduous journey. A very unpleasant shoemaker's apprentice masquerading as the father of all Christendom, why he could quite easily turn the fox away. How merciful I am, in comparison, mused the lion. What a difference lineage makes, what a difference.*

And he turned to Reynard and pronounced imperiously, 'Sir Reynard the Fox, you stand here before me, accursed in the censures of the Church. If I went about with you in public, I'm afraid my crown would become tarnished, blackened with the soot of villainy. I shall take Cuwaert the Hare, or some other courtier with me to Kriekeputte. It matters not. What matters, Reynard, and in this matter I must counsel you strongly, is that you put yourself out of this curse. Get this lifted, Fox, as soon as you can.'

Reynard kissed his psalter and then kissed Noble's feet. 'Therefore, I will go to Rome as hastily as I may! No lazy sojourning in Lyon or Marseilles or Nice for me, no, I will not rest by night nor by day until I have my pardon.'

'Reynard,' said the King, 'I think you have finally turned a corner. You're on the right path at last, old chap. May God give you grace to accomplish your desire.' The two awkwardly embraced, whiskers tangling, and then the lion walked over to the courtiers, who were all agog at the few tantalising if confusing fragments which had carried on the sweet summer air. Buried treasure! Excommunication! The South of France! Beef stew!

There was a high stone stage next to the pair of gallows, the last remaining wall of an old Roman fort, long abandoned, long forgotten, the fine-cut stones stolen for farmhouses and

* To Reynard's considerable advantage, King Noble has the real Pope somewhat muddled with the stories of Tannhäuser, which the travelling bard had actually been pronouncing.

horse troughs and the church towers of Lokeren and Sint-Niklaas. King Noble leapt up and addressed his exhausted subjects. He commanded that they should all be silent and then instructed them to sit in a wide circle on the grass around him, all according to their estate and birth, which took an inordinate amount of time and bickering and flouncing off by some of the more hierarchically sensitive animals.

Sir Reynard stood by the Queen, whom he had grown to love dearly during the past days, her kindness and unspoken understanding of the well-hidden pain which undercut his trickery moved him greatly. 'Pray for me, noble Lady,' he bowed, 'that I might safely see you once more, that I may return from my lengthy pilgrimage.' She smiled assuringly at him. Something terrible and unspoken had befallen Reynard Fox in the past, she was sure of it—a tragedy of some kind— and she prayed hard to Saint Mark the Lion Guarder to ease his jagged soul, to give him full absolution for his sins.

Finally satisfied with the arrangement of his squabbling Court in ascending importance around him, the King began to graciously declaim. 'Listen closely—poor and rich, young and old, well-born and hedge-born! Sir Reynard the Fox, one of the head officers of my house, had, as you all know, behaved so badly that he should have been gallowed by now. However, he has said much tonight, and done much, and the Queen and I have promised to him our grace and our friendship.' Noble nodded at Reynard, who had assumed a serious and weighty countenance, and was standing in his remorseful hermit pose, head bowed.

'The Queen has prayed for him and argued for him, so much so that I have made peace with the fellow. Friendship, even.' Noble laughed and the animals laughed uneasily along with him.

'Therefore, here by the side of the Doorgangstraat, under this glorious moon, I give to the fox his life and the liberty of Flanders once more, from Gent to Dowaai, from Poperinge to Sluis. He has free use of his four swift legs and his four black paws and his many whiskers and his full brush and his pointy ears and his foxish tongue, both within and without the Court, and across the Lowlands and the Wastelands and the Grapelands.'

This was an old archaic legal formula which meant that Reynard had been entirely discharged from his sentence. Sir Tybert the Cat, who was uncomfortably seated next to the flea-ridden and smelly Bruin, gasped. The bear simply opened his mouth in astonishment, then forgot to close it again. Isengrim, sprawled behind them, started a low, menacing, almost imperceptible growl. And yet, there was more.

'I also command you to honour and, er,' Noble thought of the treasure-tree by the stagnant lake, of muddy drifts of gold florins and fire beryls, 'worship, yes, worship Reynard and his wife and his children and his many nephews, when you meet them, whether it be by night or by day. And I do not wish to hear any more complaints about the Baron. He may have committed bad and wicked deeds in the past, but he is a changed fox, a turned-coat fox. He has bettered himself. Tomorrow, he will take up the pilgrim's staff and the pilgrim's scrip and travel to Rome for pardon and forgiveness of all his sins.'

On cue, Reynard produced an elaborate scarlet rosary from the depths of his cloak and began to paw it solemnly. Its beads ringed a large filigree pomander, and a heady scent of ambergris and cloves and oranges carried gently across to the stunned courtiers, perfuming their rich bewilderment at their king's peculiar volte-face.

Listening to Noble's pronouncement, perched on the gallows beam, Tiecelin the Raven, a vociferous and gloomy commentator on the comings and goings of the Court, who relished disgrace and misfortune, stretched his wings in glee, then leapt down to where the wolf, the bear and the cat were gathered.

'You unhappy folk, you wretched folk,' he croaked, 'why are you just sitting there? Reynard the Fox is restored as squire and courtier and is greater and mightier in the land than ever before. The King has forgiven him all his brokes and breaches of the law, forgiven him all his trespasses and misdeeds, even forgiven him the murder of that poor little hen. You three need to watch out.'

His hollow beak curled into a grave-rimmed smile. 'You'll be betrayed and charged and hanged yerselves. Mark my hackle-feathers, you three are for the swing, you're for the swing alright!'

Cackling and kaaking, he swooped away towards the woods. Isengrim shouted after him, 'Stupid fowl! That's not true! You're lying! You're a liar, bird!' From high over the fields, they heard a faint laughing caw-caw-caw in reply, 'Not so, not so, not so!'

The three betrayed lords scrambled up, Isengrim and Bruin rushing to join the chattering gaggle in front of the King. Sir Tybert, however, stayed behind and crept back to the top of the gallows. He was utterly terrified, flashes of his old-borne terror of execution, of slow torture, of rough imprisonment flickering before him like marsh flames in the darkness.

'Faithless Fortune is playing her old games with me again,' Tybert muttered to himself, and his eye socket began to itch and ache. I would forgive the fox even the loss of that eye, he thought, if only I could secure his friendship. The sweet safety of his friendship. Oh, how I long for the past, how I wish I could return to those easeful nights of books and writing and claret and crispy roast voles! He shook with fear and worry and wished most fervently that he'd never crossed paths with Reynard in all his life.

CHAPTER TWENTY

In which Sir Isengrim the Wolf and
Sir Bruin the Bear are arrested

Arrogant, surly, spitting venom, Isengrim stalked across the field, pushing roughly through the sycophants and the chancers congratulating Reynard. They were all wishing the fox well on his journey, patting him on the back and offering copious, conflicting and unwanted advice. They argued about the best route to take to Rome (some said take the sea route; others, the mountains, Bellin the Ram suggested the fashionable Dutch way—up the Rhine, across Bavaria to the Tyrol, then over the Alps by the Reschen Pass—'you'll need to employ a few goats to help you, treacherous up there, but wonderful views, Reynard, wonderful views'), which taverns and hostelries to avoid (all apart from the Lion d'Or in Lyon were apparently flea-ridden, plague-ridden and full of thieves, murderers and card sharps), how to engage a trustworthy sea captain in Marseilles (always draw up a proper contract and take your own food and padlock aboard), where to find a good sturdy chamber pot in Venice, a reliable donkey in Jaffa and an attractive relic selection in Rome, and what not to eat, under any circumstances (melons of any description—they'll give you the 'worst flux of yer life,' warned Sir Hamel the Ox).*

---

* Some of the animals' advice can be read in the travel accounts of the fifteenth-century Devon priest, fellow of Exeter College Oxford, and bursar of Eton College, William Wey, preserved in the Bodleian Library. Wey made three pilgrimages between 1456 and 1462—to Compostella, Rome and the Holy Land.

Isengrim elbowed his way to the Queen, and stood so close to her that she could smell dead rats and goose flesh on his breath. To begin with, he whispered to her of the beauty of her yellow fur, her dark whiskers, her sleek flanks—so easy to flatter a lioness, he thought, as she recoiled both from his words and the reek of his stained, yellow fangs. Then, white-eyed, mouth dripping with spite, Isengrim started to complain to her of the fox—a thick rasping stream of vulgar, coarse accusations, wild accusations with no basis in truth. His voice rose to an incoherent brawl, loud enough for the King to hear. Noble was furious. Reynard could now do no wrong in his eyes—he was a reformed fox and the purveyor of the greatest riches in Flanders, probably the world.

As gleefully predicted by Tiecelin the Raven, Noble immediately ordered the arrest of Isengrim, and Bruin too, who was lumbering around, confused, in the wolf's shadow. Mad wood hounds from the deep forest, foaming at the mouth, had never been treated so viciously, so publicly humiliated, as were the bear and the wolf on that endless night on the Doorgangstraat. They were trussed up together, fast bound so tightly with the hanging cord that they couldn't stir a claw, scarcely able even to roar out in pain or move a fast-numbing joint.

Wise reader, no doubt a little weary of this weedy bank off the Gent to Antwerp road, I need you to listen close once more, listen under once more, listen through. Listen to how Sir Reynard Fox hard-grinds his paws on his enemies' tails. For he hated the wolf and the bear; he loathed them with every last brass-copper hair on his brush. He took counsel with the Queen and laboured and charmed her as only he could and persuaded the tired Gente—who had cloaked the fox in her frustrated affection for her beloved battle-worn brothers, whom she never saw—to grant him a single favour.

He asked her for some of Bruin's skin from his back—one foot long of thick brown fur, one foot broad. Enough to make a pilgrim's bag, a scrip, for his great journey of atonement. She readily agreed, and the screams of the poor bear, still sore and crusted from his woodyard beating, could be heard all the way to Sint-Niklaas, waking babes from their soft feather beds and little chicks from their warm, whirled nests.

But the fox wanted more.

'I am almost ready for my pilgrimage,' he said very carefully, in a loud precise voice, 'except for my shoes. I'll need four new shoes; good, strong shoes, two for my back paws, two for my front. For it's a long way to Rome, and even longer to Jerusalem.' He then knelt before the Queen, his handsome mask a model of guile. 'Madam,' he humbled, 'I am your pilgrim. Here's Sir Isengrim the Wolf, once a dear uncle of mine, who already has four sturdy fur shoes which would be perfect for me. Surely, as a criminal awaiting charges, he could spare just two.'

Reynard moved closely and spoke very softly; unlike Isengrim's foul stench, *his* fur smelt of fresh-fallen acorns and rich peat, of sweet mint and wild betony, of the damp forest floor and the high rare cold of stone towers. 'If you can arrange this, dear lady, I will pray for you on every step of my pilgrimage; each footfall will sound clear to heaven with prayers for your eternal soul. For it is only right and proper that a pilgrim should lavish thoughts and prayers on those who do him good. Think of your soul, dear Queen, and those of your kin-lions, your dear brothers.'

At that moment, there was a sudden lull in the general hum of conversation, and then the none bells rang out from Lokeren and Hillare and Lochristi. As the animals instinctively looked out over the fields, Reynard felt a sudden tug on his cloak, followed by a she-wolf's whisper—urgent, desperate, intimate. He nodded curtly and for the next couple of moments he looked very odd, undone, uncertain, then he pulled himself together and continued, his voice wavering slightly. Gente, ever solicitous to the trauma she was now convinced the fox had suffered, paid close attention.

'I would also ask that you take...' Reynard coughed and gulped as though he was trying to swallow a wriggling earth-worm, 'I would also ask you to procure the other two shoes from, from Lady Erswynde.' His eyes looked hard and gold and tarnished, like two Rhenish guldens that had crossed one too many palms. 'This doesn't need to be done here,' he said, quickly, 'she goes out so little, and abides so much at home. It can be done later, without scene or audience.'

The Queen readily agreed, 'Reynard Fox, of course you deserve some stout walking shoes. After all, you'll need them to keep your feet whole over many a sharp mountain and many a stony rock. And you can find no better pairs than those which Isengrim and his wife are wearing, even if it risks their lives to rip them from their feet. There, my word is said, they must give up their pads and cobble your paws, for your noble pilgrimage trumps their need of them.'

CHAPTER TWENTY-ONE

In which Sir Isengrim and Lady Erswynde
have their Shoes plucked off and Sir Reynard
puts them on and sets off to Rome and the
Holy Land on his Noble Pilgrimage

So, Reynard, the false pilgrim, has his two new shoes fashioned from Lord Isengrim's feet. The King's guards ripped them off in swift, cruel movements; haled them from claws to sinews. You never saw a hen being roasted or a falcon having her eyes stitched together lie stiller than the roped Baron Wolf.* As they tore and peeled his paws, he stirred not a muscle, though thick, dark blood ran down between his toes and turned the white yarrow flowers black.

Then, from behind the thorn tree where she had been crouching, watching her husband through the fading blossom, Erswynde emerged and presented herself for a similar humiliation. Reynard started. He made to stop the guards, but she slowly laid herself down onto the damp grass, next to the bleeding Isengrim and held out her delicate, thin paws, first one then the other. In a trice, they were flayed from her, skin and nails of her dainty back feet tugged and stripped, as she tried not to whimper or cry.

Reynard the Fox started to laugh, a hollow and peculiar bark of a laugh. The other animals didn't notice. They were full of blood-jeer, delighted to see the despised wolves get their

---

* To close the eyes of a hawk by stitching up the eyelids with a thread tied behind the head was used as part of the taming process in falconry, and was a common practice in King Noble's mews.

addling for once. The fox circled the wolves, full of hoker-words and sneer, and cried in a strange, overly loud voice, 'My dear Erswynde, how much sorrow you have suffered for my sake, for which I am deeply sorry, apart from one small flicker of comfort.'

He stopped and looked down at Erswynde, tone all pike sauce for his audience, but his eyes quite the contrary. 'You, lady, are one of the dearest, the loveliest of all my kin. Therefore, I shall gladly wear your soft fur slippers. You shall be the constant partner of my pilgrimage. You shall share in my pardon, which I will fetch from far over the sea with the help of your precious shoes.' Erswynde started to sob with the pain and the horror and the violence of everything, of the unrelenting undertruths of her small, restrained life. To Reynard, she said, 'Now, you have everything that you willed. I have done my part. I pray to God that he will avenge all, wreck all, that he will stem this wickedness.'

Lord Isengrim and Lord Bruin held their peace and stayed still during Reynard's triumph. They were ill at ease, for they had been bound back together, their wounds weeping and sore. Luckily for his skin, Tybert the Cat, the moment the other two were arrested, had crept away, as quiet as a moth, running the watery field route back to Gent, to take refuge in the quiet green courtyards of the Abbey of Saint Veerle, hoping his old friend the abbot would hide him until all calmed down.

It was morning now and the land was flooded with light. The sky was the palest of blue, the blue of very old glass, very delicate glass, and a gentle breeze was nodding the poppies and mazing the trees.

The Court had returned to the city, straggling along the very same route on which they had dragged the condemned fox only hours before. This time, Reynard walked jauntily at the front, engaged in a spirited conversation with King Noble, mainly about the particulars of the treasure but also humouring the king's interminable fascination for jousting, the fox recounting an interesting anecdote about one of Sir Íñigo's cousins from the Kingdom of León, who had, with ten of his companions, set up camp next to a bridge in Castile and challenged every knight who wished to pass over to a joust, swearing to break three hundred lances before they finished. 'They fought for a whole month,' said Reynard, 'one hundred and sixty battles and a great pile of lances in their field. But not three hundred. And they were all so battered and broken; they had to give up and go home in the end. Íñigo has one of the shafts; get him to show you. He wrote a very humorous account of it as well, I believe.'[*]

In Gent, urged by Noble, Reynard reluctantly went to get his new shoes greased. Whilst he was at it, he called on the relieved and grey-faced Grimbart, who had been up all night praying for a miracle. They embraced, and the badger made him a nice herb omelette for his dinner, followed by a rich cherry torte and a glass of strong cold hypocras. Reynard told him about his proposed pilgrimage and Grimbart was cautiously approving, despite suspecting that the likelihood of the fox entering Rome was roughly the same odds as the Devil swanning unfettered into heaven. After eating they had

[*] Sir Íñigo's account was later documented by the town notary Don Luis Alonso Luengo and even mentioned in *Don Quixote* as an example of the idiocies which chivalry could reach.

a snooze, and after that Grimbart gave Reynard one of his old staffs to take with him. It was the one he'd used as a young badger on his walk to Our Lady of Boulogne, a happy April pilgrimage which he remembered as a daze of blossom and sea cliffs and mead and young love.

The fox put on his wolf-fur shoes and, waving merrily over his shoulder to his worried friend, walked the short distance to Noble's castle, sauntering past the soldiers, brazen as you like, straight into the Great Hall. He went to the King and the Queen and he bowed low, and said with great jollity and cheer, his eyes as bright as cinders, 'Noble Lord and Lady, I give you good morrow, and I desire of your graces that I may have my bear-brown scrip and my fine old staff blessed by a priest or some holy animal, as befits a young pilgrim of Rome and Jerusalem.' He stroked his bag of poor Bruin's ridge fur, and banged his staff, its base carved with a beautiful, ornamental G-for-Grimbart, and waited for their response.

'Well,' said the King, 'It had better be Bellin the Ram, I think. He knows the formula for these things.' Bellin the Ram was called from his dark beamed counting room in the Cloth Hall, where he was enjoying a restful afternoon scribing his accounts of last year's exports of the finest dickedinne broadcloth to Norfolk. In he came, puffed up in his usual busybody, know-it-all manner. The King had him sit down and ordered him some Rhenish, then said, 'Bellin, you shall do a Mass for Reynard the Fox, for he's going off to Rome soon and he needs his scrip and staff blessed, and blessed properly, as befits a pilgrim.'

'No,' said Bellin, crossing his woolly legs in a neat and irritating way. 'I can't do that, Sire. Sorry, but I dare not. He's said he's in the Pope's curse. I'm not risking my own tabart for that fox.'*

'What's all this, Bellin?' said the lion, annoyed. 'Why, hasn't Master Gelys told us that even if an animal has committed every sin in the world, if they would regret those sins, and confess all of 'em, and receive penance and do by the priest's counsel, then God will forgive them and be merciful? Reynard Fox, having done his wickednesses all over the place, is packing up and off he'll go across the Mediterrany to the Holy Land, and with all his penitence, God'll make him clear of all his sinning.'†

'That's not from Master Gelys,' replied the ram, smugly, pulling a fat tick out of his wool. 'Those are the words of Master Geoffrey Ridel, the third Bishop of Ely. I know all about him through my interests thereabouts. Good sheep in Ely Abbey, very good sheep. Wool as white as snow. You should know that, though, my Lord, you should know all about Ridel; he counselled King Henry. An advisor to the King of England, no less. Although *that* advice didn't help much did it, with Thomas à Becket's swording and all.' Bellin wiped his wine-stained mouth carefully with a fancy cloth which he untied from his belt. 'And I'm still not doing any rites or rituals unless you clear it with the spiritual courts before the Bishop Prendelor and the Archdeacon Loosewynde and Sir Rapiamus, his official.' Noble had no idea who all these clergy animals were and suspected that

---

* Reynard's excommunication has excluded him from all sacraments; hence Bellin's initial objection to the King's request.
† King Noble is referring to the popular theologian Giles of Lessines, who wrote works on all manner of subjects, from sin to economics.

Bellin had made them up just to vex him. The ram was smiling now with his self-satisfied, pedantic smile, looking around the room for approval of his superior and intimate theological knowledge.

The lion saw red, and slammed his fist down, and roared at Bellin with such ferocity that the ram's Rhenish spilt and his felt hat blew off and landed on top of one of the smaller Spanish foxes. 'I shan't ask you again, Bellin; I'd sooner hang you right now from the rafters than waste my breath all day with this nonsense, this sheepish tomfoolery.' And he signalled alarmingly to his guards. Bellin's smile fell from his face faster than a tavern-stab. He saw how angry the King was and started to quake with fear. Without saying a word, he got up, knobbled knees knocking, and went straight to the altar and, taking up whatever books were there—an odd assortment—sang over Reynard and Reynard's scrip and Reynard's staff and even Reynard's greasy wolf-shoes.

Reynard stood there nonchalantly whilst Bellin was meekly wafting incense and chanting in his shaky sheep alto. The fox didn't care one fig whether his things were blessed or not, although he was appreciative of the legitimacy which the ceremony gave his venture.

When Bellin the Ram had finished incanting his service in a high devout terror, looking nervously at Noble every other phrase, he hung the scrip, covered with the thick pine-needle-lardon-scented fur of Bruin the Bear, around the fox's neck, along with a small tatty psalter faintly embossed with a golden lioness, which the King had hurled at him halfway through the service.

Sir Reynard the Fox was ready for his journey.

He trod slowly towards the King, tears dripping down his black whiskers, flowing down his long tawn-russet face, a model of piety stung with the regret of departing from a beloved liege-lord.

Oh, Reynard played the part well, as though his heart was cleaving in two from his grief. But, really, his own true sorrow at that precise moment was simply that he hadn't managed to cause as much trouble for the other animals, as he had for the wolf and the bear. That awful, vulgar merchant-sheep; that slippery, pretentious Tybert hiding, no doubt, in some monastery or other; that awful, literal-minded beaver; and that raven, flapping around with his constant omens and auguries. By Saint Francis himself, I can't stand the lot of 'em, thought Reynard. Nevertheless, he gathered everyone around him and asked them all to pray for him, 'as I would pray for you, dear friends'.

As the courtiers somewhat reluctantly prayed for the fox's safe return, Reynard began to collect all his belongings together. He was beginning to think that he was tarrying rather too long—it had been hours and hours since he'd left Grimbart's Dassenburcht, and he wasn't sure how much more weeping and milceful holiness he could keep up—he fancied a nice sit-down, a good supper and a chat with Hermeline. He knew King Noble's mood swings well, they were as capricious and unpredictable as the wind in the Waasland, and at any moment he could whirl round to despising him again, and he just wanted to get away now whilst the going was good.

'Off so soon, Reynard,' said the King, suddenly, as the fox began to make his farewells. 'I must say it wounds me to see how keen you are to leave fair Gent behind and those who wish you well in your trials. Well, I suppose you must go sometime, Fox. Off with you, then, and God be with you.'

And he commanded half of the Court (not the better half, thought Reynard) to accompany him on his way, except for the bear and the wolf, who still lay bound in bloodied, moaning heaps. No one, not even the Queen, dared to feel sorry for them. Instead, they walked around them, looked elsewhere or pretended to themselves they weren't even animals, just sacks of cloth or turnips.

I wish you had seen Sir Reynard the Fox leaving the Court, draped in all the blessed accoutrements of the penitent's path—rough-sewn scrip on one shoulder, battered prayer book hanging precariously from another, swaggering along with Grimbart's precious staff, wolfish shoes cushioning his feet. Picture yourself, idling in the busy streets outside the castle, perhaps enjoying a spiced apple pancake and a glass of bog myrtle beer in the evening sunshine. Now look up and watch an unexpected procession of nobles led by a meek and mild pilgrim-fox in flowing brown robes, accompanied by the King in all his solar, leonine glory, and by the decorative flowers of the Flanders Court, fanning out in a ramshackle bouquet. There is no one so gloomy between Poland and Zeeland that wouldn't have been cheered by Reynard's triumphant exit.

As for the fox, on leaving the tunnelled gatehouse he had assumed a carefully considered expression of devotion suitable for a departing pilgrim, but as they all solemnly processed through the heaving bustle of the wool market, a tangle of figures and noise and activity set against the tranquil fields beyond, he thought how very comfortable he was in his new attire, and then he thought about how his fellow courtiers had been forced to walk beside him, to literally ease his passage in the final stage of his perilous escape, the very same lords who were all mob-furious with him a scant time ago, and he started to get a terrible turn of the giggles.

Mirth frothed deep inside his chest like the whirling foam under the Onthoofdingsbrug. It was all he could do to stop himself guffawing out loud. And then he thought of the King, who not one day ago had signed and sealed his death warrant, who was now his greatest champion. What a fool Reynard had made of him, what a marvellous revenge he had taken, and he permitted himself a single triumphant bark, which could be explained away as a hiccup.

'My Lord the King,' he quickly said to Noble, 'I pray that you return now, and do not go any further with me. You have two murderers arrested and fettered in your Great Chamber. If they escaped, Saint Leonard only knows what would happen; you could be very badly hurt. Oh, dear King, I pray you attend me, I pray that my words of warning keep you from misadventure!' Then he stood up on his after-feet, his elegant hind legs, and begged all the beasts, great and small, in such a humble and charming way, that they should all pray for him, not least so they could profit from his good works abroad, that they all said they would and meant it too. There were many affectionate embraces and many warm tears. And when Sir Reynard the Fox finally departed from the King (who had, as intended, started to worry about his ill-kept prisoners), he looked so sad and so forlorn that his earlier trespasses were finally forgotten, and a great wave of pity and sympathy for the poor brave fox flowed from his convoy of courtiers.

But Reynard was, as usual, thinking ahead and planning from behind. He still had unfinished business to settle. He linked arms with Bellin the Ram, who was self-importantly nodding at his cronies from the Cloth Hall, and smiled toothily down at Sir Cuwaert the Hare. Cuwaert, swigging hyssop syrup for his lungs, looked nervously back up at the fox. 'Why are you staring at me, Reynard? Aren't you meant to be walking off to Rome now?'

'Dear Friends,' smiled Reynard, 'Dear Ram, dear Hare, must we take our leave so abruptly? It is a fine evening, why not walk a little further with me? You two have always been so kind, so understanding. You have never once made me angry, unlike some of the other animals I could mention. Intelligence, wisdom and perspicacity, all ingredients for a true friendship. Such gentle company, so refreshing, so stimulating! And both beasties of such good repute amongst the Court! I do believe I have never heard one complaint levied against either of you! Temperance is your watchword, am I right? Temperance. A life of steady and sober restraint! So admirable! Why, you live as I once did as a recluse in my simple hermitage. Quite happy with leaves and grass to eat, never lusting after soft white loaves or crackling flesh or creamy sauces or fancy tartes and marchpane. Ah, the simple life is the best.'

And with these flattering words, Sir Reynard the Fox beguiled the know-it-all guild merchant Bellin the Ram and the nervous valetudinarian Sir Cuwaert the Hare. He spun them, and whispered them, and led them all the way to his fortified manor of Maleperduys, by the eel village of Rupelmonde, in the far east of Flanders, in the heart of the Land of Waas, in quite the opposite direction to Rome.

PART THREE

PILGRIMAGE

CHAPTER TWENTY-TWO

Among foxis be foxissh of Nature

The Feast Day of the Bloody and Violent Matrydom of
Saint Gervase & Saint Prothase, Saturday 19th June

Whoosh! Down the river path they went, as brisk as the East
Wind, pushing through cow parsley and nettles, drifting part
of the way in a flat-bottomed boat which Reynard appropriated
for a mile or two, before abandoning it by an old mill. The
ram and the hare scarcely knew whether they were coming or
going. Reynard flitted and sparkled and entertained. He told
them fascinating gossip about their peers and their long-dead
ancestors, scintillating stories of sin and romance and larceny,
and even hinted at the grand treasure buried at Kriekeputte.

By the time they reached Maleperduys, the two befuddled
and befoxed animals were exhausted and exhilarated in equal
measure. When Reynard reached the little stone bridge over
the moat to the main gates of his house—oh, how he loved that
bridge, that worn smooth threshold of home and happiness!—
he stopped and spoke to Bellin, who was mopping his wool
with one of his linen hankies (he had dozens of them, each
one cut from a different sample of his export cloths and embroidered with the initials *B.R.*), it being a hot and humid day.

'Bellin,' said the fox, 'I wonder if you wouldn't mind waiting out here for a little time. You can cool your fleece by the
moat, and rest a while. I'll get my nephew Nivard to fetch you
a cold drink, perhaps some barley water?' 'Well, I don't mind
if I do,' said Bellin, settling himself under one of the quince
trees near the bridge.

'Good, good!' replied Reynard. 'Cuwaert and I will go in, for I need his tact and sensitivity to bid farewell to my darling wife, Lady Hermeline, and our three young foxlings, before I leave for Rome.'

'I can comfort them, your family, I'm good at that, I am,' said the hare, 'I used to comfort my mother, when she was alive. She used to get very sad sometimes and cry and cry when my father went away to Tournai to learn his painting. Have you been to Tournai, Reynard? It's a nice city, very noisy. They like their prunes in Tournai; everything they cook with prunes and almond milk; they have it with rose petals. Just like in the Holy Land. You can try it there, Reynard. They'll have it in Jerusalem, I bet. He was a good painter my father, such images he made, such images. He painted a little portrait of the Queen once, did you know that, Reynard? He did her fur all in gold. She looked like the Queen of Midas, so she did.' Most of this was incomprehensible, but Reynard smiled sweetly and nodded at roughly the right places.

'I will see you both soon, then,' murmured Bellin, flat on his side under the spreading leaves, closing his eyes and dozing off as he spoke, 'I pray you comfort Hermeline well, Cuwaert, I pray you comfort her well.'

Having flattered the hare into his plan, Reynard knocked three times for entry and was let in by the Lady Hermeline, dressed all in black and in a rapture of relief and concern. She had been distraught at the drip-drip news of death sentences and gallow trees, which had reached their distant burg quite quickly from the ravens and the crows, but the messages of hope and reassurance sent by Grimbart had not yet reached her, having been entrusted to a very short-legged cousin of his, with no sense of direction, who took a very long time to get anywhere.

She ushered her husband and his companion upstairs to the Great Chamber, which was flooded with light, muffled shards of colour cast from the old glass window onto the flagstones, wavering oblongs of dark celestrine and vert and bright crocus. The three cubs were playing with their toys and the scene was a vision of familial comfort and innocence. And yet, and yet, there was an odd chill to the air, a sharp and unpleasant undertone, a sour, dangerous feeling, which Cuwaert felt in his whiskers, in his twig-thin bones, in his rattling lungs.

As they stood there, watching the little foxes gambol, Hermeline marvelled at Reynard's ensemble—his twice-furred feet, his pouch and his carved staff. 'Why are you dressed so, Reyner, dear one? How on earth did you manage to escape?'

'I was arrested at Court,' said her husband, 'and, after much talk and much vexation and trouble, I was eventually released. It was a close-run thing, Hermeline, as close as a flea in a blanket, and now I'm bound to go on a pilgrimage to atone for everything. Bruin the Bear and Isengrim the Wolf have pledged for me, in a manner of speaking—they're standing bail in Gent, tied and fettered like tight sheaved flax.'

Then Reynard put a paw on Cuwaert's back, barely touching, but enough to heavy his skin. 'The King, however, has given us Sir Cuwaert here to do with what we will. He said himself that Cuwaert was the first to accuse me falsely. And by my trust in you, dear Hermeline, I am still rather angry with him. Very angry with him, in fact.'

Cuwaert felt dizzy, the room seemed to expand and contract. He simply couldn't understand what he was hearing—he thought Reynard had changed, he thought they had become friends on their walk, he thought Reynard liked him, he had believed everything the fox had said to him and Bellin. And then it all came rolling back, like acrid balefire, that terrifying Credo incident. Reynard's clean, white teeth coming for his throat, the crushing panic, the claustrophobia, trapped between his thighs.

Shaking with fear, his eyes darted to the doorway, but Reynard was blocking him, and, anyway, he couldn't remember the way out, they'd come up through all those dark, low passages and winding staircases. 'Bellin! Help me! Bellin!' he croaked, and then the hare's throat caught, and dried to cinders, and he began to wheeze. As soon as the attack started, Cuwaert knew it was different from the others. He gasped and gasped and gasped, but he couldn't catch his breath, and his heart was pounding, then missing beats and jumping like a grasshopper, and the pointed faces of Reynard and Hermeline loomed near and far and then near again, dancing in an odd dislocated syncopation with his spasms, and into his whirling mind began to flow a series of jewelled vignettes of his small, slight, insignificant life in his family's red-roofed farmhouse in Oostveld, like those scenes fine-painted onto a scrine or reliquary—his beloved grandmother Haazie telling him stories—his father, the painter, showing him how to draw with thick pieces of charred wood—his melancholy mother picking curled slugs from the lettuce by the back gate—the rich loamy smell of the turned fields at dawn—the drenching dew on the seed-grass—the lovely comfort of hot sun on his fur—running, ears streaming, between the long rows of his tulipa beds—dozens upon dozens of yellow and red and white papery flowers like fiery Turkish dragons in the mud—oh, the joy of racing and leaping and rolling in the sweet cool spring air—and the still, blue summer dusks—tucked up in his little willow bed as a leveret, when the nightingales sang their sweet songs from the copse by the water meadows under a thin crescent moon, and his mother sat by him and sang to him the old Flemish lullabies until he fell asleep, and then, and then, all of a sudden, in the midst of his terror, he felt a high joyous calm descend upon him and the wretched toil of trying to breathe seemed to fall away and the bright visions faded to a deep blackness, and then to a nothingness and with the faintest of cries poor Sir Cuwaert the Hare was dead.

During this terrible attack, Lady Hermeline had rushed away to find some water for the hare, her cubs loping after her. But Reynard, oh, Reynard had acted as foxes always act. He saw Cuwaert's shaking and struggling, and he decided to end it for him, and he caught him by the neck and bit it hard in two, warm blood running into his mouth, the delicious taste of fresh prey.

When Hermeline returned, she was shocked and saddened for the poor foolish creature, then pragmatic. She knew exactly what Reynard had done—his face was red with blood—but she also knew, with her practised eye, that the hare's lungs were riddled with phlegm, and that last paroxysm would have claimed him anyway. It was a mercy, she thought. She embraced her husband, who was crying, and took up the body of the hare.

There was no meat in their castle, only the usual barrels of salted herrings and a slightly green ham hock, and a plump hare would fill all their bellies. So, as dusk fell over Maleperduys, Reynard and Hermeline and Reynardine and Rossel and Reynkin sat down at their long oak table and cut off Sir Cuwaert's head, and then ate the remains of his body, every last sinewy scrap of him. A great feast it was for the five foxes. Hermeline insisted they both toast the King—'for he sent Cuwaert to us'—and, so they did, raising cups of the little hare's own let blood, an eerie sacrament in the gloaming.

'Reynard,' said Hermeline, after they had finished, and the cubs had returned to their games, 'now tell me the truth of how you escaped.'

'Dame,' said the fox, 'I have so flattered the King and the Queen that our friendship will be right thin when they know of all this.' He gestured, stricken, to the table, scattered with Cuwaert's white sucked bones.

'Noble shall be furious, and he'll seek me out to hang me by the neck, again. Hermeline, we have no choice, we must leave Maleperduys, with the little ones, we must depart immediately for some other forest, far away. Where we may live without fear or dread. Where we may be as foxes are meant to be. I'm tired of deception, tired of guiling. I know a few wildernesses where we might go—my grandfather's old stamping ground near Düsseldörp, or there's an ancient castle deep in the woods near Mons, family long gone, ringed with a deep moat. I stayed there once as a young fox, not long after my father died. There we can live for seven years, longer even, without them finding us. At Mons, I know there's plenty to eat, lots of good meat, partridges and woodcocks, oh, and many other wild fowl, I'm sure. Hermeline! Run away with me! They'll be sweet wells and fair and clear running brooks, and, Lord God, how fragrant the air will be! You'll have a library and a desk to write and work at. We can live in the freedom of the shadows, of the heather and the myrtle, in peace and ease and bounty. But we must flee from Rupelmonde, as fast as we can, for there's more.'

'More? What else, Reyner?' Hermeline was gathering up the bones into a little silk pouch.

'I'm afraid the King only let me go because I told him that there was a vast treasure in Kriekeputte.' Hermeline snorted, 'What a place to choose!' 'Yes, well, he'll find nothing there, even if he looks for ever and a day. How he will rage when the penny finally drops, and he knows how far he's been deceived! By the chains of Saint Leonard, the number of lies, the web of deceit I had to weave to escape from him. It was indeed my most difficult escape yet. I've never been in greater peril or quite so close to death before. I swear I will never, as long as I live, come under the King's power again. Thanks to my wits and my subtleties, I have finally got my paw out of his mouth, so to speak.

Hermeline beckoned to her husband to sit down—he was pacing again—and poured him some ale. The brittle remains of Cuwaert's body was a-rattling in the bag by the fireplace, next to his severed head, frozen in its death mask of terror.

'Reyner,' she said, patting his paw comfortingly, 'I must counsel you that running away to another forest, whether in Mons or Düsseldörp, is a very, very bad idea. We should be strangers, all of us, and utterly alone. In our own castle we have everything we need, everything we desire. Here you are the lord of all our neighbours, practically to Antwerp and the sea beyond. Why should we leave our own place, and venture everything in what may very well be a worse one. Have you even visited the woods by Düsseldörp, Reyner—you know they're grey with lurks upon lurks of wolves! If we stay, I think we'll be far safer. If the King attacks us or besieges us, we have so many tunnels and side-holes through which we can make our escape. And we know all the byways and crooked paths and turn-streets through the woods and the wolds. Imagine how much help Noble would need to conquer us here? He'd never be able to do it. But over all of that, the thing that worries me most is that you have sworn to go on this foolish pilgrimage overseas!'

Reynard knocked back his ale, and poured some more, occasionally glancing over at the fireplace.

'Madame,' he said, swaggeringly, kissing her paw, 'my sweeting, my dearest heart, do not worry yourself over that, it is insignificant. As the saying goes, "how more for sworn, how more forlorn". I remember going to Cologne, many years ago, with a friend of my grandfather, a very elderly and very wise fox named Reinhold, coat as white as moonshine. Anyway, he said to me that an oath forced—a bydwongen oath—was no oath at all. It simply doesn't count.' He took off his scrip and his psalter and laid them carefully down by his cup.

'If I should actually go to Rome, to the Holy Land, it wouldn't do me any good at all, Hermeline, it wouldn't avail me a cat's tail.' He smiled at her adoringly. 'I shall stay put, my dear, in Maleperduys, and follow your counsel if the King hunts after me. We shall mount the siege together! I shall keep myself as well as I may, and if he comes after me with all his might, then so be it. I will undo him and beguile him with my usual subtleties. I've done so before, why not again? I will unbind my sack of tricks. If he will search harm, he will find harm.' And he slammed down his ale and kissed his wife.

Caught up in their outlawish passion in the aftermath of the hare's death, the happy pair had, however, forgotten something, or rather, someone: Bellin the Ram, who was still waiting outside. His nap long finished, he was sitting on the stone bridge, tapping his feet, getting crosser and crosser that Sir Cuwaert the Hare was taking so long. The moon had risen by now and was perched in the quince tree branches.

Eventually, he knocked on the gate and called out, baaing at the top of his voice, 'Come out Cuwaert, in the Devil's name, how long is Reynard going to keep you in there! Come on! Hurry up! Make haste! Let's go!' As a sheep, Bellin hated being out after dark, and the pull of his comfortable house in the city, lit with a hundred rush lights, even on a summer's night, was unbearable.

When Reynard heard his cries, he raced down and opened the wicket door, and said very softly to Bellin the Ram, 'Precious Bellin, lief Bellin, lord of all creamy wool, why so angry! This is most unlike you! Calm yourself! You mustn't be displeased, for Cuwaert is speaking kindly with his dear aunt Hermeline. He bade me say to you that, er, you should, um, go on ahead. Yes, go back to Gent—you can use that boat I set aside, it'll still be up there by the mill. And Cuwaert will come after you, he's lighter of foot than you, and he must tarry awhile with my wife and cubs. They're weeping something terrible about me going away.'

'I don't know, Fox,' said Bellin, who was far sharper than Reynard gave him credit for, snobbishly thinking of him as just a stolid town burgher. 'I thought I heard him calling for help, calling my name. There was definitely a scream, for it woke me from my forty winks! What's happened to him, Reynard? I know something's happened, I can feel it in my waters!'

Reynard the Fox, peering out of the wicket, answered very carefully. 'What's all this you're saying, Bellin? Of course he hasn't come to any harm! What nonsense you speak! Now hark to what he's been doing. He came into my hall, and whilst he was having a thimbleful of wine I told my wife and foxlings of my pilgrimage. When Hermeline understood I was to go overseas, she fell down in a swoon, hard on the stones, and so Cuwaert cried out for help. 'Help, Bellin, help!' he yelled, 'Help bring Lady Fox out of her faint!' It was her scream you heard, and his call for succour.' He grinned innocently.

'Oh,' said Bellin the Ram, 'Oh, I thought he was in great danger. That's what it sounded like to me.'

'Goodness me, no!' smoothed Reynard. 'I would truly rather my wife and children should suffer the torments of hell than little Cuwaert ever come to harm in my house!'

CHAPTER TWENTY-THREE

The Head in the Scrip

The Feast Day of the Beheaded Martyr Saint Alban,
Sunday 20th June

'But before you leave, dear Bellin,' said the fox, pleasantly, with
an air of calm, day-to-day, kitchen-hearth normality, 'do you
happen to remember that King Noble asked me yesterday, in
the presence of a number of nobles, to write him a couple of
letters before I left Flanders. I wonder if you wouldn't mind
delivering them to him; they're already written and sealed.'

'I can't say I do recall; nor do I know if your inditing or your
writing are any good or if they're trustworthy, for that matter,'
bleated Bellin, still irritated. 'But I don't mind taking them,
I suppose, if you can give me a bag or some pouch or other.'

'Of course, of course! You shall not fail to have something
to bear them in, rather than they remain unborn!' charmed
Reynard, wittily. 'I shall give you my very own pouch which
I take everywhere with me and place the King's two letters
therein. You can hang them around your neck, and the King
will reward you extravagantly. You'll have all his gratitude,
even that meant for me, which I relinquish gladly!'

And so, objections defeated, Bellin the Ram formally promised Sir Reynard the Fox to carry his urgent letters to Gent.
Can you guess what happened next; have you caught the
sharp-cut threads of the fox's plan?

Reynard closed the wicket door and went back inside, up
to his Great Chamber again. Hushing Hermeline's concerns,
he then placed the severed head of Sir Cuwaert the Hare

into his scrip, tucking the silky brown ears in as gentle as a mother. 'God be with you, little hare,' he said, then fastened the pouch as fast as could be, in case he got an answer back from the head.

Then he took it out to Bellin, and pulled the scrip over his thick, woolly neck, and charged him *not* to open it and *not* to look at the letters before he presented them to the King, if he wanted to keep Noble's friendship. Thus, with one rough fur bag, a bag sewn for atonement and the discard of sin but stuffed with wickedness, Bellin the Ram, Honourable Mercer of the Fair County of Flanders, had his most gruesome fate sealed and hung right before him.

'Oh, and by the way,' called Reynard, casually, just as Bellin was turning to leave. 'If you like, you may say that you composed the letters and counselled me on how to best write them and advised me on turns of phrase and embellishments and what-nots. I don't mind one ounce and you'll scoop up all the praise from the King, so you will. They're very prettily written, very pretty indeed.'

Bellin liked the sound of this plan very much. He enjoyed being admired, mistakenly thinking it was a common occurrence, and how impressive it would be to arrive at Court with these important and thewful letters composed in what was, no doubt, a highly elegant French, or even Italian, script, formed by the richest and reddest of inks. He imagined himself telling his friends at the Cloth Hall, a circle of black-robed rams nodding in approval at his eloquence. (In reality, his paw-writing was abysmal, and centuries and centuries later would cause many late nights and reoccurring ocular headaches caused by eye strain for a retired historian in Leiden transcribing the voluminous records of the sheep's cloth exports from Gent to Norwich and London.)

'Reynard,' Bellin exclaimed, 'I'm most grateful and look forward to the praise. It may surprise you, but I lack a certain finesse and skill with a feather.' Reynard feigned amazement. 'But, Fox, you know, often it happens that God suffers some to have the worship and thanks for the labour and skills of others, and so it shall happily befall me. But what d'you counsel, Reynard, my friend, should Cuwaert come with me to the Court now, as I must get going?'

'No, no' said Reynard, eyes narrowing, a slight prickling of guilt in his belly, as it rumbled for more fresh meat, 'he can follow along later, after he's helped my poor wife. She's still sorrowed and not a little giddy from her fall. Now off you trot, Bellin, I need to go and have a few quiet words with Cuwaert, which I'm sure he'll share with you when he finally shows his face.' And with that, Reynard slammed the wicket gate, and rattled the locks.

'Farewell, Reynard! My best to Hermeline!' called Bellin and off he ran to the river path, whispering credos and paternosters under his breath to protect from the nasties and the goblins and the spirits down by the water at night, blissfully unaware of the source of the unexpected weight of the scrip.

He went as fast as he could, Cuwaert's head, heavy as an apple, banging into his chest, his fleece and his good ciclatoun robes and his brown hose catching on the brambles, leaving a trail of white wool and scraps of torn cloth all the way to Dendermonde, where he started to follow the main highways again in the bright and comforting morning sun.

He found himself back within the grey turrets and arches of the Court at midday, and found the King sitting in council with some of the barons, fanning himself in the heat and sampling a dish of honey sherbet, made to a recipe brought back from Syria by Bruin's Uncle Adalbern. Dragonflies and water spiders were darting over the moat, and the castle cuckoo and his wife were calling brightly from the rose gardens. For once, in that turbulent reign, all was drowsy and peaceful, until Bellin came bowing close to Noble's throne and the King saw the pouch dangling from his neck, the very same pouch scrapped together from Bruin Bear's fur.

The lion continued to lounge on his throne staring at the bag for few moments, then, remembering its form and history, leapt up and roared to high heaven. 'Where've you come from, Ram? Where is the fox? Why doesn't he have his pilgrim's scrip with him? Answer me, Sheep, now!'

Bellin, taken aback, stuttered his well-rehearsed piece, 'My Lord, I shall tell you all that I know. I accompanied Sir Reynard into his house, into Maleperduys, and when he was readying to leave for Rome he asked if I would, for your sake, at your request, bear two letters to you. I told him, *bien sûr*, for your Sire's pleasure and worship, I would carry seven letters; nay, seven hundred if needed. And Reynard brought me this fur scrip, wherein the letters be.'

Bellin cleared his throat and prepared for the lie. 'And you'll find those letters to be veritable marvels of composition and script, with many fine words and sentiments. I advised on both of them, you see; they were mainly mine of the making. I taught them and a-shaped them, you see. Yes, whatever you find in that there pouch is most certainly a joint production,

Sire, a joint production. My part in the matter was close and invaluable.' He looked around, beaming, pleased with his speech, little realising that he had just confessed enough to hang himself thrice over.

The King nodded, and instructed his secretary, Botsaert, to open the pouch and retrieve these two astonishing examples of the epistolary arts. Botsaert was a better linguist than anyone else at Court, and always used to read any letters or documents which arrived for the King or Queen.* Today was no exception, and as the King and the other lords leaned in, vaguely interested, licking sticky sherbet from their paws, Botsaert, together with Sir Tybert the Cat, who had returned to Court at the bequest of a benevolent Noble, slowly unfastened the scrip.

Botsaert pulled out Cuwaert's head, and screamed, 'Alas, what letters are these? *Mon Dieu, mijn God!* Is this the head of Lord Cuwaert the Hare? *Ya ilahi, ya ilahi!* It is, it is! By Saint John the Baptist, this is his head! Woe, King, that you put your faith in Reynard!' And, shaking in horror, the monkey dropped his grim discovery, which tumbled and rolled across the flagstones, coming to a standstill at Bellin's hoof.

The King stood up and with the most uncharacteristic gentleness, picked up the severed head, ears loose and drooping like a dead flower, and cradled it tenderly.

---

* Botsaert was a self-made monkey from Montreuil-sur-Mer. Of indeterminate birth, he had been raised as a mysteriously funded orphan in the Abbey of Saint-Walloy. The monks there taught him well, and he excelled in languages. He was fluent in French, Greek, Latin, Arabic, Hebrew, English, Aramaic and Dutch, and had a passing knowledge of a dozen other tongues, which his confrères had barely even heard of.

'He was a strange creature, not quite of this world, but such a merry heart, such a good heart. He never told a falsehood in his short life, not once. He thought everybody was his friend. Such a trusting little fellow, a gentle friend to all, loyal to the last. That I ever believed that fox, that I ever believed him! Oh, Cuwaert, how can you forgive me, I have failed you, failed you little hare, poor little trusting hare.'

The King placed the skull with exaggerated care on the carved griffon arm of his throne, from where it looked out like a sad, accusing gargoyle, and then hung his great golden maned head down for a very long time. Queen Gente stared silently out at the river wrens, warbling songs of love and loss to each other from the willow trees by the Leie.

Around him the other lords were exchanging looks; some were sobbing, some had been sick, others were whispering urgently about Bellin, who was mired to the spot, horrified and ashamed in equal measure, his shattered mind slowly beginning to piece together what must have been the true trajectory of events deep inside the yellow-creepered walls of Maleperduys, during those hours he was idling under the quince.

This unnatural whispery silence continued for a considerable while, until the King finally let out such a cry that all the beasts were terrified and cowered low before him. Nobody quite knew what to do; certainly nobody dared move the head of Sir Cuwaert nor attempt to engage Noble.

Eventually, Sir Firapeel the Leopard stretched forth a tentative paw. A highly aristocratic and clever animal, and a close relation to both King and Queen, he thought Noble was being wildly excessive and, frankly, hypocritical, in his grief over that milksop wood-cat. He had, after all, just polished off several large dishes of coneys in wine-currant syrup for his dinner.

'Sire,' he ventured, 'why d'you make a such a noise? You're making sorrow as much as if the Queen herself had perished! Let this peculiar grief go and be of good cheer. It is not seemly. It is downright shameful to feel so much for that pipsqueak gardener. Are you not the Lord and King of all this land? Is not all of Flanders under your control?

King Noble groaned. Truth be told, it was more the bludgeoning humiliation of the fox's complicated treachery than the hare's unfortunate demise which had propelled his bellowing. 'But Sir Firapeel, how can I suffer this false fox, this deceiver! That scoundrel has tricked me and bewitched me and led me so far down his tangly path of lies and deceits that I have betrayed and angered my dearest friends and allies. Stout Bruin the Bear. Poor wronged Isengrim the Wolf. I am shamed by that skulking Tod, shamed, SHAMED! I have attacked my best barons, my most loyal barons, grievously harmed them, all because I trusted and believed that wicked son of the Devil, Reynard the Fox. Gente, wife, I blame you, you prayed and argued for that slippery red field-rat as though he were your own kin. Damn that bloody flea-fretten fox, damn him, damn him, damn him.'

Sir Firapeel slunk around the King. The leopard ardently believed in the superiority of lineage and guarded unpleasant and incoherent views about the seigniory of the cattish races, who, he would argue, rose in society as lightly and as surely as cream with their fine-bred, intricately recorded bloodlines, their agility, their natural sovereignty, their superiority of mind and wits. He admired Reynard, his intelligence, his aggression, his lack of subservience, but, whilst more or less accommodating foxes, wolves and bears, whom he regarded as a tolerable, if sometimes uncouth, middling class, he held little sympathy for the massed sheep and rabbits and poultry of this world. They were disposable, irrelevant, passive. Engaged entirely in the quotidian. Natural farmers and shopkeepers, grubbing about with money or manure. Their ennobled ranks might make for pleasant, even stimulating, discourse now and then; they might suggest a fruitful investment or scribe up a competent will or charter; one might even become friends with one; but their blood was still as weak as Dunkirk ditchwater, and no amount of gold or titles could change that.

He sniffed and started to wash his ears. 'What does it matter, Noble,' he purred; 'whatever is amiss, can be amended. All wrongs can be righted. Peace can be clawed back easily enough. We can make reparation to Bruin the Bear for the fur ripped from his back and compensate Lord Isengrim and Dame Erswynde for their torn feet. Moreover, to ease their distress and pain, to smooth their humiliations, which have been very vile indeed, I suggest you offer them the ram Bellin. He's already confessed his guilt in the murder of Cuwaert; he counselled Reynard and shaped the attack. He told us plain enough. Why, he carried that cursed corpse head all the way back from Rupelmonde, swinging against his heart. What a ruthless biller he is!'

Firapeel jumped up and reclined on a cross-beam, his curled tail lashing. 'And as for Sir Reynard, let's all go and fetch him together. We shall arrest him and hang him by the neck, without law or judgement, without trial. Enough is enough, the time is past for the slow workings of the law. Gallow him once and for all, and everyone will be content at last.'

CHAPTER TWENTY-FOUR

In which Sir Bellin the Ram is slain

The Feast Day of the Wrathful Saint Leutfridus,
Monday 21st June

As the Sun travelled into the dominion of the crab, red and
blazing with its gripping, pincered power, so events moved
on in the fair county of Flanders. Strawberries were ripening
in the beds by the river walk and the air was sweet with the
drift of cut grass from the fields. Furious with the fox and
even more furious with the Janus-faced ram, the King had
readily agreed with Sir Firapeel on all counts. The leopard was
dispatched to the foul-stenching prison quarters of the castle,
where, holding his nose with distaste, he untied Isengrim and
Bruin, who were thin and coughing and covered in sores.
Their cell was dank and dark and dripping with water.

'Lords,' he said, as they stretched and licked their wounds,
'I bring to you a fast pardon and the King's love and friendship. All has been resolved in your favour. He has repented
and is very sorry that he has spoken or trespassed against you.'
He stalked to the open door to get some air and examined his
claws. 'He's going to give you some excellent appointments in
recompense, probably some silver as well, I should imagine.'

He looked up, pausing before he delivered his *outrepass*, the
rare prize he'd secured, which would place them delightfully
in his debt, 'And he also wants to give to you Bellin the Ram
and,' he held up a paw at their exclamations, 'and not just
Bellin, but his lineage too, every last ram, ewe and lamb,
from now until Doomsday. In the open fields or in the green

woods, you may freely bite them and attack them and eat them without any forfeit or penalty. The King also particularly wanted me to tell you that he has granted you the rights to hunt down and do the very worst you possibly can to Reynard the Fox, and his lineage too, without any trouble from the Crown. You may trouble *him*, though, ruin him, turmoil him, abase him, torture him if you like, without being charged with a single crime. And King Noble grants this great privilege over the Maleperduys foxes for all perpetuity.'

Baron Isengrim laughed his low, husking laugh, and howled with his good fortune, dark spittle dribbling down his jaws in gleeful anticipation of the torments to come, the roast lamb suppers and the fox strung up by his brush, his home destroyed, his family killed, his foxling cubs fed raw to the wolf pack. Bruin, on the other hand, simply looked astonished at the news. Whilst he was relieved and happy at his release, he had no interest in hurting others; he just liked a nice, friendly sort of life of simple pleasures—good food, lots of sleep, jolly friends, and an exciting tale or rousing song round the fire of an evening. He shuffled away from Isengrim, whose pleasure was making him very uneasy, and reminding him not a little of Reynard's crowing over his injuries at the river that horrible Whitsun day.

'But to gain all this, you must both swear never to do the King harm, to give him your full homage and truefastness and loyalty. D'you both swear?' 'Aye,' spat Isengrim. 'Er, yes—yes, of course,' bumbled Bruin the Bear, making a hasty retreat back to his comfortable quarters in the castle before anyone could change their mind.

The wolf's descendants still hold some of these now ancient privileges, passed gleefully down along his line, through grey clan and pack, abused for centuries across forest and meadow, bog and salt marsh, and to this very day they still devour and eat the sons and daughters of Bellin the Ram. Bruin never married, however, his direct line ending abruptly with him, and he was pleased to relinquish these grisly rights. He deliberately omitted them from his will, which left his considerable estate to his nephew, Alfbern, an outward-looking cartographer who had no interest in the old-fashioned, claustrophobic court politics of his uncle's day, moving with his new-found wealth to Aix-en-Provence, to learn from a master cartographer at the university and to improve his heart, which had been weakened by youthful military service in Burgundy.

Thus was a fragile peace restored to Flanders by the machinations of Sir Firapeel the Leopard. A peace, however, which cost Bellin the Ram his tabart as well as his life. He was executed that very afternoon, watched by his poor wife and six children and a sombre line of merchant sheep from the Cloth Hall, their heads bowed in respect for their friend and colleague.

CHAPTER TWENTY-FIVE

Peace for Our Time

*Midsummer. The First Day of the Feast of Saint John
the Baptist, Thursday 24th June*

King Noble the Lion was so delighted by the restoration of
his Court that he announced a great feast, in part to mark
his renewed love for Baron Wolf and Baron Bear. It would
commence at Midsummer, on the Baptist's day, he declared,
and last for a full twelve days and twelve nights.

He sent heralds out across the entire kingdom, polecats
and weasels liveried in bright saffron with fine polished black
leather boots. Without pause, without rest, they rushed from
Dendermonde to Gravelines, from Ypres to Aardenberg, from
the Somme to the Schelde, casting invitations to every village
and hamlet, to every farmhouse, townhouse and burcht, and
soon the country lanes were eagerly bustling with all manner
of beasts heading for Gent in their very best clothes—rich
silks and samites and tinsels and taffetas embroidered with
golden grapes and meadow flowers, curling leaves and little
birds in flight—their ears and tails ringed with fashionable
amorettes and fresh green garlands of periwinkles and daisies
and damask roses and meadow wort. As night fell on Saint
John's Eve, bonfires and wakefires and Baptist fires in the
fields, on the low rises, guided their path through the darkness, beaconing the festivities ahead.*

* Back in Reynard's day, fires were always lit on Saint John's Eve and
Saint John's Day, serving to repel witches and elves and ghosties of all
shapes and forms, as well as offering a focus for dancing and celebration.

Oh, how I wish you had seen the glittering spectacle of Noble's grand fête! There was more joy and mirth and happiness that summerstide than had ever been known amongst the animals before! The Hall and Chamber were bedecked with sweet branches of orange blossom and white lilac and briar roses, and the banners and ensigns of King Noble (sable lion rampant on gold) and Queen Gente (argent lioness rampant on azure) and Saint John the Baptist (severed head in bowl on field of foliage), in equal measure, fluttered from every *échauguette* and beam and stave.

All manner of court dances were performed, which everyone, from the smallest grey goose to the largest brown bear, entered into with the greatest of enjoyment and enthusiasm. There was the wild and whirling hove-dance, accompanied by frantic shawms and trumpets and tabors. Then the graceful basse-dance, adored by the lions and the leopards, who spent many a happy hour gliding elegantly like swans about the Great Chamber, which had been laid with carpets of cloth of silver, glimmering like the moon in water under the stately movements of their paws: 'Come, come,' cried Noble, beckoning to the shyer courtiers, 'it's very easy. Three paces forward, a single, double, reprise and braule.'*

The Navarre foxes taught the younger Flemish courtiers how to dance the charming and complicated palace dances from the court in León. The *Zapateta*, the *Giraldilla*, the *Baile del Pandero* and Sir Íñigo's favourite, *Los Polos*, which made

---

* King Noble's dance can be found in *The Manner to Dance Bace Dances*, printed in 1521 and translated from the French by Robert Coplande. It was appended to a French grammar housed in the Bodleian Library and is the only treatise on basse dances known to exist in English.

everyone weep with laughter. The Navarrese dances were so successful, in fact, the spinning and clapping and tapping and making giddy continuing for so many rounds, that it reminded some of the more elderly animals in the Court of the mad dancers of the plague years, who danced and danced through the corpses and the bones and the dying, unable to stop until they too dropped down as dead as their black-sored fleabaned neighbours.

As each night drew in, torches and beacons were lit in the courtyards and on the high battlements, and floated in a slow-spinning fleet of coracles on the moat and the River Leie. On the third evening, these hundreds of little fires produced so many crackling clouds of sparks that Sir Tybert, in a drunken and whimsical mood, commented that the very air itself seemed flush with wandering stars, drifting over the trees and buildings, casting strange fates and destins on all below.

When the courtiers were tired of dancing, they reclined on thick Syrian carpets and soft feathery cushions of Venice gold, and listened to all manner of minstrelsy. Every musician and wait in the city had been commanded to play, and play they did, from sunrise to moonset, weaving ethereally, sometimes dangerously, between the carousing guests, with their lutes and psalteries, their rotes and gitterns, their pipes and harps and symphony.

The food and wine flowed without stop! The King had ordered an abundance of meat, enough for every animal in attendance. And such delicacies! Sugared almonds from Verdun! The sweetest of cherry puddings strewn with sugar and clove flowers! Pies of sparrows! Pies of blackbirds! Pies of wild duck! Bourbonnais pastry with rosewater and cream!

Lombardy omelettes coloured saffron yellow, turnsole red, spinach green!

There were plays too, and other esbatements and amusements, and pageants of such grandeur and such unearthly magic that they were recounted in many a Gentish hearth-tale over the years.

For each of the twelve feast days a different subject was chosen, some traditionally performed by the Court or the guild animals on Midsummer, others drawn quite randomly from Noble's rather lurid imagination. Despite Botsaert's urging, they had no particular unifying theme or order, but were mapped like a peculiar stroll through the lion's belligerent and discordant mind. They fell as follows.

The Hanging of Judas A gloomy and threatening opening to Noble's festivities, for reasons which will become apparent. The lion bade his barons hang up a model of a fox, wearing Reynard's usual apparel. It was generally considered distasteful, but everyone was too scared of Noble to object openly. Grimbart quietly took it down, once the King was distracted with food and a crate of violet wine brought by one of his relatives, a retired military lion from Amiens.

Leo Belgicus A lavish reenactment of one of Noble's many royal progresses around his kingdom, in which the lion bade allegorical representatives of each town and city greet him effusively and present him with local vegetables. One poor old bear had to shuffle around as a Chalice of Holy Blood—actually claret—representing Brugge's most famous relic.

The Tree of Jesse A complicated pageant, adapted to celebrate Noble's triumphant genealogy stretching back to the very first Lion of Gent, Baldwin Ironpaw, re-enacted in a series of striking tableaux, each introduced by the figure of Saint John the Baptist, pre-beheading. Grimbart reluctantly took this role, but refused 'to put any flourish in it' and stolidly stumped around each ancestral scene as though he was inspecting hulls for barnacles on a drizzly afternoon or collecting a dull civic tax on Mary Day.

Christ disputing with the Doctors Noble loved gossiping about unpleasant illnesses. Wildly misunderstanding the theological significance of the subject, he had Sir Tybert dressed up as a black-wigged Jesus demonstrating a variety of horrible sores to a group of the apothecaries' guild, their physiognomy made to look more medical with false beards and eyeglasses.

The Life of Saint Bavo A spectacle of three parts. The first, Saint Bavo as a dissolute young soldier, involved much disorganised marching around the castle and many cannons. The second, Bavo giving away his wealth to paupers, took the form of Noble, dressed as the saint in dashing black satin with silver paper shoes, giving alms rather randomly, surrounded by a group of lion cubs dressed as cherubs with peacock feathers for wings. The third was a still arrange-ment of Bavo posing in his tree-trunk hermitage, enacted principally by a visiting squirrel, Sir Rodulfus from Dijon, roped in at the last minute on account of his well-known arboreal experience.

Noah's Flood A complicated tableau enacted mid-river. To create a suitably imposing ark, King Noble compelled Lord Grimbart to fetch his boat from Brugge. Aided by the shipwrights and the water drawers and the water leaders of Gent (guilds of rough and militant voles and rats), the poor Badger was to transform that serious, working sea-boat into a fancifully festooned pleasure craft for the afternoon. Even worse, he then had to stage the timed release of an extremely nervous dove, coordinate forty pairs of courtiers playing the rescued animals, and manage the dramatic emergence of King Noble at the finale, adorned in the silvered robes and spiky pewtered headdress of a thunderous, wrathful God.

The Trials of Saint Margaret A crowd-pleasing pageant featuring a fire-breathing dragon, fuelled by barrels of aqua vitae and accompanied by the diminutive figure of the saint, played by an extremely anxious cousin of Sir Cuwaert from Ingelmunster.

The Wild Merciless Forest A dusk parade of English giants: extremely tall ferocious ones carrying cudgels, and slightly smaller hairy woodwoses with rings of dripping candles on their heads, casting noisy fireworks and squibs at the crowds. They in turn were followed by a battalion of Green Beasts draped in vines, the Court wolves dressed up as rustic woodcutters, and the only unicorns Noble's pageant-masters could scrape up at the last minute—two elderly aunts visiting Sir Brichemer the Stag from Chartres, where they lived quietly and piously as invalids next to Notre-Dame.

The Nine Worthies After discussions between Sir Botsaert and Sir Tybert so fierce and so spitefully personal that they almost agreed upon a duel of honour by the Leie to settle the matter, the identity of the Nine Virtuous Figures were eventually decided upon and their roles taken by Noble's Council, with further squabbling over who was to play whom. In the end it was agreed that Hector would be performed by Musart the Camel, King David by Íñigo the Fox, and Alexander the Great by Bruin the Bear trussed up in a very tight approximation of a Macedonian chest plate. Courtoys the Hound would enact Julius Caesar during his Gallic period, the somewhat histrionic Sir Eghel the Hedgehog would take the part of Joshua, three dozen fat grapes to be spiked onto his prickles to symbolise those carried out of Canaan, and Sir Godfrey of Bouillon, the prodigiously powerful crusader Baron of the Holy Sepulchre, would be embodied by a delighted Isengrim. Finally, both King Arthur and Charlemagne were to be portrayed by King Noble, who simply couldn't decide between the two.

The Parliament of Bees Accompanied by groaning melodies on the *vielle à roue*, what had been conceived as a light-hearted frolic would turn sour after the castle beehives were involved and a group of young weasels from Lens, dressed in gold tissue and striped hose, were badly stung.

The Fair Hope of Flanders An elegant distraction insisted upon by Queen Gente, who felt that most of Noble's entertainments were vulgar and silly. It consisted of a coterie of ten maidens, all lionesses and leopards, dressed in linnet-white pleated gowns of silk with greening branches unfurling from hollied bands around their ears, signifying the springing of Hope.

John the Baptist and Herod This was to be the grand conclusion of their festive nod to the Baptist. A highly technical representation of the decollation of the poor saint, involving trapdoors and a pulley system. However, as we shall see, despite complex preparations, events intervened, and the denouement never came to pass.

There was no beast, great or little, in all the land, that did not enjoy the wonder of King Noble's Midsummer feast. Even the seabirds from the desolate mudflats and saltings far, far to the north, even the fowl and the long-toothed boars and the amber-eyed polecats from the secretive black forests of the Ardennes. Everyone who had ever desired the King's friendship came to Gent that fair June in the tenth year of his reign.

All, that is, except for one. Reynard the Fox, the red thief, the copper-tailed outlaw, who was staying behind the stout walls and towers of Maleperduys, thanks very much, and had no intention of setting foot anywhere near Gent.

And so the feasting progressed. Night after day, day after night, they bowsed and caroused and sang and quassed and fiddled and trod the boards, up until noontime on the eighth day, the first of July, when in staggered Sir Lapreel the Rabbit, hobbling straight up to where the King was reclining on a couch. He was in the middle of eating an enormous pile of *flampoyntes*—little fried triangular pastries of pork and cheese and cinnamon—and was not best pleased at being interrupted, but Lapreel was desperate, sobbing and wailing as loud as a purgatory ghostie, his ears all bandaged up, raw scars slicing his face.

'My Lord,' cried the Rabbit, who in normal times was a calm, sensible country fellow, with a substantial network of homes scattered across the eastern Waasland, 'have pity on my complaint. It is all about the great force and murder which Reynard the Fox would have done to me yesterday morning. It was early and I was travelling to Court from one of my burrows up by Schiphoek, and my path led me right past the fox's borough at Maleperduys. Well, there he was, stood outside his door, looking just like a pilgrim, in those same old sparrow-brown robes he had on before. I supposed that I could just pass by him in peace, I was only going to the Feast, nothing else. I had no ill intent to him. When he saw me coming, though, he moved towards me, all the while saying his beads.

'I saluted him, and said "Good Morning, Reynard Fox!" but he said not one word, not one single word. He just kept walking, pawing his coral beads, then suddenly he raught out his right foot and dubbed me in the neck between my ears so hard I thought I should have lost my head. Fortunately, praise our Lady of Coneys, I am as light as a feather and as nimble as a lop, so I sprang away from him, and, with much pain and hurt, away from the grip of his sharp claws. His face went all ugly and grimmed; he was so angry that he hadn't gripped me tighter.' Lapreel unravelled his bandages. 'I escaped alright, but look, I lost one of my ears and I have four great holes in my head.' He gingerly touched his wounds. 'His nails were so sharp, the blood it was pouring out, and I thought I would die; I actually thought this is it. There was so much blood that I almost swooned away, I did, but I was so afeared for my life that I just ran for it, as fast as I could, so fast he couldn't overtake me.'

The rabbit limped closer to Noble, 'See, my Lord Sire, see these great wounds he made with his sharp long nails. I

pray you to have pity on me, and that you will punish this
false traitor, this murderer. Else no one will be able to come
and go over the heath in safety, with Reynard Fox haunting
around the place, sneaking up on animals, wielding his own
lawless rule.'

Noble, who was heavily wreathed from mane to tail in
leaves and twigs for the evening's entertainment, inspected
the weeping gashes, and thought hard about the fox setting
himself up as the king of the eastern Wastelands, and began
to assume a most thunderous look upon his painted face, like
an old god of blasted oak and splintered elm.

CHAPTER TWENTY-SIX

The Death of Lady Sharpbeak

The Eighth Day of the Feast of Saint John the Baptist,
Thursday 1st July

At that very moment, just as Sir Lapreel had finished display-
ing his wounds, Sir Corbant the Crow flew into the Hall
like a ragged, rough-torn strip of black haberjet. He landed
on top of an ornamental tree trunk, freshly painted by the
pageant committee for the Wild, Merciless Forest, and stared
around, desperately, madly, eyes as pale as milk. Corbant was
a tough bird, a noisy, sociable Zeelander whose wings were
stiff-mottled with salt and sea winds, but something was
terribly wrong.

'Dear Lords, dear Barons,' he croaked, 'hear me, hear me,
hear Corbant the Crow, for he brings today a most piteous
complaint. Early this morning, when the fields were all a-
glistening with the sun's gold, my wife Lady Sharpbeak and
I went to play upon the heath. And there we stumbled across
Reynard the Fox, lying down on the ground like a dead keytyf,
like a dead wretch, like a dead, discarded hound. His eyes
were staring and his tongue was lolling, hanging long out of
his mouth. We felt his belly, we even pecked at it, but there
was no sign of life.' Corbant stopped. He staggered a little on
his perch, and let out a low caw, a groan of terrible despair,
of sealed desolation.

'My wife, my wife, my dear wife, she hearkened and laid
her ear right next to his mouth to see if he still drew breath,
just as they tell you to, physicians and, and, priests, and, and,

grandmothers. My wife, she put her beautiful black beak next to his muzzle, and, I wish by God, by all the feathery dark angels of Michael above, that she hadn't, for a great evil misfell her. For that fox, that false, felle fox, that cunning creature, had waited well his time, and when she was just close enough, just trusting enough, he, he, he caught her by the head, and he, he, he bit it right off.'

The crow stopped and sat motionless on the pageant tree. Then he wiped a single tear from his eye with a wing, and proceeded to cry a cacophony of notes from deep within his little puffed chest, which hushed the background chatter, hushed the musicians, hushed the King and hushed the Queen. It was a lament of such unimaginable sadness that afterwards hardly a soul remembered it, for it was too painful and too raw and too dangerous to recall. The King, as gentle as he could, but curt from rage, bade the crow continue, and poor Corbant croaked on.

'I was in the greatest of sorrows, I couldn't believe my eyes! I cried out wildly and as loud as loud can be, "Alas, Alas, what is going on here! What has happened here!" Something like that, I can't rightly remember. But I do remember what happened next. That fox, he stood up as hasty as anything, and raughted so greedily after me that I trembled and quaked like an aspen, and flew up as fast as my wings would carry me, up to a nearby tree.

'What I saw from there, from that branch, was the most dreadful sight. I can barely recount it. Reynard Fox, that cold, cruel keytyf, he ate her and he slonked her, until my little wife's body had collapsed into nothingness. He was in such a vicious hunger that he left neither flesh nor bone, no more than a few tail feathers. Even her smaller feathers he slung down with her poor flesh; he gobbled them down. He would've eaten her twice over if he could. Then he simply went on his way, down that thistle street to his castle. As though she meant nothing. As though she were just mullock on his haughty paws. As though she wasn't my moon and my firmament, the companion of my branch, of the high air, of the earth-sewn field. She was my everlasting, my everlasting, d'you all hear! My everlasting.' Quite undone by sorrow, the crow began to fly around and around and around the chamber, knocking into banner and beam and wall, hurting himself, cutting himself, shedding his sloe-black feathers on the worried courtiers below. At last, exhausted, he came to a staggered, jolted halt in front of the King.

'After I watched the fox for a long time, and saw him safely away, I flew down wracked of sorrows, distraught, mourning my Lady Sharpbeak. And in that morning light, that light the colour of honey and syrup, amidst the clover and the poppies, I mantled her with my wings for the very last time, and then I gathered up her feathers—black as night they were, as beautiful as the sky. I gathered all of them up to show you, Lord King, Barons, what became of my wife.'

Corbant began to shake and he harsh-crawed again; his tears were flowing without stop now. 'I tell you all here, I would never be in such peril and fear and pain as I have been these past hours, not for a thousand marks of the finest gold that ever came out of Arabia!'

The sobbing crow then took a fan of tattered, broken feathers out of a little pouch, velvet black, close-hanging around his chest. One by one, he placed them on the stone floor. No one has placed rubies or emeralds, or the truest pieces of the Holy Cross with such care as Corbant placed the fragments of his wife that day.

And as he lay the feathers, he spoke to the King. Corbant was a wise bird, even in his distress, and he knew the path to the King's heart was not through pity, but through narcissism and the spectre of faded popularity.

'My Lord, see here this piteous work of the fox. These be the feathers of Sharpbeak my wife. You are worshipped, Sire, as our great King, the most just and noble in Christendom. If this be so, then you must punish Reynard for what he's done. You must give justice, you must minister swift judgement, you must avenge us all for this wicked crime, so the animals of Flanders may look up to you with fear and love and allegiance. Lord Reynard has become an outlaw, Sire, the most wicked of highway foxes, and safe conduct is no more in this land. We cannot travel without danger; poor country folk cannot pass quietly to their cottages, barons to their burgs, and you yourself may not even go peaceably along the highways without threat of harm. Think of my Lady Sharpbeak, but think also of your reputation, King Noble. Before God, those who do not punish thieves and misdoers and murderers are their accomplices, partners in those misdeeds and trespasses and evils.'

And having said his speech and having done his best, Sir Corbant the Crow slowly and carefully picked up the broken feathers of his beloved. One by one, he kissed them tenderly, then put them back into his little bag, and patted it with his wing. 'Safe now, my lief, my darling, safe now,' he whispered.

CHAPTER TWENTY-SEVEN

The King is sore angry

King Noble the Lion was sore mad and angry after he heard the complaints of the coney and the crow. He was so fearful to look upon that even his eyes glimmered like smith-fire in his huge Old Testament face. He raged and he brayed as loudly as a stampeding bull, and the whole of the Court, still dressed in their greenwood pageant garb, trembled in terror, their paper leaves a-whispering as they shook.

At last, roaring like a Martinmas gale, he cried, 'By my crown, and by the truth I owe my wife, I shall so awreak and avenge those trespasses that it shall long be spoken of, not just by the animals of Flanders,' he waved a branch wildly, 'but by our cousins of Hainaut, of Artois, of Holland, of Brabant. I was overnice, a fool of a lion to believe so lightly that false shrew of a fox, and let the safe conduct and my commandment of the land be so easily broken, our peace slashed by his idle claws.' Noble flung himself into his throne, leaves and blossom scattering.

'His flattering speeches convinced me. What's that expression, eh? Flattery is like friendship in show, but not in fruit? Reynard told me he was going to Rome, and then overseas to the Holy Land. I gave that fox a fine fur male and a psalter illumined with such fresh colours and much gold. I made him a pilgrim. I believed every word he said, had every confidence in him. But truth turned to treachery. O, what false touches he had, what trickeries. He stuffed those long sleeves of his with valueless fluff, words as transient and meaningless as flocks of cotton.' Noble then turned on Gente, growling like a common tabby-cat.

She stared at him with a contemptuous face and silently prepared to ignore his insults, and place her thoughts elsewhere, to the next day's diversions, perhaps, or further back to her childhood home in Toulouse, and the green, cool waters, the stony clarity of the Garonne.

'It was my wife that caused all the trouble,' yelled Noble, jabbing his paw at the Queen, his face far too close to hers. 'It was all by her counsel. I'm not the first to be deceived by a lioness's talk, and I won't be the last. What miseries and catastrophes and wars are caused by the unformed advice of females!' He leapt up and started storming around the Hall, occasionally barging deliberately into a baron or treading angrily on a tail.

'I pray and command,' he urged, as though breach-poised to battle, 'that anyone who desires my friendship, any knight dependent on me for protection or money or position, throws their weight behind me, not simply with lank chamber-talk, but with bold action to take vengeance against Reynard the Fox once and for all, so we can all live in honour and truth again—to slay that outlaw of the Wastelands, so he no more trespasses against our safeguards, our safe passage! Together, we must set free the fields of Flanders, which he has crafted into a patchwork of murderous sneak-holes and ditches. As your King, I will, of course, help in every way I can.'

Dressed respectively as a woodcutter and an English giant, Sir Isengrim the Wolf and Sir Bruin the Bear listened well to the King's words and hoped to be avenged of Reynard at last, but neither of them dared utter one word, so fierce and unpredictable was the lion that humid afternoon.

At last the Queen spoke. Nothing she had heard had swayed her against Reynard. He remained as a brother to her. She spoke in her own tongues, in French and in Latin, her fine-wrought tongues of high sun and mountain and subtlety. She had to foil her husband's vulgarity, his simple-mindedness, his belligerence, his inability to hear behind and through and around a tale, however convincing, however piteous the narrator. 'Sire, *pour Dieu, ne croyes mye toutes choses que on vous dye, et ne jures pas legierment.* A beast of worship, of God, should not lightly believe everything he hears, nor swear any oath until he knows a matter clearly. By right, he should also hear the other party speak. There are many, many animals who would convincingly accuse others when they themselves are the villains.' She brushed invisible crumbs from her immaculate kirtle, and then said in her most authoritative tone:

'*Audi alteram partem.* Hear the other party. I have truly believed the fox to be a good and truthful animal, and I do not think he meant any falsehoods. Accordingly, having such faith in him, I helped him as far as I might. But whatever happens, howsoever it cometh or goeth, whether we find he is evil or good, I think, not least for your own honour, you shouldn't proceed against him overhastily. That would be a base and a very sinful thing to do, for he cannot escape from you—you may imprison him or flay him or torture him, even, and he must obey your judgement, however mistaken. Trapped, utterly trapped.'

In the uncomfortable lull following the Queen's admonishments and before King Noble could start up again, Sir Firapeel the Leopard grasped his nettle. The complaints of the rook and the rabbit had left him unmoved. He despised their low-born sentimental hysteria, their manipulation of the Court with their ugly scars and their feathers and their rattle-bones. 'My Lord,' said he, 'I think my Lady here has told you nothing less than the truth and has given you very good counsel. You would do well to follow such wise and considered advice. If Reynard is found guilty, then by all means let him be punished according to his trespasses, hang him if you want, but only if he is found to be unquestionably, doubtlessly at fault. And if he doesn't arrive here before the feast is ended—as he should rightly do to defend himself—well, then listen to your usual counsellors. But even if the fox is twice as wicked, twice as false, twice as cunning, then we still shouldn't punish him more than his crimes dictate.'

Whilst Firapeel had been labouring his point, Isengrim the Wolf had padded slowly and silently to his side. He was determined not to let Reynard wriggle out of trouble once again and he interjected as soon as the leopard paused in his urgings.

'Sir Firapeel,' he spittled, 'I think we're all agreed, if the plan pleases the King, then it cannot be bettered.' He bowed obsequiously. 'But listen. Even if Reynard Fox was here to fight his corner, even if he was cleared twice over of all these accusations, that wretch has forfeited his life through his behaviour. I am an honest wolf, Sire, a reasonable wolf. I may be a little rough around the muzzle, I may speak my mind more than most, but today, on the matter of the fox, as he's not here to defend himself, as our Queen has so delicately reminded us, I know I should be as silent as a tomb.' He slapped a paw hard over his mouth, then slowly removed it. 'And yet, on top of these murky stories of murder and tussle, he has also told the King of a pile of gold lying in Kriekeputte in Hulsterloe, of all the God-forsaken places in this land! Pile of gold, my tail! A pile of falsehoods more like! How can I stay silent when he fables so extravagantly!'

Baron Isengrim jumped up onto the high table and began to pace up and down, growling, voice rising, knocking over wine glasses and heaps of pastries and fancies, dyed green with parsley. 'Never, never, never was there a greater liar. He hath us all beguiled with his ill-woven nonsense. He hath sore-wounded and half-killed me and the bear. I would dare my own life on him never having said a true word. He's a false-sayer, a gabber, a fabler, a leasing-monger. His very name will come to spell trickster and deceiver, mark my words. He's robbing and stealing and attacking everyone who passes his house on that heath. Nevertheless, Sir Firapeel, who am I to bend the course of Reynard's fate, whatever pleases the King, and pleases you, Leopard,' a fierce sneer, 'must be done. But, remember, that fox could easily have come to Saint John's feast, he had the knowledge from the royal messenger the same as the rest of us. He chose not to come. Why, is the question you should ask yourselves.' And with that, the wolf knocked back a bottle of twenty-year-old spun-nettle wine and sloped off, leaving his sour scent of privies and raw meat and decayed teeth clouded behind him.

The King yawned. He hadn't really been listening very closely to any of them, even the Queen. No, he'd simply been stuffing himself with more of the rich, fatty, salty *flampoyntes* and slurping great frothing tanckaerts of beer. In preparation for the Nine Worthies pageant, he'd had some of the Saint Nicholas waits, a group of elderly sheep who had retired down on the water meadows, sing the *Chanson de Roland* to him, and despite their wavering and less than heroic voices he was rather taken by the idea of a skirmish against the fox to rival the Battle of Roncevaux Pass, with himself cast as Charlemagne, *bien sûr*. The fact that Roncevaux was Charlemagne's only real defeat in years of war was lost on Noble in the stirring descriptions of glittering swords of Vienna steel and winged arrows and saddles silver-wrought. Assuming his most imperial, imperious face, the face of a toughened commander of a thousand faithful knights, he bellowed out his judgement on the matter of the fox.

'We will not fetch him ourselves, we will not send erindberes for him, but I command all those who owe me service, all those who crave my honour and worship, that they should be ready for war at the end of six days. All archers with bows and arrows and crossbows and bolts, chevaliers and foot soldiers and those with cannons and bombards and *gunnes de cupro* and *gunnes de ferro*, make ready to besiege the castle of Maleperduys. If I be a king of any kind, I shall destroy Reynard the Fox. What say you! Will you all do this with a good will?'

All the barons cheered and all the musicians cheered and the pageant committee cheered and all the hangers-on cheered. They raised their sloshing cups to the fever-eyed King Noble and to the destruction of Sir Reynard the Fox, the blazen-tailed outlaw of the eastern Wastelands.

CHAPTER TWENTY-EIGHT

In which Sir Grimbart hurries to Maleperduys
to warn Sir Reynard the Fox

*The Feast Day of Saint Otto of Bamberg, the Great Reconciler
& Diplomat, Friday 2nd July*

Deeply troubled by the King's warly threats against the Fox,
Grimbart rose before dawn, took his usual cup of steeped
hawthorn leaves, made a quick *omelette de ver de terre*, packed
his travelling male, and set off for the eastern Waasland, and
Reynard's fortress of Maleperduys.

Under a clear sky, faint-ringing with the rising and tumbling
of lark song, he followed the King's Great Highway, then the
crowded village routes, then the dusty wagon roads as straight
as hop poles. For the sake of speed, he avoided the pleasanter
tracks along the rivers and streams, and through the tangled
backwoods, and shunned the ancient ramble-ways through
bushes and hedges and haws.

He did not halt, not even for water nor to rest a little
from the sun; he just kept on going. He ran most of the way,
clutching his chest when he had one of his cardiacles, mopping
his brow from the pouring sweat. For it was a blazing July
day, as hot as the fires of hell, and you could cut the air with
a rusty blade. And as Grimbart hurried on, his mind turned
over and over the matter in paw and he sorrowed and fretted
for his dear friend.

Under his breath, he muttered to himself as he panted
along, 'Alas, what danger is a-coming for you, Reynard, what
perils. What hardnesses. What shall you become! What shall

befall you! Shall I see you brought from life to death or else exiled out of the land? Truly, you are the fiery head of all my kin, the greatest fellow of my acquaintance. My oldest friend. O brave, illustrious Prince of Foxes! You be so very wise of counsel, if unusual and unfettered in your guidance. You be always ready to help your friends when they have need. I have never enjoyed greater friendship, greater kindnesses, not even amongst my own classes. And your mind, your understanding! When you speak, you carry all before you; when you argue, you never lose. You lay your shrewd reasons out before us like the gilden scales of a dragon's tail, each point close-locked and fallen stiff-meshed to another, and we are all undone and we follow in your wake. O Reynard Fox, what shall I counsel, what shall I counsel.'

Eventually, Grimbart found himself on the yarrow heath, then at Reynard's woods, dark even in summer, where he followed the crooked lob-web-paths he knew so well, through drifts of traveller's joy and spite-faced nightshades, until, exhausted and half-weeping from worry and pain, he reached the gates of Maleperduys, where he collapsed listening to the klokka–klokka–klokka of the chapel bell.

Quite coincidentally, Reynard had also just arrived back home. He'd been down by the river for a brief constitutional and was extremely pleased with himself, as he had managed to catch two pigeons. They'd been taking their first outing from the nest, urged on by their proud parents, to see if they could fly. Unfortunately, their wings were all downy pin feathers, and far too short for flight, so they had both plunged horribly to the ground, from where Reynard picked them up, cracked their necks, and slung them over his shoulder

261

for dinner and a nice hot pigeon pie. As he skipped home, he blessed the saint of lazy hunters; would that be Hubertus, he idly wondered—he supposed so, as he remembered that Hubert was very particular about hunting etiquette—*le Grand Code de venerie*—and Reynard hadn't even killed the little birds, only put them out of their misery. Such compassion, thought the fox.

He wasn't in the slightest bit surprised to find Grimbart by the gates; he knew that trouble was brewing for him at Court, but felt a little cold and clammy inside at the obvious distress and sickness of his friend. He helped the badger to his feet and kissed him. 'Welcome! *Willecome! Bel-acceuil!* Best beloved nephew, best beloved of all of my kindred! But Grim, you're covered in sweat; are you ill, have you been running? All the way from Gent? Come in, come in! What's the news?'

After thrusting his pigeons at Nivard, Reynard took the badger, who was rubbing at his sore ribs, into a cool high chamber on the east of the castle, where he gave him barley water and an orange and held his paw, until the aches subsided. 'Well, Reyner, dear,' panted the badger. 'It's not good news, but you will have guessed that. I'm afraid you're between a stone and a shrine, old friend, a stone and a shrine, and you stand to lose not only your goods, again, your castle, but also your life, Reyner; your precious life is very much at risk once again.

'The King has sworn he will give you a most shameful and undignified death and has commanded all his folk to gather at Gent in six days, two days after his festives finish.' Reynard chuckled and made to ask about the pageants, but Grimbart glared and snuffle-snouted at him.

'You must take what I tell you to heart, lieve Reyner. It is very serious, very serious indeed, worse than before. His lords and barons are marching on the city with all their companies. Archers and foot soldiers and chevaliers and prickers and goodness knows how many in wains and wagons. And he has gunnes and bombards and tents and pavilions. He has torches, too, hundreds of them, all being made ready in the cellars; he had ordered the tallow and sticks before I left.' Reynard dropped Grimbart's paw and jumped up to look out through the narrow loophole over the woods to the river-lands—the cross-hatch of dyke and stream and ditch, their waters ribbons of flint and quicksilver and fennel in the heat. The windmills were turning slow; they look like rows of sugar cones, thought Reynard and then he let out a great sigh. He really hadn't quite expected this much bother.

Grimbart, not much revived by his tisane, carried on, his voice hoarse with pain. 'Lord Isengrim and Lord Bruin—are you listening, Reyner?—the wolf and the bear are now closer to the lion than I am to you! All that they will is done! Without question, without check! With the foulest of words, Isengrim has persuaded the King that you are a thief and a murderer. He loathes you, dear Fox, I'm sorry to say. And Sir Lapreel the Coney and Corbant the Crow, they also cast the most pitiful and heartful accusations. By Sint Pieter of Flanders himself, I am very frightened for your life. I am sick with dread, Reyner, sick.' Grimbart put his head in his paws, exhausted. He felt like a wanderer in the garden maze of Daedelus; with so many dark halkes and hurnes, he knew not where to turn.

Reynard delicately brushed pigeon plumes from his breeches. 'Puff! Pouff! Pff!' he said, sitting down next to the badger, back against the wall, and placing his paw gently on the brock's arm. 'Dear friend, is there nothing else? Is that all you're afraid of? Cheer up, old sailor! Come now, mine lieve das! Don't be downcast! We've weathered worse. The King himself and all the Court may have called for my death, but I shall triumph above them all. Soar up like an eagle, I shall. They can jangle and clatter and give counsel as much as they like, but I've said it before, and I'll say it again, Grim, the Court can't prosper without Reynard and his wiles and fine subtleties.'

PART FOUR

LYING

CHAPTER TWENTY-NINE

Sir Reynard the Fox's Philosophy of Lying

After Sir Grimbart had reclined in a companionable silence, his cramps and cardiacles slowly began to settle, his distress to ease. Through the high loopholes there began to drift stark and beautiful songs of the sea intoned by a sunning of cormorants, passing through Rupelmonde for the oily river eels and the tavern scraps and the tasty moll-fish. Some of their plainchant told of their homes in the mudflats and sea marshes of the great estuary to the north-east, of the heaving tides and the cold grey water and the moon rising over the sea, and both fox and badger were moved to tears. Eventually the singing died away, and Reynard heaved Grimbart to his feet.

'Come on,' he said, as they padded down the winding stairs, floor after floor after floor; mine-dark, lit by occasional blinding shafts of summer light. 'Let all these troubled things pass, and come down with me to the kitchens and see what I can serve you this fine afternoon. A good, fat pair of pigeons. I do love pigeon meat. So easy to digest, since their bones are half blood, they may almost be swallowed in whole. I always eat one with the other. You know, Grim, I get terrible encumbered in the stomach if I don't have light meat. I need the whitest and most delicate of viands. Always have done, since I was a cub.'

Reynard paused on the turn and looked back up at the badger. 'By the way, Grimbart, Hermeline will be delighted to see you, of course, but d'you mind not telling her anything about this, er, matter, for she would take it very heavy, d'you understand? Just don't mention it at all. She is so tender of heart, she might fall into some horrible fever or sickness from the worry. I can't risk it, I just can't risk it. Even the littlest of things goes sore to her heart, let alone, well, let alone talk of gunnes and galloping chevaliers and tents.' Grimbart nodded, 'Of course, Reyner, of course. I would not hurt Hermeline for the world.'

Reynard took the badger's paw and patted it, then started down the stair again. 'Tomorrow, early, before first light, I will go with you to Gent, I promise. If—if they let me address them, and if I'm properly heard, then I am certain that I can fable a plea which will move them as deeply as the laments of those thieving sea-marsh birds did move and weepen us. And Grim, nephew, promise you'll stand by me, won't you? As a friend ought to do.' 'Yes, truly, I will,' said Grimbart, tears pricking his eyes once more. 'All I have is yours, Reyner, my very life is yours, should you need it.'

'God bless you,' cried the fox, and embraced Grimbart, clinging onto him like son to father. 'God bless you, dear friend! If I live, by Saint Christopher, I'll pay you back and more, I promise.'

Grimbart tried to rally. 'You may well come before all the lords, Reyner, in which case, I have no doubt, that you'll be able to excuse yourself. You have your great treasury of words, your *woordenschat*,' they chuckled, 'and once you've cast 'em out in the right order, you'll be free again of trouble. None of them can arrest you or hold you until you've made your speech, until you be in your words. The Queen and the leopard secured that all for you. They fought your corner well, Reyner.'

'Then,' said Reynard Fox, 'I am glad. I don't give an Italian fig for the rest of them, but I admire the Queen. She's a very gentle lioness, very kind to me. With her help, I will, God willing, save my life again.'

And they spoke no more about the matter. By now they'd reached the wide and shallow semicircle of steps leading down to the kitchens, which overhung the dark moat, a grilled iron hatch opening up for drawing water, and casting down slops, and pulling up deliveries of flour and wine and salt and wood from the oar-rats and the night voles, and, also, of course, for riverine escapes and skin-of-the-teeth re-entrées, of which there had been an unsurprising number over the years.

Grimbart loved the Maleperduys kitchens. There were two pairs of stone-hooded hearths, with huge blackened cauldrons suspended at different heights and well-built bakers' ovens for the fox's favourite meat pies and the cubs' morning brioches and Hermeline's famous prune cakes. Pottery louvers in the shape of pouncing foxes, fitted to the roof by Reynard's grandfather, let out every last coil of cooking smoke, and a big *couvre-feu* bell meant no fox ever forgot to put the fires out at night. A battery of polished copper pans hung from the ceiling, and along the whitewashed walls were chopping boards of every size and wood, from greening birch to an old heft of yew, and an armoury of the sharpest cleavers and knives and rasps. In the centre of the room was a great oak work table, twice the width of the dining tables in the Hall and scarred with knife-marks and scaldings. By the moat-hatch sat barrel upon barrel of salted herrings—for no self-respecting Flemish fox household would ever run out of herring fish.

Arranged in red-glazed earthenware tubs daubed with pictures of chickens and geese was every conceivable tool—mortars and pestles, oven shovels, basting spoons, ladles, mallets, birch whisks, graters and sieves. A narrow winding corridor led from the corner opposite the stairs, where a series of specialist rooms lay. There was the dairy, the brewery, one of Reynard's wine cellars (barrels of malmsey and Poutou and Rochelle and Bastaert from Sanlúcar), and the Badger's favourite place to thrust a muzzle, a heady-scented storeroom just for herbs and spices. Here, were the great aromatic and medicinal herbs—fennel, rosemary, brotherwort, St John's grass, wittewort, sage, lavender, borage, tansy, dittany and meadowsweet, and all manner of the rarest and priciest spices and resins—ginger, cloves, frankincense, spikenard, pepper, cinnamon, cardamom, myrrh, mace, grains of paradise, and saffron—each kept in its own special drawer in a large Florentine chest locked with a filigree key, which Hermeline wore around her neck for safekeeping on a green velvet ribbon. Grimbart thought the cupboard smelt like the Bierhoofd Wharf in Antwerp, or as he imagined the streets of Alexandria or Damascus or Mosul. It always made him want to tar and trim and ready his boat and set sail by a strong nor'easterly to destinations unknown.

Sometimes the Maleperduys kitchens were cold and bare, with only potage and pea soup and coarse dark bread and lean scraps of bacon and dull, cheap dishes like peas-on-a-stick. Other days, in the dark depths of winter, the hearths would be all aglow, with suckling pigs and venison a-roasting and gingerbreads and pies and tarts in the ovens. This particular afternoon, however, it was full of an extravagance of summer food and much bustle and chattering and laughter. Reynard's grandmother's beautiful rust and green Ferrara bowls and platters were piled high with wild strawberries and oranges and cherries and soft white rolls and elderflower fritters, and, wearing their long starched brown aprons, working at the enormous oak table, Lady Hermeline and Reynard's nephew Nivard. The three cubs were sitting at one end, eating their *Duijtse pappe*, sweet lumpy cream, which their mother said would make them as strong and as handsome as their father.

Lady Hermeline was delighted to see Lord Grimbart, and greeted with him with warmth and kindness, and not a little anxiety, as she of course knew full well why he was there. The badger salued her with a very old-fashioned bow and ruffled the three cubs. Even in his rush that morning he had still made time to pack little treats for Reynard's family—peacock feathers left over from the Life of Saint Bavo and paper wraps of Verdun almonds (pink! yellow! gold!) for the little foxes, elegant black swan plumes and a bolt of silver tissue for Hermeline, and several bottles of the syrupy violet wine from Amiens for Reynard and Nivard.

They sat down to supper, all around the kitchen table, eschewing formality in their easy affection. Nivard had made two tasty pies from the young pigeons, and the humid air was dense with Samudra nutmeg. Hermeline served a dish of broad beans and peas with costmary to cool their blood, and they all helped themselves to the berries and the crisp-fried elderflowers and the blanche-bread, and Reynard brought in yellow butter and creamed goat's cheese, and comfits of aniseed and fennel. Each took their helpings as far as it all would stretch, and there was very little left afterwards.

As they were eating, the fox said to Grimbart, 'Look at your godsons, Grim! My Reynardine, Rossel and Reynkin! How d'you like what you see? Well, I would wager! They shall do worship and honour to all our lineage, make us all princely proud.' The three cubs were sitting in a row, their faces covered in sugar and cinnamon and pastry flakes and raspberry. They loved their father and thought he was the best father in Flanders. He never beat them or shouted at them and he played with them whenever he could. He taught them hunting and all about the stars and the weather, and he had even begun to tell them the secrets of some of his tricks and subtles.

Right now, across the table, Reynard was in full and em- barrassing parental flow to their beloved old god-badger. 'They're beginning to all do really well, Grim. They're so clever, VERY MUCH cleverer than their contemporaries, so quick to pick things up. Reynardine caught a great fat chicken the other day, and Rossel a young pullet. And they've also learnt to duck right down into the water after lapwings and dive-fowls! I would like to begin to send them out into the woods and fields for provand, but I need to teach them how to keep away from danger—traps and gryns and men and the forest-ghosties. Once they become a bit wise, specially the older two, they'll bring back so many different viands, I dare say, even ones we've never had in the castle before, eh!' Reynardine and Rossel started shouting out silly animals— 'Griffins!' 'Phoenixes!' 'Elf-worms!'—and giggling so much that they fell off their stools.

'And you know, Grim,' Reynard continued, welling up a little, 'they like and follow me so well. They have Hermeline's wits alright and not a little of my cunning. They can pretend to be all grimming and angry when they're playing and then, when they hate with a fury, they are the very visage of merriment and friendliness! With all these tricks and wiles, they bring their bewhaped prey right under their feet, and bite their throats asunder!' Reynard beamed. 'This is the nature of the fox, though, Badger. Cunning. Can't change that or go against the laws of God and the angels. But my little ones, oh, they snatch as swift as fox-fire, and talk twice as fast as that!' Reynard shouted over to them, 'You please your father very well, you three, very well indeed!'

Grimbart, whose pain had returned, smiled as best he could and nodded, and when Reynard had finished said, 'You may be glad that you have such wise children, Uncle. And I am very glad of them also, as they're my god-foxes.' He mopped his brow and winced. Hermeline rushed over with some cold hippocras. The badger looked terrible, sick as sick could be. She hoped it wasn't the plague with all this rushing around the countryside. She had heard rumours from some of the otters of there being a case or two up in Mechelen; a new graveyard was being dug, they'd said, always a bad sign.

'Grim, you're sweaty and so weary, it is high time that you were at your rest,' urged Reynard, quickly, trying to damp down his old bleak fears of Grimbart's mortality, not to mention the sharp needle-pricks of conscience at his not inconsiderable role in causing his heart-grip in the first place. 'Oh, Fox, dear, yes, I think a nice rest would do me some good,' panted Grimbart.

They helped the old badger up to a bedroom high in the east turret, where the air was fresh as the sea and greened with the scent of scythe-grass and meadowsweet, and laid him down on a litter made of straw, and covered him in a cold white linen sheet. He smiled up at them and thanked them, and fell into a deep sleep. And Hermeline and her little ones went to her wide bed of white poplar and walnut veneer and goose-feather mattresses and red velvet coverlets. But whilst Reynard went to his bedchamber, he was unable to rest. Despite his reassurances to Grimbart, he was exceptionally worried about everything. He fretted and he fevered, he tossed and he turned, he sighed and he sorrowed about what he should say, how he should spin out his excuses, and how on earth he was going to wriggle successfully out of this particularly knotty tangle.

Nevertheless, very early the next morning, just as he had promised, Reynard, sallow-eyed from lack of sleep, left the safety of his castle and set off to Gent with Grimbart.

First, he took leave of Hermeline and the children, bravely swaggering around them, lifting Reynkin high in the air, solemnly asking Reynardine to protect Maleperduys from invaders and Rossel to check the locks at night, and embracing his wife as though she were as precious as saffron, as fragile as a little finch.

'Don't think too much about me whilst I'm gone, my dears, I must just visit the Court for a short while with your godfather. If I tarry there, do not be afeared, and if you hear any ill tidings, then please believe the best, for no harm shall befall me, I swear. And look after yourselves, and keep the castle well.' He held Hermeline again and whispered, 'I shall do the best I can at Court, darling, my sweet honeycomb, and we shall see where we are after that.' 'Reynard,' she whispered angrily back, 'why have you taken it upon yourself to go there again? The last time you were in Gent, you were almost gallowed, Fox-lief! You were within a whisker, A WHISKER, of the hang-rope! Dreadful, dreadful peril, Reynard Fox! And you pledged to me by all the saints that walk this land that you would never, ever go there again!'

'Hermeline,' said Reynard, 'as you have often told me, the machinations of Fortune in this world are strange and mysterious, her wheel is turned by gerishness and chance, if not cruelty, and many a time things are taken from our very paw's grasp by one of her caprices. And, more often than not, we believe something will go our way, and quite the opposite unfolds, and vice versa. But, dear lady, not all is determined by Fortune, nor by Providence above—we animals, we foxes, can be our own cause of well and woe, our own saviours too. Now I must go, but be content that it is all without dread, that I will do my best, and that I will be back within five days, no more.' And with that, Reynard left and Hermeline went back into the castle, and entrusted the cubs to Nivard and spent the rest of the day trying to be brave and distracting herself by reading Chrétien de Troyes, sniffling at the scene where Sir Yvain, the Knight of the Lion, bids farewell to his wife Laudine to adventure with Sir Gawain.

Reynard had been persuaded by Grimbart to go against every foxish instinct and take the fastest and most straight-forward route to Court. The same route the badger had travelled the previous day. Reynard reluctantly agreed and they found themselves amongst a prattle of folks heading about their country business—indeed, all manner of animals were afoot that lovely bright morning. Bakers, powdery with the morning's flour; butchers in blood-splattered aprons; brewers gathering nettles and yarrow; rattling, jangling tinkers; pompous-faced toll-collectors; masons wheezing with stone dust; and haywarders measuring hedges.

When they were padding across the heath, Reynard said 'Grim, since I was last shriven, I'm sorry to say, but a few more things have, er, cropped up. Given the circumstances, I do believe I must confess my sins once again.' Grimbart steeled himself; there couldn't possibly be as many as last time, he thought to himself, doubtfully, fishing in his bag for one of the fresh strawberry *darioles*, dainty custard tarts, which Hermeline had given him to keep his strength up. He offered one to the fox, who thus began his solemn shriving with his chops covered in custard.

'Oh dear,' sighed Reynard, 'where to start. I suppose I made that bear, Bruin, have a great wound on his back for my pilgrimage male, my scrip, which was cut out of his skin. And then I made Isengrim and,' his voice quivered, but the normally sensitive Grimbart, still maunging his rich cake, didn't notice, 'and his wife, his wife, Lady Erswynde the Wolf, they took her little feet too. I placated the King with a great snarl-sheaf of lies and persuaded him that the wolf and the bear would have betrayed him, even slain him, which, of course, made him right wroth, right furious with them, which they certainly didn't deserve.' He paused as they pushed through the hawthorn hedge to the highway, scrabbling across the dyke down to the bustling road.

'I also told the King that there was a vast treasure in Hulsterloe, by that dismal lake called Kriekeputte, the one by that unlucky avenue of black poplars. Of course, he was neither the better nor the richer for it, as I was lying in every-thing I said, every word an untruth, Grim, every single word. And there's worse. When I claimed I was going to Rome to see the Pope, I led Bellin the Ram and little Cuwaert the Hare with me, but we came back to Maleperduys instead.' Reynard stopped to take a sharp pebble from his foot. 'And he had an attack of his consumptives, but I killed him. I bit his throat. I don't know if he would have died anyway, but I certainly slew him. And I sent his severed head,' Reynard shuddered, looking behind him for thin grey chattering ghosties, 'I sent his head to King Noble the Lion, in a very scornful way, carried, without knowledge by Bellin, in that very same scrip made of Bruin's fur.' Grimbart groaned, 'Oh Reyner! What a thing to do!'

Reynard nodded curtly at the passing miller from Temse, a very portly boar who was taking some sacks of flour up to Sint-Niklaas in his wagon. Grimbert frowned at the fox, gave the miller a friendly wave and time of day, and asked after his daughters, of whom there were twelve. 'Carry on, then, Reyner,' he said when the wain had rattled far enough away.

'What else? Oh, yes, I dowed that rabbit, Lapreel, between the ears, and almost took his life, but he's so swift of foot, he escaped—very much against my will, I have to admit. I sup-posed that maudlin old rook might complain about me too, as I ate Dame Sharpbeak his wife, and very tasty she was too. Don't look at me like that, Grim, I don't care. Both of them are awful, always complaining and glooming about everything.'

It was still very early, but the sun was getting hot and they sat for a little while and rested under a broad oak tree, listening to the last sweet notes of the Lady Bells ringing out over the sheep pastures. 'Also,' said Reynard, chewing on some grass,

'I forgot something the last time I was shriven to you. An incident, which I've been thinking about and fretting over. I really need to get it off my brush, Grimbart. It was right deceitful of me.' 'Go on,' said the badger, leaning back and closing his eyes.

'I was walking with Isengrim away in the west, between Houthist and Elverdinge.' 'Near Ypres?' asked the badger. 'Yes, that's right. We were on the King's business, delivering letters and gathering some gold and attending a few banquets with some merchants. You can imagine the sort of thing. Anyway, the wolf and I had just come out of the forest onto a rough trackway. It was early October, and very muddy, I recall, and there was a strange feeling along there, like someone was going to pounce on you, like you had to keep your wits about you. So I did.' Reynard helped himself to another custard tart.

'A little further up the road we saw a beautiful red mare, accompanied by a good, fat black colt or foal of about four months old. Isengrim was half-starved for hunger and he begged me to go up to the mare—for she would less likely run from a fox—and ask her if she would sell us her foal.' 'Ha! Not likely! A mother sell her own child!' exclaimed Grimbart. 'Quite,' said Reynard, 'but I had a plan, so I ran up to the mare and just plain asked her. Loudly like, so the wolf could hear. She looked at me hard and then said yes, she would sell it. I asked how much, and she replied that the figure was written on her hind hoof. "If you're one of those clerks or scholars who can read, you may come and see and find it out," she said.

'I understood precisely what she was up to—and admired her for it, incidentally—and I says, "No, no, I can't read, plain and unlettered, me! I don't want to buy your little horse, either, it's that long streak of drear lurking over there by that rock, that miserable-looking wolf, Isengrim. It was he who sent me hither, and wants to know the price and all." "Let him come over here himself, then," said the mare, snorting, "and I'll let him have a peek."

'I hastily went back to Isengrim and said, "Look, Eme, if you want to eat your belly full of this colt, then you had better go over there quick before she changes her mind. She says the price is written under her hoof. I would have read it myself, but, you know me, the opposite of my Hermeline, can't understand a single letter. Unlearned, that's what I am, much to my regret. I never went to school, you see. In short, then, my dear Wolf, if you want to buy that foal and you can read, then I should think it's in the bag, so to speak."

"'Of course I can read," said Isengrim, very snootily. "I know all my letters. I'm fluent in French and Latin and English and Dutch. I went to Oxford, no less. I have been in the audience when very old and very ancient doctors have given their venerable opinions and arguments, their pleas and sentences, and have given my own. I am licensed in both laws, the civil and the canon law. Whatever manner of writing an animal can devise, I can read it as perfectly as my own name. Now, you wait here, Reynard. I shall go over and retrieve the price. As a scholar, it will take me no time at all." And he swanned over to the mare, black cap a-flapping, a-fronting all Oxonian, as though he were Walter de Merton himself!

'I heard the mare say the same to him as she had to me. "The sum of the money stands written on my hoof." Then the wolf cried, "let me read it then!" And she lifted up her foot, which had been newly shod with curved iron and six strong nails, and she kicked him hard, with a true aim, straight in the head, so hard, in fact, that he fell down as though he were dead. Anyone could have ridden a mile or two before he got up again, I could have strolled to Elverdinge and back.'

Reynard chuckled and Grimbert, still with his eyes shut, resting against the tree, tried very hard not to smile.

'The mare, she trotted away with her colt, leaving Isengrim lying badly hurt and wounded. He was bleeding and bleeding from his head and howling like a hound. I went up to him and pretended complete innocence, as though I hadn't been watching like a sparhawk. "Sir Isengrim," I says, all solicitous, "how are you now? Have you eaten enough of the colt? Is your belly full? But why give me no part of it? I did your errand, didn't I? Why that face, Wolf? Have you been sleeping your dinner off? I pray you, tell me what was written under that mare's foot? What was it? Prose or rhyme? Metre or verse? Come on, I must know! I think it was cantum, an unusual ecclesiastical melody, for I heard you sing from all the way over there. You were right, Isengrim, no one could read that scription as well as you."

'Isengrim, spitting blood, heaved his body up and growled. "Alas, Reynard, alas! Leave your mocking! I'm so foul arrayed and sore hurt that even a beast with a heart of stone would take pity on me! That bloody horse with her long leg had an iron foot. I thought the nails were letters and she whacked me at the first stroke. Six great wounds in my head! It's almost cloven! Letters carved in this manner I shall never desire to read again."

'"Dear Uncle Wolf," I said, "have you been telling me the truth? I am flabberghasted! Amarvelled! I had you for one of the most learned scholars that ever did live! For the wisest clerk in the whole of Oxenford! But now I know it is true what I have long since read and heard, that the best scholars are not the wisest of beasts. Indeed, we lay-people, the great unlearned and unlettered, I would wager, are much more advised and learned in the ways of the world. For you clerks, you study so much of conning and science, endlessly learning by rote and repetition, that you become slow and dull-witted."

'Thus, by the dark woods of Houthulst, that strange gloomy place, I tricked Isengrim, brought him such hurt and harm that he barely escaped with his life.'

Reynard stood up and stretched, and shielding his eyes looked across to the distant river curving through Lokeren below. 'Well, Grimbart, that's it. That's all of 'em. I've told you all of my sins that I can remember. Whatever befalls me at Court, and I simply don't know what will happen, I don't feel so afraid now, for I am clear from sin. I gladly come to mercy, Grim, and receive penance from your counsel.'

Grimbart sat up and sipped fresh medicine from his flask— to calm his heart, Nivard and Hermeline had mixed him a very strong and complicated concoction of diamargariton, made with ground pearls and water lilies and red roses and myrtle berries—and he thought for a while.

'Your trespasses have been great, Reynard, dear, but nevertheless those who are dead must abide dead. There's no changing that. We must be pragmatic. And therefore I will forgive you all your sins. I do hereby absolve and asoil you.' The badger stood up and brushed himself down. 'Really, though, Reyner, the most hindrance you'll have in your case will be that you sent poor Cuwaert's head to the Court—that was a very cruel and very rash thing to do, and, of course, you also blinded King Noble and Queen Gente with all those foolish lies. Equally stupid, in my humble opinion.'

Reynard linked arms with his friend and they set off along the highway. 'Badger,' he said, in a philosophical voice, 'what is Life after all? We animals walk through the world as you and I walk down this white, dusty road—we hear many things and we see many things, but what, pray, is the true nature of experience? To understand, to interpret and to recount all one hears and sees is a slippery, crooked affair. It is difficult to comprehend Life in its wildered midst, and no one animal's account ever quite mirrors that of their fellows.

'Complexity, ambiguity and the continual pull between God and the flesh—that is our lot on this earth. How should one handle honey, they say, without licking his paws? I am sometimes roared and pricked at by my conscience, telling me to love God above all things, my fellow Christians as myself, to act always according to what is acceptable to God himself, only in line with his law. There's been a many a time when that inner reason has fought so fiercely with my outward will, like two giants wrestling on a cliff, that I have stood still thinking I might have lost my very wits—my thoughts are churning and wilding, and I don't even know what's ailing me! But of course, Grim, I have been fresh-shriven of my trespasses now, I have left them all behind me, back by the poplars on the way to Sint-Niklaas, and I can say with perfect honesty that I truly hate and adjure all things that are sinful.'

They were passing the pleasant hamlet of Bergendries, on the high ground, just before the crossing over the River

Durme. The day had become one of great beauty. The landscape was green and golden and lusty, with the sweetest of birdsong and the lazed hum of bees. A gentle breeze stirred the corn and the leaves and the blood of the fox and the badger, who beamed at each other with the simple joy of being alive on that glorious morning. But, listen close, Reynard has more to say on the nature of Being.

'You know, Grimbart, sometimes, when I am alone, I have a special grace bestowed upon me, and I climb in high, lofty contemplation above God's commandments, like a hawk soaring above the sea. But a short while afterwards, when the world comes swift for me and I find myself thick in the chittering crowds and the busyness of it all, thrust out of my solitary retirement, I find so many stones and rocks blocking my path, so many damned obstacles. I end up following in the crooked foot tracks of those lax, thin-lipped prelates and rich, snoot-nosed priests, miraging redemption but leading to nothing but strife and a tip-tumbling into the quagmires of this sinful realm. And, just like that, whoosh, I am taken again. In floods the world and carries me away in its dirty waters. My will is quite lost to it again. Oh, the flesh wants nothing more than to live for pleasure. It lays before me so many delicious delights that I lose all my good thoughts and moral purposes. I am beguiled and bewitched by songs and pipes and laughing and playing and all the mirth that this fleeting life can conjure.

'And, *bien sûr*, I hear those lax, thin-lipped prelates and rich, snoot-nosed priests preach one thing, but think and do entirely the opposite. In this way, I learnt swiftly how animals lie, Grim. I learnt the lies most used in the noble courts of

Flanders and Burgundy, Brabant and Hainaut. For the biggest liars are not only the priests, but the lords and the ladies, and the scholars too. Nobles live out entire lives mantled in falsehoods. Nobody dares tell them the truth anymore. If they have a fault or defect of character, if they have badly sinned, then both their inferiors and their fellows say to themselves, "I must flatter and I must lie also, or else I shall be shut firmly outside the door," and they doff their caps and spin their obsequious fables.

'Almost worse than these bare-faced fawners, however, are those animals who broadly tell the truth and rightfully so, but then fabricate a lie linked to their purpose. They weave it into their argument, more or less skilfully, to make their case seem fairer or more convincing, or simply to add ornament and colour to their rhetoric. This lie often enters their speech rashly, thoughtlessly, on the turn of an idea, falling into the matter unwittingly. A well-clad falsity, in other words, slips easily into a bed of truth.'

Reynard fell silent as they crossed the river, and took some wine from his red leather bottle and one of the venison-and-sage sausages packed by his wife. But his blood was up and he continued as soon as he'd wolfed down his meat. Grimbart was interested, enthralled even, by his ideas and encouraged him warmly to continue.

'So, dear Nephew,' intoned Reynard, raising his feathered cap to a passing gaggle of geese and goslings heading to market who hissed nastily back at him, 'all animals lie here and flatter there, and menace and implore and curse. Always, always pressing hard upon the feeblest and weakest points of their fellows. How otherwise can one flourish in the world without devising the fairest of falsehoods and bewimpling them with kerchiefs in such a way that they lie undetected in the rich folds of an argument, and animals take them for the truth. This, my friend, is the only way to escape a life enslaved to others.

'If a beast can be subtle and wily in such a way that he doesn't falter in his words, and is heard in a bold flow and a flourish, then that beast may work veritable wonders! He will wear bright scarlet and soft gris! He will win in whatever business he has! Triumph in both spiritual and temporal law!' Reynard reached for another sausage.

'There are many scoundrels in this world who get in a terrible state about grasping and clawing hold of great privileges and advantages. They think they have a talent for lying, that they lie well, and they make a habit of their falsehoods. Those sorts of animals always think they deserve the best and fattest morsels for themselves, but are never actually trusted or believed or properly listened to. You know precisely to whom I refer, Grim!' Grimbart nodded, with a wry smile.

'And then, of course, there are those who are so foolish that when they are pronouncing away, gesticulating wildly, and come towards the grand finale, the denouement of their case, they get completely muddled and drop and tangle the threads of all their lies, one after the other. They simply cannot help themselves. They leave their arguments without tail nor head, and are reckoned by all for a fool, and are mocked and derided. Any more tarts left, Grim?' 'Just the one, and some rather hard pears,' said the badger, passing them over. They had just reached the Doorgangstraat turning, where Reynard had almost been gallowed, a night which

Grimbart was hoping he might forget in the fervour of his diatribe, so, again, he persuaded him to keep going.

'Now,' continued Reynard, 'the animal who can give to his lie a firm and well-crafted conclusion, who can pronounce it without stammering or stumbling over his words, as though it were written before him, who can so blind his audience that his lie is better believed than the truth, now *he* is the animal, the king of liars, the fabler par excellence!

'What skill and honour, or perhaps stupidity it must take to simply tell the truth! How these tricksy gabbers and false sayers laugh to themselves as they sly-cobble together their lies and release them into our fair world.' Reynard leapt up, dashingly, onto a milestone (10 miles to Gent) and shouted to the sheep and the carts rumbling by and the embarrassed Grimbart trying to hush him. 'They turn night into day! God into the Devil! Flax into gold! They make unright go above right! Lies above truth! They write bills and libels and rolls and letters and insert things that were never thought nor said! They teach animals to see through their paws! Men through their fingers! And why? All for money! They put their tongues out for hire to maintain and strengthen their falsities! Scoundrels and shrews, the lot of 'em! Lying well is an evil cunning, Grimbart, mark my words, it causes nothing but trouble, nothing but hurt and misfortune, and death, yes, even death!'

Reynard was swigging rather liberally from his bottle of wine, and a small crowd of passers-by had gathered around his rock—some voles, felt-makers, carrying piles of colourful hats, a couple of bored donkeys, a small procession of pious ermines on their way to Sint-Pieters and a boar covered in very painful looking sores, who started to clap when he thought the fox had finished. Grimbart helped his friend down, shooed everyone away and, arm in arm, Reynard a little unsteady on his feet, they set off once again.

'My old friend, I cannot deny that witful animals must jape, bourd, mock and, more to the point, lie in small things, for those who only speak the truth, they get nowhere in this world. Nowhere, Grim, nowhere. There be many that play placebo, play the flatterer, the sycophant. They tell their lords whatever they want. Half of Noble's Court, I'd warrant. Whosoever always tells the truth, they find so many obstacles and lettings in their way.' He gestured at a wood-rotten old cart lying abandoned in the road. 'And some of us may lie only when it's needed, and then afterwards amend it all with counsel from our fellows.' He smiled at Grimbart. 'No animal is beyond redemption. Mercy is available for all trespasses, for all our sins, including lying. There is no beast so wise that he doesn't do stupid things now and then, after all.'

'Goodness, Reyner, dear, no obstacle on earth could block you!' exclaimed Badger. 'You with your through-seeing eyes. You see behind and under and right round the back of words, so you do! You grasp the core of things at their narrowest, their faintest, their slightest! You see form in the shadows, in the gloaming, in the cast-gloom, as clear as noon. Your reasoning passes my simple understanding; you leave me far behind, my friend, far behind. My wits are a mere sparrow to your hawk. You don't need me to shrive you, to absolve you, Reynard! You could shrive yourself! By rights, you should be the priest, and let me and all the other sheep come to you!

You know the state of the world so well that no beast can play false in front of you!'

All this talk and philosophising had sped their journey, and as the badger was talking they entered the gates of Gent, and making swift passage through the bustle and stench of the fish market soon came walking into King Noble's Court. There were no guards; everyone of a menial status was far too busy with preparations for the Parliament of the Bees pageant. They passed the group of weasels from Lens being fitted for their striped costumes. There wasn't much excited chatter; everyone had rather wearied of Noble's festivities by this point.

Reynard's wine had worn off by now, and he was trembling not a little, and sorrowed and sore-fretted in his heart. He was scared this time, really scared. But, being the fox he was, he braved it out, and striked forth through all the gabbering, pointing, gossiping courtiers until he came into the inner chamber where the King was holding court, playing chess with Sir Firapeel on a table piled with delicacies.

Kind, loyal Grimbart was always by his side. A presence of such goodness and such solidity, he could not fail but calm his friend. 'Be not afraid,' he whispered to Reynard, squeezing his paw, 'make good cheer! Adventure favours those who have courage, *mon oncle! Audaces fortuna juvat, timidosque repellit!* Fortune aids the bold, but repels the timid! Very often, the events of one day can be better than a whole year!'

Reynard looked at Grimbart with rare, unmasked love. 'Grim, all of this is very true, very true indeed. God thank you, old Brock, you comfort me so well.'

And so Sir Reynard the Fox went forth, his travelling cloak flowing behind him, his handsome brush copper-gilt and black and chalk, the colours of the heath by Maleperduys. As he stalked through the throngs, he looked fiercely from side to side, daring the courtiers to question his presence there, daring them to question his God-given nobility, his God-given right to speak, to defend himself—'What will you! Here come I! Here come I!' he seemed to say with each glance.

Many of his kin who were there wished him but little good, and muttered and swore and spat as he passed by—Sir Pancer the Beaver, the otters, and many others; Grimbart counted ten at least—but we will return to them a little later on in our account. Dotted amongst the fox's enemies and *adversaires*, however, there were those, too, who loved him.

So, into the lion's den went brave Reynard Fox, and he fell down onto his knees on the fresh-strewn meadowsweet in front of the King and began to speak.

CHAPTER THIRTY

In which Sir Reynard the Fox
excuses himself before King Noble

The Tenth Day of the Feast of Saint John the Baptist,
Saturday 3rd July

Reynard began as he meant to go on and assumed an expression of which Saint Bavo himself would not be ashamed. 'O God, from whom nothing may be hidden, who is mightier than all things, than all of us lowly beasts, I implore you to save my Lord the King and my lady the Queen, and to give them the grace to know who is right and who is wrong! For there are many in this world who seem otherwise outward than they are within. Their mask belies the corruption beneath. I would that God would openly show every animal's misdeeds, and that all their sins and trespasses were written across their foreheads, even if it cost me more than I now can say.' Reynard sighed.

'And I would that you my Lord, my King, knew how loyally I have conducted myself both early on and later in your service. If only you knew everything I have done for you. And yet I have been bombarded by accusations from evil rascals, with whose lies I am cast out of your grace and good opinion, and undeservedly charged with great offences, accusations which go against all that is good and right and just.

'Therefore, I, Lord Reynard, do cry harrow against my false accusers; I denounce all their lies, the lies which have caused me so much trouble. I hope, indeed I know, that both you my Lord, and you my Lady Gente, are so wise and so discreet that you would never be led astray or believe such lies and false tales. It's simply not your way. Therefore, dear Lord, I beseech you to cast the bright rays of your vast wisdom upon my case, every aspect of it, every deed, every word, every speech. All I desire is that you punish or pardon each animal according to what is right, according to the laws of Flanders. Before I depart this Court, all shall know who I truly am. I am quite unable to flatter and will always show quite openly, more than most, the workings of heart and mind, the truth cradled in the matter.'

Reynard stopped and bowed his head solemnly. The entire palace was still. The chatter had stilled, the malicious mumbling, the minstrels' music, the preparations for the masque, all had stilled. Everyone stared at Reynard Fox. No one could believe it. He spoke so stoutly, with such courage and austere elegance. The King, however, was having none of it, and who, frankly, could blame him?

Noble blew his nose noisily and then moved a bishop and took Firapeel's knight. 'Ha—Reynard,' he said, 'how beautifully, how prettily you present your salutations, and all your bloody lies, but your fair words won't help you now. Before this day is out, I think you'll be hanged by the neck for all your evil works. But, I won't rebuke you, I won't chide you much. Instead, as your compassionate king, I shall shorten your pain. You have shown us how well you love us with your conduct towards that rustic young rabbit, Lapreel, stealing his ear, trying to kill him, and murdering and eating poor Corbant's wife, Lady Sharpbeak. Terrible affair. Your falsities, Fox, and your false intentions will lead you straight down the gallows path again.' Noble sneezed.

He was suffering from very bad hay fever, which was not improving his mood. 'A pot,' he blazed at Reynard, 'a pot can only go so long to water, without coming home broken! I think your pot that has so often deceived us is most certainly about to crack.'

There was a pause as everybody thought about King Noble's metaphor, imagining Reynard as a large broken pot. Reynard himself was very much afraid of the lion's words. Oh God, he thought, I wish I was anywhere but here. Paris, Lyons, Genoa, London, Reims, Ypres. Anywhere at all. I wish I was in Cologne, sitting outside a nice friendly tavern having a nettle beer or perhaps in my great-uncle's farmhouse near Rouen, with some chicken stew and a big bowl of sugary burnt teurgoule. Then he looked up and caught Gente's eye. She faintly smiled at him, a ghost of a smile, but nevertheless a smile. And he thought to himself, 'Rally, Fox, rally; just keep going.'

'My Lord, the King,' he said in his most determined and grave voice. 'There are many reasons to hear my words out. I may be damned to death, yet you should *still* hear my words out. In the past I have given you much good counsel. Profitable, valuable. And in need, I have always stood by your side, when other beasts have walked away, gone off and deserted you.' Reynard turned around to look pointedly at Isengrim, who was sitting looking daggers at him from across the crowded Hall. 'If those evil beasts have sharp-battered you with so many lies that it is impossible for me to present my excuses amidst the debris of my reputation, then ought I not be able to complain? In the past I would have been heard again. In the days of your father, and grandfather, I would have had my turn. Can things not change, and return to the fair and gentle courtliness of old Flanders?'

King Noble harrumphed and took Firapeel's other knight with his Queen. The leopard yawned; he was letting the lion win, and very boring it was too.

'And all my good deeds of the past should be marked and remembered.' Reynard sat up in a very proper, very upright and very old-fashioned way—tail curled, ears pricked, paws close together—reminiscent of the more formal style of the Burgundian courts and, as such, cocking-a-snoot at the lounging Noble and his barons. 'I look around here today and see many of my lineage, many of my oldest friends standing around as though they don't even know me, as though they set very little by me.' There was a good deal of uncomfortable shuffling at this.

'But nevertheless,' the fox went on, 'I know that many of them would be most upset, their hearts would ache and ache and ache, if their King should wrongfully destroy me. And in doing so, incidentally, he should destroy the truest servant that he has in all his land, for not if you walked all the way from Zeeland to Bapaume would you find a more faithful fox.'

King Noble signalled for yet more gallons of his never-ending Rhenish wine and turned another pawn into a queen. He was still deliberately not looking at his treacherous, pleading subject from the Land of Waas, who should, by all rights, be dead and buried deep under the Doorgangstraat by now.

'Sir King,' argued Reynard Fox, 'would I really have returned from my safe and impregnable fortress to the dangers of Court, knowing myself guilty of any feat or breach of the law? Would I really have come to stand trial in front of a veritable storm of all my gathered enemies? Nay, Sire, nay. Of course not. Not for all the red gold in the world. I was free. Free! Free and at large! Why would I come to Gent? God be thanked, I know myself so clear and innocent of all misdeeds that I can dare to come out into the bright, searing daylight of the Court—and the Court, moreover, in the great bustle-midst of all its festivities'—Reynard waved a paw at the many bee-embroidered banners and sticky heaps of honey cakes and dripping casts of honeycombs and flagons of ambery mead already laid out for the Parliament of Bees, 'and openly and frankly answer to all the complaints laid against me.'

'When Sir Grimbart first brought me tidings of all my troubles and the fierce accusements against me, I was in a terrible state, half out of my mind with worry and care. I started to wildly pace up and down, and then leap here and leap there, and rip my fur out with my teeth, as though I had gone quite, quite mad. Had I not been under all of the censures of the Church, cursed and banned and excommunicated and everything, then I would have come straight to the palace without any tarrying whatsoever, but instead I went to the yarrow heath by Maleperduys woods, and sat mournfully under a willow tree, quite distraught. I was so upset, I didn't know what to do.

'And then, quite coincidentally, Mertyn the Ape, my dear uncle, happened to be walking past, on his way to Sint-Niklaas. A great theologian, a very impressive animal, much wiser in canonical matters than many here present. He's been the advocate for the Bishop of Cambrai for nine years, in fact.

'Anyway, he caught sight of me in my fit of weeping, and hurried over and cried, "Dear nephew, what *can* be the matter, you're not well in yourself! Very ill, indeed, I'd say, very ill! Tell me, what is ailing you? What has displeased you so? Things that cause so much distress should be shared in knowledge with one's friends! A true friend is a great help! He can often give much better counsel than one can oneself, mired as one is in the stagnant fen of a problem. Yes, sometimes, when charged with burdens, one is so heavy and so encumbered with them that one cannot even begin to find the remedies, and sinks down into the darkest of sorrows, as though one had quite lost their wits."

'I replied: "Dear uncle, you speak the truth, very much so. I am in exactly the position you describe, weighed down with misery and so many dilemmas, I can't see the bush for the thorns. Despite being wholly innocent and undeserving, I have been put in a position of enormous danger, and by an animal to whom I had always been a great and magnanimous friend. I refer to that rabbit, Lapreel, who came to see me yesterday in the morning, as the bells were calling matins across the fields, and I was saying my prayers in the cherry orchard, just next to my house. In my paw, I believe I had my coral beads, which my dear departed mother acquired on a pilgrimage to Aachen. The coney told me that he was just off to Court, and he greeted me in a very friendly way, and so I returned his salutations. Then he said, 'Good Reynard, I'm very weary and very hungry, d'you happen to have any meat?' And I replied, 'Of course, of course, come in, dear Lapreel.'

'"We went into my manor and I took him to the kitchens and gave him a couple of slices of Hermeline's best manchet—bread as white as snow, made of the finest flowers of wheat—and the sweetest, creamiest butter. It was a

Wednesday, you see, when I try not to eat any flesh. And also I was fasting, of course, because Whitsun was approaching. For those who will taste of the highest of wisdom—the loftiest plains of what we foxes like to call *wisehede*—and live according to the spirit, to the ghost rather than the flesh, keeping the commandments of our Lord, they must fast and make themselves ready for the High Feasts and the Holy days. *Et vos estote parati*—You must be ready."'* Pleased with the insertion of this very apposite, godly reference into his narrative, Reynard briefly grinned at his captivated audience, who were all busy trying to piece together his new account with that of the wailing Lapreel a few days past.

"'Oh, such delicious white bread I gave that rabbit, really it was, and that butter, so rich, so yellow. If an animal was really hungry, it would hit the spot very quickly. Very tasty indeed.

"'But, things took a sudden turn for the worse. When Lapreel had eaten his bellyful, then Rossel, my middle son, asked very politely if he might have the leftovers. Young cubs are always so very hungry. But when he put out his paw to take a slice, that nasty rabbit punched him in the mouth! So hard that it knocked out one of his teeth! It bled and bled and my poor little one fell down in a fainting swoon! When Reynardine, my eldest, saw what had happened, he sprang at Lapreel, and caught him by the head, and would have killed him, had I not rescued him at the very last moment. And how

---

* Reynard, who had an excellent memory for quotations, is citing Matthew 24:44: *Et vos estote parati quia qua nescitis hora, Filius hominis venturus est*, 'Therefore you too are ready, because in the hour you do not imagine, the Son of man will come.'

d'you think the coney repaid me? By going for Reynardine next, and thrashing and beating him sore!

"'Lapreel then has the nerve, the absolute nerve, to run pelly-melly all the way to Court, to my Lord the King, and declare that I, Reynard, tried to murder him! Him! See, see how I am placed! False words brawling my name like storm-drops, laying a trail of blame in his slanderous twist-lies! And yet he complains, and I complain not!'" There were a few gasps at this point. Reynard was beginning to unsettle some of his detractors, casting doubt over the rabbit's somewhat wild and shaky account of the same events. But he had a lot more work to do, and he knew it.

"'After Lapreel had run away, up flies Sir Corbant the Crow, cawing and railing in the most lamenting of tones. I came hastily to the gates when I heard his cries and asked what ailed him. 'Alas, my wife is dead,' he wailed, 'there's a dead hare lying yonder full of maggots and flies, and she ate so much of it that those foul worms have bitten her throat in two.'

"'I asked how that could have happened, it seemed rather odd to me, but he wouldn't speak another word and just flew away, leaving me standing, staring after him." Reynard shrugged. "And now he's saying that I was the one who bit her and slaughtered her! But how could I even go near the lady? For she has wings and can fly, and I can only go by foot! There you are, you see, dear Mertyn, this is how I am hounded and despised and slandered. Oh, I am indeed a very unhappy and ill-starred fox. But perhaps it's all on account of my old sin? If that's the case, then I wish I could just learn to patiently suffer it all."

'The Ape sighed and shook his head and said, "Reynard, you need to go to Court straightaway to clear your name in front of all the barons."

'"I'm terribly sorry, Uncle Mertyn," I said, "that's not possible. The Archdeacon put me in the Pope's curse; he excommunicated me, all because I counselled Isengrim the Wolf to leave the monastery at Elmare, to forsake the religious life, which wasn't suiting him, and forsake his habit. He had told me that he lived so narrowly, so sternly, so austerely as a monk that he couldn't bear it any more. All the long fasting and continual reading and chanting and singing. It was just too much. He couldn't endure it. He told me if he had to live a moment longer, he would just die. Simply curl up and die. I felt very sorry for him, very worried for him, and advised him as a true friend to leave Elmare and return to his old life.

'"How I regret that concern now, for now he labours against me, persuading the King to have me hanged. Thus, he returns evil for good. D'you see Mertyn, how I am at the end of my wits and out of ideas and counsel. For I must go to Rome for an absolution, but if I do journey there, then my wife and my three children will be in terrible peril, and will be shamed and attacked and goodness knows what else. For these evil beasts who hate me will do to my little family all the hurt they wish to do me—they will torture them and drive them out from their home, from the Waasland even. I could defend them if only I were free of the Pope's curse, for then I could travel to Gent and excuse myself and explain what really happened that day. But I'm so afraid, for if I go in front of godly animals in my current state of exile and sinfulness, then I fear that God will punish me and plague me!"

"'Nephew, nephew, nephew, don't be afraid, I won't leave you to suffer in your torments a moment longer. Look, my dear Fox, I know the way to Rome extremely well. I'm an old Italian hand, Reynard, I understand how all of this works. I know everyone and they know me. I know the puppetmasters and the players and the audiences. I know their tricks and their cunning wires and where the bodies are buried, so to speak.

"'As I've said to you before, I'm very well known about San Pietro as the Bishop's clerk. I'll tell you what I'll do. I'll just accuse the Archdeacon. He runs the courts, all that legal stuff. I'll fire off a plea against him, and before you know it, Fox, I'll come back with a nice, clean, shiny absolution for you, no questions asked. The Archdeacon won't dare go against it, he has too much to lose. My Uncle Simon dwells in Rome, you see, he's extremely wealthy and powerful. He helps anyone who can, how shall I put this delicately, slip him something of interest. And he's fast—he'd do it *aussitôt que*, immediately.* I have other contacts, too: friends, allies, associates all over the city, in every holy house from Santa Croce to San Pancrazio—Prentout, Wayte-Scath, to name just a couple of fellows. I'll need to take some cash with me, of course, a small sack of marks should suffice. I may not need any, but a pocket of coins certainly adds a certain heft to a petition. The course of justice, of righteousness, is always helped along with a scatter of silver. A true friend put his life

---

* Martyn the Ape is referring here to the practice of simony, the buying or selling of ecclesiastical or spiritual benefits, especially the sale or purchase of preferment or office in the Church. In medieval texts it is frequently written with a capital, as a result of its continuing association with Simon Magus, after whom it is named.

and his money and his all worldly goods on the line, and so shall I for you, Fox, so shall I for you.

"'Now make good cheer, Cousin. I'll set off tomorrow, and I won't rest until I arrive in Rome, where I shall solicit all your matters, smooth them all out like a beaver's hat. So off you go to Gent as soon as you can. All those misdeeds, all those sins which swept you under the Pope's great curse and sentence—I'll take care of them all myself. Don't even think of them. And when you get to the palace—and this is important—go and seek out Dame Rukenawe, my wife, her three sisters, our three children, and the rest of our family. You can speak to them all in complete confidence, they're very discreet. My wife, particularly. She's immensely wise. A thousand times cleverer than me. And she'll gladly do anything for her friends. Any animal—any *sympathetic* animal —in need of help will find great friendship in Lady Rukenawe. Always remember, Reynard, to seek out your friends, even if you might have once angered them. Kin will always struggle on, no matter the difficulties—crawl through the very mud in service, if it can't walk upright. Remember that, Reynard Fox, when you're in Gent.

"'If you find yourself in an even worse situation where the charges are coming thick and fast, and you are not being properly heard, and justice is not being carried out, then send for me by night or by day at the court of Rome and let me know what's happening. I'll be with the Bishop. I'm easily found. And I shall bring the entire festering palace of Flanders under the Pope's curse should I need to—king or queen, lord or lady, mouse or lion, it makes no matter to me, nor, I can assure you, to San Pietro. What is more, by return of messenger, I shall issue an interdict, forbidding all ecclesiastical actions. All of 'em. No priest of Gent, no animal, shall read nor sing nor christen cubs nor bury the dead nor receive any sacrament until my dear old friend, Baron Reynard, is given the treatment he deserves. Everything grinds to a halt, the singing bread is silenced, until justice is restored to King Lion's den. Where justice is not, the most fertile land becomes barren, so they say. Well, I shall speed that barrening, Fox, with one word from you.

'"The Pope, of course, is so old and decrepit that no one pays much attention to him anymore. It's the Cardinal Puregold who holds all the strings, who grips the might of the court. He's young and virile, with hundreds of friends, a beautiful mistress whom he adores. Whatever she desires, she gets with a quick tap-tap of her curved claws. She, dear Fox, is my niece, and so whatever I want is swiftly granted also. I have a considerable deal of influence in these circles, a great deal, so you can press King Noble for justice, and be assured that you have the whole of Rome allied behind you. He'll not deny you.""

Reynard paused with his account of the ape's visit. The entire Court was staring at him with their mouths as wide as Saint Amalberga's fish.*

'My Lord, King Noble,' he said, measuredly, 'when I heard all this, I laughed and with a heart full of gladness, rushed

---

* Saint Amalberga of Temse (b. c. 741, d. 10 July 772) was venerated across Flanders, particularly by the river animals. For she was known for miraculously crossing the River Schelde on a giant fish, the largest sturgeon in the Low Countries. Her relics are kept inside the little church of Temse close to Reynard's castle, Hermeline often popping in to pay her respects.

to Court, where I have faithfully recounted the unwemmed truth. Things have changed, Sire. The wind blows sweet and strong from the south. If there is any other animal here today in this chamber who can lay further charges against me, produce sound witness, and prove the matter as it ought to be proven in the case of a noble fox, then let me make amends according to the law. If he still pursues and grapples me after that, well, then, set the day and set the place, and if he be my match in birth, then I am happy to fight. Whoever's the victor, whoever wins the worship of our battlefield, then that shall prove the right or wrong of the matter. This is how the law has stood since the time of Baldwin Ironpaw, and it should not be broken by me! Law and Justice do no animal wrong.'

When the fox spoke so stoutly and plainly, there was a stillness and a stealing fear among the gathered animals, as though they could hear the faint bells of Rome, as a mistle thrush hears the muffled jangling of a sparrowhawk in the wildering dew-mists of a Michaelmas morning.

The rabbit Lapreel and Corbyn the Crow were so sore afraid that they didn't dare speak a word, but crept out of the Court as quickly as they could, making their way to the empty water meadows to try to make sense of it all. Isengrim and Bruin both saw them go, the wolf scowling at their cowardliness, the bear nervously wondering if he should follow their example.

Down by the irises and the tall reeds and the dark lap-lap of the Leie they felt a little safer and they both started to hop around and exclaim as one: 'God grant this foul, evil murderer of a fox may get his just deserts! He wraps and wreathes and covers his lies so that his words seem as true as the Gospel!

No one knows this better than us! How can we find good witnesses? The only witness is dead! It's better that we flee than we should stay and get mingle-mangled in a field-fight with him. He's so shrewd and cunning, if there were five of us, we couldn't defend ourselves. He'd slay us all before we'd even drawn our iron.' And they nodded at each other, crow and rabbit, and awkwardly embraced as brothers scarred and bonded forever by foxish wounds, and then returned to their quiet country seats away from the dangers of Lord Reynard of Rome.

King Noble had listened quite carefully to Reynard whilst finishing his game. Unusually for the lion, had a moment of clear perspicacity—undoubtedly aided by the intellectual cold drench of the chess—and had decided to take the fox's Italian threats with a very large grain of salt. He stretched, one great paw, whoomph, another great paw, whoomph, and then yawned in a very lionish way, showing his long, sharp, yellow teeth.

'If any courtier wants to complain against Reynard, they'd better come forward sharpish, and we'll hear them out,' bellowed Noble. 'There were so many of 'em yesterday, where are they all now Reynard's here, eh? Scuttled away, I don't doubt?'

'My Lord Lion,' said Reynard in a very grave voice, 'there are many animals in this castle who are happy to point the pen feather or the clawed paw in my absence, but when they actually come face to face with their adversary, me, they keep as still and silent as a lich-rest. Look at Lapreel the Coney and Corbant the Rook, moaning and groaning to you when I was back home in Rupelmonde, but now I'm come into your presence, as bold as a bell—nothing! Gone! Fluttered away!

Bavo knows where! Daren't stick by their words! And if folk should start to believe these rascally liars and troublemakers, then good, honest animals are the ones who will suffer. As for me, I don't listen to scoundrels; I neither believe them nor indulge their games.'

Reynard fished his fancy scarlet rosary beads from his cloak and began to smooth and play with them absentmindedly. 'Nevertheless, Sire, if you commanded my detractors to apologise and beg forgiveness from me, then I would, as a loyal subject, I suppose, regardless of the weight of their trespasses, for your sake, pardon them. I am, after all, a most charitable fox, and never hate nor complain about my enemies. Instead, I place them firmly in the capable hands of God, so that He can work and avenge and grind down as He sees fit. As its pleases Him. Better God to judge and punish than a humble old fox from the eastern Wastelands.'

The King had moved over to his throne, which was almost entirely hidden by grand swathes of Italian velvet in beely, drumbledory colours—soot black, brun-burnt gold and a pollenish yellow—and garlanded in orange blossom and woodbine. Noble's temper, however, had not been ameliorated by his honeyed surroundings, and he was as cross as a wasp.

'Reynard, you look as grieved as you say, but are you within, as you seem outward? Are you, Fox? Are you, you red-faced witherwin! Things are never as they seem with you, Reynard! I have learnt that much over the years. None of this is as clear or as straightforward or as open as you have presented it. And I am obliged as your rex and your kine-lord, in the old tongue, to tell you a few things. I start with my own grief, which is considerable and waxing as we speak. Your very life and honour are at stake, d'you hear me, eh?'

(When Noble was in this ferocious mood, he often started to resemble his grandfather, Baldwin the Just, who was a terrifying lion, keen on torture and grisly executions. Some of the elderly courtiers remembered him and his bloodlust well, and shuddered bone-deep at the likeness.)

'Reynard Fox, you have committed foul and shameful misdeeds. When I had pardoned your string of loathsome offenses and trespasses, you promised you would go abroad, first to Rome, then beyond-sea to Jerusalem on a pilgrimage. I gave you that magnificent scrip, sewn from Sir Bruin's oiliest and blackest and thickest fur. And what d'you do with it, eh? You send it back to me, by that merchant ram, Bellin, with the head of Sir Cuwaert the Hare of Oostveld stuffed inside it. That poor little chap! How dare you! How dare you, you miserable flea-bitten scarlet shanks! You could not have performed a more reprovable, a more reprehensible crime.

'You dishonoured me, Fox, shamed me in front of all my barons and ladies. Is it not an act of extraordinary evil to send to a King—your liege-lion—his servant's head! Evil and treason are pretty damned close together and you can't wriggle out of this, Lord Tod, for we heard the whole, miserable tale from Bellin—once our chaplain, now decorating the gates of Gent with his skull. Such was the reward *he* had when he brought your message. You'll get the same, if justice follows its rightful course.'

Reynard gulped. His brush slipped between his legs. His heart began to pound in a heavy angular sort of way, saw-edged and ragged. For the first time in his life, he did not know what to say. Reynard, a fox of thousands upon thousands of eloquent utterances cast together in different combinations of truths, half-truths, falsehoods and subtleties. Reynard, who had glossed his way out of every hole and tight place, wielding words as deftly as any sword. Reynard, whose *raison d'être* was shuffling the shift-layers of meaning of a word, of a phrase, of a tale. How many things can one foxish sentence shake into being? How many can it evoke simultaneously to different ears? Oh yes, Reynardian rhetoric is a delicious and dangerous confection, a crackling *millefeuille* of signification and soothfastness rooted in a single belief—that a fox can only ever be a fox, should only ever act according to his God-given vulpine nature and those who disagree deserve all the obfuscation and trickery a tod can throw at them. Understand that basic truth and you understand a great deal about Reynard.

But every animal, even a linguistic genius of a fox, has their breaking point, and this, for some reason, was Reynard's. Perhaps it was the unmoved Noble or the thin, grey ghost of the hare, but he simply could not grasp another word to utter. And so he began to shake, as he had done once before, but this time emptied of every last coin of word-gilt as surely as if he'd been stung in a tavern gamble. There, in front of the carved thrones of Flanders, before the King and Queen in all their might and ceremony, he stood, as mute as a swan. He was at his wits' end. He looked about himself piteously, searching out many of his kin and allies, but they, who had heard all, said nothing either. He was as white as a shroud, but no one proffered a paw to help him.

The King leaned forward and growled at him, 'You crafty, subtle fellow. You false scoundrel. Why don't you speak. Have you been struck dumb?'

Grim-faced, marble-faced, Reynard the Fox stood in his great dread, blinking up at the lion—without his unsurpassed eloquence, he was nothing. He was doomed. A shorn Samson, his strength lost, the blindness of the dead before him. And sunk in these gloomy thoughts, he sighed, a great sigh which echoed around the Great Hall. All heard it, all felt a twinge of pity—all, that is, except for the wolf and the bear, who were very, very glad.

CHAPTER THIRTY-ONE

In which Dame Rukenawe the Ape
answers for Sir Reynard the Fox

Dame Rukenawe the Ape was not best pleased. She was an old and intimate friend of Gente, and knew of the Queen's affection and sisterly concern for the fox. Rukenawe, in turn, appreciated Reynard's fire. She had fought her own way up from a comparatively humble start in life. The daughter of a wealthy vintner from Brugge, she had entered the béguinage of Saint Elizabeth as a young ape, passing her girlhood in an austere but benign world of gilt candlesticks and blanched linen and long woollen cloaks and boxwood hedges and constant singing, which also offered the rare opportunity to plunge into much textual study. There she also met the young Hermeline, and together they pledged to dedicate their lives to scholarship, to gramarye and learning.

Hermeline was particularly interested in comparative philology and what she termed 'the aventure' of translation, which she saw as a perilous journey over the gaping chasm between two languages, a gulf that could be bridged or leapt, but never filled or closed, and with each passage, each transfigured word, endured the subtle fractures and fissures of meaning and signification. Rukenawe, on the other hand, developed a fervour for the intricacies of law, both civil and canon, for which her quick-wittedness and sagacity were well suited.

Everyone was always glad of her presence, and indeed Reynard was very fortunate that she was there, not simply for her considered and well-trenched wisdom, but for her eloquence and strength of argument. Unlike most of the other courtiers, she knew exactly when to speak and when to stay silent, not for the sake of courtly etiquette, but for the furtherment of her own interests and plottings.

Rukenawe stood up. She always dressed simply, but had a love of jewellery, pierrerie and proud gems, which she often used to convey the subtexts, the faint intimations and underwords which flowed beneath each of her legal cases. Today, she wore a pendant formed of an onyx cameo bust of Minerva wearing an elaborate helmet and surrounded by enamelled forget-me-nots and odd-shaped rubies the pink of lark's foot flowers. She spoke directly to Noble and she did not mince her words.

'My Lord the King, you ought not to be angry when you sit in judgement. It does not become your noblesse. An animal who sits in judgement should put from themselves all wrath and anger. Anyone who sits in justice must have discretion and discernment. I may be a she-ape, but I know the points of the law better than those who wear furred gowns and hats. I am an expert in both branches of law, having studied them in depth for many, many years.

'When I was visiting the Pope's Palace at Woerden, I had the finest bed of sweet hay, whilst all the other creatures had to make do with the hard, cold, miserable ground. Whenever I desired to speak, I was heard first and listened to with the greatest of care, because of my intimate knowledge of the law.'

She regarded the King and sniffed in a superior manner.

'Seneca writes that a lord should administer justice, do what is correct and proper, across his kingdom. He should charge no one to whom he has given a safeguard above the right and law; he must never step outside the clear bounds of his jurisdiction. And the law ought not to halt for no beastie. Anyone who does wrong should be repaid for his wrong, and there should be no favouritism.*

'If every courtling present here this afternoon thought hard on their past days, on their past deeds—performed an honest review of what they have done, what they have been driven to do—then they would certainly have a great deal more patience and pity for Reynard the Fox. Let every animal know himself or herself, that is my counsel. There is no one who stands so surely that they cannot fall or slide. Of course, a fellow who has never sinned, nor committed a misdeed, is bright and holy and good, and has no need of reparation. But when an animal does do something wrong, something amiss, then makes amends through prayer and counsel, that is precisely as it should be. However, if a beastie persists in wrongdoing and trespassing without showing any remorse, without any form of self-reformation or correction, then that is truly evil, a life of scorch-marked devilry, in fact.'

Dame Rukenawe turned to address the room. Everyone was silent and carefully listening. If truth be told, they were all a little scared of her.

'Mark well what is written in the Gospel—*Estote misericordes*—Be merciful. Have pity. Have clemency. But wait, there's more—*Nolite iudicare et non iudicabimini*—Damn no one, and you shan't be damned yourself.† I would also like to remind you all of how the Pharisees once brought in an

---

* A reference to Colossians 3:25: 'But he that doeth wrong shall receive for the wrong which he hath done: and there is no respect of persons.'
† Luke 6:37: 'Judge not, that ye be not judged.'

adulteress and would have stoned her to death, had not they asked our Lord first what His thoughts were on the matter. As I hope you would recall, He cried out that "He who is without sin among you, let him cast the first stone."* Not a single Pharisee remained standing there after this devastating remark; all of them had some awful sin or other that they immediately thought of, and so the poor, terrified lady was left alone and unharmed.

'I think we have a very similar tale at Court today, unfurling before us, with the fox as the main player and, I shall argue, the victim. For there are many here that see a straw in another's eye, that cannot notice a hulking baulk of timber in their own.† And there are those too who judge others, when they themselves are by far the worst. If one falls and falls and falls, but picks oneself up, and comes to mercy, then they are not damned! Far from it. God rescues all those who ask for help, who desire His mercy.

'Let no animal condemn another, even if the accused has plainly committed the worst of crimes. Instead, we must turn to our own faults, and correct those first. If we adhere to this simple precept, then Sir Reynard the Fox should not be treated harshly, he should not have to suffer. And we should not forget, either, that his father, Lord Reynardius, and his grandfather, Lord Rodevacht, have always been far more loved and respected in Flanders and in this Court than Isengrim the Wolf or Bruin the Bear, or any of their kin for that matter.'

* John 8:7: 'So when they continued asking him, he lifted up himself, and said unto them, He that is without sin among you, let him first cast a stone at her.'
† Matthew 7:3. 'And why beholdest thou the mote that is in thy brother's eye, but considerest not the beam that is in thine own eye?'

Both Isengrim and Bruin cried out at this slur. But one thorn-sharp look from an unsmiling Dame Rukenawe, and their cries lowered to grumbles and then tailed off entirely. They were both quite aware that it was impossible to win an argument with the brilliant ape.

'There has always been the most unfortunate contrast between the wisdom of Reynard and the honour and glory he has brought to the Court and to the fair county of Flanders, and the idiocy and ill-considered counsel of the bear and the wolf, for they have little grasp of how the world turns. This Court itself is upside down too, in my opinion. The scoundrels, the shrews, the flatterers and the deceivers rise up effortlessly to yet more exultant heights, advanced to the highest ranks, their power and influence waxing as the flood-fields creep in Zeeland, whilst the good, the true and the wise are cast down, for all their stout advice and loyalty and hard work. There's no rhyme nor reason to it and I can't see how this can carry on for much longer. Something is rotten in this Court and needs rooting out.'

Rukenawe nodded at the King and then sat down on a wooden stool carved with angry-looking angels next to the Queen. Noble sighed and thought a little.

'Lady Rukenawe,' he said, at last, 'if Reynard had done the same to you as he has done to others, you would be just as aggrieved, I can assure you. Is it any wonder that I hate him? He regularly breaks my safeguards, without a thought for the consequences. And have you not heard all the petitions and complaints against him? Murder. Theft. Treason. Do you really have such trust in him?' He jabbed a paw towards the chapel and began to shout.

'You think he's so good, so clear from sin, as innocent as a new laid egg, then why don't you set up an altar to him? Eh? Why don't you worship and pray to him like a saint? Saint Reynard of Maleperduys! Ha!'

Gente beckoned to her husband and whispered something angrily, and he whispered something back, then swiftly quietened down and tried to look a little more sympathetic to Rukenawe.

'Look,' he said, 'I have no quarrel with you, Lady Ape, but you must understand that there's not a single animal in the world that has anything good to say about Reynard. You can protest on his behalf as much as you like—praise him till Judgement Day, if you want—but you'll find out in the end, as we all have, that he's worth nought. That he's an utterly worthless fellow. He's so corrupted, so caught up in his criminal racket, his scams and schemes, that he has no kin nor friends who can or want to help him. I marvel at your support of that fox. I never heard of anyone who fellowshipped with him who ever thanked him or said anything good of him afterwards, except for you, Rukenawe, except for you. He's always striking them with his tail.' For emphasis, Noble enacted a vicious swipe of a fox's brush.

And where was Reynard during this intimate assassination of his character? Just where we left him. Frozen, shaking and mute. Sitting on his haunches like a painted papier fox from one of the King's masques. Attended by Grimbart, who did his best to help without making matters worse.

The ape walked over to him and placed an elegant hand, laden with toadstone and sapphire finger rings, gently on his back. 'My Lord King,' she said, 'I love this fox, and hold him in great fondness. I also recall an unusually good deed he performed in your presence, of which you may not know, but could profusely thank him, though things have turned and twisted so much since. In the end, to balance the push and pull, the ups and downs of friends and enemies, I would suggest that temperance is the path to follow. We must love our friends in a measured fashion, and not hate our enemies too much. Howsoever the world turns and Fortuna spins her wheel, steadfastness and constancy should be the watchwords of a noble. One should not praise the day, until the evening has come. Good counsel is only spent well on him who actually follows it.'

And having delivered her succinct aphorisms, Dame Rukenawe of Brugge sat down on her stool again, took a good long draft of her mead, which was made from black honey and borage, and began her tale of a Man and a Serpent and Reynard's Good Deed.

CHAPTER THIRTY-TWO

The Story of the Man and the Serpent

'Once upon a time, about two years ago, a young man and a serpent came to this very Court to seek judgement. The serpent, an adder, brown and lozengy, had found himself stuck in a hedge. He had meant to slither straight through, but had been caught in a snare by the neck so tightly that without help he wouldn't be able to escape and would certainly lose his life.

'The young man happened to pass by, however, on his way to Desteldonk to visit his sweetheart, and the snake cried out to him, "Please, I beg you, help me from this trap or else I'm afraid I shall die here, in this here hawthorn hedge!"

'The sun was shining and he was in love, so the kind young man took pity on the glint-eyed serpent and said: "If you can promise me that you won't envenom or poison me or do me any harm or hurt me in any way, then, yes, I shall help you out of your peril and release you from your snare." The adder was ready for this and he swore a great and solemn oath that he would certainly not, under any circumstances, hurt nor do any harm to the young man whatsoever.

'Somewhat gingerly, as you can imagine, the young man unloosed him and delivered him from the hedge. He slithered gratefully out and they accompanied each other along the road for a fair number of miles. However, as the midday bells rang out from village and abbey, the adder's belly began to grumble and rumble. He hadn't eaten all day and, reminded of his dinnertime, he was suddenly overwhelmed by a ravenous hunger. Without warning, he turned and violently struck at the young man, as though he wanted to kill him. The poor boy stumbled backwards, terrified. "Are you trying to slay me, serpent!" he gasped, "Have you forgotten the oath you just made, that you wouldn't harm me in any way?"

"'I am sorry," replied the adder, "but the whole world would understand why I did that, and think it reasonable and right. The great necessity of hunger may cause both men and animals to break their oaths. That is the way of things."

"'I disagree!" cried the shaken man, "I disagree most ardently! And I would ask you to give me some time to find someone knowledgeable who can settle this between us! Someone to judge who of us is right and who is wrong!"

'The snake, flushed with an unshakeable belief in the hegemony of hunger, readily agreed his request, and off they trooped to find some arbitrators for their argument. After a while, perched in an ash tree on the Oude Veldstraat, they found Tiecelin the Raven and his son, Slyndpere. The young man and the serpent presented their respective cases and the two birds listened from their branch. Tiecelin, fatalistic as ever, immediately agreed with the serpent. "He should have eaten the man," he pronounced, "I would've done and my son Slyndepere would have had his part too." "There you are," said the adder, puffed with success, to the man, "I've won, wouldn't you say?"

'The young man shook his head. "No, no," he cried, "it's well known that this bird and his shifty son are robbers; we can't just listen to them alone. We need some other opinions. There should be two or three other judges together, judges who are well versed in rights and laws and can administer a sentence with enough weight behind it. No, I don't accept

Tiecelin's pronouncement—with his dubious character, it simply doesn't hold up."

'The adder reluctantly agreed and they set off again on their search. Eventually, outside a run-down tavern in Hijfte, they came across Isengrim and Bruin having a couple of cool river-ales together in the balmy afternoon sun. They related the matter in full, but unfortunately for the young man the same conclusions were swiftly reached. Both bear and wolf judged that the serpent was right and should kill his companion. For the need of hunger in the animal world surpasses everything else, even an oath—it trumps all such promises.

'Hearing this judgement, the snake started moving towards the frightened young man, spitting and casting his venom like a fountain of poison. The young man managed to leap away just in time, falling and hurting himself in doing so. Lying on the road, he shouted up at the adder, "You're doing me a dreadful wrong, lying in wait to attack me. You have no right to do so!"

'"The case has been judged twice! I have every right!" hissed the adder straight back at him.

'"Judged," retorted the man, "by two animals who habitually lie and rob and murder! Who break every oath and promise they ever make! There's only one thing to be done. I will appeal this matter in a court before our Lord the King. You can't forsake a judgement given there. And I pledge that I shall abide by whatever conclusion is pronounced—I shall obey and suffer it, whatever it may be. I won't do anything even slightly contrary to it, I swear."

'Having moved on to the nightshade mead, the wolf and bear made no objections and said, "Yes, yes, we agree, let that be so, whatever you want," and the serpent said that he desired nothing better.'

Lady Rukenawe adjusted her pendant. 'You see, King Noble, they all assumed that if the case were to come before you, then you would automatically side with them; it would all go exactly as they wanted it to. I believe you must remember this very well yourself.

'Everyone came to Court to present their arguments. If you recall, it was a bit of a procedural mess to begin with. The wolf brought two of his children with him, Emptybelly and Neverfull. Isengrim was readying them to eat part of that poor young man—offered them a leg apiece. They howled and yowled for hunger, in a noisy, unregulated cubbish way, and you commanded them to be taken out. D'you remember it now?' Noble humphed and nodded.

'The young man stood there in great dread, trembling like a rose blancmanger and calling upon your great grace and wisdom, King Noble. He told how after he had saved the snake's life from a tight gryn, the ungrateful adder had tried to kill and devour him, after solemnly oathing not to harm him in any way.

'The serpent spat back immediately, "I have not trespassed, though, that is precisely my point and I shall account for myself wholly before the King. I did it to save my life. For need of life one may break an oath or promise."'

Rukenawe cleared her throat and took another swig of mead. 'My Lord, that time more than any other, you and all your counsellors were sorely troubled and tangled by this case. Burdened by its moral complexities. For, on the one paw, your noble grace was profoundly moved by the great sorrows and sufferings of the young man and could not bring yourself to sanction a death sentence in exchange for his gentleness and generosity to the serpent. And on the other, the stark import of that snake's hunger and the urgent need to preserve and continue life had also to be heeded, of course. The Court was, not to put too fine a point on it, in an impossible stalemate, a philosophical snare which was proving as difficult as the adder's to escape. There was nobody in Court who could see a way out. Some animals favoured the young man; I see a flutter of them over there,' she gestured at a cluster of kindly faced otters and ermines leaning against a stone pillar in their new yellow velvet breeches. 'Others supported the serpent'—she looked disdainfully at the wolves chewing their bones in the back. 'The only thing all could agree upon was that there seemed to be no way to decide the matter.'

'King Noble, you then commanded—do you remember?— Sir Reynard the Fox, my dear nephew, to come to the front and give his advice. At that time he was very well thought of in Gent, and was heard more, and, indeed, believed more than anyone else. Everyone thought him very sage, a bit of a brass-tailed Solomon. You bade him give judgement, Sire, and assured him that we would all follow him, without question, for he had proved many times how well he knew the deep grounds of law.' Rukenawe stood up again and went to Reynard's side.

'And this is what Reynard said,' she continued, smiling briskly and encouragingly at the still-shivering Fox, 'and it was quite, quite brilliant.'

'"It's not possible to give a true and fair verdict," said he, "just from their spill of words—for lies are always lashed tight into the fabric of language, unravelling and hard-knotting the thread of truth. But, if I might see, with my own sharp eyes, the serpent in the same peril, the same desperate need he was in when the man found him and unloosed him and unbonded him, then I would then know exactly what to say and how to pass judgement on this difficult case. Taking any other course of action would be going against what is right, transgressing against Dame Justice herself."'

Rukenawe examined her rings. 'Then you, Lord King, said to him, "Well spoken, Reynard Fox, we are all in agreement with you; no animal could say better."'

'Is that so,' mumbled Noble, 'well, well, well.'

The ape smiled briefly and carried on with her account.

'Off went everyone to the tangle-hedge on the Oude Veldstraat where the young man had come across the trapped adder. And Reynard asked that the snake be put back into the snare, in exactly the same strictured position it was in before. And it was done. Then, Sire, if you recall, you asked the fox, "Reynard, what do you think? What judgement will you give, now we're here looking at old zaggle-skin in his noose?"

'Reynard replied as follows: "My Lord, both man and serpent look just as they did before. We have folded back the hours as smiths fold red iron. Neither has won, neither has lost. Sire, please notice how I will aim to file-shape—to forge—a right and fair judgement to please your Noble Grace.

"'If the man now wants to unbind and unloose the adder from its trap, upon the same promises uttered earlier, then he is free to do so. However, if he thinks that he will be troubled and venomed again, if he thinks hunger will provoke the serpent to break his word and strike, my judgement is that he is equally at liberty to simply walk away. In which case, he would leave the snake still latched in his snare, as he might have done right at the beginning, when he first passed him on the way to Desteldonk. Or the young man might yet save the serpent a second time from certain death, but, as before, he could very well attack him and drop his oath againward like a hot crab apple.

'"This I think is the rightful judgement, which you and the Court have searching for, Sire. The young man shall have his free choice once more, just as he had bright and early this fair and innocent morning."'

Dame Rukenawe moved in for the kill. 'Both you, my Lord, and your wise counsellors, who were also in attendance at the hedgerow denouement, were impressed by Reynard's ingenious and practical ruling. You followed it, without question, and praised the fox for his wisdom in justly giving the gentle young man his freedom. Indeed, Reynard acted as a true servant is bound to do for his lord—keeping your honour and reputation whilst skilfully achieving a resolution pleasing to all, even the snake admitting its fairness.

'When has the wolf or the bear ever honoured you in such a way? Those two crooks only know how to conceal and protect themselves, how to blow their own half-piped trumpets, how to steal and lie and rob, and how to eat the fattest of morsels and fill their bellies to bursting point. And they grumble and judge and insist that very minor thieves who rustle hens and chickens should be hanged, whereas they, who steal great hulking oxen and the finest of horses—black dappled Spanish destriers and palfreys as white as milk—should be entirely let off, free to enjoy themselves as the most privileged and idle lords in Flanders. They pretend to be as wise as Solomon, or Avicenna or Aristotle, and constantly demand to be lauded for their courage and their great deeds, their hardiness. But put them in the storm-blast middle of a battle, and they'd be the first to flee. Cowards to the core, they'd push the smallest animals, the humblest, the lowest ranking to the vantward, right to the arrowy fore, whilst they slink to the rear and hide.

'Och, my Lord, these beasties and others like them are neither wise nor judicious; quite the contrary. They care nothing for others. They destroy towns, castles, lands and whole communities of animals. They don't care whose house is burning down, as long as they can warm themselves by the burning timbers. They seek nothing other than their own selfish-hearted interests and their own singular profits. Whereas Sir Reynard the Fox, his friends and lineage, sorrow for the misfortunes of others. They put the honour, profit and well-being of their lord above themselves, the pursuit of his advantages outweighing their own. Instead of falsely puffing him up through pride and boastfulness, they offer good and measured and truthful counsel, to strengthen and consolidate his power and reputation. Yet poor Reynard receives no thanks for any of this. But, at length, it will be known, it will come out, I assure you, who is the best for Flanders, who profits us all the most.'

Rukenawe fixed Noble sternly in her gaze and pressed further. 'You have stated, my Lord, that because of his wiles, his trickery and swikleness, Reynard's kin and his kith have drawn away from him, shunned him, no longer stand with him, tail to tail. How I wish any other courtier had said that, so we might take our revenge on the Scariot and punish them so sorely that they would whimper like a newborn cub if ever they saw even the barest flick-flash of a fox brush.

'We will forbear you, though, my Lord—as the King you may say whatsoever about whomsoever you like, and I'll not pass judgement on a single word. In fact, I would protect you from any soul who rebuked your speeches and utterances. I'm not afraid of fighting. Och, words, words, words—the blurred imprecision of our language—the gape-hole between intention and phrase—that's at the bottom of all these troubles.'

King Noble the Lion, Flower of Flanders, opened and shut his mouth, and was about to say something, but the ape was too experienced a lawyer for that, and launched straight into the next artful sequence of her defence of the fox.

'My dear Lord, this leads me to a simple request. By your leave, may I guide you through the rich ranks of Reynard's many friends and kin. For there are many who would risk their life and all their worldly goods for his sake. I know myself for one. I am a wife. If Reynard needed the sacrifice of my life, I would happily give it. I am a mother. I have three, full-grown children, brave and strong, whom I would cast into the fury of untamed adventure and peril, if it would save Reynard from destruction. Even though I would rather die than see my little apes come to harm, I would do so for love of the fox.'

CHAPTER THIRTY-THREE

The Friends and Kin of Sir Reynard the Fox

Lady Rukenawe the Ape had been playing a long and clever game with the lion, adeptly shifting his perception of Reynard from rascal to loyal servant with expert skill. She had uneased him and silked him with story and moral fable and back-handed compliment and sudden peculiar shifts in perspective, until he followed her unthinkingly as a clear, bright star within the overwhelming and shadowy complexity of a situation she had entirely manufactured, which had been, in fact, as clear as day to him only hours before. In the florid imagination of the Court and the mead-addled mind of the King, she had successfully conveyed Reynard the Fox from a figurative prison of villainy to a blossoming garden of virtue and faithful knightlihood.

She had returned to Reynard's side—he was showing faint signs of returning to life, asking for a 'very small glass of Rhenish' and nibbling a *crispel*, a fried honey pastry—and after stroking his ears in a brisk, motherly way, launched into her naming and assembly of his formidable pack of allies, starting with her own apen.

'My first child's name is Byteluys—you will know him, Sire, from his exquisite fur of gold and white and his fine dark eyes, the blee of crakeberries. He is much cherished by his family and very playful, full of sport and games, which is why we give him the biggest trenchers piled high with his favourite foods—Makerouns! Moules! Mutton chops! So much good meat, too much sometimes, which goes to the profit of his brother, my second son, Fulrompe. My third child is a daughter named Hatenette. She is already well versed in Roman law and skilled too in picking out lice and nits deep-burrowed in our heads and coats. These three apelets are true and gentle to each other, and I love them very well.'

The courtiers of Gent, who were all very sentimental and excessively fond of children, beamed at Rukenawe and her sweet little apen. She called them all up from the crowd, saying 'Welcome, my dear ones! Don't be shy, come and stand by Reyner, your beloved cousin!' Up they all came and formed a charming tableau centred on the fox, who smiled wanly and coughed into his sleeve.

Dame Rukenawe then clapped her hands and cried, 'All those of my kin and of Reynard's kin, come forth! Let us all pray to our great and just King to do right by our valiant fox, right by the laws of fair Flanders and right by this Court!'

There was a swell of excited chatter and glaver and exclamations, and many beasts started to make their way to Reynard's side, shoving and pushing each other in the crush. His supporters included:

Sir Eenkoorn the Squirrel,*
Sir Musehout the Weasel,†

---

* An important squirrel of Brugge, involved in restructuring the composition of local government, making it a regulation, for example, that alderanimals were not allowed to work with their paws, thus excluding the manual labourer from power.
† Wealthier than the other courtiers, a great connoisseur of tapestries, having recently commissioned, from the Grenier atelier in Tournai, a three-part weaving of the old story of the Swan Knight (*Le Chevalier au Cigne*), a legendary ancestor of Musehout, through Godfrey the Weasel of Bouillon.

Sir Fluwijn the Stone Marten,*
Sir Maerter the Pine Marten,†
Lady Genetta the Genet,‡
Sir Pancer the Beaver,
Dame Ordegale the Beaver,§
Sir Ostrole the Stoat,¶
Sir Boussyng the Polecat,**
and Sir Foret the Ferret.††

Last came Baron Otter and Lady Panthecrote his wife—Dame
Rukenawe almost forgot to mention them, for along with Sir
Pancer the Beaver they had been enemies of Reynard for a

---

* Fluwijn was never quite the same after losing his family—a wife and
three kits—during a nasty bout of summer pestilence. He haunts the
taverns of Gent, gambling and drinking, and occasionally being dragged
out and taken home by Grimbart.

† A rather brisk sort of fellow, often away travelling. Part-owner of the
family banking business, handling loans in Gent, Brugge, Lokeren and
Sint-Niklaas.

‡ An Italian genet, educated in Latin, painting and music at court in
Ferrara, Genetta had travelled a number of years ago to Gent with her
husband, who died under mysterious circumstances when buying a horse
in Hulst.

§ According to Reynard, Ordegale is as dull and as tiresome as her
husband. She vociferously disapproves of Hermeline's scholarly pursuits
and is always raising the rents on her many tenants in Gent and Brugge
and Blankenberge.

¶ A slightly mysterious figure, Sir Ostrole was usually holed up in his
elaboratory on the Quai de rosaire in Brugge, where he worked on
chymical preparations and Gelenical compositions of surprising innova-
tion, according to Tybert, who knew about such things.

** Boussyng was as keen on poultry as Reynard and despised by some
members of the Court as a dissolute rascal for his predilection: a 'poule-
chat' of the worst order, it was muttered.

†† Again, cursed with a similar lust for *poulleterie*, Foret had pressed
Reynard to consider establishing an Order of the Golden Chick (Orde van
het Gulden Kuiken) to promote their shared interests.

considerable number of years.* But they didn't dare gainsay the ape, being trembled of her formidable intelligence—she was, without doubt, the wisest of all the fox's kin, with a scouring ability to detect weak points in any tale, argument or character.

More than twenty animals stepped forward after the otters, in awe and fear of Rukenawe, having been moved by her eloquent tongue to reappraise their ties and trueship to the fox. Dame Atrote the Ape† hurried over with her sister, Dame Quanteskieve,‡ and her two friends, Lady Weasel§ and Sir Hermel the Ermine of the Far North.¶ The Navarre Foxes, of course, led by Sir Íñigo, needed no persuasion; nor did the Water Rats, the Flittermouses or the Hedgehogs. Sir Grimbart the Badger, we need hardly mention, as he had not left his friend's side. Even old Sir Watermael the Bittern, secretive and taciturn Knight of the River Leie, trod carefully over to the growing throng around Reynard, raising his long brown neck as far as it would go to peer over ears and tails into the inner sanctum of fox and ape. For

---

* Their once concordious families had fallen out some twenty-two years earlier, when, furious over a perceived slight, one of the otters had hurled a full chamber pot at the front door of Reynardius's townhouse in Gent.

† A wealthy and prudent widow, Dame Atrote owns considerable property in Hulst. With no desire to remarry, however, she spends an irritating portion of her time repelling aggressive suitors.

‡ Dame Quanteskieve considers herself a widow to all intents and purposes, her gullible husband having been held in prison for nine months in Rupelmonde for counterfeiting money.

§ Belette, wife of Sir Musehout the Weasel, shares his artistic sensibilities and is highly skilled in painting manuscript borders and miniature backgrounds, having trained in Paris with her cousin, Anastasia.

¶ A whiskery adventurer for the King, Sir Hermel had just returned from a long six months in Kargopol on the Onega river in Muscovy.

by now, over forty courtiers had pledged their allegiance, a substantial number—which gave the King considerable pause for thought.

'My Lord the King,' said Rukenawe, the laughter and conversation falling away with her authoritative cadence, 'come and see if Reynard Fox has any friends! This company, you observe, are all true subjects, who would gladly sacrifice life and goods in the service of the Crown.' She thin-smiled, with a strong whiff of malevolence. 'Of course, you are hardy, mighty and strong. You have nothing to fear from a band of such allies. Our well-willed and good-natured friendship can not hurt you nor your throne.

'Allow Reynard to think about these matters you have laid against him. And if he cannot excuse himself, then, by all means, do what you will with him according to the strictures of the law. We would be sorely grieved, although we would desire no better. But Lord Reynard the Fox must not be denied the right of self-defence, we are all agreed on this point.'

She looked sharply around, and an immediate chorus of 'Aye, aye' bloomed from the press of supporters.

The Queen then spoke up: 'I said all of this to him yesterday, Rukenawe, but he was so fierce and angry, he wouldn't listen to a word of it.'

Pleased with the tide turning in favour of his old fiery pal, Sir Firapeel the Leopard, lying on his favourite beam above Gente, spoke too: 'Sire, you cannot judge any further than the Court's verdict allows. If you storm ahead, past all legal bounds, by will and might and wrath alone, then you will disgrace your position, disgrace the Crown of Gent itself. Hear both parties, both sides of the tale, and give your verdict measuredly, soberly, and according to the most exalted ideals of justice.'

King Noble was quite overwhelmed, head spinning with mead and rhetoric. He had caught Rukenawe's warning, but it hadn't been necessary. Dressed in their bloom-bright bee costumes for the pageant, Reynard's supporters were clustered around him like a dangerous swarm, and Noble had a horrible feeling they could turn on him at any moment.

He cleared his throat and adjusted his crown and pronounced carefully and in favour of the fox: 'This is all true. I'm afraid I was so furious when I was informed of Cuwaert's death and saw his poor pathetic head that I was hoot and hasty and acted without thinking. I shall hear the fox. If he can answer well and excuse himself of all his accusations, then I shall gladly let him go quietly. I can see how much support he has, how many friends rally.'

Reynard the Fox, sitting happily in his throng of well-wishers, was very glad of these words, and dozens of thoughts raced through his head: Thank God for my aunt! What skill she has! What brilliance! She has made dry, wintered twigs blossom again! She has rescued me from the darkest, deepest hole of my foxish career! I now have a good foot to dance on! I shall look out at them all straight and sure, and compose the fairest lies which ever a beastie did hear! As intricate and beautiful as Mechelen lace! I shall prick my design, then weave my falsehoods with hundreds of fine silvered threads. Oh, I will twist the bobbins so skilfully that pattern and ground will be indistinguishable, and so I shall bring myself full out of all danger!

PART FIVE

JEWELS

CHAPTER THIRTY-FOUR

The Jewels of Sir Reynard the Fox

*The Eleventh Day of the Feast of Saint John the Baptist
and also the Feast Day of Bishop Ulrich of Augsberg,
Patron Saint of Master Weavers, Sunday 4th July*

The following afternoon, bright-eyed and raring to go, papers
fanned in his paw, Reynard the Fox addressed the Court. In the
morning, everyone had watched Queen Gente's sophisticated
performance of 'The Fair Hope of Flanders'; its themes of
redemption and promise hitting a nerve in an audience eager
for Reynard's testimony. After the ape's machinations of the
previous day, the entire castle felt fresh and clean, as though
a brisk east wind had blown all the corruption and fury
and violence away. The fox could not have enjoyed a more
fortuitous setting for his appeal.

Reynard launched straight into his defence, no holds
barred. 'I am horrified and desperately sad to discover that Sir
Cuwaert, my dear, strange little friend, is dead. And what of
Bellin? Is he here?' He looked around convincingly, as though
searching hopefully for the curled mercantile head of the ram
(which he knew full well was spiked on the watery Rabot gate
north-east of the castle).

'Please tell me, what did he bring you when he came again?
I had entrusted three jewels to him. I would very much like
to know where they are. One of them, he should have given
to you, my Lord the King. Another, to my lady, the Queen.'
He half-bowed, and kissed her paw.

'There were no jewels!' exclaimed Noble, surprised. 'Bellin brought us nothing else but Cuwaert's head. As I said to you before—d'you not recall, Fox?—I took my vengement on him alright. I had him killed for all his wicked deeds. That foul keytyf had told me that he himself had counselled the making of everything in that furry scrip of yours. He told me there were just letters in there. Letters! Foul mangy creature.'

Reynard looked distraught: 'Alas, my Lord, can this be the truth? By the chasuble of Saint Ulrich, I wish I'd never been born. What a wretched thing!' He clutched his chest dramatically. 'My God, I think my heart is breaking, shearing into two halves, for the loss of those jewels. I am very sorry to be alive, I truly am. What will my wife say when she hears the news? She'll go out of her very wits with sorrow! I fear I may lose my gentle Hermeline for ever.' He covered his face with his paws and made a series of muffled, baleful yelps.

'Come now, Reyner, dear nephew,' cried Rukenawe, briskly, 'what on earth is the profit of all this weeping and wailing? Let it pass, young Fox, let it pass. It's not doing you any good; nor is it helping the situation. I suggest instead you tell us what these jewels were? If they aren't buried deep in the earth or thrown down a well or plunged into a chasm or some such pit, then I don't see why we couldn't find them still? We can get Master Akeryn Flittermouse, the old library-keeper at Sint-Pieters, to help us. He can labour for them in his books— trace their history, their past owners, their peculiarities and properties. And we can also put a powerful curse upon them in all the churches and holy houses, until they turn up or we have knowledge of where they are. Don't lose heart, they may not be lost, Reyner, they may not be lost!'

Reynard blew his nose and shook his head sadly. 'Aunt Rukenawe, I daren't believe it, for I'm afraid that once someone has their paws on these jewels they will never let them go. Never did a king, not even Charlemagne, own gems such as these. Nevertheless, with your kind words, you have somewhat eased and lightened my heart. Alas, alas, alas—this terrible affair shows how we are always betrayed by those we trust the most. Even if I have to journey and adventure across the whole world, I will find those jewels. They are far too precious to let go.' He blew his nose again and paused. Everyone was agog, and pressed him to continue. 'Tell us, Reynard, tell us about the jewels!' Reynard smiled bravely and nodded, 'Well, I can hardly bear to, but if you insist...'

The Ring of Gold

'The first was a ring of the finest gold. Inscribed inside the ring was a series of letters, enamelled in sable as dark as ash buds and azure as bright as a damselfly. There were three names written in Hebrew, which I could not read, nor write for you now, as I do not know that language. However, after many months of searching, travelling many hundreds of miles, I eventually found someone, a wise man, who managed to decipher it.' He beckoned the fascinated courtiers closer, and dropped his voice to a stage whisper.

'His name is Master Abrion of Trier. He resides in that city in a very old, very tall, red-brick house next to the synagogue on Jakobstraße. He speaks all manner of languages fluently and knows the virtues of every kind of herb. There is no beast so fierce or so strong that he cannot subdue and tame them. He only needs to see a wild animal once and he can do as he will with them. When I visited him around Lent, two salamanders and a manticore were sitting down to a supper in his chambers, and I shared a Tart de Brymlent with them. Very nice it was too. Delcious salmon. Yes, Master Abrion is, without doubt, the most learned man I have ever met, the most cunning man alive. The reason why I had searched him out especially, however, was because of his unrivalled knowledge of the properties and powers of stones. Their strange magic was of particular interest to Abrion.

'When I showed him the gold ring, he told me that the inscriptions were the three names that Seth brought out of Paradise when he took the Oil of Mercy to his father, Adam. Whosoever bears these three names will never be hurt by thunder or by lightning; nor shall witchcraft or spells have any power over them. And they won't be tempted to commit any sin, not even the minor ones, which are so very easy to slip into, like thinking about playing boules or jousting on a holy day, for instance. Nor will they be harmed by the cold, even if they slept for three long winter nights in the frost-hoar fields, even if road and sky and land were blanched white with snow and the drifts were six-foot deep, and the Schelde and Leie were frozen hard as iron all the way to the sea. So much power held in three little words, Master Abrion warned me. So much power.

'Decorating the outer band of the ring was a stone of three distinct colours. First, a red crystal which shone as though a fierce fire raged inside. If you were about on a dark moonless night, you would need no other light, for it emitted a radiance as bright as midday, illuminating road and sky and land, like the golden flames of Phoebus.

'The next part of the stone was as white and clear as if it had been burnished. If your eyes were sore or smarting, if you had a strange swelling in your skin—a nasty boil or amper or bulch—or a bad headache—perhaps one of those choleric ones that begin with flicker-patterns like fortress walls in the corner of your sight, then hammer and pound and pierce like a rusty longsword's been thrust through your temples then hard-twisted—or any pernicious, outward malady for that matter, common or rare—then all you needed to do was to stroke the stone gently over the afflicted place and you would instantly be whole and well again.'

'Completely cured?' asked King Noble, who was very interested in his health. 'Completely cured,' nodded Reynard.

'And, equally, if you were poisoned by venom or hemlock or rancid meat, or had a bad case of colic, or strangullion— when your throat swells up like a turnip—or tormented with spreading cancers or stones or fistulas or any other sickness, save only death itself, then all you would have to do would be to put the stone in a little water, then drink it and you would immediately be healed. Alas,' sighed the Fox, 'we have good cause to be very sorry indeed to lose that jewel.

'The third colour was green like glass. But there were also some unusual purple sprinkles—odd little specks and marks scattered in its depths like pollen. In our stormy world, this was perhaps the most important hue, for Master Abrion told me truthfully that whoever bears the stone can never be hurt by their enemies. No one, however strong or daring, could harm you, and wherever you fought, you would always be victorious, whether by day or by night. That is, advised my wise man, as long as you had made yourself sufficiently pure by fasting rigorously before viewing the stone. Wherever you went, whatever fellowship you kept, you would be greatly loved when wearing the ring, even if you'd been loathed and derided before—the moment the fine gold band slipped over your finger, they would forget their anger as soon as they saw you, as though it were as insubstantial as marsh-mist. Even if you were completely naked on a battlefield facing one hundred armed soldiers, you would swell with flamed courage and escape from them with honour and style. However, in addition to the fasting, the ring only works for a bearer who is noble and gentle,' Reynard sniffed and winked at Sir Firapeel, 'and has no low-born, no earth-born connections, no churlish qualities of any kind. For them, the stone would hold no might at all.'

'Did you wear it, Reynard?' asked Fluwijn the Stone Marten. 'Oh no,' replied the fox, 'I decided that because the stone was so precious and so good, I really wasn't a worthy enough fox to carry it. So, I sent it—or at least I thought I had sent it—to my dear Lord the King instead. For he is the most noble animal who has ever lived, I said to myself, and as our great country's welfare and honour lies entirely upon him, he should be kept from all fear and need and *ongheluck*, as they say in the Waasland where I live—from the worst of the evil fortunes.'

The Panthera Comb

The Stone Marten looked impressed. Everyone looked impressed, in fact, as Reynard Fox continued his account. 'I found the ring in my father's treasure hoard, and from the same place I took a looking glass or mirror and a comb, which Lady Hermeline wanted at any cost, being interested in its properties and its beauty. Any animal who saw these two treasures would stand and wonder. They were marvellous to behold. I put them also in the scrip, to be delivered to the Queen, for she has been so good and gracious to me.

This comb cannot be overpraised too much. It was made from the bone of a pure and noble beast named Panthera, who lives somewhere between Great India and the Earthly Paradise. He is an exceptionally beautiful animal, and the hues and tones and shades of his fur! The colour! Oh, there is nothing to match it under the starry heavens. And he smells so sweet that his perfume salves all sickness. Because of his beauty and this intoxicating fragrance—which has elements of roses and orris root and jasmine and orange flowers and frankincense and cloves and hart's tree, combined with other subtle notes from far beyond-sea, which my Flemish foxish nose could not even begin to guess or identify—all the beasts would follow him, for it was by this sweet savour that they were mended of their illnesses.

'The bone of this panthera is also very beautiful—broad and thin. When it is slain, all this precellent odour resides in this bone, which cannot be broken; nor can it be destroyed by fire or water or by smiting or sawing it—it is so strong, so dense, so fast. Yet it is notably light in weight, as light as silk or the feather of an owl. Its perfume is so mighty, however, that whosoever smells it loses all other worldly lusts and desires, is eased and cured of all manner of diseases and infirmities and their heart filled with gladness and mirthfulness and a joy which are not quite of this earth.

'The comb itself is polished to a high sheen, as though it were made of silver, and its teeth are very narrow and very straight. Between the greater teeth and the smaller, there are wide hollows and spaces where many an image is subtly carved and enamelled about with fine gold.

'The carvings were exquisite. They told the history of how Venus, Juno and Pallas strove for the apple of gold, which each of them wanted for their own. It was decided that Paris should be chosen to settle this controversy and give the gleaming fruit to the fairest of the three.

'Paris was at that time a herd-man, a shepherd who kept his father's sheep and other beasts just outside the walls of Troy. When Paris was given the apple by Jupiter, the three goddesses put their cases to him one by one. Juno promised to him, if he should award her the apple, riches beyond imagination, hoards of gold and silver and gems. He would become the wealthiest man in Troy, nay the wealthiest man in the whole world, with just one click of her fingers, one swish-swoosh of her peacock feather. Pallas was next. She had an even more tempting offer. If she might have the apple, she said, she would reward him with vast wisdom and strength and make him so great a lord that he would overcome all his enemies and anyone else he felt like defeating into the bargain.

'Venus spoke next. "Whatever do you need with riches or with strength?" she laughed. "Are you not Priam's son? Is Hector not your brother? Together, they have the whole of Asia under their power! Are you not already one of the possessors, one of the powerful barons of great Troy? If you present the apple to me, I shall give a treasure more valuable and more desirable than all others, and that shall be the fairest woman who ever lived on earth. No woman will ever be born who is fairer. With her beauty by your side, you will be richer than rich, and shall climb above all others, for that is the treasure that no man can praise enough. For honest, good and beautiful women can put away many a sorrow from the heart. They are virtuous and wise, and bring a man love and bliss and every good thing."

'Paris heard Venus's honeyed proposition of joy and love and beauty in a rapture of excitement, and begged the goddess to name the lady who was so fair and to tell him where he might find her. "It is Helen, the wife of King Menelaus of Greece," cried Venus, "and there is not a nobler, richer, gentler, nor wiser lady alive in the world today, nor was there, nor will there be." Without a second thought, Paris gave the golden apple to Venus, goddess of Love, and declared her the fairest of the three. How he won Helen with the assistance of Venus and how he brought her into Troy and wedded her, and the great love and jolly life they had together, was all carved in the hollows of that comb. Every detail of the story held in perfect miniature form, vignette following vignette until the whole tale was told in perfumed white bone.'

The Mirror of All-Seeing

With the entire Court from King Noble to the smallest harvest mouse enthralled, Reynard clattered on with a yet more fantastical historiette, which, truth be told, he'd heard at the Burgundian court a couple of Christmases ago at a very good party to celebrate some ram or other being entered into the Order of the Golden Fleece.

'Now, you shall hear all about the mirror,' said the fox. 'Its silvery glass is of such virtue, such power, that when you look into it, you can see everything happening within a good square mile—every single beast, every single human, everything they're saying, everything they're doing, everything they're not doing. You can see anything you would desire to know or discover, or perhaps find blame and fault with.

'The moment someone looks directly into the glass, if they have a disease—with their eyes, say—a pricking pain, an irritating mote, a scatter of floating stars or blinding pearls like milky elven cawls—it would be healed at once, without pause or prayer. Such is the uncommon magic of that looking glass. Is it any wonder I rage with fury, madness even, at the loss of these bold treasures?

'The wood which framed the glass was light and hard and stern as a stone, and came from a peculiar tree called the Cetijn tree. It endures forever, before it succumbs to rot or is eaten by worms. Wise men value it far higher than fine gold or saffron. This is why King Solomon himself sealed his temple with the same wood—every gleaming beam and rafter and joist. It somewhat resembles the tree of ebony, from which, you may remember, King Crompart made a wooden horse for the love of King Morcadigas's daughter, a desperately beautiful lady, whom he won with his fine-carved gift. But the horse had a secret. It had been so cleverly made by Crompart that when his beloved rode it, if she wished she could cover a hundred miles in less than one hour! No matter how muddy or boggy or stony her route!

'And this was well proved. The King's son, Cleomedes, a stubborn, know-it-all young man, refused to believe that a horse made of wood could possess such miraculous properties. Despite his failings, or perhaps because of them, Cleomedes was very courageous and full of a violent sort of vigour, and desired more than anything to prove himself in the world by performing great deeds of bravery and heroicalness. So, he leapt onto the horse made from the solemn black tree and turned a gold pin on its wooden breast. Immediately, the horse lifted him up into the air and they flew straight out through the window, into the cold night. Before you could say a paternoster, he was gone more than ten miles in a storm of hoofbeats and thundered earth and sheer white terror. For Cleomedes thought he might never return and would gallop to the end of the world and beyond. The rest of the tale—how he began to learn the art and craft of turning and slowing and calming the horse, how joyful he was when he learnt its ways, how worried his sister and father and brother-in-law were for him, and how he finally managed to return to Court, all of this I'm afraid I will have to skim over for lack of time.*

A great groaning echoed around the chamber—stories about magical horses always went down well at Noble's court, particularly ones with a touch of Burgundian swagger. Reynard ignored them. He couldn't remember the end of the *roman de cheval de bois*; that was why he had stopped, nothing to do with timing. Like Scheherazade, and for much the same reasons, he was determined to carry on spinning tales and excuses as long as he possibly could.

'All of this happened, of course, by virtue of the qualities of the wood. Let us return to our lost mirror, however, and I will describe its wonders to you. Its Cetijn frame was very large—around a half-a-foot broad,' Reynard described it in the

---

* The wooden horse features in *Cléomadès* by Adenes le Roi, a favourite of Henry III, Duke of Brabant, and so would have been very well known to Reynard and his fellow courtiers in Flanders.

air with his paws, 'and was covered with paintings depicting a collection of strange stories in a rich palette of colours: gold, sable, silver, yellow, azure and the blood-red earth of Sinope.* These six colours were wrought in such a way to bring the histories unsettlingly to life. Under each illustration, there were also words, graven and enamelled, so that every onlooker would understand which tale was which. In my humble opinion, there was never a mirror so costly, so lustly, nor so pleasant to behold.

'The first picture and tale were of a strong, well-built horse, a little round in the girth.' Given the enthusiastic reaction to his last tale, Reynard thought he had better return to equine subjects. 'He was very envious of a nimble hart, who ran so swiftly and so far ahead in the fields that the horse was unable to catch up. Furious and rather wheezy, he decided to try to catch and subdue the stag, however much pain and trouble it would cause him. Without further ado, he went to speak to a herdsman. "Excuse me," said the horse, "if you would like to capture a hart, one which I can easily show you, then I'll make sure you profit greatly by it. You can sell his tangled horns, his skin and his flesh, and make lots of money at market." The herdsman hadn't eaten well for a while and so was interested in the proposal and asked, "How may I come by him, horse?" The horse replied, "Sit on my back and I'll carry you there, and we shall hunt him together, until he be taken." The herdsman sprang up and sat astride the horse, and seeing the deer in

* Whilst Sinope indicates vert or green in heraldry, Reynard here is following Pliny and Isidore of Seville, and referring to the brownish-red of the pigment dug in the city of Sinope in Turkey. For a fox, it was, of course, a favourite hue.

the distance galloped after him, but once again the hart was light of foot and as swift as the east wind and easily outran the horse. The herdsman rode and rode, until the moon rose high over the fields and the shadows lengthened, and still they hadn't caught him.

'The horse was weary and could barely stand. "Please climb down," he gasped, "I need to rest for a while. I shall go on after I catch my breath." "No," said the herdsman, casually, cruelly. "I've arrested you now and you cannot escape from me. I have a bridle on your head, and spurs on my heels. I can do what I like with you. You'll regret ever offering to help me. I shall subdue you and rule over you for ever more, however much you swear the contrary."'

Reynard switched from his storytelling to his didactic voice and looked down his whiskers at his audience—this part was important. 'See how this foolish horse brought himself into thraldom, tricked himself into servitude, trapped himself in his own net, never to taste the sweet honey of freedom again! How easily one is swept up in the chesil-rough tide of envy! The horse let himself be taken, he let himself be ridden, he let himself become enslaved. And the moral, my courtly friends, is that there are many animals who would wound and torment, even try to kill others, only to end up hurt themselves—rewarded with precisely the same treatment as they would happily mete out.

'Next on the looking glass frame, painted so true to life that I thought for one moment that the figures were moving and breathing, was the story of Boudewijn the Ass and the hound, who both dwelt with a very, very rich man. It was quite obvious that the man adored his hound, for he played with him all the time, as folk do, of course, with their cherished barkers. And the happy dog would leap up, tail wagging nineteen to the dozen, and lick his master on the face, great slobbery licks all around his mouth.' Reynard shuddered; he immensely disliked the subservience of dogs. 'Boudewijn the Ass would sit and watch all this affectionate romping and, in his heart, a great ball of envy and spite grew and grew like a canker.

'One day, he said to himself, "How on earth has it come to this? Whatever does my lord see in this foul, smelly hound, who never does anything good or productive or profitable, except for springing on him and kissing him! I, on the other hand, am put to work without stop. Labouring away from dawn to dusk, pulling carts and carrying heavy weights, drawing and bearing, drawing and bearing, until my back aches and my knees tremble with pain. I do more work in one week than that dog with ten or fifteen others could do in a whole year! And yet there he is, sitting next to our master at dinner, eating bones covered in juicy flesh, presented with huge trenchours fat with food—bigger helpings than anybody else at the table, whilst I have nothing to eat but thistles and nettles. At night, I have to lie on the hard earth—scorned and insulted! I refuse to suffer like this anymore! I will think of a plan to get my lord's love and friendship, just like the hound has—perhaps even try to supplant him in his affections. Why not!"

'The next morning, along came the lord; Boudewijn, seeing his opportunity, lifted up his tail and sprang up, putting his forefeet onto his master's shoulders. He then opened his mouth wide and stuck out his tongue and began to sing, and with his hooves made what felt to the lord like two enormous boils or bulens, or something most peculiar and most unnatural, crushing his ears. A hideous and unwelcome embrace, which ended with the ass putting forth his lips and trying to kiss his master square on his mouth, dribbling as much saliva as he could muster, just as he'd seen the hound doing.

"'Help! Help!" screamed the terrified lord, "This ass has gone mad and is trying to kill me!" His servants came tumbling out of the kitchens, armed with heavy staves and beat and struck Boudewijn so badly that he almost lost his life. Afterwards, he hobbled painfully back to his lowly stable and quietly ate his thistles and his nettles, and went to being just an ass once more, as he had always been.

'Just like the history of the foolish horse and the hart,' the fox admonished, 'this clearly demonstrates that those who have the spitting envy and the curdled spite of another animal's joyous life deserve to have that same hatred served upon them tenfold! After his comical efforts, I think we can all conclude that it was quite right for the ass to return to his proper station in life, to his thistles and his nettles, to bearing his heavy sacks. Even if he were honoured and lifted to the highest echelons of society, he would not understand its subtleties and rules, and would continue to use his old unseemly manners. Where asses receive lordships is seldom seen good rule. For they take heed of nothing but their own singular profit in life. Yet those kind of beasts are often raised up to the detriment of other nobler animals.' Reynard sighed and looked distracted for a moment or two. 'Carry on, Fox, carry on!' encouraged Noble, who was very much enjoying his afternoon.

'Well,' said Reynard briskly, 'I can tell you another tale, one which concerns Sir Tybert over there.' Everyone turned to look at the cat, but Tybert was fast asleep, curled up underneath the high table, his embroidered eye patch slipping as he gently snored.

'Before my father, Reynardius, died, he passed a great deal of time together with the cat, becoming the closest and dearest of friends. Indeed, they swore to one another that they would never separate; both in times of love and in times of hate, they would stick together like sap in a pine tree. Whatever they got, they would carefully divide it into two parts. Everything was equal and just as true friendship should be.

'One cold winter morning, they were taking a constitutional and my father was inspecting the bounds of our property, when suddenly they saw hunters coming over the frosty-furred fields with a pack of ferocious-looking hounds. Afraid for their lives, they leapt up and ran away as fast as their legs would carry them. "Tybert, Tybert!" whispered Reynardius, "where would be a favourable place to hide out? They've spied us, without a doubt! What shall we do? How shall we get out of this! Where shall we go?" My father was a good fox. He trusted Tybert like his own brother, trusted in their shared promises of faithfulness and fidelity. He would never have abandoned the cat, no matter how much danger they found themselves in. "Tybert," he said, seeing the cat blanching with terror, "calm yourself! I have a great sackful of wiles and tricks and dodges we can dip into. As long as we stick together, we needn't be too afraid of those hunters, nor their pack of dogs."

'But Sir Tybert began to sigh and moan and tremble in fear. "Oh, Reynardius, how do words avail us at this point! And I only know one wile—one certain trick—and I plan to use it!" With that, he scurry-climbed up a high tree, right up to the very top, under the leaves, where neither hunter nor hound could harm him. And in doing so, he deserted my father, left him all alone in the snow, his life in jeopardy—for the hunters set the eager pack upon him, barking in their bloodlust. And the men blew their horns and yelled and urged and hallowed the hounds: "Slay the fox! Take him! Kill him! Tear him into scraps!"

'From his elevated position of safety and superiority, Tybert looked down on the mayhem far below. But instead of expressing concern for his old *ami*, he hailed down a storm of insults. He mocked and scorned my father, and sneered at him, saying "Hey, cousin Reynardius, open up your sack! Fish out your wiles and tricks! Now's the time to help yourself, Fox—show us how clever you really are!"'

Reynard pointed a paw at Tybert. 'All this vulgar jeering from a so-called clerk! A scholar of Pliny and Boethius and Ovid, no less! Despicable! My poor dear father forced to listen to such a cruel bombardment of taunts and gibes from the animal he loved and trusted most in the world.

'He was almost taken, on the verge of being ripped apart, when he managed to scramble away, letting his leather bag slide off, so he would be a little lighter in his escape. And as the red sun sank into the snow, he ran and ran and ran for his life. Yet it was not enough; the dogs were too swift, and they almost caught up with him, and he was stumbling and slipping on icy puddles, until finally he reached a familiar old hole, deep and sound and safe. In he crept, and waited until the sounds of baying had slowly died away into the night and he knew for certain that they had given up and gone home to their hot suppers and blazing fires.

'This was how Tybert upheld the oaths he had sworn to my father! That false deceiver! Alas, how many are there nowadays who don't keep their promises, and don't care a pomegranate kernel if they break 'em or not! Though I despise Sir Tybert for doing this to my true-hearted father—and who can blame me—I have a fine care for my eternal soul as well. If I came across the cat in trouble, floundering in the middle of a dangerous mishap or trapped in a life-squeezing bind, I admit that I would not care so much as if someone else was suffering. I'm sorry to say this, but it's true. Nevertheless, I refuse to hate or envy him, and shall, for the love of God, forgive him—and yet, his behaviour has cast a thick, weighty shade upon my sin-cleansed heart, a grey shadow of ill will which stirs whenever my remembrance touches upon that bleak winter's day. I think of my *père* shivering in his tunnel, and the bile rises once more. Always the base sensuality of the flesh which betrays us, railing and scratching against reason and godliness. We try to rise and are pulled down, over and over again.'

Reynard suddenly stopped and wiped an unexpected tear from the end of his nose. Whenever the figure of his father tiptoed into his fables, his phantom always unsettled him, and he had to fight to dissolve the inked memories—the stiff body in the snow, rust-black-copper against the blinding white, the knot on the noose rigid and pearled with ice. But he pulled himself back and boldened on with his next tale of wonder—he was fighting for his own life, after all.

'Another vignette on the mirror,' said Reynard Fox, 'was dark and slight, limned in tones of lead and cinders and ash. It told the story of when a wolf found the body of a dead, flayed horse upon the heath one summer, midst the fallow gorse and the adders.

'All the flesh had been eaten, but the wolf slunk up to the corpse and bit great morsels out of the old nags' ribcage, white and rickety as a storm-wrecked fishing skoute. He was so ravenous that he swallowed three or four shards at once, gobbling them down as fast as he could, until one of the bones got stuck thwartlong, right across his throat from side to side. The wolf was in agony, he could barely breathe. Frightened for his life, he frantically searched for wise doctors and surgeons, promising them the world if they could make him better and remove the rib bone. At last, after a fruitless search, marked by incompetent short-fingered physicians or heavy slammed doors, the wolf suddenly had a brilliant idea. He rushed to find the crane with his long neck and beak, who lived by the water in Tielrode. At his riverside hut, the wolf begged the crane to help him. He told him he would love and reward him so well that he would be better off for the rest of his life. He offered him gold cups and sturgeon fish and silk fans and a feather mattress and silver spoons and sugared frogs and a bolt of sorrel taffeta and the Duchess of Burgundy's psalter and a wide-brimmed sun hat and a relic of Saint Amalberga. All manner of enticing gifts and trifles.

'The crane was intrigued by this array of riches and readily agreed to help. He put his head into the wolf's throat, and brought out the bone with his bill. The wolf started and jumped to one side with the plucking and howled with pain: "Ow! You're hurting me, crane! But I forgive you as long as you never do it again. I wouldn't suffer that kind of rough treatment from any other creature though!"

'The crane stepped back, spat the bone into the River Durme, and then addressed the wolf, bowing with a well-plumed wing: "Sir Isengrim," he began.' In the Flanders Court, everyone laughed at this and Reynard traced a little flourish with his paw. It was very amusing for the courtlings to have that grumpy old wolf baron unexpectedly tumble into the tale. It wasn't really Sir Isengrim, of course; the fox had just made the crane use his name for comic effect and for more subtle and twisty reasons, which will become readily apparent. In any case, let us return to the crane.

'"Sir Isengrim," he said very politely, "go off and be merry, for you be as right as rainwater and as whole as a wheel-loaf now! Before you go, can you give me all my treasures please. All the fancy goods you promised me." The wolf, still coughing from his extraction, looked at the crane with an arrogant frown. "Well, I never! Just hear what he said! The nerve of that fisher-bird! I'm the one who has suffered from a painful and clumsy procedure! I'm the one who has cause to complain, and yet he wants me to compensate him! He doesn't even consider thanking me for my great kindness in not biting his head off when he put it down my throat. I am quite shocked! He hurt me very badly—if anyone should have a reward it should be me!"'

'Thus, the story and its picture reveal a sad truth,' preached Reynard the Fox, 'that this is how unkind and cruel animals treat those who do them good. This is how they pay those gentle souls back—with broken oaths and insolence. This is what happens when the false and artful and unprincipled are advanced, and arise and assume importance in society—any thoughts of courtesy and consideration for others are cast aside. There are so many who ought to reward and do good to those who have helped them in need, but instead they pluck a dozen reasons and causes to claim the opposite—that they are ones who have been injured and who deserve honour and recompense. Therefore it is said, and very true it is too, that whoever chides and chastises and punishes others should make sure that they themselves are in the clear first.

'I can remember all this and much more was wrought into the looking glass. The master craftsman who made it was a cunning man and a profound scholar in many sciences. A marvel, it was, a marvel.' Reynard sighed. 'As you can see, these jewels were far too precious for me to keep for myself and my wife. Therefore I sent them to my dear Lord the King and my dear Lady the Queen. I defy you to find any liege-animals these days who give their lords such gifts! My three children were very sorrowful when the mirror was gone, for they, as all cubs will, had taken to looking at themselves to see how fine their clothing looked, how sweet their masks and brushes, and to make merry with all the magical properties which I have described to you. One foxling would wander off into the Maleperduys lands, and the others would watch him in the mirror, as he made his way through wood and orchard and meadow. When he returned, they would all laugh and gasp as they told him his exact movements and pathways, seen from afar.'

Reynard regarded the King. Now was the time, he felt, to tighten the pattern and weave in the lies. He pulled his plain, unaffected gown, made from a dark russet summer cloth to match his fur, close around himself and bowed low before the King. 'Alas,' he said quietly, 'I had no idea Sir Cuwaert was so near death when I gave him the scrip containing the jewels. His asmyes had been very bad, but he had his medicines with him.'* The fox pushed down the memory of the little hare's delicate neck, blood flowing from the ripped artery. 'I could not imagine a better animal to entrust them to, though. It should have cost me my life, rather than him and Bellin the Ram. They were two of my best friends.'

Reynard circled in anguish and cried, 'Out, out, foul murderer! I swear I shall find out who it was, though I should run through all the world to seek him! I will search every house and abbey from Gent to Salamanca, from Cologne to Norwich if I have to! For such a scoundrel cannot hide for ever! What's that old saying? Murder will out in the end, that much is certain. Perhaps he's here in this very company, the fellow who knows what really happened to Cuwaert, hiding in full sight of us all. Many villains walk with good animals— mingle amongst them, befriend them. And it is very difficult to protect oneself, for they know their false-craft so well that they can cover and cloak their lies and misdeeds with ease.'

---

* The fox's word for asthma. The first written reference can be found in one of the Maleperduys foxes' most used texts, Bartholomaeus Anglicus's encyclopaedia, *De Proprietatibus Rerum*, of 1398.

CHAPTER THIRTY-FIVE

The Finest Fox Physician of Montpellier

Dusk and a storm was brewing. The air was heavy and humid, and the great bells of Gent were tolling across the city, thunder rumbling in from the sea. As the chamber darkened, Reynard's tone also changed, and he assumed a grave and weighty authority, which had been lacking before in his light mercurial storytelling.

'The greatest wonder I have,' declared Reynard in a saturnine voice, 'is that my Lord the King has stated so felly, in such cruel terms, that my father Reynardius and I have never done him any good—that we have not been faithful servants to him. I suppose that so many pressing matters come before your attention, Sire, that certain things, including important and impressive acts of loyal service, cannot help but slip your mind. So it fares with me.

'Dear Lord, don't you remember when your father the King, Blessed Baldwin the Mild, was still alive, and you were a mere youngling of two years old? My father had just returned from Montpellier, where he had spent five years at the Universitas medicorum studying the art of medicine—Salernitan, Arabic and Hebrew practices.

'Reynardius was particularly knowledgeable about the teachings of the master surgeon Abū al-Qāsim Khalaf ibn al-'Abbās al-Zahrāwī al-Ansari, and knew his entire œuvre by heart. Every word of his thirty volumes of treatises, the great *Method of Medicine*, the *Kitab al-tasrîf.* And my father had become an excellent diagnostician through his labours.

He knew all the tokens of urine as well as he knew the claws on his own paw. He was also learned in the nature of herbs—which of them were sticky and viscous, and which of them were laxatives. Indeed, he was a distinguished magister of that university with the right to practise medicine *hic et ubique terrarium*—here and anywhere on earth. Accordingly, he would wear the cloth of silk and fur and golden belt indicative of his scholarly rank. Never was there a finer fox physician!

'When he came to Court, he found Baldwin in a troubling sickness, which pained him deep in his heart, as he loved the King before all other lords. The King, equally, trusted Reynardius more than any of his other physicians and surgeons, and dismissed them the moment my father arrived.

'King Baldwin was shaking and shivering with fever, tucked up high upon his featherbed, draped in Rennes sheets and piles of fustians and that scarlet coverlet with a crowned lion at its centre, which I believe you still possess, my Lord? My father lovingly described every detail to me—he adored the King so. And there the sickened Baldwin sat, propped up by pillows of down and a head-sheet of the softest ermine—but in such excruciating pain that nothing could bring him comfort.

'"Reynardius," he groaned, "I am sick and I fear it's getting worse."

'My father held his paw gently and said, "My dear Lord, here's a urinal. Make your water in it, and as soon as I can examine it I will be able to tell you what's wrong and how we might be able to cure you."

'King Baldwin did as he was counselled, for he had complete faith in my father and trusted no living creature more.'

Reynard put a paw up before Noble could say anything. 'It is true, I concede, that Baron Reynardius acted very badly towards you, Sire, after that dark night of tavern-plotting near Hijfte, but that whole coup was prompted by the cursed properties of the treasure, and by the evil urgings of those foul and wicked beasts with whom he'd surrounded himself. The whole incident astonished me, but it took place hard up against his death, and his melancholic decline had already disturbed his judgement and possessed both body and soul. I do not recognise that later fox as my father. He bore no resemblance to the kind and moral animal whom I knew and loved so greatly as a cub.' Reynard looked down and studied the pads of his front paws and straightened his whiskers.

'So, back then, back when he was still my father, Reynardius carefully examined Baldwin's waters. He put the flask up to the light, and held one paw behind it, to first check for its opacity and thickness. My father sighed at his observations, for the addle was troubled by flames of pus and a certain unpleasant viscosity, and, at the bottom of the murky Jordan pot, it was heavy-clogged with grains of sand. Next, he tasted it. It was sharp and salty, with the foul-fish smell of the bottom of a herring barrel after a North Sea crossing. He tutted to himself. Finally, he assessed its hue, comparing it to the wheel of urinary shades he himself had drawn up and painted with a colleague whilst in Montpellier. The royal urine was, unfortunately, blood-coloured, bruise-coloured, a nasty shade of *rode wijn*, the darkest, strongest red wine in Flanders.

'He returned to the King's bedside. "I'm sorry to have to tell you this, Sire, but you are suffering from a serious malady of the liver. All the signs are there: sanguinolent urine, salt, sand, and traces of corrupt purulent matter. Moreover, my Lord, these urinary symptoms are coupled with a high fever and yellowish, pale eyes. Taken all together, this indicates a highly dangerous illness, which requires a strong medicine to avert a swift and fatal decline."

"'I will take anything, do anything," cried poor liverish Lord Baldwin, thoroughly alarmed, feeling his hardened belly. "There is only one cure I can recommend," replied my father, 'but if you follow it, you will find yourself hale and hearty and whole before the month is out. You must eat part of the liver of a wolf who has reached the age of seven years. You must do this, otherwise you will certainly die, your urine shows that plainly."

'Isengrim the Wolf was standing in the bed chamber when Reynardius was telling the King all this, but kept as quiet as a snail at dawn and said nought. But the King saw him lurking and shouted over, "Sir Isengrim, did you hear that? I must have your liver if I'm to be cured!"

'Isengrim looked horrified and quickly replied, "No, no, my liver wouldn't do, my Lord. I'm too young! I'm not yet five years old! I heard my mother say so."

'My father, irritated on behalf of the King, interrupted the wolf: "Ignore these excuses, my Lord! Let him be cut open, without further ado, and I'll know straightaway whether his liver will be any good for you or not."

'The wolf was taken down to the kitchens, and his insides were slit wide with a carving knife, and a bloody slice of his liver torn out and placed in a shallow earthenware basin, decorated with vines and yellow blossoms. Mantled with a starched white cloth, the pretty bowl was then carefully carried up to the King, who ate the wolf's liver in one big gulp, washed down with a glass of cooling anisette, which my father said would help to ease his fever. By the morning he was entirely healed of his sickness, and thanked my father a hundred, nay a thousand, times and commanded all his household to call him, for evermore, there to continue to perpetuity, *Master Reynardius, the Finest Fox Physician of Montpellier*, or their very lives would be in jeopardy.

'My father stayed with the King after this triumph of physic, and became his most trusted advisor, privy to all matters, great and trifling, and obliged always to be by his side. All forgotten now, all forgotten! Instead, these covetous and ravenous scoundrels, these undeserving, low shrewish lords, have been taken up and advanced and set on the high bench, where they have been listened to and pampered and treated as the greatest barons in Flanders. Wise animals, noble and true animals, are ignored, trampled over, cast off with much suffering and sorrowing.

'Gentleness and courtesy are easily silenced by the discordance of rapacity and greed. For when a beast of low birth is made a lord, raised to great heights of power and might and rank above his scraggle-tailed neighbours, he quickly forgets himself and his muddy sabots and his unmapped lineage. He knows not himself, nor where he comes from. He has no pity for any poor creature's pain; he has no ears for any poor creature's requests, unless, of course, those petitions are attached to a hefty reward, a deep sack of gifts, an advancement yet higher. His only intent is to amass more money and fancy goods; his only desire to wield yet more power, yet more privilege. Who cares whom he crushes along the way?'

Reynard broke off as a jag of lightning lit up the Hall, followed by the deep whurl-bellowing of the thunder, angrily rolling over the flat yellow velds and the swelling rivers and the lonely salt marshes to the east. Whilst he was talking, the courtiers were eating and drinking and flirting and playing cards as usual, but such was the fox's oratorical magnetism that every animal in that chamber was nevertheless hanging upon his every word, desperate for more of his amusing fables of morality and vice, more of his soaring rhetorical flights and, as the evening progressed, more of his piquant accounts of Isengrim's cruelty and self-interest.

'Oh, how many grasping, avaricious animals are there now in this and other palaces? Holland, Artois, Brabant, Hainaut—all stuffed full of greedy, low-born lords, in their brand-new silks and damasks and furs. They flatter and smeeke and please their prince for their singular gain. But if that prince ever had need of them, or their estates, they would let him die or suffer appallingly, then raise a soft-padded paw to help! Just like the wolf, who'd rather King Baldwin had died than have given him his own liver! Yet I, Sir Reynard Fox, would see twenty such selfish wolves killed, before any harm befell the King or the Queen. Their loss would be small in comparison.

'But, my Lord, all this took place in your youth—it seems that you have long forgotten my father's good deeds and noble obeisance. And I too have gladly carried out many services for you, performed with reverence, honour and courtesy. But I shall leave any complaints as well alone as an unroused falcon in her darkened mews. You may thank Reynard but little, I don't mind. I don't mind one little bit. Not a scrap of worry furrows my brow. But perhaps you've forgotten what else I'm likely to say? Not that you would find any reproachment from me, Lord Lion—for you are worth all the worship, devotion and love that any fox could impart. From Almighty God, by the inheritance of your noble progenitors, back to Baldwin Ironpaw himself, your rare and esteemable qualities are as long as your fine golden mane, as your black tasselled tail. These princely virtues bind me happily as your humble subject and servant, dutifully fulfilling any command or request with a merry heart!'

Reynard bowed low, and as he did so the rain, pouring hard for a while now, increased to a deluge—bursting the moat and flooding the courtyards and belling the Leie till its banks were fierce-broached; fleaming on the roofs and fast-fleeting on the towers and drenching the bed linen drying in the orchards. But they were used to flooding in their watery, low-lying world, and the castle was sound and safe, and meat was roasting in the dry kitchens and wine flowed free in the Great Hall, so only the smallest lords—the mice, the hedgehogs, the weasels—looked concerned, or those, like Sir Grimbart, whose cellars marched close by the river.

With the flood-rain as plainsong to his weave-woven prick-song, Reynard continued apace.

'Once upon a time, I was walking with Baron Isengrim the Wolf, a couple of miles to the west of here. Between us, we had managed to capture and overpower a wild swine, long-toothed and savage. Because of his screeching and squealing, we bit him hard until he bled to death. Sire, if you recall, you approached us then, coming up from the hazel grove down by the Hare farm, near Oostveld. My Lord, you were most friendly in your greetings, and said, very pleasantly, that we were most welcome there. Then you announced that you and Queen Gente, who was following close behind like Flora through the bell-flowers and the primroses and the fair-in-sight, were ravenously hungry, but had nothing to eat. You begged us to give you part of our winnings, part of the fresh-killed boar. Isengrim replied so softly that an animal could scarcely hear him. He wanted all of that tasty swine-flesh for himself! I, however, spoke out so loudly that the hedge sparrows scattered to the skies. "Yea, my Lord!" I cried, with the best of wills. "I only wish we had more, but I am delighted for you to take the biggest part—do have a hunk of belly-fat or a tallowy hind leg or his head, if you will!"

'The wolf then loped away a little, as he always does. But in going, he took half the pig for himself, only passing you and the Queen one quarter! The last quarter, he chewed and swallowed as hastily as he could, leaving me only half the lungs for my supper! What a creature! I prayed to God then and there that evil would come his way, so I did! Thus, Isengrim the Wolf showed his true nature. How often it is that the smallest, most seemingly insignificant of our actions reveal our inner workings, whether for good or bad.

'Before a beastie could have sung the Credo, you and the Queen devoured your piece of swine. You were so famished. And yet you both still wanted more, as you were not yet full. Hunger and starvation make any animal rage, so when Isengrim proffered no more blood-dark meat, no more scraps of fat or flesh, you lifted up your right foot, and hit him smack between the ears, then slashed his skin raw with your bitel-sharp claws. He bled and bled and bled, almost as much as the boar, and ran away, leaving the remains of his part behind him, his tail cocked between his legs, howling into the greenwood.

'My Lord King, remember? You roared after him, saying: "Make haste, you worthless cur! Come back here straight-away! Get us some more fresh meat, Wolf, and learn how to better deal and part, learn how to equal the cuts this time!"

'I interrupted then, to ease the matter. "Sire, if it pleases you, I will go with him. I'll make sure he does what you ask." Off I went into the gloaming woods where Isengrim was hiding. Milky spring blossoms had fallen into his gashing wound. He was very quiet though. He was in pining agony with his dripping cuts, but had forced himself to groan only as soft as the wind in the trees, for he didn't dare howl or cry too loudly, for fear of what might happen.

'So, off we went a-hunting, as fiercely and as far-ranged as if our very lives depended on it, and brought back a plump calf from the river pastures. And when you saw us heaving it through the grass, you were so pleased that you laughed and laughed, and you complimented me, saying: "What a swift hunter, you are, Sir Reynard! What excellent quarry you find when you're leading the chase! You're just the animal to send in need! Well done, well done! That calf is good and fat alright—you carve it up, Fox, you be the dealer. I trust you to be fair with your divisions, unlike that greying slink-dog over there."

'"With great pleasure and a good will," said I. "The one half, my Lord, shall be for you. And the other half for my lady, the Queen. The muggets, liver, lungs and the innards for your children."'

(The Fox nodded in the general direction of the nursery.

The royal children were barely seen at Court, Noble fretted too much about their safety. There were two princes, Leontius and Lenaert, who lived with their lioness nursemaid Mathild, and a tutor—an elderly Bavarian beaver, Master Hinz—in the south turret. Reynard had met them a couple of times and felt rather sorry for them. Compared to his own rambunctious, three, always in the middle of Maleperduys life, the lion cubs seemed thin and sallow and sad and half-forgotten by both parents.)

Reynard went on with his detailed description of the scissoring: "'The head," I said, "can go to Isengrim the Wolf, and I will have the humble feet." "Reynard," you exclaimed, my Lord, "who taught you to divide so courteously!"

"'That would be the grey priest who sits here with the bloody crown." I pointed at Isengrim. "For he lost his skin with his discourteous disporting of the swine. Such greed and selfishness, such hoggishness, leads to nothing but punishment and shame. Alas, there are so many wolves these days, skulking in every manor and wold, every castle and abbey—wolves who, without right or reason, destroy and gobble up anyone they can overpower. They spare neither flesh nor blood, friend nor enemy; they take what they can get wherever they go. Woe be to those sorry lands where the wolves run and have their power unchecked!"'

Reynard had finished the main thrust of his case. He was exhausted. He had been talking for hours and hours, shouting near the end through the bells and the rain and the thunder. But he pressed on with his closing remarks, binding off the subtle patterns he'd delicately and skilfully woven over the tempestuous afternoon.

'My Lord,' he said, 'this and many other good things I have done for you over the years. I could recount them for you now, if it would not take such an unconscionably long time. In any case, from what I hear, you seem to remember very little about them indeed. If perhaps you oversaw the matters of Flanders yourself a little more, you may recognise everything your loyal Fox of Rupelmonde does for you, year by year, both here and abroad.

'In the old days, no great matter in Court of any importance would have been settled without my advice. After all my troubles are over, I hope fervently that my words may be heard and believed and acted upon once more—along with the wise counsel of all the other true and loyal courtiers who have been discarded or rusticated or falsely accused of something or other.'

The rain had stopped and a sudden shaft of evening sunlight illuminated Reynard's brass-russet coat as he turned, catching him and gilding him like a limning of a fox in the margins of an old book of fables. He looked to the King and to his friend, the Queen, and pleaded with a passion and sincerity evident to all:

'If there be anyone who can say and prove by sufficient and reliable witnesses that I have committed a crime, without a shade of a doubt, then I will abide by all the usual workings of Flemish justice. However, if there are accusations but no witnesses can be brought, then let me be judged upon after the law and custom of this Court.'

The King stood up and stretched, looking quite bewildered. He'd been thoroughly transported by the fox's stories within stories within stories, bewitched and amused and horrified and ashamed in turn. He quite saw now how corrupt his kingdom was and determined to pursue change and reform. He padded over to Reynard and hugged him, kissing him three times in the old Gent way. 'Lord Reynard, you have argued very reasonably that I know nothing more of Sir Cuwaert's death other than that his head was brought here by Sir Bellin the Ram in that scrip of bear fur. Therefore I hereby release you. I will let you go quietly and honourably, without any further process, as there are no witnesses to any crimes. Good for you, Fox. I'm glad you had a chance to explain yourself.'

Trapped in the lion's embrace, Reynard inhaled the King's heady scent of frankincense and roast venison and sugar syrup and marigolds. He sighed. He felt like his father must have felt that day with the treacherous Tybert and the hunter—lungs burning, slavering hounds nipping at his brush, then the sudden embrace of enclosed earth tunnels. Quietude and incolumity after the clattering edge-lands of death and destruction. He sent up a quick prayer to Genesius, saint of tricksters and thieves, then addressed King Noble and the court.

'My dear Lord,' he exclaimed, kissing Noble's whiskery face, 'may God thank you a thousand times over! Most assuredly, your judgement is the right one, for Cuwaert's death makes me so sad and sorrowful that it feels like my heart will break in two. When they both departed from my castle, my chest was so heavy I felt I was going to swoon. I suppose it was a token of the loss which was full fast behind, as close as night.' Reynard shivered at his membrance of white sucked sparrow-thin bones and stare-eyed blood-drippled head, and resolved silently to pay for a Mass for the hare.

366

Apart from his enemies, all of the palace animals who had heard the fox's stories of his wondrous, magical jewels and had followed his well-argued and heartfelt defence against his accusers believed him. They believed him absolutely, without question, without doubt. They were sincerely sorry for his unfortunate misadventures, and felt great compassion for his loss and his sorrow for the little hare. The King and Queen, in particular, pitied him and counselled him not to lament overmuch. 'Try not to upset yourself,' entreated Gente, worried for the fox's nerves, ordering him soothing skullcap infusions and urging him to pray to God, who was 'a friend most excellent' to the grieving.

They also urged him to search for the jewels. For he had praised their properties so imaginatively and skilfully that both lion and lioness were craving their possession, sharing a great will and desire to have them brought to Gent and make high use of their magic. They were grateful that the fox had tried to send the jewels and, despite never having received them, thanked him over and over again and offered all their help in his search—money, horses, servants, letters of introduction.

Reynard crouched before the thrones. He understood their meaning very well—their kindness a through-shine veil for their greed—and thought but little good of them for that. But he said, 'God thank you, my Lord and Lady, that you comfort me so well in my sorrow. You are true friends to me. Neither I nor my supporters here,' he waved vaguely at the raggle-taggle crowd which Lady Rukenawe had assembled, 'will rest, day or night, until those gems are found. We'll run and we'll search and we'll pray. I will threaten and question and beg in all four corners of the world, from Alexandria to Bjørgvin. And I swear on my father's tail that I shall look for them without stop, until they be found and properly restored to the jewel house of the palace of Gent.

'But, I pray to you my Lord King that if they did happen to be concealed in some place from where I couldn't summon them by prayer, or by might, or by request, then you would still help? Still assist me and abide by me and offer all that support you mentioned—money and horses and servants and letters of introduction? For this affair touches you more than anyone! The mirror and the comb and the ring are your goods and yours alone. They are no longer my property. And it is your responsibility, Sire, to take revenge on the theft,' Reynard's voice shook, 'and the—the murder, which have dispersed these precious ornaments, possibly for ever.'

'Of course, Reynard,' said the King, 'I won't fail you. You will always have my support.' Noble spoke magnanimously and gestured with a graceful flourish he'd observed at the court in London once, when the King of England was distributing alms to the poor and ancient. With Reynard's help—and, later, with the strange sorcery of those jewels—he would launch a new age of princely virtue, of attentiveness and care for his lands. A golden *siècle* for Flanders, he thought to himself, lost in a hazy reverie of power and kingship, imagining the worship and envy and obeyance from neighbouring courts.

'Oh, my dear Lord,' wept Reynard, 'this is too much. You give me too much! If only I had the power and might, I would repay you a thousandfold!'

Yes, patient reader, clever reader, who will have seen straight through his patterning and twisting, Reynard had managed to utterly befox the lion, his master. He'd got him fast and fair. He'd got him in his paw. He'd got him just where he wanted him. In fact, Reynard couldn't really believe how well things had gone. He'd laid out his bobbins and he'd woven his threads of fables and romances and histories and truths and half-truths and out-and-out gabbings, one over the other over the other, until a piece of word-lace of such beauty and craft had emerged that no one could see its irregularities and anomalies and ill stitches. The lies had been woven that tight. So many lies, in fact, that he could move freely as he wished from now on—travel anywhere he liked, do anything he wanted to do—without anyone complaining about it.

That is, except for Isengrim the Wolf.

Unlike the rest of the Court, who were placidly going about their business now the fox had been forgiven—some sipping the crow-garlic soup which had just been brought up from the kitchens, some playing dice, others readying the many contraptions for the final day of the pageantry—the Decollation of Saint John the Baptist—Isengrim was angry and highly displeased at the felicitous turn of Reynard's fortunes.

The great grey wolf hauled himself up and slunk spitting and growling across the Hall, his beads and amulets and relics rattling from his belt, and a smell of pine tar and sour urine and maggoty carcasses seeping into the air as he moved. He leapt up onto the high bench and knocked Courtoys's bowl over, the scalding soup spreading over the table and dripping over everyone's breeches and gowns. Isengrim ignored the yells and curses and started to shout himself.

'O noble King! O stupid King! Are you so cubbish that you believe this false and subtle-tongued rascal? Are you so foolish that you let him deceive you and run rings around you with his preposterous lies? Look at him—pretending to be grieving! Shreward! Knave! Swike! Sly pautener of a fox! In faith, if I were Lord, if these were wolf-lands, then Doomsday could come and go and I still wouldn't believe him, for he is wrapped in murder and treason. He's mocking you to your very face. But I'm glad to see him here still, for I have a few tales to tell and all his lies won't help him when I've finished in the telling.'

PART SIX

COMBAT

CHAPTER THIRTY-SIX

The Wolves accuse the Fox

The Twelfth Day of the Feast of Saint John the Baptist
and the Feast Day of Saint Zoe of Rome, the Silenced,
Monday 5th July

It was midnight now, tharky and humid and dripping after the rain. The air smelt of wet mud and of the sweet white flowers of the *Arbore triste*, a jasmine which grew profusely in the Queen's sheltered garden by the ramparts overlooking the river (some of the more poetical courtiers called it the sorrowful tree, as it only bloomed on the darkest and most desperate of nights).

Isengrim was holding court. He stood, heavy-pawed, on the table, hackling, low snarling, snapping at servants nervously mopping soup and clearing basins around him. Sir Courtoys and his entourage had since quietly moved to the lower benches away from his stench and unpredictability.

Poor Erswynde limped to his side from the Lady chapel, where she'd been silently lying by the altar during Reynard's interlude, staring up at the limned blue vault with its precise measured march of gilden, dory stars. She was not well. Harrowed, thin as famine-time, her clever mind and delicate body were exhausted from beatings, scoldings, brutings, deceivings—the ceaseless torments of her unhappy marriage.

'My Lord,' growled her husband, 'I demand you take heed of me, the head-wolf of all the Low Countries. All of you, you low-born rabble-beasts. That fox, that false thief, that swikel-tongued rogue, has betrayed my loving Erswynde in

373

the most foul and dishonest manner.' He nipped Erswynde hard to make her nod in confirmation.

'It happened one winter's day, when the snow was bitter and the land was rimed with frost. They journeyed together to a great lake, by an old meander of the Schelde—Donkmeer, they call it, the Dark Lake. Eel-black and as shallow as a font. The fox made my wife believe that he was going to teach her how to fish with her tail. All she had to do, he said, was to let it hang in the water a good while, then so many fish would cleave on it, that even four wolves would struggle to eat 'em all.

'The stupid little fool, my wife, fell for this nonsense and supposed he was telling her the truth. She stepped into the boggy mire at the edge of the lake, squelching and sinking and picking her way through the mud, right up to her white belly it went, before she finally reached the water itself. And when she got to the deepest murkiest part of the lake, he told her to hold her tail still, until the fish came.

'Well, she held it steady for so long, the idiot, that it became frozen solid in the ice, stiff as a brush, and however hard she tried, she couldn't pluck it out.' Isengrim bared his teeth and glared over at the fox, who was sitting next to the Queen, staring daggers back at him, and a strange, guilty sort of look flickered over the wolf's cruel face.

'When Reynard Fox saw how she was, he came right over and sprang up onto her body and kissed her and did things he should only do with his own wife. She couldn't defend herself as she was stood crane-deep in the mud. I see you shaking your head, Fox, but it's all true, and I know it's true cos I sniffed it out with my own nose, saw it with my own two eyes, heard

374

the howls with my own two ears. I was a witness to the ruin of Lady Erswynde and you can't argue with that, Reynard, however much you try. I happened to be walking along the bank by the reeds, and saw you both embracing, her struggling to get away, you foxing her and pecking her. What anguish I suffered up on that dyke, I thought I'd faint away into the ditch. I fair lost my wits. And I shouted out to you. I cried out as loud as I could, "Reynard, what are you doing down there!"

'When he suddenly saw me so near, he leapt off and ran away as fast as he could, the coward, sloshing and stumbling through the letch. By the she-wolf of Saint Anthony, I went to her with such a heaviness and misery. Deep footed in that slaggy mere and that freezing water I toiled, trying to break the ice around her. She suffered the worst of pains, agonies upon agonies, before she could finally heave out her tail, and even then she left a gobbet of it behind her.

'And we almost lost our lives whilst we were struggling. My doltish, stupid wife was yelping and galping from the smarting pain, crying so loudly that the men of the village came out. A long line of them up on the dyke with flails and pitchforks and staves and bills covered with spikes, which give the worst wounds of all—proper battle wounds, not farmyard wounds. And their ugly wives were up there too, following them, waving their distaffs and crying without pity, "Slay! Slay! Slay the wolves! Slay the wolves!" They stormed through the mire, and reached us in the middle, and started to beat us and strike us, as mean as you like. I've never been so afraid in all my life.

'It wasn't an easy escape. We ran so fast we were sweating, and our breath was raggedy thin. There was one villein who kept staking us with his pike—he was so strong and so swift of foot, he hurt us mighty sore. If it hadn't been night, certainly we would have been slain. Those foul old hags, they didn't care, they would've gladly beaten us to bloody death, right there in that frozen mizzy. They said we'd bitten their sheep. They cursed us with many a curse. But at last we squeezed into a field full of broom and brambles, and we hid there from the peasants, who didn't dare follow any further by night, but returned home again.' Isengrim jumped down from his table pulpit and stalked between the long benches where the rest of the courtiers were seated, watching him with revulsion and the anxious fearful hush conjured by the wolf whenever he took the floor. 'See, my Lord,' he snarred, 'this foul matter, this murder, this treason, this attack upon my wife—justice is needed, sharply, without pause.'

At this point, Sir Reynard the Fox raised himself, and smoothed down his parsley-green silk robes, a beautiful old houppelande embroidered with silver falcons, which Gente had given him to change into the moment he was pardoned. 'If any of this was true,' he said, 'it would ruin the respect and honour in which I am held, shred my reputation, as a hawk shreds its prey. God forbid that such lies be proved! Now let me sort the wheat from the chaff in this roughly fabled account. Firstly, I *was* indeed there and it *is* true that I taught Lady Erswynde fishing—as Queen Gente, our finest fisher-lion, has tutored me in the past. In fact, it was the Queen who showed me the lake in the first place.'

The lioness inclined her head in agreement and smiled at the fox—she couldn't quite remember, but she had indeed taught Reynard how to fish, so it was very plausible that she had taken him to Donkmeer many years ago.

'So, yes,' Reynard continued reasonably, affably, 'I showed Isengrim's wife the best way to fish there, and I also pointed out a good route to get straight to the clearer water without getting stuck in the mud. However, poor Erswynde was so keen to start, so excited when she heard me say the word *fish*, that she rushed off pelly-melly on a great wave of hunger and desire, didn't stick to my instructions nor to any safe route, and ended up caught in the worst of the ice, in which she was frozen fast. And that was only because she abided there too long. She had enough fish, if only she'd been happy with that measured amount, but like all of us she wanted a few more. Being over covetous is never wise; one often ends up with nothing. We animals can never really be satisfied. But I can quite understand her cravings—Donkmeer has such fine cold, oily river fish with flesh as soft as butter—twisty eels as black as the Styx, dogdraves and lampreys and trout and tench.

'When I saw her stuck fast in the ice, I waded over as quickly as I could to help—very difficult going, you understand—and I heaved and shoved and strained; I even stabbed and pierced the ice here and there, but it was no use, all that pain and exertion was for nothing, it proved impossible for me to pull her out.

'Then Isengrim arrived, towering like the very devil on the dyke ridge, and saw how I was pushing and hefting, trying to do my best in a difficult situation, and he started shouting at me with all this nonsense about hurting dear Lady Erswynde. He slandered me most indecently, with such lewd and base language, trying to cause as much trouble as possible, just as worthless loons, rude unthrifts like him are always wont to do.

'But my dear lords, my dear ladies, nothing was as he said—everything was as innocent and as pure as the snow blanketing the fields that night. Perhaps his lies were unintentional? Perhaps his eyes were dazzled as he looked down from above? I don't know. But, in any case, he was screaming and cursing and shouting so many oaths that he was going to punish me and kill me, that when I heard all these threats I thought I'd better leave, at least for a while, and let him calm down. And off I went, promising to return, the insults still echoing in the freezing air.

'Isengrim stumbled down into the water and forced Erswynde out, ripping her poor tail in the process, he was so rough. And then I saw them running and leaping towards the blackberry meadows, warming themselves up, I imagine; otherwise they would have died from the cold.

'Everything I have said is as true as the fixed stars above,' said the fox, settling himself comfortably on a vast pile of velvet cushions, not in the slightest bit concerned by the wolf's accusations. 'For a thousand marks of fine gold, I wouldn't lie to any of you, for lying is not a fitting pursuit for someone of my rank and background. As I have said many times, when something befalls me, I always tell the truth, I cannot help it; it runs deep in my blood. Just as my elders have always done, since the time they reached the age of reason. Indeed, the very first Reynard, for whom all others are named, though we are but passing shadows of his greatness, was entitled Sir Reynard the True—he was cousin to Baldwin Ironpaw, d'you recall, King Noble?'

'Aye, that's right,' replied the lion, who didn't recall anything of the sort, but didn't want to look foolish in matters relating to his illustrious and blessed ancestor, whom he worshipped possibly more than Charlemagne, which was saying something.

'I propose,' said Reynard, curling his sharp black whiskers, 'that if you're doubtful about anything I've said, then give me respite of, say, eight clear days to take counsel, and I will bring you written accounts of of such reliability, marked by good truth and sufficient record, that you, Sire, and your counsellors shall believe and trust me for the rest of my life and the rest of yours, into the bargain. But I am shocked, I'll be frank, that, after my recent ordeal, my actions are even being questioned. It is most irregular.'

There were murmurs of agreement and enthusiastic nodding from the exhausted courtiers, who much preferred Reynard's luminous wit, spine-tingling tales and heart-rending confessions to Isengrim's drawn-out dour complaints, built around his madful suspicions and envies and rivalries, and delivered with an uncouth viciousness, which was very unpleasant and sometimes rather frightening to listen to. Lady Erswynde hadn't moved. She was staring at the trampled meadowsweet on the stone floor, head sunk in her misery.

'I made my opinion of Isengrim plain in my speeches earlier this evening, which told of everything I have had to do with him in recent years,' said Reynard, measured, sane, composed. 'He is a vile and villainous caitiff, an unclean, immoral beast, as was shown when he divided up the wild swine, to give one example out of many. But now it is known to you all, by his own words, what has been clear to me for years, that he is a defamer of ladies—a slanderer of one of the gentlest animals in Flanders! For who would want to play those kinds of horrible games with such a steadfast wife in so great a peril of death? Ice-bound and desperate?' Reynard leapt to his feet, his anger at the wolf was getting the better of him. 'You must ask his wife if it's true,' he shouted, 'and she'll say no! She says as I do.'

Erswynde lifted her head and pulled herself up, and stood swavering, as though she was about to faint clean away. Her gown was grey and tatty and she looked a little like the ghostie that was said to haunt the castle wine cellars round Christmastide. She took a deep breath and was about to speak, when Isengrim snarled at her and jumped down.

'Now, look here,' cried Reynard, holding the hilt of his dagger, 'you really shouldn't talk to your wife so! You're not fit to be a member of the noble Court of Gent with such a want of manners! How dare you treat a lady with such contempt!'

'I don't care a damn for what you think, Reynard,' spat the wolf, 'I know what my wife was going to say and I shall have the saying of it.' And in this casual way, Isengrim stole Erswynde's voice once more, thieved it without a second thought, without a pang of conscience, as so many have done before, and so many will do after. And, having pinched her words, Isengrim spoke over Reynard, spoke over the King, spoke over the Queen, and in the end his bullying arrogance worked, his aristocratic drawl convinced, and he was listened to, as has happened many times before, as will happen many times after.

'Ach, you felle fox, wicked fox, she would say,' leered Isengrim, tongue lolling, 'no one can protect themselves from your fancy words. Oh, you can talk so fine. Your utterances, your words spilling out of you like steaming mig from a jordan. Your falseness and reason are set forth so cleverly, you veil your traitory so well, but you'll be punished for your evil one day, mark my words.'

'There is nothing new in any of this, Isengrim,' retorted Reynard, 'these are all old insults, and I for one am tired of them. If you have nothing of note to say, then stand down, help your wife—she is poorly and sickening—and let us all go to our beds.'

Isengrim stalked over to Reynard, and carried on, close-faced, saliva dripping from dirty teeth. 'What about the well, eh, what about the well?'

'Well, what about the well?' said Reynard, stepping back from the wolf's fetid breath.

'When you lured me down that wretched well at Baudeloo Abbey!'—the wolf spat out each word like a curse. 'There were two buckets, hanging from one cord running through one pulley—one bucket goes up the well, as the other comes down. It was a sleety night, last Candlemas, I came past the Abbey on my evening stroll, and heard you wailing and moaning deep down in the well shaft. I ran over and looked down into the darkness, and there you were, sitting in a rusty bucket, frightened out of your skin and sobbing away like a motherless cub. I asked how you came to be down there, and you said that you'd eaten so many good fishes out of the water that your belly was about to burst wide open like King Henry of England, who died from stuffing too many tasty lampreys

381

down his royal gullet. I was famished, hadn't eaten for hours, so I asked you how I could join you down there.

'"Spring into the bucket hanging up at the top, and you'll be with me in a trice," you said. So in I jumped and went down fast—rattle-clattle-rattle-clattle—faster than I thought I would; but as my bucket tumbled down, yours rose up, and there I was, stuck down the bottom of that dank old well at Baudeloo. I was furious, and you mocked me from on high, sneering, "Thus fares the world, one comes up as the other goes down!" Then you clambered out and went on your merry, blasted way!'

Everyone laughed, including Reynard. Not the reaction that Isengrim was expecting. His wife crouched down and sorrowed quietly to herself, knowing exactly who would bear the brunt of their easy mirth.

'You all mock me too, but that fickle fox left me alone in that miserable place, stuck in a rusty old bucket for a whole day, sore and hungry and very cold. Then the monks found me the next morning, when they pulled their morning water, and I had to endure many a hard blow before I could escape.'

More laughter from the court.

Reynard, having noticed Erswynde's pain, held up a quietening paw and said seriously, 'Baron Wolf, though the strokes did you considerable harm, I'm pleased they fell on you rather than me, for you're far better placed to bear them and one of us had to be beaten. Those cloister-monks are scared of you, they would have killed me. I am only a feeble fox, after all, and you're a great vicious, fang-spiked wolf. This is a useful lesson I've taught you, Isengrim—try to understand and think about it for future reference. Next time, take more care in your dealings with the world; don't believe any animal overhastily, even your friends or cousins. For every creature seeks their own profit, their own convenience in the end. And if not, then they are fools, especially if their own life is in danger!'

CHAPTER THIRTY-SEVEN

The Wolf throws down the Glove

Despite Reynard's somewhat half-hearted attempts to cool the situation, the wolf was scalding-angry, raging with the humiliation of years upon years of foxish tricks, culminating with the King and courtiers' languid dismissal of the incident at Donkmeer, and their mockery of the bucket story, which was meant to turn them fast against Reynard once again. He had had enough.

'I can bear your mocks and your scorns,' he howled across the chamber, 'and even your vile and venomous words, loathsome brass-tailed knave that you are. But the infernal lies—the lies without end—I cannot withstand them any more. Over and over again, you scrape away at my honour, clawing at the respect my fellows once had for me, skinning me to the very bone with your tricks. How many a spity word have you conjured with your falsehoods? How many humiliations must I suffer at your slick tongue! To have the slink-fox nerve to claim that I conspired to kill the King! That I would have murdered Lord Noble just to seize the treasure you said was in Hulsterloe! And you have shamed and slandered my wife—she will never recover from the disgrace. I must avenge her, if not myself—try to salvage the gobbets of her honour, if not my own.

'I have endured you, Reynard the Fox, for long enough, but now you shan't escape me. I might not be able to produce witnesses or testaments for my stories, but by God's entrails, by his rusty, hammered nails, I can certainly declare before

King Noble the Lion of Flanders, and all you fiking, fawning courtlings, that you are a false traitor, a common murderer. And I will carve my proof of this into your flesh, into your bones, into your very marrow! Then shall our strife finally have its end.'

And Isengrim, whipped up by envy and spite and blasphemy, stramped over to Reynard, who was sitting crossed-pawed on his velvet cushions, and slowly and dramatically removed one of his stinking black leather hawking gloves—which he wore for effect, as he had neither the patience nor the intelligence for falcons—and tossed it at the fox's face. 'Therefore,' he gnarled, 'I cast my glove at you—I'll have my justice or die in the attempt.'

Reynard the Fox removed the glove from his head and glared defiantly at the wolf, who was shaking with raw nerves. A fight like this hadn't taken place for years, not since the reign of Noble's belligerent grandfather.

Eyes glazing as he stared at Isengrim, the fox thought desperately to himself: How on earth has this come to single combat! To a grand *kampen*, a beast-to-beast camp-fight! We're scarcely matched—he's thrice my size! My God, I haven't got an ermine's chance in hell! Fat lot of good all my exquisite rhetoric was, if we're reduced to wraxling each other in the mud. I'm a fox of words not of swords! I always thought the dash of my well-honed arguments would release me from the rumble of tooth and claw, but it seems that I was wrong.

CHAPTER THIRTY-EIGHT

The Fox takes up the Glove

Yet, mused the fox, and yet, I have one advantage. Isengrim's forefeet are still raw and tender after his claws were ripped off for my slippers. That makes him considerably weaker than he used to be.

After that somewhat cheering thought, Reynard came to from his reverie, suddenly aware that everyone was staring at him, amidst their outraged chatter, expecting him to say something, do something.

He stood up with the dash of an old-fashioned chevalier and, clutching the hilt of his dagger again, exclaimed, 'Whoever calls me a traitor or a murderer, I call *him* a plain liar! I refer especially to Isengrim, who has brought me to a place of reckoning, where I have often desired to be!'

Reynard removed his own beautiful and immaculate gauntlet—soft cream kid edged with sage-green lace and decorated with vignettes of running foxes and heliotropes and miniature lions embroidered in silver and gold gilt thread— and tossed it to the floor in front of the wolf.

'Lo!' said the fox, all a-flourish, 'Here is my pledge that your acoupements are false. I shall defend myself and prove that all your words are nothing but lies.'

King Noble received both pledges and, as a sporting lion, was delighted to accept the proposed combat. According to the Flemish courtly tradition, he asked two lords to step up as sponsors—borrowers they called them back then—who would make sure that both fox and wolf came promptly first thing in the morning to do battle, as they had promised to do. Sir Bruin the Bear and Sir Tybert the Cat vouched for Isengrim, and standing up for Reynard were his loyal friends Sir Grimbart the Badger and Sir Byteluys the Ape, Rukenawe's eldest son.

CHAPTER THIRTY-NINE

Dame Rukenawe the Ape
trains Sir Reynard the Fox for the Fight

The Feast of Unhappy Saint Godelieve, Murdered
by Her Husband, Tuesday 6th July

Dame Rukenawe, Grimbart, Byteluys and Reynard had removed to Queen Gente's chambers high in the west turret. They were comfortable and spacious rooms. In the day, you could see far, far across the low waterlands—first, the close towers of Gent, then the grey windmills and painted farmhouses and long straight lines of green poplars and skeining dykes and channels and reedy streams, stretching fifty miles or so to Brugge and the rough, heavy waves of the North Sea in the west. But now, in the deep night, that falconish vision was veiled, and should you gaze from the windows all you could see were high stars in the rain-washed sky and a few pin-pricked lanterns in the abbeys and watchtowers and city gates.

Rukenawe was a brilliant strategist and, as such, had put herself in charge of Reynard's training. 'Reynard,' she said, 'my dear nephew, if you want to win tomorrow, you must pay good heed to my advice and recommendations. In your battle, you must be cold, composed and dispassionate. And clever, extremely clever; don't let your guard down for a single moment. Your uncle Mertyn once taught me a prayer which is very useful, full of power and virtue, for those about to fight. The then abbot of Baudeloo, a great master and scholar, taught it to him. He said that whoever utters it devoutly, whilst fasting of course, shall not be overcome in fighting that day. Therefore, dearest Reyner, do not be afraid! I shall read it over you tomorrow morning before you leave, then you can be sure that you'll be triumphant against the wolf. And remember, nephew, it's far better to fight than to swing by the neck.'

Reynard was immensely thankful for the wise ape's help. Tricking and talking his way out of a skirmery, even from the gallows, was one thing; being obliged to duel to the death in this very formal manner was quite another. 'Thank you, dear aunt,' he replied, embracing her. 'I do believe that my quarrel is just, and I'm right to pursue it, and I hope I win, but I certainly need all the help I can get. I'm most grateful for the prayer from Mertyn; he's always brought me good luck.'

His three friends stayed with him throughout the night, keeping a vigil and helping to drive away the time. Grimbart told some tall tales of sea monsters and the wonders of the many ports he'd visited as a younger, seafaring badger— Lisbon, Bordeaux, Bayonne, Cley-next-the-Sea. Byteluys sang old Zeeland folk songs about love and death and herrings. Rukenawe had no time for any of that, however. She was far too busy thinking of how they might increase the fox's advantages and fordeals.

First of all, she had every last hair of his fur, from the tips of his ears to the end of his brush, shorn off as smooth as a new-born chick. Then she anointed his body all over with rich oil of olive, so it became so glat and so slippery that the wolf wouldn't be able to get a hold on him. Reynard was a well-built fox, and this, she thought, would help him wriggle away from Isengrim's claws.

Second, she told him to drink as much as he could, 'so that tomorrow, you'll make lots of urine. But try to hold it in until you come to the field, then, when a good moment arrives, you can let loose a whole sour bladderful into your rough tail, and spray the wolf straight in his beard. Or if you could aim for his eyes, then you'd have a fighting chance of blinding him, and even for a short while that would hinder him considerably.

Next, Rukenawe had some very specific tactical tips for fighting a large brutish wolf:

TAIL. Always hold your tail fast between your legs, so that he can't catch you by it.

EARS. Hold your ears down flat against your head, so he can't grab you by them.

PROTECT. Watch yourself and protect yourself—at the beginning, flee from his strokes.

DUST. Let him spring up and chase you, and make sure you run to where the most dust is and stir it up with your feet so that it flies into his eyes, and again that will blind him momentarily. Whilst he's rubbing his eyes, take your advantage, and smite him and bite him where you'll most hurt him.

PEE. Keep hitting him continually in the face with your brush full of pee; that will make him so wild and confused, he won't know where he is.

WEARY. Make him run after you for as long as possible to make him tired and weary.

FEET. Remember that his feet are still excruciatingly painful since you took half of them for your shoes.

HEART. Whilst he appears full of vigour, his heart is not as strong as it seems.

'There is my counsel then, nephew. Now, don't forget that cunning always goes before strength, so use your wits at all times. And put yourself in a wise and defensive position, so you can win and bring us all glory and honour! I would be very sorry, as you know, to see you come undone and lose this battle. Now let's have some more wine, and I'll teach you the power-words that Uncle Mertyn taught me to overcome an enemy.'

She made Reynard sit on a little stool and stood over him, and laid her hands upon his head, saying the following magical words:

Blaerde Shay Alphenio
Kasbue Gorfons Alsbuifrio

'Now you're safe, my dear Reyner, from all mischief and dread and your tremble-fears. I would suggest that you feel better disposed to fight if you rest a little now, as it's almost day. We'll wake you in plenty of time.'

'Auntie!' said Reynard, slightly tearful, 'I feel so much better. Full glad inside. God thank you for doing me so much good. I don't fully deserve it. I don't think anything can hurt me now you've said those holy words over me!'

Then down the spiral stairs he padded, to the Queen's garden, where he lay under his favourite tree—a spreading linden tree in full leaf, its wide branches stately and cool and soothing in the hot night. And there he slept in the long grass until the sun had risen and was glittering gold on the gush-water of the Leie below.

Wreathed in weeds, a river otter came and woke him, and told him to get up. He was an old friend of Grimbart, who often crewed his boat. The otter, whose name was Erasmus, after the saint of sailors, was desperate for Reynard to win. He loathed Isengrim, who had taken one of his nephews, his sister's little pup, many years ago up by Dendermonde.

Once the fox was awake and sitting up, he gave him his breakfast—a good young duck. 'Grim told me what's been going on and I saw them lanterns up in the tower. I've been up all night too, cousin,' he said, as Reynard stretched and yawned, 'I had to make many a dip and a dive and a plunge before catching that fat quacker for you. I pinched it from a fowler by the Minnemeersbrug. Go on—take it, eat it, Reyner!'

'What a marvellous duck! A handsel of great luck and good fortune, no doubt!' said Reynard, 'I thank you for remembering me, cousin, and if I live I promise I'll shower you with gifts!'

Then the fox took a napkin from his bag, and began his breakfast, watched eagerly by the otter. He ate the duck without any of his usual rich sauces or soft white bread, but it tasted delicious and went down very well, and the otter was delighted. Afterwards, Reynard went down to the riverbank and drank four long draughts of water, as instructed by his aunt Rukenawe. Thus readied, he set off towards the battlefield, down on the water meadows, and all those who loved him went close by his side.

CHAPTER FORTY

Sir Reynard the Fox enters the Battlefield

Stands had been erected overnight by Noble's carpenters, with three viewing boxes on stilts prepared for the many spectators; fancy courtiers and working town-animals mingling together. The central box for Queen Gente, the King and their cubs was draped in yellow silk, with *de Leeuw van Vlaanderen*, 'the Lion of Flanders', blazoned across the curtain in fresh gilt paint. On the right, benches were draped in deep russet for the fox's supporters, with one of his many Reynardian family proverbs written in scarlet on the lean-rail below: *Laat elke vos op z'n eigen staart passen*, 'Let every fox take care of his own tail.' The wolf's left-hand box, filled with his glowering, squabbling allies, was decorated in black-and-white checks; his house's dour legend, *Dood en wraak*, 'Death and Revenge', scrawled in a wobbly attempt at black letter.

When King Noble saw Reynard approaching, all shorn and oiled and ugly, he chuckled and nudged his wife, and said to himself, 'Ey, ey, Fox, how well you do look after yourself. Ey, ey, ey, clever old Reynard!' But the fox said not one word, and unsmiling he knelt down low to the earth in front of the King and the Queen, then striked off to the field of battle.

The wolf was ready too, surrounded by his pack, laughing and boasting and showing off in his loud, brash, tavern voice.

The Rulers and the Keepers of the Field were the leopard, Sir Firapeel, and Sir Antheunis the Lynx. Between them they were carrying the huge and ornate royal Bible, on which the wolf swore that Reynard was indeed a traitor and a murderer, that there was no one falser in the whole of Flanders and that he would prove these claims in blood and claw on Reynard's body. Lord Reynard, in turn, swore that Isengrim was a miserable liar, a false knave and a cursed thief, and it would be he who would prove all of that on the wolf's nasty worm-ridden scrub-furred bone-house.

Once they had finished with all their oathing, the two Governors of the Field cheerfully bade them do their best, and then gave the precious Bible to Botsaert the Monkey, who scampered back to the castle to lock it up again, in case things got nasty.

Everyone then left the Field, apart from Dame Rukenawe the Ape. She stayed close by the fox, and urged him to remember all the instructions she'd given him. *'Tails! Ears! Protect! Dust! Pee! Weary! Feet! Heart!'* she counted them off on her fingers, one by one.

'Don't forget, Reyner, dear, when you were only seven years old, a mere scrap of a cub, you were already clever enough to scout around at night without a lantern, winning all the best food and treats to be had, from right under the muzzles of much older beasties. And everyone is always saying how subtle and wise you are! So, follow my counsel, remember your worth and your talent, and work as hard as you can to win the prize, and you and your friends will bask in the honour and glory of it for many years—nay, forever after.'

Emboldened and embarrassed by her words in equal measure, Reynard mustered, 'Dear Auntie, I remember that very well, sneaking out at night, and I promise I'll do my best today as well and put your counsel into play—the pee and the feet and the dust—everything. I'll endeavour, however difficult, however much it pains me, to triumph, and bring renown to all friends of Maleperduys—and to my enemies, nothing but shame and confusion!'

'God grant it you!' cried his aunt, thumping him on the back affectionately, as the King's waits began to blow their trumpets for the commencement of the combat.

CHAPTER FORTY-ONE

The Fight

Having bolstered her nephew as best she could, Dame Rukenawe walked to the stands, leaving the Field entirely to the two champions.

The wolf immediately attacked without the King's sign or any of the usual chivalric niceties. He jumped at Reynard, deep-snarling in his fury, forefeet opened wide to seize the fox's body. But Reynard sprang swiftly away from him, for he was far more nimble and lighter on the feet than the heavy-cast wolf. Isengrim leapt after him, and, whilst the courtiers watched in a fever of excitement and horror from the boxes, chased him round and around the field without stopping, bared teeth snapping at his brush and hind quarters, sometimes stumbling over himself in his bloodlust, wild and vicious in his hunt.

As he was so much broader, his stride was wider, and he often overtook Reynard, at one point circling around and lifting up his foot to strike him, but Reynard saw it coming and in that fragment of a moment smacked the wolf in the face with his rough and urine-soaked tail, exactly as advised by his aunt. Isengrim staggered back; the sharp-acid fox pee stung his eyes so badly, he thought he'd been full, plat, stark blinded.

Whilst Isengrim was rubbing his eyes, desperately trying to clean them, Reynard immediately seized his advantage. Remembering his training, he stood with the stiff river breeze behind him, skrabbing and casting up the dust with his feet, so it also flew straight into the wolf's eyes, blinding him even more. What with the yellow pee and the dense clouds of dry gritty sand, his eyes were smarting like the very devil, so bad in fact that he had to abandon the chase. As he was pawing at them, Reynard grasped his chance again, and hurled himself at Isengrim. Fired up with a violent anger flamed over years and years of enmity, he bit the wolf as hard as he could, leaving three great gashes on his head.

Tumbling back, the fox laughed and, gasping from his exertions, started to mock his adversary: 'What is it, Sir Wolf? Has someone bitten you? How's our *mêlée* treating you so far? It's not over yet! Hold fast, and I'll produce another fighting trick or two. You've stolen many a lamb, many a young cub, and destroyed many a simple beast. For decades you've ruined lives, ruined families, and now you've falsely accused me and brought me into all this trouble. I shall avenge all today! The mills of God may grind late, they may grind slow, yet they grind as fine as the dust soiling your face!

'I, Reynard the Fox, have been chosen to repay you for your old wicked sins, for God will no longer stand to suffer your greed and your cruelty. Me, I shall assoile you! Absolve you! And that will be right good for your soul, so you should take the penance patiently, for you haven't got much longer to live, and the flicker-fires of hell shall be your purgatory! Thy life is now in my mercy, in my very paws. But if you'll kneel down and ask for my forgiveness and acknowledge that I've won our combat, then even though you're as wicked a wolf as ever walked this earth, I will spare you. For my conscience, fine-tuned from my time as a hermit, counsels me that I shouldn't kill any of God's creatures, even a low-down, sinny-boned, litherhead like you!'

Isengrim was almost driven out of his wits by the fox's spitous and contemptuous words. He was so angry and in so much pain that he didn't know whether he was coming or going; he was neither buff-ne-baff, not one thing nor the other. His wounds were spurging blood and smarted sore; he cursed the fox and, gathering his scattered wits, thought how he might take revenge and fast.

Arrogance had been hammered into rage, and he lifted up his foot and hit Reynard's head with such a violent, heavy-clawed stroke that the fox collapsed into a limp heap on the ground. The wolf scrambled round to capture him, but Reynard was so light-footed and wily that he leapt up as agile as a monkey, and turned and faced him fierce and bold, initiating a long and grindingly repetitive round of the battle. It was excruciating to watch for Reynard's followers and dull for the wolf's allies, who'd expected a quick snap of the fox's neck at least half an hour ago.

That Isengrim loathed Reynard was as plain as the morning sun now beating hard down onto the exposed, treeless Field. He sprang after him a full ten times, one after the other, each time grabbing him and trying to pin him down, but the fox's skin was so oily and sliddery that he kept slithering out of his grasp and escaping.

Over and over this happened. So subtle and snelly was he that many a time the wolf thought he'd finally got him, the fox would slip between his legs and under his furry belly, then swift-twist round to give Isengrim another flick of sour-addled brush, swish-whoosh in his face again, murking and blinding him with effortless ease. And as soon as the pee was trickling down Isengrim's muzzle, Reynard would leap back onto the dry ground and raise another cloud of powdery sand to fill up the wolf's red-streaked, blear-watered eyes once more.

The wolf grew increasingly woebegone, desperate—the fox was quite literally running circles around him. Yet, and yet, he had a wolf's body, a wolf's fangs, a wolf's heft, a wolf's strength, and whenever he could reach the fox he bombarded him with agonies of blows, slashing and cutting and grushing and thumping him with all his wolvish might. Yet, and yet, Reynard gave as good as he got, and together they swapped many a stroke and many a bite whenever they found the slightest chance or advantage. Each did his best to destroy the other.

What a battle it was! A battle the like of which was not seen again for many a century. One so wily, the other so strong; one fought with brute force, the other with artful subtleties. It was the age-old fight between Brains and Brawn, Muscle and Reason, but who would win nobody yet knew, and the courtiers and the townsfolk were on the edge of their benches, cheering and yelling and clapping and screaming and howling in turn.

Isengrim was wrothy that the fox had managed to endure so long against him. And, just as Rukenawe had hoped, Reynard's resilience had a great deal to do with the unhappy state of the wolf's feet—his sores were still open and weeping, making it difficult for him to run, particularly now the dust had also worked its way into them. This also meant, of course, that Reynard could move around the Field more easily—halting, launching, ducking, diving, freezing, turning—all were easier with two pairs of working feet. And the fox didn't stop torturing the wolf with his sodden tail either, so much so that

Isengrim thought his eyeballs might tumble out, they were so murky and inflamed.

At last, tired of this fruitless chasing, Isengrim said to himself, 'I need to make an end of this endless battle. How long can this keytyf, this weakling scoundrel keep going against me? Why isn't he dead yet! I am Baron Isengrim, by God's sinews—the greatest wolf in Flanders. Nay, the greatest wolf in Christendom. If I laid on top of that fox, I would crush his wretched body to death. It's embarrassing that I've spared him so long. Animals will mock me and point paws at me that I'm on the losing side, being beaten by that dirty, low-born tod. I am sorely wounded and bleeding like a pig at Martinmas and he's drowning me in his pee and casting so much dust and sand in my eyes that soon I really will be blind. What can I do but take a gamble and see what happens?'

And so, just as Reynard was turning to attack, Isengrim hit him unexpectedly, as hard as he could on the side of his head, so hard that the fox crashed backwards onto the ground once again. But before he could struggle up, the wolf caught him in his feet, and laid down on top of him to press him to death with his weight.

For the first time in the fight, unable to catch his breath, Reynard was sick with fear, his heart pounding in his ears. His friends were equally frightened when they saw him lying under the wolf, his aunt and Grimbart rushing down to the side of the Field from the stands. Isengrim's supporters, on the other hand, lounging in the chequered box, drinking dead-nettle ale and chewing on kiken legs, were delighted, joyfully cheering the wolf on. Reynard defended himself as best he could from his awkward position, clawing and kicking his legs upwards and pummelling and punching the wolf wherever he could. Isengrim didn't dare to do much harm with his feet, in case the fox slipped out, but with his teeth he snapped and snatched at him, trying to bite his neck as he writhed below him. Reynard was terrified of being clamped by those huge, slavering jaws—even his considerable courage began to falter whilst pinned underneath a raging, murderous wolf. He began to feel dizzy and weak. 'I am going to die,' he thought, 'I can't keep him from killing me much longer—I don't have much breath left, much strength left—Oh God, I'll never see Hermeline or my cubs again.'

The beloved faces of his little family as sharp and lively as paintings in his mind, the fox made one last gigantical effort, and struck Isengrim across his head with his fore-claws, ripping the skin off between his brows and his ears so violently that one of his eyes was torn out and hung bobbing against his muzzle, like a golden grape on a stem, before it fell.

The pain was like an arrowhead. The wolf howled and wept and cried and made the most piteous noise imaginable, for the blood was flowing like a flood stream, crimsoning his fur and pooling wide on the hard parched ground.

CHAPTER FORTY-TWO

In which Sir Reynard the Fox
flatters Sir Isengrim the Wolf

Paws shaking, the wolf wiped the blood from his eyes. Taking
his chance, Reynard wriggled out from under him and sprang
to his feet, gulping air into his lungs. Isengrim was raging with
fury, and despite his wounds and all the bleeding he managed
to hit and smack the fox before he could escape and clasped
him fast in his arms. The fox was plunged into peril again.
The two wrestled for a long time—violent, brutal, tough it
was, and no pleasure to watch. Isengrim was so wrathy and
angry, he forgot his pains and his smarting eyes, and threw
Reynard flat under him.

In the scuffle, the forepaw which the fox threw out to break
his tumble somehow ended up in Isengrim's mouth. Reynard
was terrified he would lose it, one hard bite and that would
be the end of him.

'Now choose,' said Isengrim, 'whether you'll yield to me as
overcome, announce to everyone you've lost, or I'll slay you
here and now. Not the scattering of the dust, not your foul
pee, not your mockery, not your defence—none of these will
help you now. You can't scape me, Reynard. You've done me
so much harm, done me so much shame—badly wounded
me—and now my eye—you've taken my precious eye, you
miserable thief.'

The fox understood only too well the trouble he was in,
caught between a wolf and a hard place. He had either to
submit to Isengrim, admit he was beaten in front of the

whole court and half the town, or be killed. He knew he must say one thing or another, and the way he answered was vital, a question worth ten marks, as foxes used to say back then. However, this was Reynard, Lord of Maleperduys, not an everyday fox, and he wasn't so easily conquered. Indeed, he had already concluded what he would say, and it was not exactly what Isengrim was expecting. Far from it.

He began with a cascade of fair words: 'Dearest Uncle, there is a third way which lies between these two choices, as clear as a fresh-paved road lying between two muddy, gnatty ditches! I, Reynard, will become your fox—with all my goods and talents attached, *bien sûr*! I will serve in a myriad ways. I will travel for you all the way to the Holy Grave in Jerusalem, and will secure pardons and great spiritual benefits for your cloister, from all the many, many churches in the Holy Land.

'From Bethlehem to Nazareth to Damascus, I will roam at your command. My journey will not only greatly profit your soul, but the souls of all your ancestors, wolf ghostie after wolf ghostie going back all the way to Wicked Wulfstan of Loon, who still needs all the help he can get after his rampages and all those papal curses. I don't believe there's ever been such an offer proposed to even a bishop or a king! Indeed, I would serve you as I would serve our Holy Father the Pope. Everything I have, all my property—not only Maleperduys but all my other land and manors, including my hunting lodge in the Ardennes—will be yours. I will be your servant in every possible way and will command all my kin and lineage to serve you also, from my tiniest cub to my most elderly aunt. Then you shall be a lord above all lords! Who would dare to lift a paw against you!

'Furthermore, everything I acquire in my nocturnal wanderings, whatsoever it should be—also yours! All the pollaile! All the poultry of your dreams—the plumpest of geese, partridges, plovers! All the fish—rich and oily tench and eel and luce! And all the meat—the tenderest of swine, venison, calves! Everything you might desire! You and your wife and your children will always have the choicest cuts before us foxes. And from now on, I will always be by your side, I'll be your shadow, your loyal companion, your wardecorps, protecting you from all hurts and scathes. You're strong and I'm wily. You've got the brawn and I've got the brains. One with the counsel, the other with the deeds. Together we'll be unbeatable—nothing bad could ever befall us with such a compatible union!

'We are kin, Isengrim. Family. We shouldn't be fighting. There shouldn't be any enmity between us. I certainly wouldn't have fought against you if I could have escaped. But you appealed me into a battle, in which I was required to participate according to the laws of Flanders. I would not have taken part, I have not done so gladly. But in our combat I have been most courteous to you. I haven't used all my strength, all my cunning, as I would have done if you'd been a stranger to me. The Nephew ought to spare his Eme, says the old custom, and I stick by it. And, mark well, that when I ran from you to spare you, I couldn't have done otherwise; my heart would not let me. I could have hurt you much more than I did, but I never even thought of it. Indeed, I have barely touched you, barely wounded you save for that unfortunate accident with your eye, for which I am extremely sorry. Truly, it wounds me to the very bone, it cleaves my poor heart in two to witness your pain, dear Uncle Isengrim. I wish it had happened to me, rather than you, at least then your anger would have been soothed by my misery. There are advantages to losing an eye, of course, as Sir Tybert can tell you. For when you fancy a nap, you need only shut one window, whilst the rest of us must shut two.

'My wife and my three children and all my many friends and relations and allies and supporters, as one, will fall down before your feet in front of the King—and in front of anyone else you'd desire them to prostrate themselves in front of, in fact—and pray most humbly that you will allow Reynard Fox, your closest nephew, to live. And not only that, I will also acknowledge that I have trespassed against you and told many, many lies about you. How could any lord have greater honour or respect than I am offering you now? I wouldn't think of doing this for anyone else. Therefore, I pray for you to be pleased with it all!'

Reynard's patter, designed to confuse and flatter and lull the listener into a state of malleability, did not seem to be working on the wolf, who was standing half in agony, half in turbulence, glaring at him like Achilles once glared at Hector outside the walls of Troy—the fox's paw still trapped in his mouth, blood still a-trickling, right eye still a-missing, left eye still a-clogged with sour pee and sand. The fox sighed, but pushed on regardless.

'Look, I know very well you could kill me if you wanted to. But if you did slay me now, what would you win? Forever after, you'd have to hide from my friends and my family, who would commit themselves to most grievous and glorious revenge. As the Ancients tell us, he is a wise animal who can measure himself in his anger, not be overhasty, but look to see what might happen or befall him in times to come, before making his judgement. A beastie who stands back in his fury, and calmly contemplates the best path to take, is a beastie flush with wisdom, indeed.'

Reynard shuffled his weight onto his other backfoot; he really was in a most uncomfortable position. 'Yes, there are many fools in this kingdom, in this world, who rush in without thinking in the heat of their raging, then repent afterwards, when it's too late, sometimes for the rest of their lives. But Eme, I think you're far too wise a wolf to do that.' The fox looked up at his enemy. He was at least listening. 'Isengrim, isn't it better to be praised? To have honour, peace and a restful, untroubled life? And better to have friends who are ready to help than to have shame, hurt and unrest, and enemies lying in wait to do you harm? There is no honour in killing a fox whom you've already overcome! No honour at all! It scarcely matters to me—if I were dead it would be but a little hurt—but your shame would be mountainous…' Reynard tailed off, realising he was overdoing it, and Isengrim was beginning to bite down. He closed his eyes, but the wolf was too cross to do anything other than yell.

'Ay, you stinking thief,' he shouted, 'how you would love to be freed, to be loosed and discharged by me! That much is clear from your gildy, flowery words! You might have blinded me, but even with one eye I can still conceive a liar and a cheat. If I let you go and you were gadding about on your free feet, you wouldn't price my worth as much as an eggshell. Though you promise me the world of finest red gold, I still wouldn't let you escape. I set little by you, and less for your ranks of kith and kin—they mean nought to me. Less than nought.

'Everything you've said to me has been nothing but fables and feigned falseness. You thought you could deceive me? Think how many years I've known you! The Holy Grave? Damascus? Giving me your best poulets? Magged tales, all of 'em. I'm no bird to be locked into a cage, or muddled by chaff—I know good corn when I see it, just as I know a fat bushel of lies!

'Oh, how you would mock me if I let you escape! Someone who didn't know you might have been taken in by all this; not me. Not Baron Isengrim. All that flattering and sweet fluyting is wasted on me, for I can see straight through to the subtle lying tales crouching behind. You've so often tricked me in the past, I'd be a fool to heed your nonsense now.

'You foul stinking knave, you said you'd spared me in this battle. Look at me! One eye gone! Gashes all over my head—more than twenty, I'd say! How is that sparing me! You didn't even give me pause to catch my breath before another blow! I would be a complete fool to spare you now or show you any mercy at all! You've spun confusion and shame all around me and I have had enough. Enough! And what wounds most of all, gives me the most pain, is how you've dishonoured and slandered Erswynde my wife, whom I love as well as myself! I shall never forget how you forced yourself upon her, how you deceived her! Every time it comes into my mind, my anger and hatred for you are renewed tenfold!'

As Isengrim was speaking, he was getting more and more agitated, and the fox was thinking hard about how to disentangle himself and get his forepaw back from the knifey dangers of the wolf's mouth. He managed to move his free paw between Isengrim's back legs and, just as the wolf was reaching the peak of his invective, gripped him fast by the cullions, before wringing them as hard and as viciously as he could.

Isengrim's screams! My goodness! Sailors in the middle of the North Sea could hear them! The Mercers having a nice dinner at the English Merchants' House in Brugge could hear them! Even Hermeline, in her study at Maleperduys, sucking the end of her quill whilst struggling with a particularly difficult line of Hebrew, heard them and wondered what on earth her husband was up to now.

As Isengrim was howling and crying and baying with pain, Reynard managed to finally pull his other paw from his mouth. The wolf didn't even notice; he started rolling in the dirt, spitting blood and wetting himself in his agonies.

CHAPTER FORTY-THREE

Sir Reynard the Fox Wins the Battle

The pain was even worse than that pinsing and torturing his eyes, which were still bleeding freely, made worse by all his rubbing. It was so bad, in fact, that Isengrim the Wolf fainted dead away. He'd lost so much blood, and the thresting and crushing of his cullions had squeezed out every last drop of stamina and energy and fight. The moment he was down, Reynard leapt on him with all his might. He caught him by the legs, and pulled him roughly across the Field, stopping in front of the stands, so everyone could see, and proceeded to pummel and pound and thump him sore.

Isengrim's friends, once so arrogant, were bowed down by shame and grief and raw fear for the wolf, and went weeping to the King. They begged him to stop the battle and decide the winner himself. Noble, who had thoroughly enjoyed the contest and was delighted at the unexpected upturn in the fox's fortunes, readily agreed and muttered animatedly for some time to the Keepers of the Field, the leopard and lynx, who then, in turn, went to speak to Reynard and the limp form of Isengrim.

'Our Lord the King would like to speak with you,' declaimed Sir Firapeel, self-importantly. 'It is his will that the battle be ended and its resolution be taken up into his own paws. For if either of you were slain by the other, it would be a great shame on both sides. King Noble feels you have both fought well, but have gained as much honour and glory on the Field as is possible without an unpleasant end.' He turned to

Reynard the Fox and bowed. 'Lord Reynard, all the beasties, both Crown and Town, who have witnessed this battle have decided to give you the prize. You have won, Reynard Fox! Well played! You have defeated Lord Isengrim fair and square!'

Covered in Isengrim's blood, battered and bruised, Reynard surveyed the Field, a great flood of relief and happiness and sudden exhaustion flowing over him. 'Then I thank every last animal here,' he said beaming, 'and whatever it pleases my Lord to command, I shall not gainsay. I desire nothing more, nothing better than to have won the Field. Let my friends come to me now!' He stood up and waved and opened up his scratched and bloodied arms, shaking from his sudden happy deliverance. 'I shall take their careful advice as to what to do next. Sir Grimbart—ah, there he is!—Grim! Grim! Come here!—Sir Grimbart always tells me that it's wise for a fox to take counsel from his friends in weighty matters!'

Down they all came from the box and the stands, some waving Maleperduys banners, others singing rowdy songs, all exuberant with joy and relief.

First was Sir Grimbart the Badger, rushing as fast as he could, crying and laughing and shaking his head all at the same time; then came a triumphant Dame Rukenawe with her two sisters, and her two sons, Byteluys and Fulrompe and her daughter, Hatenette. Akeryn Flittermouse, the librarian at Sint-Pieters, was next, thrilled to be part of the winning party; then Hermel the Ermine from the Far North, who wanted to talk to the fox about his unusual tactics, which he felt had more than a smack of the chronicles of Troy. More and more animals came to congratulate Reynard, along with twenty or so others who certainly wouldn't have come if he had lost.

Oh, the fickle nature of fame and glory, thought Grimbart, as he was squashed and pushed and trodden on by the throng of well-wishers. Whoever wins a great victory can be sure of the praise and admiration of the unworthy. Nobody ever gladly goes to the loser, of course. Amidst the crowd there was also:

Dame Ordegale the Beaver,
her husband, Pancer the Beaver,
Lady Panthecrote the Otter,
her husband, Baron Otter of Leie,
Erasmus the River Otter, their cousin thrice removed
    (by situation as well as lineage),
Íñigo the Fox and his usual rakish young Navarrian cohort,
Sir Ostrole the Stoat,
Sir Fluwijn the Stone Marten,
Sir Maerter the Pine Marten,
Boussyng the Polecat,
Foret the Ferret,
Sir Eenkoorn the Squirrel,
Sir Musehout the Weasel,
Lady Genetta the Genet,
and the Mouse, Prince Myš, who was visiting from Novgorod,
    and didn't really understand what was going on.

There were many, many more, some of whose names even Reynard didn't know. And they all had come because he'd won the Field. Some came who had even laid complaints against him before, terrible accusations forgotten in a puff of victory. Now, of course, they were suddenly his best friends, his closest kin, his longest standing supporters. And they, who once sneered and spat at him, booed him, slandered him and whispered about him behind his back, were full of praise and fluttering compliments.

'What hypocrites they are!' said Erasmus to Grimbart. 'Horrible to Reynard for years, and now showing him right friendly cheer and countenance!'

'Aye. Thus fares the world these past years, Erasmus,' replied Grimbart. 'Whoever's rich and high on the Wheel, he has many kinsbeasts and friends eager to enjoy his wealth and position. Whilst those who are needy or in pain or in poverty find themselves lonely and deserted, eschewed by kin and friend alike. Fickle creatures, animals, fickle and cruel as the sea.'

Afterwards, a great feast was laid out on the grass. Long boards and trestles were heaved out from the castle, and dozens of benches and the two portable thrones and some scissor chairs for Reynard and the higher lords, and a mass of silk cushions in Reynard's colours—russets and scarlets and vermicles and crimsons and hazel-nut browns. Trumpets were blown and bagpipes played, and there was singing and dancing and some animals even jumped in the river. The food mainly consisted of poultry, in honour of the fox, and very good it was too—cold chicken with sage sauce, twenty large crustades, chicken and egg pies with cloves and mace and saffron, roasted heron with ginger and galingale, and a fine selection of plovers, mallards, teals, larks, finches and buntings with fritters and brawn.

During their banquet, they all said to Reynard, 'Dear Nephew, blessed be God that you have won! We were all so frightened when we saw you lying under the wolf!' Reynard thanked them all in a charming and self-deprecating manner—'No, no, no, please, it was nothing at all, really, nothing at all'—receiving each and every one of them with joyfulness and great gladness, friend, kin and former enemy alike.

When they had reached the cakes and spiced-wine stage, Reynard asked his most trustworthy companions what he should do, whether he should give the judgement of the Field over to the King or not. 'Oh yes,' said Dame Rukenawe, 'of course you should, Reyner. You'll win honour by setting the whole matter in the Crown's paws now, great honour. You can trust Noble well enough.' His other friends agreed, so they all went with Sir Antheunis the Lynx and Sir Firapeel to the King, who was in an extremely good mood, after a highly enjoyable fight and an excellent dinner.

Reynard went in front, accompanied by trumpets and pipes and all manner of other minstrelsy, playing loud and merry tunes. He knelt down before King Noble, who immediately bade him stand and said to him, 'Lord Reynard, you must rejoice at your great victory—for you won the day most gloriously! I thus discharge you and let you go freely quite wherever it pleases you! And that old debate between you and the wolf, well, I'll take it over now. I'll hold it on me. Don't you worry, eh! I shall discuss it by reason and by counsel of the wisest and most noble of Gent, who aren't necessarily those animals you see gathered about me at Court. In any case, we'll wait until Isengrim is healed of all his wounds, then I shall ordain whatever justice is necessary, send for you to come to me and, by God's grace, give my final sentence and judgement on the matter.'

The fox could not quite believe that he'd managed to pull off another miraculous escape, avoiding doom by the tip of his brush, largely through the stratagems of his clever aunt, he thought gratefully, turning to salute her with his paw. Then, before the King could add anything else, he flourished a low bow—looking most handsome thought the Queen, with all his battle wounds and heroic scars—and said in a humble voice: 'My Lord the King, I am in complete agreement with your judgement, which is most pleasing and most wise. And I must declare I love you with my heart above all other lords. I have always done my best for you and the Queen, and will continue to do so for as long as I shall live.' Reynard bowed again and smiled sweetly at Lady Gente, who whispered something urgently to her husband.

PART SEVEN

HOME

CHAPTER FORTY-FOUR

In which Sir Reynard the Fox is made the Most Powerful Lord in Flanders

Noble helped himself to another cake and a dollop of cream and looked at Reynard trying not to smile too broadly in front of his King. Remembering how the fox had tricked Isengrim, all that insolent wolfish arrogance felled by a pee-sodden tail and a swirl of dust, he began to laugh, first a little, then a great booming imperial laugh which rumbled around the water meadows like a smite of midsummer thunder.

'Oh, Reynard,' he half-roared, half-chuckled, wiping his streaming eyes, 'you owe me homage, Fox, an allegiance which I hope you'll pay for the rest of your life. But seriously, I would like you to become a permanent member of my Council, available to your sovereign at all times, early and late, for advice and wisdom on all manner of judicial and administrative matters and concerns to me and to Flanders. Moreover, I'd like you to assume the role of one of my Justices, with all the powers which that implies, dishing out just deserts and whatnot, eh? But you'll have to clean up your act, Reynard, no more misdoings or trespasses. Back to the hermitage for you, what!' He laughed again, and slapped the table heartily. Reynard smiled politely, stunned by his promotion.

'No more crimes, though, d'you understand, Fox? And I will also restore all the power and authority and privileges you enjoyed before. Now, make sure you judge wisely, according to the strictures, the detail, of the law. Don't just fudge it or make things up, like some of the lazier animals.' He nodded at Bruin Bear, snoring under the stands.

'For when you set your fine mind, your brilliant wits, and your excellent counsel to virtue and goodness, then our Court simply cannot do without you. For there's no one quite like you, Reynard. You've demonstrated that today. What a victory! Overpowering one so much stronger and mightier than you, simply through your brilliance and sharp thinking. No one can equal you in clear-sighted advisement, no one subtler in finding remedies for mischiefs and offences and troubles.'

Noble knocked back another couple of drinks. 'Be true to me, Fox, true to me and righteous in all your dealings, and from now on I will act entirely on your advice. Anyone who hurts you breathes their last. I will avenge all for you, Fox, and inflict the very worst punishments on all your enemies.

'With your eloquence and word-wielding, I'll have you to speak for me as well, I think—yes—you can say all my words and speeches for me.' The yarrow wine was sinking at an alarming rate, and Reynard hoped that Noble would remember all this the next day. 'And in all of my lands, you shall be sovereign above all other beasties, and stand in as my bailiff, the King's representative. Yes, a fox and a lion working together will be a great partnership—my power and your wits, we could set our sights further afield than just Flanders. In any case, I invest you with that office, which you will, I have no doubt, occupy with great honour and verve.'

Reynard's friends and his kin and his old and extremely new supporters came running up to thank the King lavishly and indeed hastily. (Reynard was evidently not the only animal with concerns that his sudden meteoric rise in Noble's

418

estimation correlated rather too closely with the lion's consumption of the summer wine cellar.) The King beckoned to Dame Rukenawe, and grasped her hands. 'I would do more for all of you as well,' he cried, 'but look after the Fox, promise me you'll watch out for him, keep him on the straight and narrow.'

Rukenawe recoiled a little from Noble's pungent breath, then said, 'I can assure you, my Lord, that we will always look after Reynard the Fox. That shall ever be. If he did anything wrong, anything at all, which I'm sure he wouldn't, then we would completely disown him.' She extracted her hand from underneath an enormous lion paw. 'I would give the Fox up for ever, use all my power to hinder him, but that really won't happen, Sire.' Noble nodded. 'I've always liked you, Rukenawe. Reynard's trainer, eh? Good job, good job. Well done. I say, any bottles of the myrtle wine down there, Firapeel?'

A deliriously happy Reynard thanked the King with an outpouring of fair and courteous words, delivered with his finest foxish swagger, notwithstanding the lingering smell of his brush. 'Dear Lord, I'm not worthy of all these honours. But I shall ponder very hard on everything you've said, and listen to my auntie also. Be certain, though, that I will faithfully serve and obey you for the rest of my days. I will be your most loyal subject and my counsel will be hard-thought and as advantageous and beneficial as you would wish it to be.'

And with that, Sir Reynard the Fox took leave of the King, and went to prepare himself for his journey home the following day.

The first thing he did was to have a cooling dip in the river, where he floated on his back for a long while, watching the wispen clouds drift across the endless blue flax of the summer sky. And he suddenly recalled being a little fox and his father telling him about all the different parts of heaven, of air and of ether and of clouds. They were walking along a beach just along the coast from Brugge, at a little village called Oostende, where the skies were huge over the North Sea. These thin, torn clouds he called curl-clouds or gallop-horse-tails. 'I wish he could see me now,' thought Reynard, 'the grandest lord in Flanders. I wish I could grasp back into the old times, and pull him through to me, scape him through one of his old muddy hiding-tunnels, well and whole once more. I wish he hadn't fallen to despair.' And the burden of that terrible discovery in the snow cast its old weight once more. Even on the fox's day of triumph, even in the shimmering glory-heat of July, he was never quite free of that hard, frozen death, that creaking gallows-tree, that aching bone-deep loss.

But what of Isengrim? You are probably wondering what happened to him at the end of the battle.

Somewhat reluctantly, Bruin the Bear, Tybert the Cat, and Erswynde and her cubs, along with a few straggling pack-wolves, pulled Isengrim from the Field, and laid him on a litter of hay. They covered him with cotton blankets and made him warm, and his wife tended his cuts, which numbered over twenty-five, such had been Reynard's bombardment. Masters of physic and the best surgeons were called for, and they came after dinner, and tutted and inspected and washed and bound his wounds. He was so sick and weak and feeble that he'd lost all feeling in his body, and just lay there, moaning quietly to himself. So they rubbed and wrived him under his temples and eyes, until, all of a sudden, he sat bolt upright from his swoon, and started to cry so loudly—shouting and yelling about Reynard and something to do with a bucket and the head of Saint John the Baptist—that they were all terrified, thinking the wolf had entirely lost his wits. But the physicians gave him a drink that soothed his heart and sent him straight to sleep. They also comforted Erswynde, telling her that there were no mortal wounds and he was quite out of peril. He simply needed sleep, no special care.

That comfort was misplaced but useful. For freed from guilt and duty, her cage bars briefly parted, Erswynde left that very night. She readied her cubs, who were finally old enough and strong enough to travel, and packed her small collection of jewellery, her psalter, her herbs, some toys, and a letter of introduction written by Queen Gente to her remaining brother in Toulouse, asking him to protect and shelter the Lady Wolf, for as long as she required. Finally, sewn into her travelling cloak was a little silk pouch of gems, including a curious gold ring inscribed in an old Hebrew script, slipped to her by Reynard the Fox just before the battle, his sleight of paw unnoticed by the rest of the Court.

Running as hard as she could with her bad leg and aching feet, the cubs barking encouragement all the way, Erswynde reached Mons at daybreak, staying the following night at the Abbey of Saint-Michel-en-Thiérache. By the end of the following week, travelling steadily by night, and sleeping during the day, they reached Aquitaine and safety.

She and her children were never seen in Gent again, but once a year Reynard would receive a letter faintly scented with mimosa and orange blossom, carried to Flanders from the far south by the swallows, and with only ever one word written inside, in Occitan: *Mercés*—thank you.

CHAPTER FORTY-FIVE

Home to Maleperduys!

*The Feast Day of the Translation of Saint Thomas à Becket of Canterbury, Wednesday 7th July**

The following day the Court broke up, and all the beasts departed and headed back to their townhouses and manors and farms and castles.

Reynard himself took his leave of the King and Queen with elegance and full ritual, and an unfamiliar dash of plain honesty, highly invigorating to the fox, like a very, very good cut of meat with only a smear of melted butter, rather than a rich cream sauce. He didn't have to weave words or thread new falsehoods; he was free to go—important and honoured and respected by all. The past had dimmed behind the smoke and noise of the battle.

They asked him to return to Gent as soon as he could, and the Queen presented him with a large shield to commemorate his victory. It was freshly painted, gleaming with varnish, decorated with his new coat of arms, which had been hurriedly devised by Sir Ostrole the Stoat, who acted as the King of Arms, assisted by four heralds and three pursuivants, also ermines, as was the custom at the time. The device comprised a *renard de goules, passant la tête de face* (a striding red fox turning to face the onlooker) over two crossed keys, one *argent* (silver)

---

* The Feast of the Translation of Thomas à Becket marked the transferral or 'translation' of the provocative martyr's relics, on 7th July 1220, from the crypt of Canterbury Cathedral to a magnificent state-sanctioned shrine in the newly constructed apse at the east end.

and one *or* (gold), to represent his new positions as justice and a bailiff of the King, as well as signifying Sint-Pieters in Gent. 'Very clever, those ermines, very clever to do it overnight,' praised Noble, as Reynard held up the shield to the Court.

'Dear King and Queen,' the fox declaimed, 'I will finally take my leave for Rupelmonde, but I shall be ready for any commandment, however small or trifling. Fair Maleperduys is less than a day's walk or river-sail away and easily reached. Send erindberes for anything you need; my body and my goods and my soul are at your disposal, as are my dear friends and my gentle lineage. May God grant you both good grace and exceptionally long lives for your kindnesses to this humble fox. And now I simply desire your licence and leave to return home to my Hermeline and my children at last. Should Your Grace require me, he will find me ever attentive.'

With these fair words and pretty sentiments, the fox departed for Maleperduys, accompanied by a festive party of forty friends and companions, dressed in rich silks and taffetas with rustling garlands of leaves and flowers around their ears and tails. Reynard led the way with Sir Grimbart and Dame Rukenawe, and the journey was delightful. Walking without haste through goldening fields, under a delicate reeded patchwork of lark song, each animal told a story or sang a song or set a riddle, according to their talents. They stopped for a long, rustic dinner at Lokeren of cheese pancakes and cold ham and onions and thick slices of *ontbijtkoek*, spiced honey cake, then walked in groups of twos and threes, laughing and philosophising and putting the world to rights until they reached the yarrow heath and the woods and the wild briar path, and then, finally, the stagnant moat and bold gatehouse of Maleperduys, two lanterns burning sulphur-bright in the darkness.

What a jovial scene of friendship and fellowship was then enacted! Reynard was exceptionally courteous to each and every one of them, as he had, after all, freely offered their services to the King. Many embraces and promises of visits and more congratulations to Reynard and felicitations to Lady Hermeline were proffered and accepted, until finally just Reynard the Fox and Grimbart the Badger remained.

Before waking up Hermeline and the three cubs to give them all the wonderful news, they paused for a moment to take the sweet night air, standing under the old statue of Reynard's great-grandfather dressed as a bishop, his foot firmly placed on the recumbent figure of Isengrim's great-grandfather, stone tongue lolling.

Grimbart the Badger looked up and laughed: *'Plus ça change—plus c'est la même chose,'* he said.

'Very true,' replied Reynard the Fox, 'very true.'

THE END

LADY HERMELINE'S
GLOSSARY

The linguistic landscape of Reynard's tale is almost the same as that of our world, but not quite. The animals' speech is richly descriptive and onomatopoeic, rooted in their courtly and country lives in old Gent and the Waasland. It is peppered with lovely old medieval and early modern words and phrases which have long fallen out of favour, such as *nuncheon* (a snack between meals) and *gerishness* (wildness, waywardness), *singing bread* (the wafers used in celebration of the Mass) and *cry harrow* (to denounce someone's tricksy doings).

It is perfectly possible, of course, to read Reynard's book without consulting his wife's glossary—the meanings of the more obscure words can usually be understood by their context or sound. Indeed, first letting the flowery language of Flemish foxes and hares, badgers and bears, polecats and pine martens, simply wash over you is a fine approach, as though listening in to spirited tavern conversations in a foreign tongue in which you are almost fluent, but still a little unsure of colloquialisms and idioms. Then, if your interest is piqued, turn to the back and you'll find all the meanings and dates and explanations you might require for further study.

Of course, etymologies of English words are complicated and twisty, but Lady Hermeline has kindly provided the general language of origin for each word, where appropriate: D = Dutch; E = English; F = French; Fl = Flemish; G = Germanic; Gr = Greek; It = Italian; L = Latin; O = Obscure; OE = Old English; P = Persian; Sc = Scandinavian. The dates following a word's origin relate to its first recorded use in that particular sense in English, which may not always be the same as its first actual use, of course. Abbreviations in front of dates are the usual *a.* = *ante* (before), *c.* = *circa* (around) and e = early. As the adventure is set in Flanders, there is also a heavy seasoning of Flemish, Dutch and Anglo-Dutch words, many first transplanted into English by William Caxton in his 1481 translation of Reynard, which is indicated by Cax. 1481 in the Glossary.

For more detailed etymology, Hermeline says please to refer to the *Oxford English Dictionary* or similar.

Finally, in addition to words and phrases, she has also included a sprinkle of historical, topographical and literary notes, again for those readers who like to be thorough and well informed.

Aachen	Aachen (Aix-la-Chapelle), in the Rhineland, was a preferred Imperial residence of Charlemagne, and, gilded by that heady association, where thirty-one Holy Roman Emperors were subsequently crowned between 936 and 1531.
Accusement	The action of accusing; an accusation (F; *a.* 1393).
Addle	Urine, particularly infected urine, with an associated smell of foul, rotten eggs (OE).
Albespyne	Common Hawthorn or Whitethorn, *Crataegus monogyna* (F; ?*a.* 1425).
Amorettes	Love knots or garlands (F; *c.* 1500).
Amper	A swelling on the skin, especially a boil, pustule or pimple (eOE).
Aspen	Tremulous, quivering; quaking, timorous; 'aspen fear' (OE; *c.* 1412).
Asunder	To separate, divide, split (OE).
Avicenna	Avicenna was the name used in Western Europe for Ibn Sina (Persian: ابن سينا) (*c.* 980–1037), a Persian polymath regarded as one of the most significant physicians, astronomers, thinkers and writers of his time, and of huge import and influence in the history of medicine.
Baardkriel hens	An old Belgian breed of bearded bantam chicken, first bred in the village of Uccle.
Batrachomyomachia	The *Batrachomyomachia*, the 'Battle of Frogs and Mice', was a mock-epic poem written by an anonymous poet at the time of Alexander the Great, broadly imitating the language and style of Homer.
Baudeloo	The Abbey of Baudeloo was founded in the year 1197, when Boudewijn van Boekel (a monk from Sint-Pieters Abbey in Gent) installed himself in the village of Klein-Sinaai as a hermit. The local Flemish historian and Reynardist Maurice

427

Nonneman (1907–1979) convincingly proposed that the Middle Dutch *Van den vos Reynaerde* (1250) was written by a monk from Baudeloo.

Beaupere A term of courtesy for 'father', used especially to or of a spiritual or ecclesiastical 'Father' (F; *c.* 1300).

Bebled To cover or stain with blood, make bloody (OE/G; 1230).

Béguinage A *béguinage* or, in Flemish, *begijnhof* was a Flemish architectural complex created to house *béguines*: lay religious women who lived in community without taking vows or retiring from the world (F; *béguine*, 1483; *béguinage*, 1815).

Bewhape To bewilder, amaze, confound utterly (E; 1320).

Biller A ram (F; *c.* 1560).

Blechure A wound. First used in English by William Caxton in his *Golden Legend* (F; 1483).

Blede A flower, blossom or fruit (OE; 975).

Blee Colour, hue (OE; *c.* 888).

Boudin A blood sausage, black pudding or forcemeat shaped like a sausage (F; 1845).

Bote A type of tool used in carpentry (O; 1450).

Boudinsbrug An important bridge over the River Leie in Gent. Now called the Zuivelbrug (Dairy Bridge). Until 1476 it was known as Boudinsbrug after the Boudins, who lived in the Suvelsteghe (eventually renamed Meerseniersstraat).

Bourd To say things in jest or mockery; to jest, joke or make fun (F; 1303).

Bowse To drink to excess or for enjoyment or goodfellowship. To swill, guzzle or tipple (E/D; *c.* 1300).

Brandewine Brandy. From the Dutch *brandewijn*, 'burnt' (i.e. distilled) wine (D; *a.* 1640).

Braule A particular pace or movement in dancing (F; 1521).

Bubastis An Ancient Egyptian city dedicated to the worship of the cat goddess Bastet, situated south-east of modern Zagazig.

Bulch A hump or swelling (F; *c.* 1300).

Buskling Eager activity, bustling; scuffling, agitation (Sc; 1546).

Bydwongen Forced. Past participle of *bedwynge*, to restrain, to control. Used by William Caxton in both his *Metamorphoses* of 1480 and his *Reynard the Fox* (Fl; 1480).

Cardiacles Palpitations of the heart, suffered grievously by Grimbart (L/F; 1377).

Celestrine A kind of sky-blue cloth (It; 1435–36).

Chalybes The Chalybes were a people cited by classical authors as living in Pontus and Cappadocia in northern Anatolia. They occupied a position of mythical blacksmiths within the classical imagination; Pliny cites even their mice as having an overwhelming predilection for metal.

Chape The tip of a fox's tail, from its resemblance to the tip of a scabbard, the word's earlier meaning (F; 1677).

Chaperon A form of hood or cap worn by nobles (F; *c.* 1380).

Ciclatoun A costly cloth of gold or other rich material (P/F; *a.* 1225).

Clary A sweet liquor consisting of a mixture of wine, clarified honey and various spices, such as pepper and ginger (E; *c.* 1300).

Cloisterer One who dwells in a cloister; a monk or nun (F; 1340).

Cocket A style of wearing a hood in a manner resembling the shape of a cockerel or its comb (F; *a.* 1500).

Cogboat	A type of flat-bottomed boat used on the Schelde, and across northern Europe from the eleventh century (F/Fl; 1376).
Compline	The last service of the day, completing the services of the canonical hours; also the hour of that service (F/L; *a.* 1225).
Coquin or cokin	A rogue or a rascal (F; *c.* 1330)
Couvre-feu or curfew	An evening bell rung to prevent conflagrations arising from domestic fires left unextinguished at night (F; *c.* 1320).
Crede, Creed or Credo	The Apostles' Creed; also a repetition of the Creed, essential to Christian doctrine, as an act of devotion (L; *a.* 1000).
Crouse	Bold, audacious, daring, hardy, forward, full of defiant confidence, 'cocky' (E; *a.* 1400).
Cry harrow	To denounce someone's doings (F; 1340).
Courtling	A frequenter of the Court, a courtier; a creature of the Court; a young or petty courtier (F/E; 1616).
Courtnoll	A contemptuous or familiar name for a courtier (F/D; 1568).
Crake-berry	The black berries of *Empetrum nigrum*, a small evergreen shrub; also known as crowberries.
Cullion	A testicle (F; *c.* 1386).
Dainteously	Daintily (F; *c.* 1380).
Das, Dass or Dasse	Badger. Used repeatedly by Caxton in *Reynard* when referring to Grimbart (D; Cax. 1481).
Demon blue	Dark blue was often perceived and interpreted as close to black, and as such was used for painting demons. This was undoubtedly due to racial prejudice. See, for example, M. Lindsay Kaplan, *Figuring Racism in Medieval Christianity* (Oxford University Press, 2018), p. 88.

Diamargariton A restorative medicine, principally made
with powder of pearl (Gr; 1362).

Dickedinne Medieval broadcloth from Gent, made
with the finest English wools, which was
popular in the fourteenth century.

Dogdrave A mysterious type of medieval fish,
possibly like cod (E/D; 1227).

Dory Of a golden colour; bright yellow
(F/L; 1398).

Dow To press, squeeze, wring (D; Cax. 1481).

Drenkle To suffer submersion or drowning
(OE; *a.* 1325).

Drightfare The march of a host, procession or throng
(OE).

Drosen Dregs (OE; *c.* 1000).

Drumbledore A clumsily flying insect, especially a
bumblebee (E; 1567).

Duijtse pappe 'German Pap', a porridge consisting of a
combination of sweet cream, wheat flour
and lots of eggs, which makes it lumpy
when heated. Usually given to very young
cubs.

Dwale The deadly nightshade, *Atropa Belladonna*.
Sable or black in Heraldry (Sc; 1393).

Échauguette The French term for an overhanging,
wall-mounted turret projecting from the
walls of late-medieval and early-modern
fortifications.

Elmare Now long-drowned, Elmare was a village
in the frontier region of the present-day
Zeelandic Flanders. It was once centred
around a small monastery, a priory,
founded in 1144 by Sint-Pieters Abbey in
Gent. Due to flooding, the foundation was
destroyed after 1375.

Eme Uncle or old friend. Used in *Beowulf*, in
Chaucer and throughout *Reynard* by
Caxton (OE).

Erindebere	Errand-bearer (OE; *a.* 1250).
Esbatement	Amusement, diversion (F; 1477).
Ewery	The apartment or office for ewers, especially within a royal household; a room where ewers of water, table linen and towels were kept. A ewerer provided linen and water to those dining (L/F; *c.* 1460).
Fance	Grimbart the Badger's word for fancy.
Fazart	A very obscure word meaning cowardly, dastardly. King Noble changes it to 'fazartly' in his anger (O; 1508).
Felly	Cruelly, fiercely, harshly (E; 1300).
Flawn	A kind of pancake, custard or cheesecake made in various ways (F/L; *c.* 1300).
Flèche	French word for a slender spire, especially one placed over the intersection of the nave and transept. Typical of Flemish *béguinages*.
Fleech	To beguile, cajole, coax, wheedle; to entice, wheedle into going to a place (O; *c.* 1425).
Flitch	A 'side' of bacon (OE; *a.* 700).
Flower-de-luces	Irises, especially *Iris pseudacorus*. Also known as fleur-de-lis (F; 1352).
Foin	An animal of the polecat or weasel variety; particularly a beech marten. In Noble's retinue, they often act as sentries (F; *c.* 1394).
Fortune's Wheel	Mentioned casually by Caxton in his *Reynard*, the great wheel turned by the goddess Fortuna, an ominous emblem of treacherous mutability, was a constant in the medieval imagination, popularised by Boethius's *De consolatione philosophiae*. Depictions of the Wheel typically described four stages in its revolution; figures climbing to triumph or descending

to ruin around its rim. These four stations were often paired with the mnemonic Leonine hexameter: *regnabo* ('I shall reign'), *regno* ('I reign'), *regnavi* ('I have reigned'), *sum sine regno* ('I am without a kingdom').

Foxery   The character, manners or behaviour of a fox; wiliness, cunning (G; *c.* 1400).

Fraked   Wicked, vile (OE; *a.* 900).

Frike   Lusty, strong, vigorous (F; *a.* 1400).

Frith   A rather poetic way of describing wooded country (OE; ?826).

Frory   Covered with foam or froth (E; 1600)

Gabber   A liar or deceiver (F; *a.* 1325).

Galantine   A sauce served with fish or poultry, originally made from the jellied juices of meat or fish, and typically flavoured with spices and thickened with breadcrumbs or soaked bread (F; 1304–05).

Galping   Yelping (D; Cax.1481).

Gerishness   Wildness, waywardness (O; *a.* 1513).

Gibbe   A popular name for a tomcat; probably the shortened form of the male name Gilbert (E; 1400).

Gipon   A close-fitting tunic, usually padded and bearing heraldic arms (F; *a.* 1387).

Gittern   An old form of guitar, strung with wire (F; 1377).

Glat   Smooth (D; Cax.1481).

Glaver   Chatter, loud noises (O; *a.* 1400–50).

Gleiming   Sticky (O; *a.* 1387).

Glister   To sparkle; to glitter; to be brilliant (OE; *c.* 1380).

Gnar or Gnarl   To snarl or growl: onomatopoeic (G/D; 1496).

Godfrighty   God-fearing (E; 1225).

God wot   Used to emphasise the truth of a statement (G; ?*c.* 1225).

Gong	The contents of a privy; excrement (eOE).
Grate	The backbone of a fish (D; Cax.1481).
Grim	To be angry, look fierce (D/G; *a.* 1400–50).
Gryn	A snare for catching birds or animals, made of cord, hair or wire, with a running noose (OE; *c.* 825).
Gunnes de cupro	Guns of copper or brass (E; *c.* 1365–70).
Gunnes de ferro	Guns of iron (E; *c.* 1365–70).
Haberjet	Known as *haubergetum* in Medieval Latin, haberjet was a very, very old worsted of high quality, mentioned in *Magna Carta*. It has been suggested that the cloth name may derive from its similarity in appearance to chain mail (O; 1216).
Halkes	A corner, recess or hiding place (E; *a.* 1300).
Handsel	Indication or omen of something that is to happen; an animal's fortune or luck (eOE).
Hardiesse	Boldness (F; 1300).
Haywarder	An officer of a manor, township or parish, having charge of the fences and enclosures (OE; *c.* 1225).
Hippocras	A drink made from wine sweetened with sugar or honey and flavoured with spices and other ingredients, typically drunk as a restorative or a digestive (F; 1400).
Hindberries	A very old name for raspberries (OE; *a.* 700).
Historiette	A short history or story; an anecdote (F; *a.* 1704).
Hornblende	A mineral closely allied to augite, having as its chief constituents silica, magnesia and lime. Usually a dark brown, black or greenish black colour (G; 1770).
Houppelande	A highly dramatic long and extremely full outer garment, which first appeared in Europe in about 1350. It was worn by men over the top of a tunic and hose and by women over a long underrobe. Reynard

the Fox has *houppelandes* for every season (F; 1392–3).

Hurnes A corner, nook or hiding place (OE; 897).

Hypocras A drink made from wine sweetened with sugar or honey and flavoured with spices and other ingredients, typically drunk as a restorative or a digestive (F; *a.* 1400).

Incolumity Safety, soundness, freedom from danger (F/L; 1534).

Inditing To utter, suggest or inspire a form of words which is to be repeated or written down: dictating (F; *a.* 1340).

Jordan pot A kind of rimmed pot or vessel formerly used by alchemists and physicians, the latter particularly for urine samples. It originally referred to the bottles of water brought from the River Jordan by crusaders and pilgrims (O; 1377).

Jurvert A piquant green sauce from Catalonia, made with parsley, marjoram, mint, sage, garlic, toasted bread, hazelnuts and walnuts.

Kaaking An imitative word meaning cawing (E; 1606).

Kercher A kerchief or neckerchief (E; 1380).

Keytyf A base, mean, despicable wretch; a villain, a piteous case, a captive, a prisoner (F; *c.* 1325).

Kinestool A throne (OE).

Kirtle A woman's gown (OE; *c.* 995).

Klompen Wooden shoes or clogs made of a single piece of wood, usually willow, poplar or alder, shaped and hollowed out to fit the foot. Associated with peasants and working people in Flanders. See also *sabots*.

Lamber Amber (F; *a.* 1400).

Latten-brass A mixed metal of yellow colour, either identical with, or closely resembling, brass; often hammered into thin sheets (F; 1677).

Lauds   The first of the day-hours of the church, the psalms of which always end with Psalms 148–150, sung as one psalm and technically called laudes (F/L; *a.* 1340).

Leo Belgicus   The Leo Belgicus (Belgic Lion) was used in both cartographic design and heraldry to symbolise the Low Countries.

Letch   A stream flowing through boggy land; a muddy ditch or hole; a bog. Also a pool (usually of blood) (OE; 1138).

Lich-rest   A place for a corpse to rest, a burial place (OE; *c.* 1000).

Lickerous   Pleasing or tempting to the palate (F; *c.* 1275).

Lief   Beloved, dear (OE; *c.* 897).

Lither   Bad, wicked; base, rascally unjust, ill-tempered (OE; *c.* 893).

Loophole   A narrow vertical opening, usually widening inwards, cut in a wall or other defence, to allow both for the passage of missiles and for the admission of light and air (D; 1591).

Lour   Of the sky or weather: gloominess, a threatening appearance (E; 1596).

Lowrie   A Scottish name for a fox, taken from the name Lawrence (L; *a.* 1500).

Manchet   White wheaten bread of the finest quality (F; *a.* 1450)

Mandements   Commandments or orders (usually written) (F; *c.* 1325).

Marchpane   Marzipan (It or G; *a.* 1513).

Maunging   Devouring greedily and noisily; munching, chewing (F; *a.* 1500).

Mazer or Maselyn   A bowl, drinking cup or goblet, usually without a foot, made from a burr or knot of a maple tree and frequently mounted

	with silver or silver-gilt bands at the lip and base (F; *a.* 1200).
Meechering	Sneeking, furtive (E; 1615).
Menour	A stolen object found in the possession of a thief when arrested (F; *c.* 1436)
Mercer	A person who deals in textile fabrics, especially silks, velvets and other fine materials; specifically a member of the Worshipful Company of Mercers, of which William Caxton took the livery during the 1450s, having trained with the wealthy and influential merchant Richard Large (F; 1230).
Meulevijverstraat	Meulevijverstraat was known for centuries for its wild packs of marauding wolves.
Milceful	Merciful, gracious (E; *c.* 1225).
Mig	Urine or draining from manure. One of our oldest words for pee (eOE).
Misprisions	An offence similar to, but less serious than, treason or felony, usually relating to the accused's concealed knowledge of those crimes (F; 1425).
Mizzy	A bog or quagmire (E; *c.* 1400).
Moil	To wet, soil or bedaub (F/L; *a.* 1425).
Muggets	The intestines of a calf or sheep, particularly when cooked as food. Also the uterus of a deer (D; Cax. 1481).
Mullock	Refuse matter, rubbish (E; *c.* 1390).
Murder will out	The belief that 'Murder will out' is recorded in a number of literary works from the fourteenth century onwards, often associated with the superstition that a murderer's presence might be revealed by the bleeding afresh of the murdered person's wounds.
Musket shot water	A preparation of agrimony leaves, seeds and other herbs, used to treat gunshot wounds. Stocked up by Pancer the Beaver

rather unnecessarily in case of war or civil insurrection. Also known as *Eau d'Arquebusade*.

Nef A table ornament in the shape of a ship, usually of intricately worked silver and used to hold condiments or table napkins (F; 1567).

None One of the daily offices in the Western church, forming the fifth of the canonical hours of prayer and originally appointed for the ninth hour of the day (about 3 p.m.) (F/L; *c.* 1525).

Norfolk tumblers Norfolk tumblers were a dog breed similar to a small greyhound or a lurcher, used to catch rabbits. So called from their tumbling action when taking their quarry (E; 1607).

Nuncheon A drink taken in the afternoon; a light refreshment between meals; a snack (E; *c.* 1260–75).

Omelette de ver de terre Earthworm omelette. Phrase first coined by Grimbart the Badger, who conceived the dish.

Outrepass A person who, or thing which, surpasses all others (F; 1477).

Paternosters The special beads in a rosary that indicate that the Lord's Prayer is to be said, of a different size or material from the rest and occurring at regular intervals (L; eOE).

Pautener A rascal, a villain, a rogue (F; *c.* 1330).

Pennon A narrow swallow-tailed flag, usually attached to the head of a lance or a helmet, originally the ensign of a knight (F; 1380).

Peradventure Expressing a hypothetical, contingent or uncertain: perhaps, maybe, possibly. Once a very popular qualifier (F; *c.* 1300).

Pilche An outer garment made of animal skin with the fur used as a lining (L; OE).

Pimpernol A kind of small eel (F; 1251).

Plitching Plucking, pulling or snatching (G; *a.* 1400).

Plowngy Rain-bringing, stormy. Famously used by Chaucer in his translation of Boethius, *Boece* (*c.* 1377–83): 'The firmament stant dirked with wete, plowngy cloudes.'

Poffertjes Small puffed pancakes, eaten at celebrations, with their origins in the weekly communion bread.

Pottle A pot or tankard (F; 1310).

Precellent That which excels or surpasses others; surpassingly excellent, pre-eminent (F/L; *c.* 1384).

Preen A decorative pin, a brooch, a clasp (G; OE).

Pricksong Music sung from notes written or pricked, as opposed to music sung from memory or by ear. Also a descant or melody devised to accompany a plainsong, or performed as such an accompaniment. Often used figuratively, as in our tale (E; *a.* 1450).

Prickers A light horseman employed as a skirmisher or scout (E; *a.* 1350).

Provand Food, provisions, or provender (F; *c.* 1341).

Provend An ecclesiastical stipend or revenue (F/L; *c.* 1300).

Psaltery A stringed instrument with a sounding board or box, similar to the dulcimer but played by plucking the strings with the fingers or a plectrum (F/L; *c.* 1330).

Pullaile Poultry (F; *c.* 1400).

Putou Red wine from Poitou.

Quadrivium Taught in European schools and universities after the initial trivium (grammar, logic and rhetoric), the quadrivium consisted of the four mathematical sciences: arithmetic, geometry, astronomy and music.

Together the subjects comprised the seven liberal arts (L; *a.* 1626).

Quarefoure A quarefoure or carrefour was a place where four ways meet, a 'carfax'. Formerly quite naturalised in England, naming, for example, the main crossing-point in Oxford, but now treated only as French. Used frequently by Caxton (1477).

Quass To drink copiously or in excess; to quaff (G; 1549).

Ramp To creep or crawl on the ground, particularly plants and animals (F; *c.* 1390).

Raught To reach after, to grasp at (G; eOE).

Rote A stringed medieval musical instrument, with a soundboard, bowed or plucked (F; 1330).

Ruffin A devil or fiend (OE/L; *c.* 1225).

Sabots Wooden clogs. See *klompen* (F; 1607).

Sackbut A bass trumpet with a slide, like that of a trombone, for altering the pitch (F; 1503).

Saint Monacella Saint Monacella is the Latin name for the Welsh patron saint of hares, Saint Melangell. Melangell saved a little hare from the hunt of Brochwel Yscythrog, Prince of Powys; impressed by her compassion he granted her a parcel of land as a sanctuary. After her death, hares flocked to her relics, becoming known as *Oen Melangell* (Melangell's Lambs).

Salue A greeting or salutation (F; *c.* 1430).

Samite A rich silk fabric worn in the Middle Ages, sometimes interwoven with gold (F; *c.* 1366).

Scat Treasure, money (OE; *a.* 1182)

Scranch To crunch: onomatopoeic (E; 1620).

Screak To utter a shrill harsh cry; to screech or scream (Sc; *a.* 1500)

Scrip A small bag or pouch, especially one

carried by a pilgrim, such as Reynard, a shepherd or a beggar (F/L; *c.* 1300).

Serge A durable woollen fabric used for bed covers, hangings and humble robes, such as those favoured by Grimbart the Badger (F; 1382).

Sexte One of the daily offices, or canonical hours of prayer and worship, of the Western church, traditionally said (or chanted) at the sixth hour of the day (about midday) (L; *c.* 1450).

Shaffle To shuffle about; to make excuses, to prevaricate (E; 1552).

Shaw A thicket, small wood, copse or grove (OE: 755–7).

Shawm A medieval musical instrument of the oboe class, having a double reed enclosed in a globular mouthpiece (F; *c.* 1350).

Sherbet A cooling drink made of fruit juice and water, usually sweetened, often cooled with snow (P; 1603).

Shrab Strong wine or spirits (P; 1477).

Shrive To impose penance upon a person; hence to administer absolution to; to hear the confession of. Also, to be confessed; to make one's confession and receive absolution and penance (G; *a.* 776).

Siede To boil. From the Middle Dutch *sieden* (D; Cax. 1481).

Sile To glide (probably Sc; *c.* 1400).

Singing bread The round cakes or wafers used in the celebration of the Mass. The name possibly derives from the custom of singing during its preparation (E; 1432–3).

Skirm To fence or skirmish (F; *c.* 1225).

Skirmery Skirmishing, fencing (F; 1500).

Slidder Slippery (OE; *a.* 1000).

Slike Mud (OE/D; *c.* 1425).

Slike	To slide, glance (G; *c.* 1400).
Slonk	To swallow greedily. Probably from the Dutch *slokken*, to swallow (D; Cax. 1481).
Smeke	Flatter, sooth or fawn (D; Cax. 1481).
Smolt	To make off, go or escape (O; 1400).
Snaphance	An early form of flintlock used in muskets and pistols; a musket or gun fitted with a lock of this kind (Fl/D; 1539).
Snepe	Foolish, silly (O; *a.* 1250).
Soothfastness	The fact, condition or quality of being soothfast, of being true or truthful; truthfulness or veracity (OE; *c.* 825).
Schuyt	A flat-bottomed, shoal-draught sailing barge, used for carrying fishy cargo, particularly eels, in the rivers of Flanders and the Netherlands (D; 1666).
Skrabbing	To scratch or claw, both literal and figurative (Fl; Cax. 1481).
Shrewish	Wicked, ill-disposed, malignant (OE; *c.* 1480).
Sties	Paths or narrow ways (OE; *c.* 725).
Stockfisch or Stockfish	A name for cod and other gadoid fish cured by splitting open and drying hard in the air without salt. Very popular in Reynard's Waasland (D; 1290).
Strop	A loop or noose (OE; *c.* 1050).
Supping	A liquid taken into the mouth in small quantities or using a spoon, such as a medicinal draught (eOE).
Sweven	A dream or vision (OE; *c.* 897).
Swikedom	Deceit, fraud; treachery, treason (OE; *c.* 893).
Symphony	A collective name for different musical instruments, after the late Latin *symphonia* (L; *c.* 1290).
Tass	Heap, pile, stack (F; *c.* 1330).
Teurgoule	Rice pudding, a speciality of Normandy, particularly Rouen.

Teumessian fox	The Teumessian fox was a giant fox in Greek mythology, sent by the gods to ravage the countryside around Thebes as punishment for various terrible crimes. But the fox was wily and destined never to be caught, so eventually the Theban general Amphitryon, stepfather of Heracles, unleashed the magical dog Laelaps, who always caught his prey, in pursuit. Inevitably, the pair were bound in an unending chase, and eventually Zeus, annoyed by the sheer paradox of their situation, turned them both to stone, then cast them high into the stars as *Canis major* (Laelaps) and *Canis minor* (Teumessian fox)—fox and hound fixed fast in an eternal hunt through the dark and glittering heavens.
Tharky	Dark (E; *c*. 1275).
Thester	To become dark, grow dim (OE; *a*. 900).
Thewful	Full of or characterised by good qualities; good, virtuous, moral (OE; *c*. 1225).
Thraldom	The state or condition of being a thrall—a villein, serf, bondman or slave; bondage, servitude; captivity (Sc; 1175).
Thrutch	To thrust, squeeze or push (OE; *c*. 888).
Thwartlong	Crosswise, transversely (Sc/E; 1600).
Thyvel	A bush or thicket (OE; *a*. 1000).
Tierce	The third hour of the canonical day, ending at 9 a.m.; also, the period from 9 a.m. until noon (F; *c*. 1450).
Tod	A very old name for a red fox (O; *a*. 1200).
Tree of Jesse	The schematic depiction of the genealogy of Christ, from 'the root of Jesse' of Bethlehem, the father of King David. The original example of a family tree, it represented a popular iconographical subject within almost every medium of

medieval Christian art, from stained-glass windows to illuminated manuscripts (E; 1463).

Trencher A slice of bread used instead of a plate or platter (F; *c.* 1380).

Trindle Something rounded; a roll or coil of wax taper, used for light in medieval churches (E; 1537).

Unchancy Ill-omened, ill-fated, unfortunate. Principally Scottish (E; 1533).

Unwemmed Spotless, pure, immaculate (OE; *c.* 950).

Vamplate A plate fixed on a spear or lance to serve as a guard for the hand in tilting (F; *c.* 1350).

Vantward The vanguard of an army (F; 1297).

Vermendois Vermendois was a county in Northern France which belonged for some time to Flanders (1156–86). It has been proposed that the land of Vermendois (*lant van Vemendoys*) mentioned in the old Reynard tales is actually an abbreviated reference to the watery area of Oostkerke, between Brugge and Sluis, where the Abbey of Saint-Quentin (located in the county of Vermendois itself) had a number of possessions, including presumably Bloys, the village mentioned in Reynard's tale. See André Bouwman's translation notes to *Van den vos Reynaerde*, p. 133, line 1510.

Vielle à roue A French wheel fiddle or hurdy-gurdy, used as a melodic instrument in dance music, especially during festivities, such as Noble's Midsummer revels.

Villein One of the class of serfs in the feudal system; specifically a peasant occupier or cultivator entirely subject to a lord or attached to a manor. They were usually rabbits or mice in Reynard's world (F; *a.* 1325).

Vizying	Looking at closely or attentively (F/L; *c.* 1425).
Vos	The Dutch word for fox.
Waasland	Also known as the Land van Waas or Land of Waas, the Waasland is a flat, marshy area stretching from Gent to Antwerp along the left bank of the River Schelde. The etymology probably derives from 'waas', meaning muddy, soggy, damp, with a further sense of a haze or mist.
Waits	A small body of wind instrumentalists maintained by a city or town, playing particularly on ceremonial and celebratory occasions, such as King Noble's lengthy Midsummer festivities (F; 1298).
Wakefire	A ceremonial fire by which a night watch was kept (OE; *c.* 1400).
Wandelard	A criminal or traitor (F; 1338).
Wardecorps	A bodyguard; an armed personal attendant (F; *a.* 1330).
Warly	Martial, bellicose, ready for battle, skilled in war (OE; *c.* 1400)
Waterzooi	A famous stew dish from Flanders. The second part of the name derives from the Middle Dutch term *zode*, relating to the act of boiling or the ingredients being boiled. You can still sample it today in Gent and across Flanders, and very nice and warming it is too.
Wawish	Turbulent: of the sea (OE; *c.* 1450).
Wellaway	An expression of sorrow or lamentation. (eOE).
Wentling	Rolling or tumbling about (D; Cax. 1481).
Wether	A male sheep, a ram; esp. a castrated ram (G; *c.* 890).
Whister	To whisper (OE; *a.* 1382).

Whitsuntide	The church season of Pentecost; the weekend including Whit Sunday, or the week beginning on that day (OE; *c.* 1275).
Wight	A supernatural, preternatural or unearthly being (OE; *c.* 888).
Wisehede	Wisdom (OE/D; 1340).
Witherwin	An enemy, adversary, especially the Devil (OE; *c.* 897)
Wood-hagger	A wood-cutter, wood-hewer (OE; 1295).
Woodwose	A wild man of the woods; a satyr, faun; a person, or animal in this case, dressed to represent such a being in a pageant (OE; *a.* 1100).
Worthly	Having great value or importance; noble, fine, excellent, worthy (eOE).
Wraxling	Wrestling (OE; *c.* 1000).
Wrothy	Wrathful, angry (E; 1422).
Wraw	To miaul, as a cat; to mew (D; Cax. 1481).
Wrive	To rub (Fl; Cax. 1481).
Yirr	To snarl or growl (E; *a.* 1796).

ACKNOWLEDGEMENTS

Writing this book would not have been possible without the support and expertise of friends, colleagues and institutions from across the United Kingdom, the Netherlands and Flanders.

The idea for a new and expanded retelling of *Reynard the Fox* was born and nurtured within the historical outreach project *North Sea Crossings: The Literary Heritage of Anglo-Dutch Relations, 1066 to 1688*, a collaboration between the University of Bristol, the Bodleian Libraries and Aardman Animations, principally funded by the National Lottery Heritage Fund. From Bristol, I would particularly like to thank Professor Ad Putter and Dr Sjoerd Levelt, the lead academics on the project. They have both been unflaggingly kind, answering dozens upon dozens of questions about Anglo-Dutch history and Flemish foxes, giving generously and enthusiastically of their precious time and expert knowledge. They were also, very luckily for me, my first readers, polishing my manuscript like one of Reynard's peculiar jewels.

My editors at Bodleian Library Publishing, Samuel Fanous and Janet Phillips, have been wonderfully supportive and brilliantly insightful, and I am so grateful for having had the opportunity to work with them and the rest of the team. I virtually lived in the Bodleian whilst I was writing the book, working directly from Robert Burton's 1620 copy of *The most delectable history of Reynard the fox*, and I am very thankful for all the help I received from library and curatorial staff, especially from Madeline Slaven and Sallyanne Gilchrist, with whom I shared many a pleasant hour examining Reynardian manuscripts and early printed books. Equally, I owe a great debt to the London Library, whose 'Country Loan' service was invaluable for night-time foxish research and for the trickier parts of my core translation of Caxton. Other libraries which were immensely useful included the British Library, Bibliothèque Nationale de France, Leiden University Library, and Universiteitsbibliotheek Gent.

As part of *North Sea Crossings*, in partnership with Aardman Animations, Reynard's story has also been made into a short film by students at the University of Bristol, in collaboration with pupils at Kingsweston School in Bristol and the Ormerod at Marlborough School in Woodstock. Enormous thanks go particularly to Danny Gallagher and Katie Williams at Aardman and Dr Kristian Moen at the Department of Film and Television in Bristol.

In Flanders, I want especially to thank Henk Huisman, who kindly guided me around Hulst, a centre for Reynardian studies, and its environs, and helped me to locate the lonely site of Kriekeputte on the Dutch–Belgian border. The Oxford–Leiden Link assisted with my research trip to Leiden, Delft, and Den Haag, and I am appreciative to Roelof Hol, John Chipperfield and the committee for their advice and guidance.

The National Lottery Heritage Fund has been a wonderful partner for the Reynard project, and I must shower gratitude upon Helen Wheatley, who has been both inspirational mentor and kindred spirit for many years now.

I am also deeply appreciative of the inestimable support and encouragement from the following friends throughout the writing process: Simon Brandenburger, Brigid Hains, Lisa M. Heilbronn, Amy Hennig, Lisa Hirsch, Mischelle Hopper, Claire Ivins, Sharon L. James, Rosalind Maud, Heidi Moore, Isabelle Prim, Laura Salmon, Hazel Rattigan, Susie and Sophie Roberts, Catherine Taylor, Michaeleen Trimarchi, Sue Vorchheimer, Niamh Walsh, Heidi Wolf, and Rene Yoakum. The extraordinary generosity of Robert Siegle enabled to me to keep writing at a crucial juncture.

Finally, my late father, Dr Ronald Avery, was the first person to introduce me both to Reynard the Fox and to the Bodleian Library, and my sketch of Lord Reynard owes much to his charm, wit and unrivalled talent in talking his way out of tricky situations. I also dedicate these pages to my Grimbart, Steve Pratley, without whom nothing would be possible, and to my mother, the novelist Felicity Bridgen, known by her *nom-de-plume* Anne Stevenson, who mirrored Hermeline in her great kindness and intellect. And for Indy, of course, my dearest Reynardine, who is the reason I write.

FLANDRIÆ DESCRIPTIO

Septentr[io]

Maris Germanici Pars

Occidens

Picardiæ Pars

Arte siæ Pars

Scala miliarium

1 2 3 4 5 6

1 2 3 4 5 6 7

Miliaria flandrica magna
Miliaria flandrica parua Lens

Calæs
Ermuen
Blanckenberg
Wendunen
Ramscapell Lap
Sunke rer
Houthaue Meletke
Bru[ge]
Clemkerck
Oostende
Marienkerck
Nieuport
Westende
Snaeskercke
Staelhill
Tabeke
Oudenborch
Ergem
Meerberge
Ridder
Score Winendale
Vlaertfele Coolscamp
Werne
Prouse
Dymude Hoochlede
Clorcken Ingelmu
Staem Emels
Rousselar
Vue
Lampernefc
Fintele
Vloers bergen icmgie
Hondscote Biscot
Wmoxbergen Oostolet
Westfoletenek Paeschendale
Bierne Wormhout en Dadisele
Hospitael Popering[e] Iperen
Leregem Westhoutre Comene Menene Léye
Peene flur Lauu
Bambeke Drenoutre Moschero
Winnefeele Messene
Cassel Vleteren Dulcemont
Caestre Niewkercke Ferlngehem
Walscapelle Belle Houpines Marque
Steenbe Steenwercke Armentiers Trec
Suid Ha
Walle Beerquin Campingehem Ryssele
Merab Radingehem Tem
S. Omar Fouessart Templ
Arienn Beaupre Allene
Hann ter Tosse Waurin
Terwanen Callocne Streta Fetuber Espinoy Dou
destructum Rebeque Atricourt Winen
Lilers Bethune Ba sec Douga
Sotques Beuri

Maruuck
Greuelinge
Loon
Oyenkercke Arenboch capelle
Dunkerch Teieg[em]
Souricote Usem Adegem te more
Borborch Capelle
te Dunen
Leffenhouck
Wulpen
Caes tre
Buischa Au flu
Hospitael